The Truth Keepers

Jacqueline Ward

This is a work of fiction. Names, characters, businesses, places, events and incidents are either the products of the author's imagination or used in a fictitious manner. Any resemblance to actual persons, living or dead, events or locales is entirely coincidental.

Published by Novelesque

ISBN: 9781698681887

Dedication

This book is dedicated to those who lost their lives in the Iraq war

"None but the dead are permitted to tell the truth."
Mark Twain

Part One: Kate Morden

.

Chapter 1

I end the call and kiss Neil goodbye but it hardly registers. He knows the score by now. I kiss Sammy, his seven-year-old daughter, and Leo, his-ten-year old son. Their eyes don't leave the TV screen but I know that they'll have noticed me leaving. It's just that they're so used to it. They won't miss me because I'm not their mother. Good, I tell myself. *Good.* I need to detach myself now. I'm in this alone.

As I walk down the drive of Neil's semi-detached home, I go over the decision I've made. I've clung onto Neil and tried to make a family. It isn't working. It's interfering with my job and I suddenly realise that I need to be the woman I really am. Someone with no family, I need to be solitary. It's no use pretending any more. But it's a risk because since my father died that's my greatest fear: to be alone. It's stupid really but there it is: I'm terrified of being alone.

I walk towards the train station until the message arrives. I've been expecting it. There are no details but it's clear that it's imperative I attend. It's from the communication hub that my employers provide. MI6. I guess you could say I am a spy. Yes, a spy. I'm a secret agent and I'm high end, although lately it hasn't seemed that way, while I've been in Neil's dead wife's shoes, in her family. As I stand waiting, I know that day by day I'm becoming her and that I need to get back to me.

I slide into the back of the waiting Volvo and throw my holdall onto the seat beside me. The driver doesn't speak to me and it takes the entire journey for my heart to calm. I know that it's the end for me and Neil. I will miss him and the kids. After all, I've let myself make memories with them. But I know this is the right thing; if I'm going to do my job properly I must focus completely. So I don't look back.

In twenty minutes the car pulls up outside a three-storey building. As I prepare to step out of the car the driver hands me a mobile phone. I hurry towards the door, pulling my long coat around me to protect myself from the rain.

The door's open and I follow the noise up to a second-floor flat. A man is slumped over a dining table, a gaping wound in the frontal lobe of his head and the blood around the side of his face starting to

3

dry, connecting him to the wooden surface. A baseball bat lies on the floor beside him. I don't recognise any of the investigating officers or the SOCO team. No one notices me for a moment and I step backwards into the shadows of the room.

My skills kick in and I search for patterns, little signs that other people miss. It's what I'm good at. There has to be something here. There always is. It raises excitement mixed with dread, because this looks serious. Unexpected; I was here to retrieve data, not to deal with a murder.

I work with terrorists, sometimes in person and sometimes from a distance. I infiltrate them, one way or another. Every case I'm involved in is somehow linked to terrorism. It might be encrypted information or money laundering to support terrorist groups, or the movement of weapons. I've been part of a team that foiled a plot before it happened, sometimes only moments before.

This mission is to retrieve data, inevitably related to terrorism somewhere in the world. The dead man isn't a terrorist. I know this because he's had dealings with my department. He's probably tried to sell us something. That's why I'm here, to retrieve something we need.

I take in my surroundings. It's a medium-sized lounge and dining room, combined. There is a kitchen, two bedrooms and a bathroom, all adjoining by the look of the doors around the room. It's tastefully decorated, although it looks a little clinical, unlived in. An evening newspaper lies on an armchair recliner, open on the used car sales page.

Eventually the lead investigating officer spots me and rushes over. "DI Ringer. Can I help you?"

He looks concerned, almost afraid. We all are these days, with the heightened security levels; these days it's through the roof. He tries to exaggerate his medium height and slightly dumpy build by standing up very straight.

"Kate Morden. I'm the investigator."

Investigator isn't the right word. We both know that I'm MI6. He would have been briefed but he lets it go.

"Oh yes. Yes, right. Just here to observe, are you?"

"Awaiting further instructions," I reply.

He looks from my holdall to my handbag. I pre-empt and show him my passport and driving licence. Not that it means anything – anyone could fake them – but he seems satisfied.

"The victim's Lewis Krommer. He's been living here for about three months according to the guy downstairs who's also his landlord. Paid six months up front. Been hit over the head with the bat by the looks of it. No signs of a robbery or forced entry."

I glance at the lock on the front door behind me. I need to keep Ringer busy.

"Could you ask someone to take magnified pictures of the lock? Full forensics around the lock and a ten metre area; they had to get in here somehow. How were you alerted?"

"Landlord heard the TV as he came in from work and went to investigate. Door was wide open and he saw the victim. No one in the building saw anyone come in or out."

"CCTV?" I might as well make it look like I'm interested. In reality I'm waiting for further instructions. I'm here to do one job only.

"No. Not in here and not on the street outside."

He gives me a 'why are you here?' look and I break eye contact as the phone I was handed in the car buzzes. The text message reads: *Kitchen cupboard under the sink, cream cleaner bottle.*

Game on. Ringer's still hovering. He's determined not to let me out of his sight. Sticking to me like glue, despite the dead stare of his murder victim.

"Mind if I have a look around?"

Of course he minds but he can't really refuse. He's under orders to let me have a free run of the crime scene. He's tailing, hoping that some tiny particle of my occupation might stick to him because that's what everyone in this business aspires to: security services, full blown, high-level investigations. Spying, counterintelligence. No one to answer to. No rules and regulations. Travel. All expenses paid. What they never realise is the consequences, the trade-off: hiding away, insecurity, not even being able to tell your nearest and dearest who you really are. How a man with a split head hardly fazes you because he's not what's important.

DI Ringer would love to be me. He'd love to be a spy, anyway. He follows me into the first bedroom and watches as I look around. Then I go to the bathroom. I pull on some white gloves and look in the cabinet where I know I will find no evidence. He peers over my shoulder and I watch him in the mirror, then glance around. Shaving gear, paracetamol. No stubble in the sink. No debris whatsoever in the bathroom. Lewis Krommer hasn't been living here. My hackles rise. There's more to this than there seems.

I rummage around and eventually someone needs Ringer to sign off some forensics. He's undecided for a second but has to go. I wait until he's occupied, then I go into the kitchen and run the tap. Again the place is spotless. The cooker hasn't been used and, although the cupboards are stocked, there are no gaps. No fresh food at all. Not even a grain of rice out of place. I open the fridge and the inner light shines on the floor. Not a speck of dust under the fridge door.

I open the litre of semi-skimmed milk and sniff it: fresh. Every item in the fridge has a long-range sell-by date. Krommer only arrived here in the past couple of days. He's been preparing to live here, to hide away but he's been busted almost immediately.

Ringer's paying half attention to the forensics lead and keeps glancing over his shoulder at me. I look in the empty bin and open the waste disposal unit door.

Then I select the target cupboard. There are several bottles and I grab the cream cleaner. It feels full so I run my finger around the edges and the base. Taped underneath is a flash drive. I pull the tape away and quickly remove the back of the phone. Inside is a USB docking port and I attach the flash drive firmly so that the screen lights up. I replace the back and watch as the call connects.

Ringer appears and I press the active phone to my ear. "Yes. Oh. I must go. Someone's arrived. Bye."

He looks at the phone and I push it deep into my pocket.

"I didn't see you were on the phone. Wondered if you wanted to take a look at this?"

I lean against the kitchen cupboard and calculate my exit strategy.

"Sure. What is it?"

He leads me through and we stand in front of Lewis Krommer. His blood is congealed now and I notice that he isn't wearing any shoes. No jewellery. Not even a watch. I look around the flat. No telephone line or satellite TV. No internet connection. This was obviously a safe harbour rather than an operations centre.

"Did the victim have a mobile phone?" I ask.

"That's the puzzling thing. No mobile. No documents except a driving licence. No letters addressed to him here. Must have kept them somewhere else. But the landlord told me that he was in and out for three months. Sometimes arriving late at night or early in the morning. Thought he was working shifts. But quiet as anything."

I pick up the evidence bag with his driving licence in it. It's immediately obvious to me that it's a fake. I weigh the plastic in my hand and feel the edges. Good but a fake. It doesn't matter. He won't need it now.

I should get out of here. "So what did you want to show me?"

"The guy's fingers."

The forensics guy turns Krommer's hand over with a plastic paddle. The blood has collected along his knuckles where one hand has been folded over the other and has made no contact with the table. Livor mortis. After death blood no longer circulates and succumbs to gravity in the lowest parts of the body. Because Lewis was leaning forward with his hands face-up on the table, the blood has settled in the interstitial tissue of his hands but only where they're not in contact with anything else. It's clear that someone has moved them.

"His hands looked awkward, twisted like, so Dave here made him more comfortable. So we didn't notice it at first."

I lean in and examine his hands. The skin is soft and his nails are clean and perfectly manicured but the ends of his fingers are red raw and bloody. I look closer and see that the ends of his finger pads are missing. Someone has stolen Lewis Krommer's fingerprints.

Chapter 2

Ringer shakes his head and wipes beads of sweat from his nose. "It doesn't make sense." He's walking around the crime scene and the forensics team makes him put on a pair of white paper slippers.

I stand back a little. So someone has hit Krommer over the head with a baseball bat, clumsy and obvious, then waited a while, and then performed a delicate surgical procedure. I look a little closer at the fingertips. Tiny, neat incisions, almost scrapes but deep enough to remove the dermis and leave the fleshy pads. Why not cut the fingers off?

Then it strikes me. They didn't cut off Krommer's fingers because they wanted the prints as fresh and alive as possible. Somewhere inside me alarm bells ring and my natural instincts kick in. This isn't run-of-the-mill at all. Why would someone want Krommer's fingerprints so badly?

Ringer's team gathers around Krommer, postulating theories on his missing skin. I hurry into the kitchen and open the fridge again, then the freezer. I pull out an ice-cube tray and the water is only semi-frozen. Whoever has killed Krommer has been here before, to prepare. To make sure that the vessel they will use to freeze his fingerprints is ready for use. They even brought a replacement. This is what I'm looking for. This is the start of something.

I call over a SOCO. "Please could you analyse this tray? I believe the perpetrator may have used it."

I check the contents of the freezer to make sure that the fingerprints aren't stored for later collection. Nothing.

The phone data is still transmitting. There's about ten percent left to download. It's time for me to leave. I push my phone against my ear and hurry past Krommer and the investigating officers, shrugging and pointing at the phone as I pass. Ringer's gaze follows me as I exit.

Outside the air is ionised after the rainstorm and the street is bathed in the golden evening light I love so much. I walk up the road outside the flat to a set of traffic lights and think hard about what's just happened. The surgical neatness of the skin removal intrigues me and makes me wonder why someone would want the fingerprints alive.

This was exactly why I was recruited, to solve this kind of mystery. I'm already involved.

Less than five minutes later the black Volvo that picked me up arrives and I get in. My original mission, the file upload, has completed but there is more to this, much more. It's nagging at me. There's a message on the screen: *One. Two. Three.* One for straightforward. Two for problematic. Three for assistance.

I consider the fingerprints and the wound in Krommer's head. I would have expected poison or maybe suffocation, something that would have produced less blood loss and preserved life until the very last minute.

I would have removed the skin while he was still alive. That way, when the tissue was frozen, there'd be a good chance it would be usable. In Krommer's case there was a lapse between death and the removal. I'd seen this before in a previous case. I'd been sent to Copenhagen to covertly retrieve and decrypt some coded information from the laptop of an informant turned bad. Someone got there before I did, and he'd been drugged or poisoned to the edge of death before the sensitive tissue was removed, in this case a thumbprint, the access key to the laptop and to wipe the drive – which contained plans to blow up the Eurotunnel. The perpetrator didn't check that he was dead, simply assumed. He wasn't. He lived to tell the tale – and to identify the killer. As always, I completed my mission, even if I retrieved from the perp and not the informant.

In this case there was a clear need for Krommer to be dead, and obviously dead. The killer must have been in no doubt that he was dead. That would have been the first and most important instruction. Then the removal of the fingerprints, or possibly retrieval of the flash drive but they didn't manage that. I smile to myself. Not as smart as they thought they were. Two out of three objectives achieved. Whereas my score sheet is flawless.

I'm already engaged in a mental battle with whoever has done this.

So I press reply and the number three on the keypad. I run the risk of alerting headquarters to the loss of the flash drive when I actually have it. But I have nothing to lose. I do it anyway. I shift in my seat. I have a bad feeling about this and I'm usually right about these things. There are complications. Krommer is clearly not just a runner. No sign of drugs or alcohol. I'd bet my life that his bloods are toxin free. No. He's critical in this operation, someone who can access important places. His biometrics are valuable and no doubt his body will be seized and interrogated for any other missing parts, once I've alerted someone.

The driver starts the engine and there's a boom. For a second I fear the car has exploded, that this is the end. A split second of regret that I haven't done what I intended to. I feel the car shake then hear the blaring of alarms. I look back up the street, making myself stay in the car, even though I want to run. No. I have to see it through. I have to. A cloud of smoke clears and I see the SOCO team out on the street, with Ringer shouting into his mobile phone.

The explosion has taken out the flat above the crime scene. Smoke still bellows from the windows. The debris has reached the car and the windscreen is covered in dust.

Almost in slow motion the driver raises his phone to his ear, then turns around and drives in a different direction.

In fifteen minutes we arrive at a gated complex in Alderly Edge, about twenty minutes outside Manchester and conveniently near to the airport. I'm met by Karl Ronson, Director of Operations, who points me towards a side door. Once inside he takes my coat and the phone that contains the flash drive. He perches on the arm of a stylish brown fabric sofa and motions for me to sit on a nearby recliner. Like Krommer's flat, this apartment is brand new and pristine – no dust, and the faint smell of paint. I stand near the door. I always stand near the door.

"Kate. Thanks for that. So…"

Straight to the point. No pleasantries. Just how I like it. I quickly explain about Lewis Krommer and the missing fingerprints and he nods and smiles as I talk. Karl's charming and warm on the surface but his eyes are steel-grey cold. The smile doesn't extend to them. I've met him many times before but not as a director of any operation I'm involved in. He's watching me as I explain about the ice tray, working out what he can use me for.

I'm watching him, too, scanning his facial muscles for the slightest hint of a twitch to signal a reaction. It's only when I talk about the delay between the time of death and the removal of the skin that he frowns slightly. It's not revulsion, rather a nod to the shabby nature of the operation. Like me, he's thinking how it could have been executed better. When I finish speaking he's silent for a moment. Thinking. Considering.

"OK. This is more of a problem that we expected. The explosion. We need to get the body out of there as soon as possible. I'll make some calls. You retrieved the target and uploaded the data successfully. Good job, Kate."

I blink at him, waiting for him to continue.

"Is that it? Are they after something else, Karl? The fingerprints? Why remove the fingerprints? Why blow it up?"

As I push him for information, he taps his foot slightly. Something deep inside me shifts as I realise this must be serious. Karl was nervous. It wasn't like Karl to be nervous. It's too much of a coincidence for this to happen to someone who's a target carrier.

"No. They're after the same thing we are. I'm trying to decide who to deploy." He pauses for a moment and stares hard at me, mirroring my frown. "How's Neil?"

My hand grips the arm of the chair and my heart flutters. It always comes down to this. Fucking Neil. He was active two years ago until he began work on a case in Central America that escalated out of proportion. He did the same job as me for the security services. We called ourselves undercover agents but we were spies. That's how we met, on a shared mission. We were flexible and we worked with different agencies: armed forces, security services, and police. It depended on the case. We'd worked together and lived together for seven years in the security services, on a long case that ended badly. We'd been recruited onward separately and I was working in London when the news came through.

Neil's ex-wife had been targeted and, as the message so eloquently stated, neutralised. There'd been a car accident. His children had survived. They'd seen her blown out of the car, covered in her own blood. I felt for them profoundly because I had lost my own father and I knew at that moment I was deeply involved. Too deeply.

I wasn't with him when he got the message but I spoke to him an hour later. He'd seemed fine when he called me from Brazil but, when I met him from the flight, he broke down in the arrivals lounge. I'm excellent at my job but I hadn't anticipated how he would crumble at the death of his ex-wife. I'd begged him to stay professional, rein it in until we got home.

"You haven't got children…" he'd whispered, as we summoned a taxi at Manchester Airport. In the middle of all the chaos and drama I realised that we weren't as close as I'd thought. Whereas my dedication was to him, his was diluted by so many other people. He didn't love me. He would never have said that otherwise, even in shock. He knew how I felt about having children – or, rather, about not having them. But I'd stayed silent, knowing that it would have been inappropriate to expose my scarred heart at that moment. It would keep until we were alone in our apartment. I'd asked the driver to take us to our apartment in Didsbury but Neil had stared at me and shaken his head.

"Home? Home? No, Kate. Everything's changed now. My children need me."

So he was anchored and I was thrown out of my life and into his. What was described as a tragic accident to the press was acknowledged as a cock-up internally, and Neil was put on garden leave with full pay. Indefinitely. We never spoke about our apartment again. But I'd left my heart there. It felt selfish and uncaring but I couldn't help it. His ex-wife's house became home and I became a part-time mother, between assignments, to Sammy and Leo. None of it felt right and it was taking its toll on me professionally. I couldn't risk making mistakes in the life and death scenarios I faced when I was working.

It wasn't just my personal life that was disrupted. As if my dull, disappointed heart was on show, I'd sensed a change in how I was perceived at the agency. It's all about attachment: the more you have the less objective you are.

And now Karl is asking me outright before he gives me this assignment. I look away. "If you're asking me if I'm playing wifey to him, then the answer's no."

"I'm asking if you're likely to be running back at the first sign of trouble. There's more to this case than meets the eye and I can't risk any emotional baggage fucking it up. Yeah?"

It's irritating but I know he's right. After all, wasn't that why I had left? "Then Neil's fine. He's got it all tied up nicely on his own."

There's more truth in this statement than I like to admit. I'm more alone than I sometimes pretend I am. Or want to be.

Karl stands up. "Good. Then that's settled. But this is a tricky one, Kate. We need to move quickly. Lewis Krommer had information that is critical to a potential international incident, and the fact that he's dead minus his fingerprints means that someone else is after that information. Someone who is prepared to be killed for it."

Chapter 3

Karl gets out a slim manila file. He reads through it and passes it to me. "I didn't mean to sound harsh about Neil, Kate. It's just, well, at this level I can't afford any emotions coming into play. This is big time."

I speed-read the contents of the folder. Lewis Krommer has no background between leaving university and turning up in London about fifteen years ago. Then he got a couple of minor traffic offences in Manchester a couple of years ago. Living in Harpurhey then and still is, according to council tax records pulled last week.

It seems like we'd had an interest in him for about three months. He'd come to our attention when he directly offered some information. A couple of sensitive files which he said he found on his travels, and someone had told him they might be valuable. I get to the back of the file, and to the photographs. His college pictures don't resemble his forty-five-year-old self. In fact, I'd be hard-pressed to say it was the same person. And now there's no chance of comparing his dead fingerprints with the ones taken at the time of the traffic offences.

Karl's watching me. Waiting for a response.

"OK. And I didn't mean to snap. Neil's fine, actually. Enjoying the time out with his kids. And I'm fine. It's just that me and Neil, well, we're not fine. And I probably won't go back after this job. You know, Karl, this is the first time in my life I've felt guilty about what I do. Queen and country and all that. But now I can't discuss it with him. He's bitter and who can blame him?"

"Only natural, I suppose. He must miss it."

"I don't know if he does. I just think he wants me to be Mum to the kids and it's not gonna happen. It's not what our life together is."

Karl's icy eyes suddenly show a little compassion. "Will you go back to London then? Back to your old place?"

I feel a tingle of excitement when I think about it. My old apartment, complete with a tiny office. I used to work out of there long before I met Neil. It was left to me by my father when he died thirteen years ago. His little piece of London, he used to call it. I don't feel alone there. Oh no. I feel like he's still there with me. I picture the tiny lounge and the bedroom with its neon light outside the window, pink above a backstreet cocktail bar. But two floors up, so it isn't noisy. Tucked out of the way where no one would ever find me.

I'd reluctantly rented it out when I moved up north. I loved that place and I wanted to keep it exactly like it was. But it made no sense. The tenants were usually people working for the security services with short-term contracts. When the last one left eleven months ago, I hadn't let it again. I knew then, deep inside, that Neil and I wouldn't go the distance. I started to pine for London again, to crave the crowded tube stations and the busy pavements. Even though I was a northern girl at heart, I could still see the London streets in my mind's eye. That's what I want. Yes. London. For a while, anyway.

"Yes. I probably will."

"Good. From the looks of this case you'll need to spend some time down there. So, a bit of background. Krommer appeared on our radar about twelve weeks ago. He contacted our intelligence with something of interest."

"Source?"

"He has a contact in the service. He may have been an informant at one time or another. That's one route. He knew names."

I write this down in my black leather-cased notebook. "So what was the information?"

Karl licks his lips and swallows hard. "OK. Krommer was offering information on weapons of mass destruction. WMD. And obviously, in this day and age, that could indicate a possible terrorist threat."

I stop writing and feel the fear rise through me. My stomach somersaults and my breathing momentarily goes into overdrive. My work has involved plenty of risky situations but WMD is the biggie. The Holy Grail. Deadly on a large scale.

Was this what we'd been waiting for?

"WMD? Really, Karl? What specifically do you mean?"

He pauses. I feel a little bit sick. My hands involuntarily sink to my notebook. I might be a seasoned secret services employee but I'm prey to the same dread as everyone else. Terrorism. You just never get used to it. It's exactly what it says on the tin. I'm just as suspicious as the next public transport user that a bomb will go off in the next carriage, or in a crowded city centre. There was daily intelligence on terror threats but most were dealt with and few materialised. I was hoping that this would be solvable.

"We have information from a member of a team who worked on weapons programs. Confirmable details of the materials used in the original weapons, and all were accounted for after the weapons inspection by NATO. But there was some information relating to something other than that. That's what Krommer was selling. About a different threat."

"Right. Location?"

"Iraq. The information on the flash drive was a sample of what he was selling to us. Giving us a name to connect what he was offering. To authenticate it. Security level one. We've been looking for this information for years, Kate."

My mind runs over the scenarios, the questions over hidden weapons of mass destruction in Iraq and how none were ever found. Yes, my instincts tell me, this was the prize. Yes. This is valuable information, at the root of everything the security services did. This is what I was trained to do: locate information that lay hidden in databases for years, the final pieces of puzzles that would turn data into deadly action.

"What was his price?"

Karl pauses. He has to be sure about me before he gives me the core case information. I know he's going over the conversation about Neil, weighing the probabilities. Finally he continues. "One million for the first data packet. Then half a million each for the next eleven."

I whistle loudly. "Bloody hell. Presumably whoever killed him wants to avoid paying him?"

"Looks that way."

Then the million dollar question: "So what was the initial information, Karl?"

It's the point of no return. The place where the road narrows and you can't go back. The only sign of his doubt is his left index finger pressing against his thumb. I know that this is a well-known technique to diffuse stress because I know all the tricks in the book.

"The name given to us by Krommer is Zaki Assadi. Assadi turned informant and gave us a document about a program producing deadly weapons somewhere in Iraq. The document explained the nature of the program and some background but stopped short of giving us the exact device or the location. Or who has it now; although we strongly suspect that it's in its original position as there is no intelligence to suggest otherwise. Hidden somewhere, possibly and probably Iraq. There was a gap in his file and Assadi said it was because that information was never passed to him. Credible because Assadi worked on the Iraqi nuclear weapons program and had links with Saddam Hussein's regime until he defected. All Krommer's sample information checked out with Assadi's. We've been in contact with Krommer for months and he was all set to transfer the information, presumably with the location and the names in two days."

"Is it definitely weapons?"

He studies me again. His breathing is quick and he's flushed slightly pink. "It's definitely weapons. We have more than enough intelligence to know that. Assadi's information made it clear. Until today this mission has been on ice, until we retrieved the coded text. I'd reactivated the case, against the possibility of Krommer coming good. Now it seems we're not the only ones who want that information. But let me make this clear. This has become a matter of life or death. Krommer was murdered. He wouldn't have been able to tell whoever murdered him what the information was because it was coded. Even the sample used different ciphers. That information is critical. With the Iraqi links this has the potential to become a major threat to British security. Whoever killed Krommer has the same information as us, and may be one step ahead. And they're here. That puts us all in danger. All of us."

Fear kicks in quick and deep. Even in my job, where I know the stakes are high, I still have the capacity for fear. But I push it aside as I realise why I'm here, and focus in on one word. "Coded?"

"Yes. So even when we get to the information – which we will because we have to – even when we get it, we'll need to crack it."

I know exactly what he means. I would have to decode it.

He looks towards the door. Our meeting is over.

"I've already given you a name: Assadi. He's been questioned over and over but he's all we've got with Krommer dead. Find out all you can, yeah? It's a race, Kate, because someone who doesn't seem to give a shit about leaving Krommer in his apartment with his head split and his fingerprints missing is one step ahead of us. Think about it. They wanted us to find him there, like that. They knew we'd be there to collect the flash drive. It's a warning."

He hands me the manila file and opens the door. "Good luck. We're at your disposal. Code word: *pronto*. I'll get a dedicated phone delivered to your London apartment by morning. I'll be in touch later with a clear mission statement when we've clarified what's on the flash drive. It's all yours."

I leave and walk down the road. I can see the light cast from the open door and Karl's long shadow from the corner of my eye. Weapons of mass destruction. Missing fingerprints. Coded information. Jesus. Yes, this is it. This is where everything was leading to. This is the kind of case I'm used to. Fear or no fear, it's the challenge I need to get back to me.

I reach deep into my pocket for a cigarette but then remember that I stopped smoking because of the children. I really need a cigarette.

Assadi is my starting point. Excitement pulls at me again as I think about the resurrection of my London contacts and the open access I'll have to the Vauxhall offices as long as I am on this case. The thrill of freelance work, of no rules, is as attractive to me as it is to the security services. I can go further, push harder than your average operative and that's exactly what I intend to do to find out who Lewis Krommer is, where he's been for half his life, and how he is connected with Zaki Assadi.

Chapter 4

I'm in my London apartment by midnight, drinking a straight whisky with ice, and when I wake early the next morning the pink neon sign is still flashing. It bathes my tiny bedroom in pink light and, for a moment, I imagine that it is thirteen years ago and I'm twenty-three and my father is still alive. I can still feel him here, a stabilising presence in my life. Any minute he'll call me and tell me to come to his office for lunch at exactly twelve o'clock because he's got a surprise for me…

Then I remember about Lewis Krommer and the weapons program, the present threat, and Neil and the kids. How I always went for the bad boy and how that had backfired on me. How he'd never really been a friend, just a lover.

I flop back into the pillows and wonder how I will tell Neil that I am never going back. How I'll start again and wipe out the past eight years of my life with him, and the last two with Sammy and Leo. It's not that I didn't like them. I would even go so far as to say I love them in a way. But they're not my children and I'm not their mother. I don't belong in their world. I belong in this one. This world, that's suddenly a very dangerous place; more dangerous than usual.

Right on cue there's a buzzing noise and I look out of the window. A courier looks upwards and I signal for him to post the package through the door. He waves that he needs a signature. I wrap my dressing gown around me and rush down the two flights of stairs. As I open the door the courier pushes the parcel into my hands. I sign and he's gone.

I look up and down the street. It feels like home but it's not thirteen years ago and my father will never ring again. He and my mother were older parents, both in their forties when I was born. I had an idyllic childhood in a little village called Mossley, tucked up above Manchester just under the Pennines. My parents lived up there to preserve our family normality but my father often worked down south. It would be easy and almost true to say that he was a code breaker who worked at Bletchley Park. But he was more than that. The security service is like a Russian doll; you always think you've reached the last one but there's always another. My father was right at the centre, a kind of consultant to the code breakers. The Morden codes – they were his baby.

He'd been a lecturer in advanced maths when he was younger and I can only guess that's where he was recruited from. He became part of a go-to cell for the military, always on call and forever in his study poring over maths. New computer after new computer meant he always had the best kit – which meant that I, as I peered over his shoulder and followed his commentary, soon had his great love of maths and cryptography at my core. I couldn't get enough of problem-solving. By the time I was a teenager, he'd taught me everything he knew.

But he'd always kept his northern, down-to-earth air. And so had I. He stood out from the Cold War crowd; everyone who visited our house spoke Received Pronunciation and his low vowels marked him different. It worked that way for me, too, and helped me to gain people's trust. Friendly and northern worked every time, for both of us.

Then my mother died. One day she was in the kitchen making tea and toast, the next she was in bed with a terrible cough. The day after that, my father came out of her room and shut the door. He'd shaken his head and picked up the telephone in the hallway. We still had dial phones, even then. Everything seemed to suddenly go into soft focus, film-like, as he summoned the family doctor.

After the funeral we didn't speak for weeks. We simply carried on working on one of his projects. I went to school as usual, even the day after she died. We lived on corned beef sandwiches and hot, sweet tea. The fruit my mother had bought rotted in the uranium green fruit bowl. Eventually, after the Christmas holiday, we emerged a little bit recovered and things went back to almost normal. Whenever he came here to London to work I would stay with his sister in the village. Every day on my way home from school over the moorland, I'd go round to our house and look through the window at the computer and his desk, and pine for his return so we could 'get on' and work.

Then the day came that he didn't return. It was the first term of my Master's degree at Oxford University and I'd been staying in the flat for the weekend with one of my friends, enjoying the London nightlife, when the phone rang. It was Aunty Rose, and after a long silence she told me that it was bad news and that my father had been killed in an accident in London. It was the first time I'd felt the crushing fear of being alone in the world. When my mother died I'd still had my father.

"But I'm in London. He can't be here if I'm in the flat. Where would he stay?"

I had no idea what his life was at that point. All I knew was that I was his double, red hair and blue eyes, white-pale skin, and that I'd been his protégée. I had no idea who he worked for or what his projects had been. But I was about to find out. Within a few days someone contacted me about his work and asked to meet me. They explained that some of his work had been sensitive and that I would have to be debriefed.

I'd been scared at first but then I thought about my father's life and how he was calm, always together. And that I could be like that. Yes. I'd be like him.

After the debriefing an older gentleman came into the room and asked me if I was interested in working for the security services. He didn't say 'spy'. Not at first.

It wasn't an easy decision to make, especially just after your father has died in service. I went home and thought a lot about it. All through my Masters course, in fact. Looking back now I see that although I was always looking for reasons not to, I'd actually made up my mind that day at the debriefing. It was almost inevitable that I would continue my father's work. But this time in my own right.

By the time I finished my Masters I was working in analysis. This is how the service works, recruiting you bit by bit, skill by skill. I was given snippets of interesting codes to solve at first and, to me, it was like a game. I would shadow other agents in what I now realise was intensive training. Back then it all seemed like one big, exciting adventure. Up and down the country, then overseas. Codes, watching, analysing; all the things I was born to do. But there's more to it than that. There's instinct, gut feeling. I'm chasing the silent messages, the invisible crime scene, the hidden world that I know is around here somewhere, waiting to be discovered if only I can make sense of all the signposts, all the patterns.

Then I was asked to go on my first mission. I aced it.

The brief was to infiltrate a bank-fraud gang that was money laundering for the IRA, and to leave with my identity intact but all their secrets transmitted securely to Millbank. It was easy and fun. Not one of them suspected me, and one of the gang still tries to contact me all these years later. To them I was just a girl with expensive tastes.

In reality I rose quickly to become one of the shooting stars of the agency, with a high security level and a boyfriend in tow – because round about then is when I met Neil.

Now heavy nights of passion mixed with the excitement of becoming a spy. His children were toddlers and he saw them alone. He was careful to keep his personal life separate from me and that was how I liked it. But little by little our masks slipped – until in the end we were just two normal people with two kids. But one of us had a job that wasn't normal. And it became dangerous.

My last mission had sent me soaring to the top as the combination of all my skills finally came together. I'm a coder by nature, and most coders are happy to hole up, analysing pattern after pattern. But I'd gone farther; I'd built up a unique repertoire of both quiet, exacting cryptography and the kind of skills that suited the dangerous world of the spy. By linking the two I had, over time, developed a way to link the patterns in a code with the patterns in life. What people do, the way they subconsciously make sense out of internal chaos, is so revealing. I knew deep down inside that it was here, in people's inherent desire to preserve themselves for infinity, that the clues to even the most difficult cases lay. In memories, and in diaries, photographs and notebooks. The pattern was always there somewhere, and I discovered I could use both the micro and the macro to find it.

I quickly realised that I had the same skills my father had, and more besides; which meant I could call the shots. So I set myself up as a freelancer, just like him. Just like thousands of other people all over the country who live absolutely normal day-to-day lives but, when called upon, became secret agents.

It felt good to be following in his footsteps and I'd never once regretted it.

My last mission had relied on it. Like this one, I had been assigned to find some coded information that was critical to prevent people coming to harm. The detail involved several executives who were running an international money ring. There was little to go on initially but the small amount of evidence that we had was clear enough to implicate an MP who could influence banking policy and who was making money laundering easy. The mission's extra edge rested on the fact that the money was being filtered into Syria to fund an anti- Assad organisation.

This world is difficult to crack and often involves infiltrating the lives of those involved and secretly looking over their possessions. Luckily, people just can't help being sentimental; they keep photographs, notes on slips of paper, bank receipts that show their greed, any reminder that prompts their memories. People just love memories – which is so often their downfall.

I'd worked on the case for months, interviewing and re-interviewing the executives, following them around London and New York, and came up with nothing. Snooping and spying. Then I noticed that one of them, Ken Miller, the main contact in a Syrian financial deal, was constantly typing into his phone - either a blog or messaging someone. He'd often take pictures on trains, the underground, in the street. It was all going to some social feed somewhere. We checked his Facebook and instant messaging but he only used them to monitor his wife's social networking. Eventually I drilled it down to an Instagram account where he was making a picture diary of his life.

But the case was nearly stalled when Neil rang me on the agency phone to ask where I had put a pair of Leo's shorts. That's when I realised what my priorities were. It wasn't the first time he'd done this. I was covertly in Miller's bedroom when the phone rang. Miller was on the other side of the door. The phone was on buzz, because I knew and Neil knew that it would only buzz in a critical scenario.

Thank God Miller didn't hear it. He would have killed me. But Neil hadn't thought of that. He'd only thought about himself.

I had to put work first. I blocked Neil's number and carried on with my mission.

Among hundreds of pictures of Miller's kids and grandkids, his hometown and his plush New York apartment, there were three pictures taken on a Caribbean island with two of the known suspects. From those photographs we traced everyone who went on that trip; delving into their affairs revealed a network of encrypted documents relating to banking fraud. I cracked the code in forty-eight hours, a personal best, and uncovered enough information to incriminate and remove the MP and foil a major terror plot.

This case will be the same. They always are. I just know it. People love their routines and they love their codes. Passwords, entry keys, alarms. My life's blood. The devil's in the detail, as my father used to say.

I open the package that's just arrived. It's the phone Karl promised, and a laptop. Tucked inside the padded envelope is a dongle and a key drive. I feel a tingle of excitement as I rush back up the staircase and into the flat. I set up the laptop and switch on the phone. The moment I switch it on it rings: Karl.

"Kate. Hi. OK, where are we up to?"

"ID?"

"Pronto."

I think back to our conversation last night. "The name you gave me, Karl. I'll investigate that and I'll go over Lewis Krommer's movements."

I hear him move into another room and close the door. "Still got the contacts, Kate?"

"Always. I've been in regular employment. Haven't lost my touch."

"OK. Good. The offices will be open to you but I'd prefer it if you connect remotely. The access code's on the inside of the envelope. I've arranged for you to have full security access but you'll need more."

I know what he means. I know he means the silent messages that hang around these cases and signpost the way. "Just as well I've got more, then. I'll check in using the secure portal and keep you updated. In the event that I can't make a voice call I'll upload anything I find in the usual manner." Like I did at Krommer's flat.

Karl is unusually quiet. I can hear his breath through the silence. When he speaks his tone is measured. "I've had confirmation, Kate. The information on Krommer's flash drive matches the information Assadi provided when he defected. This is definitely connected." His voice lowers perceptibly. "Still no nearer with the coded information. Looks like it's twelve separate items with some text. So, to clarify, that is your mission: to find that information and to decode it. When you do, we'll know exactly what kind of threat this is. Nuclear. Chemical. And where it's hidden. We already know the context from Assadi's files. This is definitely some kind of weapon that could potentially pose a terrorist threat to the UK. It talks about populations, not towns or cities. Krommer was murdered here, so whoever wants the information wants it bad, and is right here on sovereign soil. This is fucking big, Kate. Scary big. There's something massive going down here. Potential for a major terrorist attack."

It's escalated so quickly. Last night Karl seemed calm and collected; now he seems spooked and afraid. The clumsy job on Krommer was a bit odd, could have been gangland but now it seems like an international incident. I suddenly realise that I'm shaking. This is potentially bigger than anything we have dealt with before.

"God, Karl. Are you sure?"

"Absolutely sure. We've hit a wall now, gone as far as we can. Any further evidence was contaminated by that explosion. In the flat upstairs from Krommer's, it turns out. We've mediated it as a gas explosion – don't want the press getting hold of anything. Follow the name, Kate. Follow the name. Like I said, you'll need more than we've got, and you'll need it quickly before someone else gets hold of it."

I know exactly what he means. The service has all kinds of listening devices and intrusion tools at their disposal and don't hesitate to use them. They have operatives all over the world, just like me, eyes and ears. But what the others don't have is my specialist knowledge. I'm my father's daughter. I learned my analytical skills from him, then honed them in my own work.

I'm his legacy. His work helped to end the Cold War; I work in a more modern world of high technology mixed with unlimited knowledge. And a little knowledge is a dangerous thing. Anyone can pull together a series of facts and list them but, as Karl pointed out, it's all about context. A code can mean nothing until you know who designed it, what it is applied to and how it will be transmitted.

I've yet to meet anyone who can match my skills of analysis. After all, I learned from the best.

Chapter 5

An hour later I'm walking quickly away from my flat on Woburn Place towards the British Library. I'd forgotten how great it was to be so central. The flat's perfectly placed, just between two major rail stations and tube stations. The whole of London is accessible from Euston and King's Cross. It's easy to reach the airport and to travel to other major UK cities in a day.

But this morning I'm meeting Carey Morrison. I'd texted him earlier asking him to meet me at the British Library at ten, and I'm right on time. Of course, he's late, which irritates me a little because time is of the essence in this case. Even at our age, as we hurtle towards forty, Carey doesn't change. We were at university together, on the same course, and we realised our common interest early. Carey stayed in London when I left for the north but I've used him in almost every project where I've needed information fast. We make a good team.

I reach the library and look around the foyer. He hasn't arrived yet so I sit outside in the chilly morning breeze. I prefer to meet outside. If I have to meet inside I sit near the door. I always need a quick getaway. I know the exits to a building before I even take one step inside.

I order a coffee and turn on my laptop, logging on to the service intranet with my secure dongle and access code, and I see that Karl was right: Krommer was setting up a big deal. The current exercise had been just a taster to prove he had the goods. The central proof point was the comparison with Zaki Assadi's information.

So I call up the files for Zaki Assadi. He's a sixty-one-year-old Iraqi professor of physics. Came to work in the UK at Cambridge in 1991 from Baghdad University. Married fellow academic Belinda Lindon in 2006. Lives in Cambridge. On his entry into the UK he exchanged information for a visa. I click through the information and it details incidents in Iraq and Syria on random dates relating to the Gulf War and later missions by UK and American forces. The incidents are numbered one to 306, and all are clickable except those numbered from 212 to 223. Just like Karl said. Twelve missing pieces of data. The files contain details on Assadi's work as a nuclear scientist in Iraq and how he worked on Iraqi and Syrian weapons programs.

My mission clicks into clear focus. The core of this information is clearly something potentially world-changing. These twelve links are my mission.

I call Cambridge University to make an appointment with Professor Assadi. He's deeply involved in this. He must know something. The collegiate secretary puts me on hold, and then the call connects. There's a pause and I can hear my own heart beating loudly above the busy London traffic.

"Hello?"

I hear a rustle of paper, then a voice. "Assadi speaking. You wanted to make an appointment?"

I wasn't expecting him to answer himself. I collect my thoughts quickly. "Yes, please. My name's Kate Morden."

"And you are with?"

I tell him that I'm with a magazine and I'd like to do an interview with him about his involvement in the Cambridge University chess team. Standard identification. Straight from his file with MI6. He pauses and takes a sharp intake of breath. "It's started, then?"

I close my eyes momentarily and regroup. I need to know what has started. "I'm sorry?"

"It's started. I'm not involved in the university chess team, Miss Morden. I've never played chess in my life."

"May I come to see you today, Professor Assadi?"

"Yes. One o'clock. In my office, Miss Morden. Will you be alone?"

"Yes."

The line disconnects and I see Carey approaching. He waves and runs across the forecourt. When he reaches me he kisses me on both cheeks and we sit.

"My God, Kate, you look fantastic."

I return the compliment. It's a while since I've seen Carey in person. "You too. Bloody hell, Carey. Is that a hint of silver round your temples?"

He touches the auburn curls around his forehead and laughs. All white teeth and a cute cleft in his chin. He has a few more lines but haven't we all? "Comes to us all. It's a wonder I'm not completely bloody grey."

I watch his face tighten and know what's coming. "So what brings you to London? Life in Manchester not matching up to the big city? How's Neil?"

Fucking Neil again. "I've left him."

Carey nods slowly. There's a long pause before he speaks. "OK. Why? Why now?"

I don't want to explain it out loud but I need Carey on my side. "He was fucking things up for me. Jobwise. Wasn't working."

Carey breaks eye contact and nods again. I change the subject. "So, the job. Something big happening and I need some info. I need you to have a look at everything you can around Lewis Krommer. He was found dead in his apartment in Manchester yesterday. Fingerprints removed and carried off for future use, as far as I can see. The service case files have him at uni, then nothing for years. Odd. Suggests that he's maybe not Lewis Krommer at all."

"Great. What's it to do with?"

I know I can trust Carey with my life. He's unbuyable and a rare person who has no living relatives to be used as bargaining chips. No partner, no pets. He's completely alone and just the thought of this makes me shudder, even though it's a prime position for a spy to be in.

I give him the key-drive that Karl gave me and he copies it to his laptop. "Krommer is somehow linked with an Iraqi nuclear scientist. Zaki Assadi. I'm going to see Assadi this afternoon to find out what he knows."

I can hear my voice shaking with emotion. I sip my coffee and wait as he speed-reads the data.

When he's finished, he looks up. His grin fades. "Big time, Kate. You hear so much about this stuff. So what's the connection between Krommer and Assadi?"

"Unclear. Just what it says in the file. Krommer was trying to flog some secrets and Assadi brought some secrets to the UK in 1991. I'm working under the assumption that they're the same secrets. Or related, at least."

I know that this is his territory. I know from past experience that Carey's skills and mine are a perfect match on this case. We've worked together on several missions and Carey's down-to-earth reasoning balances with my instinctive way of working. He's my sanity check, my rationale check, my backup. Not that I always listen to him.

"Known or unknown?"

"Known but twelve files are missing and encrypted, as you can see. The confirmation data names Assadi and we know that it's to do with WMD. Obviously that isn't in the file."

He pales. "So not your run-of-the-mill terrorism, then? God, Kate. I thought you looked worried. Jesus. This is the big one, isn't it?"

I nod. The feeling of doom is growing inside me. They say a problem shared is a problem halved but in this case sharing this with Carey has just made it worse. More frightening. "Call me later, Carey. Let me know how you're getting on with Krommer."

"This could be *really* fucking massive."

"Or it could be just another mission. I could be a small cog in a big information wheel. I can't be the only agent working on this. Let's see what I come up with."

Carey looks doubtful. Between the silences both of us are screaming internally that this is the real reason we've both committed our lives to MI6. Somehow international security has taken over and we've both been honed into killing machines. But we're still human and prey to the emotions life throws out. Right now tears prick my eyes as I think about what is at stake, the millions of people who would suffer in a terrorist attack – and if Karl is right, here on UK soil.

Carey senses it. "Someone else is after the same thing, then? Which is why Krommer copped for it?"

"Mmm. That's what the director said."

"So if we don't solve it, it's only a matter of time until they…"

"God, Carey, yes. Don't state the obvious."

But I know he can't help it. He always states the obvious, whereas I'm more prone to make it unspeakable.

He gets up to leave and then pauses and leans over the table. "Is this the right time for you to do this, Kate? You know, with the Neil stuff? You'll need everything you've got on this one."

I feel the waves of anger, which is exactly what he means. Emotions and cold, hard spying don't mix. "I'm fine. Absolutely fine. I'm a big girl now."

He knows me so well. He just raises his eyebrows and strides off. I watch him cross the courtyard towards Euston, his dark brown mackintosh blowing in the wind. Carey's a good friend and, as always, I wonder if I should involve him. We've discussed it many times before. I wonder if I'm putting him in danger, if the invoices he files to the service are traceable so that one day he'll inevitably become part of a project that goes wrong.

He's got a different perspective. He says it's his life blood. A bit like I do, really. I've no doubt that, through my links, he's working on other cases alongside the work I've fed to him. It's all he has and, by the look of him as he strides around the corner, a half smile on his face, he loves it. It gives him a life, something aside from the private students he tutors in advanced maths and technology. It gives him an identity set aside from the norm and beyond his wildest dreams, even if it does seem to prevent him from holding on to relationships. It's too late now, anyway. Carey's involved. One more person carrying the burden of what is possible.

Sitting in the British Library grounds, what Carey said makes me think about my own past and how I've lived for the travel and the complexity of the cases that have filled my waking hours and kept me awake at night. Cases that have scared me to fucking death but compelled me to take them on anyway. How, when Neil's circumstances changed, I'd been given the choice between him and my job. And how I chose my job.

I haven't told him that yet. There is still time to go back. But I can't. No.

I walk towards King's Cross station to connect with the Cambridge train and think about what happened a long time ago and far away in Iraq. A world that most of us saw through the lens of a TV camera, in which we heard only what suited the people with a vested interest in the outcome. And how I would soon meet someone with a more accurate version of the truth about what was happening today.

Chapter 6

The train isn't due for another twenty minutes, so I read through Assadi's files again. He's given information about places and people in Baghdad, mainly relating to academics who were working on weapons programs at the university in 1990 and 1991. He seems to have been afraid that people were in danger, and the intervention of the US in Operation Desert Storm gave him a chance to air his views.

He's listed academics and their affiliations, those who were involved in previous weapons programs, and asked that they be kept safe. This forms the first part of the numbered items, and then he listed members of the village council from his place of birth in a village near Dokan. Then the critical information that Karl referred to, describing a new threat, something the world had never seen before, hidden away. The threat level was international, according to the papers. Following that is the empty data that is my mission.

I check and check again. If this threat is so big, why hasn't it been investigated before, when the information was first received or later?

Then I see that it has. The file has been accessed at various points in time. But no one has been able to locate the missing information. This has been simmering on the files for decades. A clear and present danger.

Next there are accounts of conversations Assadi had in the university with people whose names appear on the first part of the list and others marked as Iraqi officials. All the information has been corroborated and cross-referenced with the accounts of other defectors.

They form a familiar picture of Iraq in Saddam Hussein's heyday, where people were controlled by the state but, as Assadi puts it, free enough to go about their business. He talks about the manufacture of weapons and the invasion of Kuwait and the effect of the regime on his village, and on students and academics in Baghdad. How he'd been forced to work on weapons research programs. It finishes with him imploring the US and the UK to intervene in the invasion of Kuwait.

Back in 1990 this would have been shocking, top secret information but with the benefit of history and hindsight it's common knowledge.

I shut the file. That's the other puzzling part. It's only natural to wonder why you've been given a mission. True, I am a coder and I have overseas experience on difficult cases but I know only as much as the next spy about weapons of mass destruction: that there is a grey area around the question of their existence in Iraq. Maybe that's the point? Sometimes too much knowledge muddies the waters. And what did Assadi mean when he said that it's started? If this happened back in the nineties, why is it only just active again now? What has happened in between?

An hour later I'm in Cambridge. Such a beautiful city. I walk along Station Road to the university. It's a familiar pathway for me; I visited Cambridge many times during my time at Oxford, mainly to take part in code-breaking competitions designed to pit our academic wits against each other. When I reach the physics department I'm led along a corridor and given directions through the winding wooden passageways, which I follow until I reach a doorway with a doorbell. I ring it and wait. The slow tick of a clock somewhere calms me.

Moments later a woman opens the door. Her eyes are vivid blue and her expression changes inexplicably when she sees me to sullen grief, which makes me all the more uneasy. This is turning into a fucking nightmare.

"Kate Morden?"

She takes my passport when I offer it and glances at it, raising her eyebrows. She leads me through a large, silent hall that smells of beeswax and makes me think of *Dead Poet's Society*. The floor is made of black and white squares that, on closer inspection, are made of black and white mosaic. There are no windows, just winking faux-candles and, at the centre of the high ceiling, a grid of blue, red and amber glass tiles that on a sunnier day would give the room colour.

We reach the end of the hall and descend. The steep steps end at a solid oak door and she knocks. I hear a bolt being drawn back from the inside and the door opens.

Assadi is tall and dark and dressed in a tweed jacket. His office is a mixture of his heritage and his life today, Middle Eastern artefacts mixed with souvenirs from London and Edinburgh. Again, no windows but a strong smell of tobacco.

He points at the chair facing the desk. "Please. Sit. So, Miss Morden. What has happened to bring you to me? Someone has died?"

He's secure. It's almost a bunker. I spot a small wooden door at the back of the room, half draped with a thick maroon and blue curtain. I ignore his question. "That woman. Is that your wife?"

"Yes." His eyes follow mine to the semi-hidden doorway. "And yes, we live here. This has been our home for many years. I expect you're here to ask me if I know what the gap in the document refers to?"

He's leading me into it. He's been expecting me.

"Yes. I am. I saw your defection file. I wanted to find out why you didn't give us the full information and why you think something has started. That's what you said on the phone. It's started."

"Oh. I see. Aren't you Frank Morden's daughter?"

So that's it. That's the only reason I'm here, because of my father. Even now he opens so many doors for me. "Yes. Frank Morden is my father. He died…"

"Yes. I know. I knew Frank a little. So you follow in his footsteps?"

"In a way. I'm sorry to rush you, Professor Assadi. But there's been an incident and we feel that time is of the essence. I really need to know what the missing information is. Where is it?"

His expression is guarded. He looks around his office here in the inner sanctum of Cambridge University and taps his foot. "I don't have it. I can't tell you what it is but I can tell you the nature of it. It's just like the other information that you have. And perhaps some names, rumour has it."

Rumour? No. *No.* It has to be more than that. "I need more than rumour."

"I never had that information. My intention was to find it and complete my list but I had to leave before I managed it."

I feel the bottom fall out of my stomach as I realise what's happened. "So you don't know anything more?"

"No. I don't. Would I still be here if I was the key to this? If it's started, I expect someone has died already. Why not me, you ask yourself, if I have the knowledge?"

I lean forward and raise my voice. "What has started, Professor Assadi? What has started?"

He laughs loudly. Then he shakes his head. "I know it has started because you are here, Miss Morden. Someone who is involved in this mess has tried to sell that information. And it's been linked to me. So the search for it is on, the search for something that can destroy my country. Only by the grace of Allah have they not yet found it. Someone has finally realised how it all fits together. I knew I would be the first port of call because my file is all you have to go on. I always knew. But don't you think that if whoever is one step ahead of you thought I was of any value, I would have been a dead man by the time you got here? I never read the information you seek. I never had it."

He has a point. Disappointing though it is, he has a point. "So have you any idea what the missing information is?"

There is an uncomfortable silence. A sliver of uncertainty has punctured his confidence. And mine.

I say, "It's encrypted. The man who died sent a fragment of it to us beforehand and that's how we linked it with you. Look, I need to know what this is about. What are these weapons? Where are they? Please, Professor."

He's sweating heavily. I look around the room again, desperate to find some pattern that I can follow up. But he has no photographs, no common theme. He's fidgeting. He's hiding something.

"I don't know. All I know is that as I left Baghdad I was supposed to receive twelve more pieces of data to complete my list. Someone was supposed to meet me to give me information that I would take to the UK government to help topple the regime. They didn't turn up. I wasn't surprised. I left anyhow, and gave your employers what I had. I don't know where the information you seek is."

"Who had it, then? Who had that information? Professor Assadi, if whoever is looking for this information finds it before we do, there is potential for a terrorist attack. We know that it's an extreme threat because of the information you gave about the weapons programs. That's why I'm here. This isn't a personal mission. People could die. So where is the information? Who had it? Who was going to give it to you?"

"I expect the people who are rumoured to be named on the list have it now. Who always had it? The people who made it and hid it. The names I have never known. One of them may have finally got greedy. I don't know."

He does know. Like Karl, he suspects that the threat is still in Iraq. He knows something else that he isn't telling me. He looks sad. I can tell he's holding back. He will never tell me that what he suspects is worse than just his village being wiped out or his colleagues killed; what I see in his eyes is fear of something just outside his imagination, just beyond the horizon of what he wants to believe is possible for mankind. That's why he's hiding here in this bunker; he doesn't want to face whatever's coming next.

He rises suddenly and rounds the desk to stand in front of me. "I don't know what the information is. But I do know the situation in Iraq. I study it. And you need to find out what it is quickly. Iraq has changed, Miss Morden. IS is a new phenomenon. Something we haven't seen before. If they are chasing the information to find the missing weapons, then you need to rethink. They don't operate like us or Saddam. They have cells. It's a different kind of war with people you would never guess were involved. And if someone has killed on UK soil and it is connected to my information, then they have a cell here."

A chill of fear runs through my soul. IS – the so-called Islamic State. Assadi is right: they don't observe the rules of engagement in any shape or form. They are different. Deadly, because we just don't know how they operate.

"What makes you think it's them?"

He shakes his head. "Who else would it be? At this time? Worst possible scenario, Miss Morden. They want those weapons and they'll go to any lengths to get them. And they could be anyone. You know as well as I do, in your line of work, that a name is just a label so we can identify what they're doing on our own terms. In reality they're fragmented. You must suspect everyone."

I stand and he shakes my hand. A shock of fear runs through me and I step backwards.

"Honour your father's memory, Miss Morden. And when you arrive in my homeland, give her my regards."

"What makes you think I'll go there?"

"I don't know what the information is. But clearly it's still relevant now, even with the regime toppled. It has started. The hunt for it has started. After all this time, someone has realised its importance, its potential. Your country is at risk and my country is *still* at risk. She doesn't give up her secrets easily. But once the key begins to turn…"

Chapter 7

I'm fuming. The fucking key is turning. What key? What fucking key? He isn't taking it seriously. He ushers me out; the meeting is over. I reluctantly shake his hand again and I leave with his wife. As I walk away I hear the wooden door close firmly and the bolts snap shut.

Belinda Assadi walks just in front of me, guiding me along the tight corridors out of the maze that leads to their hidden home. She is tall and composed and has more than a hint of elegance. Her hair still has a tinge of auburn. Before we reach the huge hall she stops suddenly and turns around. Her face is still a mixture of grief and sorrow and she points at me. "Don't come here again. You don't know what it does to him."

She turns to continue our walk but I stay still, very still. I am as tight as a drum inside, ready for the fight that is on her face. "I had to come, Mrs Assadi. I had to find out what he knew. It's important. Someone has died."

She turns and approaches. Her face, close to mine, is a portrait of hate. "Lots of people have died, Miss Morden, haven't they? Lots of people. All this," she waves her arms around at the wooden panels and the fine upholstery, "all this is just a shell. He's tortured. Have you any idea how it feels to leave your own country? To defect and feel like a traitor? In normal circumstances he has to live with it every day on his conscience, and now it's starting again."

I stare at the mosaic floor. I don't know how it feels. I can only imagine. "I just needed to find out what he knew, Mrs—"

"Belinda. Please. Look, I understand the circumstances but he will never tell you what he believes, because he knows what the bottom line is. He'll skirt the issue because he knows that whatever that information is has the potential to change his world forever."

I step closer to her. "I know, Belinda. I get the picture. I've read his file. I just need to find out what it is, where it is and who has it?"

"He won't tell you because he doesn't know."

"I think he knows something, Mrs Assadi. And until he does I, or one of my colleagues, will keep coming back."

She flushes red and moves even closer. I can smell her perfume and feel her breath on my face. "You're very much like your father, Kate. Persistent. OK. If I tell you what I know, will you stay away? You must have some idea?"

She's thrown me a little but I quickly reason that if Assadi met my father then she probably did too. "I can't promise anything. In my experience secrets usually have money at the bottom of them. Large amounts of money."

"Or power. Zaki is a nuclear physicist, Kate. I'm sure that you know that. It's no secret that he's worked on weapons programs for your government and also for his home government."

We're going around in circles. I need to draw this to a close. Get to the nub. "OK. We already know that this is about some kind of weapons program. And your husband believes that some kind of a terrorist cell operating in the UK is chasing information about it. But we also know that there are no weapons of mass destruction in Iraq."

She looks away. "Do we?"

"After two invasions and years of warfare I think they would have been either found or used by now, or at least alluded to. Everything's accounted for. It's my job to know these things."

She withers and sits on a window seat, exhausted. "You're right, of course. The missing data could be anything, anything at all. But as your father will have taught you, the probability, based on what you already know, is that this is serious and it's about defence. You know what it is in the context of the former information. Inference. Isn't that how you work in MI6? Or something worse, something that could affect the whole of mankind. The fact that you're here confirms how serious it is. This has lain dormant for decades but we always knew that someone would come after it. That someone would be a Judas and try to sell it when the demand was greatest. It was inevitable, because people are greedy. I'm just surprised it took so long. Zaki always said that a beautiful woman would precede Armageddon."

She gets up and starts to walk. She speaks with her back to me but I can tell she is crying.

"I've said enough. Don't come back. He's told you all he knows. Leave him alone now."

We reach the entrance and she looks at me again, cold, angry eyes and thin lips. She presses a card into my hand. "Phone only. Don't come back."

I won't be back but I know someone else will. I start my walk back to the train station. He's confirmed what we've all been thinking and desperately hoping wasn't true. IS. Terrorism. Moving goalposts, never sure what their next move could be. But I feel cheated. I feel like sending in someone to persuade him to talk, to push his buttons but I'd need to ask Karl for permission, and it could be a dead end anyway. What if he really doesn't know what the missing information is?

Someone must bloody know, and I have to find them.

Fuck IS, or any other terrorist organisation for that matter. On a visceral level they piss me off, the way they force terror into the hearts of the general public. But for me it's even more serious: they fuck with everything I stand for. My confidence that patterns, predictability and human sentimentality will solve the case flounders because terrorism is ruthless and rule-less. It spits in the face of predictability – and that is its success. It's the opposite of what we expect and outside the acceptable rules of combat.

Even so, people are still involved. And where there are people there are families, loyalties and therefore deeply ingrained rat-runs of sentimentality, even if it is for the spoils of war. Terrorism goes against everything I believe in: goodness, peace, respect for all human beings. In fact, everything my father taught me and everything that finally convinced me to work for MI6 so that I could make order from the chaos of unpredictable events, keep people safe.

And that's the task that faces me – to find the missing information before anyone else does and prevent anyone from wreaking chaos. And that's what I will do.

I take the train back to London and call Carey from the station.

He answers after one ring. "Whoever that guy is with no fingerprints, it's not Lewis Krommer."

I'm still mulling over my meeting with Professor Assadi, trying to push down the fear back to the bottom of my being, when Carey hits me with this. "Are you sure?" I ask.

"Yes. Absolutely. Krommer made it through university but was reported missing in 1980 and was never found. But his UK passport was applied for in 1995. So, for a start, there's a missing fifteen years with no activity on his bank account or national insurance. Nothing suspicious enough to flag him up before or during university, though. Then there's the blood group. Krommer's mother was rhesus negative so his blood group was tested at birth; it was O negative. The guy you saw yesterday turns out to be B positive. I think we can safely say it isn't Krommer."

"Great. Thanks for that, Carey. I appreciate it."

"Welcome, Kate. But I have to say, this is the tightest case I've seen. No way in. I really don't think operations know much about this. Whatever the guy pretending to be Krommer had, it was unique information."

I think about what Assadi said, that he didn't know the details.

"Mmm, it seems that way. I've had no luck either. Just an elaboration on what we already knew."

There's silence on Carey's end. I know that he is going to ask me something important. He always does this. Eventually he speaks. "So it definitely is weapons in Iraq, is it? Is that what your contact told you today?"

I look up and down the concourse to make sure I'm not being watched. Then I begin to walk. If anyone was following me, they won't be able to lip-read if they're behind me. I instinctively drop my gaze to the floor when I see the CCTV cameras. Standard procedure. "Yes. We can be sure about that. But whoever is after them is here. Right here, in the UK. It's weapons alright"

Or worse. Wasn't that how Belinda Assadi put it? What the hell could be worse? "This information is from a long time ago but still relevant today. In fact, it's more relevant now. Someone is desperate to get hold of it."

"Bloody hell, Kate. Is it IS? Islamic State? Are they after it? Didn't think they were so organised."

It's what I fear. It's what Assadi fear. But it isn't like we can email them and ask them. Or even find an informer. The hard truth is that we don't know who they were. There has been no declaration of war against us, no public announcement of intention to commit an atrocity. But psychopathic terrorists who prey on innocents rarely announce themselves. Carey understands that.

"All we know is that someone posed as Krommer, someone else needed 'Krommer's' fresh fingerprints, and 'Krommer' is connected with this mission and Assadi. We don't know who it is for sure. Assadi thinks it's IS. Maybe an active cell. But I'm going to find out for sure."

There's silence between us. Like Assadi said, IS is an unknown quantity. We're used to dealing with international fraud rings, even gangsters who would have you killed as soon as look at you. But mass murder? On the scale of the reports coming out of Iraq?

Carey needs time to process this. He says goodbye and I walk to my apartment. I'm beginning to feel spooked, like I do at the beginning of every case; the sense of fear that prevails when the initial information is scanty. But I know deep down that getting past this is what sorts the security experts from the beginners. The persistence, the hanging in there until more pieces fall into place.

I reach the door when my mobile rings again. The display flashes Karl's name.

"Kate. Good. How are things proceeding?"

I open the door and go up, making sure that everything is how I left it. My father had installed a few gadgets that would let him know if anyone had been in the flat. My instincts about this job had told me to pull a length of hair's-breadth fishing line across the bottom of the door before I left; it was still intact.

"ID?"

"Pronto."

"Hi Karl. I went to see Professor Assadi and I'm up to speed."

"Good, because there's been another incident."

This is the point I've waited for. Sometimes we are given missions that go nowhere. An initial flurry of information or action, then nothing. Dead in the water – that's what we call them. But it looks as if this has just moved up another notch. There's a link. A pattern forming, seeping into the world, little by little, and I must chase it. I feel the goosebumps and the adrenaline, my breath quickening. This isn't dead at all.

"Oh. So…?"

"Another person. Alone in a public place with their fingerprints removed."

"Here? Known to us?"

I hear him get up and close a door. "Not to us. Kaleef Ahmed. Aged 48. He was found in his flat in Baghdad this morning. Same MO. Explosion in the next apartment shortly afterwards. Known to the CIA. Shared information. Ahmed's a big deal in the university. He's the go-to for rock structure and such like. Lead petrologist for the US government up until about six months ago. Apparently he left Iraq around the time of the first invasion. Came to America and exchanged information for citizenship. But working back in Baghdad."

"Just like Assadi." I think about Belinda's words and Assadi's information. Assadi and Ahmed both working at Baghdad University. Could there be another link?

Karl continues. "Similar. Yes. So we need you to attend and to find out what you can."

"What's my angle?" I know I can't go somewhere like Iraq without backup or a story. It just wouldn't work.

"Journalist. Kate Lynch. We're getting your papers together now. I'll send you a link to your background. Degree in journalism, minor articles in well-known publications. You'll be there to find out about women's roles in Iraqi academia. That should get you in. After that you'll have to find your own way. You'll be met by a CIA agent when you've settled in. As backup. Your flight's at eleven thirty in the morning. The papers will be handed to you at the airport."

I swallow hard. My mind races ahead and suddenly it all becomes real. Jesus. I'm going in, into a country where people are murdered on a daily basis. Where only the other day an American reporter was shot through the head at his hotel breakfast table. I'm mostly hardened to risk but this is extreme.

"All we know, Kate, is that we need to get to the threat before someone else gets to it. Someone's collecting fingerprints. Here and in

Iraq. Find out all you can about Kaleef Ahmed. Did Assadi say anything that would enhance that information?"

"He talked about Islamic State. He thought that it was a cell activated in the UK to specifically retrieve Krommer's fingerprints. If that's true, then another one has been activated in Baghdad. Assadi seemed afraid. He knows something but there's no way he was telling. And his wife mentioned Armageddon. In the context of defence."

Karl sighs. "Fucking hell. *Fucking hell.* This is a fucking mess, Kate. Fucking IS? We're clutching at straws now."

Chapter 8

I've been in this situation before. A long time ago. Sent out incognito and alone on a case that seemed to be straightforward but snowballed into something else. Then I spent many years going from team to team, working small jobs within the same case. After 9/11 we tracked suspects all over the world, some of them dead ends but a few of them part of a ragged patchwork of terrorists, often working alone but joined up by common training and communications networks. The Neil years, where it took almost a decade to find a solution.

I know that I ought to be afraid but I'm not. It's in my blood to push the fear back in order to get the job done. I'm no stranger to dangerous situations and I'm well prepared.

But the fear is still inside me, leaking out in tiny signs. Like my constant nicotine craving when I'm stressed and the slight twitch in my right eye when I'm under pressure. My need to be near an exit at all times. But I hide them well. I might be shaking inside but my appearance is calm and collected. I know myself well, and I know now that I'll have to be completely focused. Not thinking about it isn't enough this time, because the weight of people's lives is on my shoulders. Lots of people, potentially. Scaring myself to death is, in a strange sense, a good way to rid me of anxiety. I imagine the catastrophic chaos of a terrorist attack on the UK. Not just the lives lost but the effect on individuals who will experience the unthinkable – the loss of their loved ones.

Thinking about the domino effect of widespread destruction pushes down my fear and raises my sense of patriotism and duty. Yes, I'm proud of what I do. More now than ever before, my expertise is needed. That's why Karl chose me, isn't it? I know this but, like all agents, somewhere inside I wonder if I've been chosen because I'm dispensable.

I pack a bag. I need to be at Heathrow by ten in the morning. I type up my report of today's work and send an email to Carey. We have our own coded system, almost our own language, and the message gives him the map coordinates, latitude and longitude, of where I'm going. I know he'll reply with something similar but I'll be long gone by then; I'll pick it up remotely.

My last task is to open a panel behind the shower and remove a small case. It contains a range of mobile phones. As I decide which one to use I wonder how my father managed without one. Life must have been so much more difficult then. Then I remember what Professor Assadi said – that he knew my father. He came to the UK in 1991. My father kept a complete list of everyone that he ever met, complete with dates and times. The list was originally written in a series of exercise books – in code, of course. Later he kept an extension of the original list in an encrypted spreadsheet.

I'm the only person able to read these lists. My father taught me his own encryption technique early on in my childhood. I open the spreadsheet on my laptop and, although it's a long series of symbols and squiggles, I read it like a second language. I search for 1991 and scan through the entries. Finally I find it. July 1991 was the first meeting between my father and Assadi. I copy the code for Assadi's name and search through the rest of the document.

He had four more meetings with Assadi in 1991 and 1992, then nothing until 2001, when there were two more meetings just before he died.

I click the file shut and push the laptop into the panel behind the bath. I'll be supplied with another one at the airport, one with all Kate Lynch's' journalistic history. One without all the hidden encrypted files. It's still niggling at me as I choose a Samsung S3, nothing too flashy but adapted to transmit information; I'm still processing the fact that my father met with Assadi, yet there's nothing in Assadi's service file to indicate this.

There's no one to ask now. Maybe they were just social meetings. The list doesn't indicate an information recovery, and Assadi wouldn't have mentioned that he knew my father if it was top secret. In any case, I need to get organised. I pack the phone, the battery and the SIM card separately – no one can track me that way. Even if the battery is in the phone and it's switched off, it can emit a traceable signal. I need to eradicate every trace of Kate Morden and become Kate Lynch, or I haven't a chance of succeeding.

I've played the journalist before. Neil was seconded elsewhere and I was teamed up with a Venezuelan operative called Nathan. We were supposedly man and wife and he would joke that we were Angelina and Brad in Mr and Mrs Smith. Nathan is why I prefer to work alone. He was fine when everything was cool and we were hiding out or watching and waiting. But it all went wrong when he hesitated for a fraction of a second in the wrong place. I'd spotted the target immediately but Nathan seemed oblivious and when we were approached he clammed up. We were on the roof of an apartment building, opposite the target's penthouse suite, when the target arrived unexpectedly and opened a side door. He was a businessman, part of a high level fraud ring, and he addressed Nathan directly: "What are you doing? How did you get up here?"

Nathan had just stared. So I flashed my press pass. "I'm just getting some pictures for the nationals. They're interested in your life, Mr Leron."

But he was staring at Nathan still. "Didn't I see you the other day at the restaurant?"

Nathan should have answered immediately. He should have answered with a question or a denial. Instead he looked at me. Leron was already dialling security; we were detained overnight by the police until our supervisor was alerted.

I never spoke about it to Nathan but I swore to myself that I would never work with a partner again. Not after Neil and not after Nathan. It was too much of a risk.

I'm fully aware of all the risks but I have to get into role, to lie. To leave myself behind temporarily. One slip in front of the wrong people and I'm alone in a foreign land with no backup. A shiver runs up and down my spine and I push the tray of phones back into the panel shelf and close the door of the safe. Then I open it again. I reach to the back of the safe and pull out an old-style Ruger SR45. It feels heavy in my hand and I hold it tightly for a full minute.

I'm not considering taking it with me. I just need to feel the reassurance of it. My father told me he never used it but when I collected his effects from the funeral director I found it at the bottom of a backpack. The funeral director had discreetly handed the pack to me, looking me full in the eyes as he did so. Be careful – that's what his eyes said. Be careful, young lady. There's a gun in there. I'd left with my father's things. Outside I leaned against the wall. I reached into the bag and there, on the street, I breathed in the smell of burnt nitrocellulose. Sulphurous. The gun had been shot recently. At the time I felt like life had gone a little awry but I thought I was coping. Looking back at that moment, with the gun at my nose in the street, I realised how affected and confused by his death I'd really been. And how suddenly alone.

The gun still smells a little. It's the closest thing I have to any clue about the last moments of his life. A recently shot gun smell. Occasionally, when I'm stressed or over-tired or in danger, I wonder why it matters so much. Why I have to chase the memories of my father, the muddled ending to his life, the contradictions and unmatched accounts of what happened to him. Why I think about the smell so often, imagine what he was doing in the run up to his car crash.

Was it a car crash? My aunt told me it was an accident; my debriefers mentioned a car and some kind of collision. But the hospital told me that he had been brought in with a head injury. I read his hospital file from top to bottom and there was no mention of a road traffic accident. It said DOA. Something about an alleyway. Then there was the small matter of my father not having a driving licence. But no matter how many times I asked, I was never given a complete answer.

By that time I'd known he was a spy. I'd been told what he did and debriefed, then recruited. In the avalanche of new information everything was thrown up in the air and it only settled slowly over the years in small pockets of downtime in my busy schedule. But the smell of the gun remains. I'm a grown woman now, with a grown woman's life but this remnant of my early life sticks.

I wrap it up carefully and replace it in the tray. In one way it awakes my suspicion about him and what happened but in another way it gives me the motivation to carry on. I expect this is what legacy really means.

I'm almost ready. Ready to be Kate Lynch.

Chapter 9

It's just past midnight when my door buzzer rings. I was only half asleep but it makes me jump and suddenly alert. For a moment I feel safe and warm, then I remember what's going on and my mission floods my mind. I pull back the curtain quickly and look outside onto the street. People are hanging about outside the club, smoking and talking. My flat is completely soundproof but I can see their lips move and their wide smiles. In the centre of the melée is Carey. He's leaning back and looking up at my window. He beckons me to come down.

I pick up the intercom phone. "Carey. It's the middle of the night and I have to be up early. Come up."

I can hear his breathing, his lips close to the Art Deco brass buzzer plate. "No. You need to come down. Please, Kate. I need to talk to you."

I listen for a moment longer but he doesn't laugh or follow it up with a Careyism. He's prone to left-field jokes that not everyone appreciates but this isn't one of them and it scares me. I pull on some leggings and a tunic top and hurry downstairs, pulling at my long red hair to untangle the sleep knots. When I open the door he eases me into the crowd and walks me a little down the road until we're out of range of the club security cameras. There are still people around; we stand near a group of Italian tourists.

"What?' I'm hands on hips now.

He grabs my arms and holds me away from him. "Don't go, Kate. It's too dangerous. Don't go."

My hackles rise. Carey can't tell me what to do. "For God's sake, Carey. You've come all this way to tell me that? I know what's going on out there. I'm well aware of IS and their threat. I won't be venturing outside Baghdad. And I've got backup."

He grips my arms and frowns deeply. I've never seen him like this before. "I got in, Kate. I got in and I've seen what this is about."

He's looking around, checking for tails and cameras. Deadly serious. My heart beats faster suddenly and I feel afraid again. I know Carey and he wouldn't have come over if this wasn't crucial.

"OK. So what did you find?"

"Nothing. Fucking zilch. But I accessed the need-to-know file log. There were two encrypted files in there and a recently added transcript of them. Recently like yesterday."

"Yeah, I already knew that. They would be the contents of the flash drive."

Sweat blooms on his forehead now and he's pacing around. The chatter of the club-goers is beginning to irritate me. And this isn't the Carey I'm used to.

"But this, Kate. This. There was a piece of intelligence. It was the data from Assadi's report. It's what you've been looking for. It was heavily coded and transmitted to RAF Akrotiri in Cyprus on 15 January 1991. Two days before Desert Storm."

"God, Carey, Assadi's contact came good! Good work. So we do have it. How did you get in?" I feel a weight lift from my shoulders. I'm not going in blind after all.

"There's more, Kate. We don't have it anymore. The day after it was received it disappeared. The file is marked Top Secret and it's only been seen by very senior eyes. It seems that we've been looking for that information since 1995 when someone realised the document had been substituted. And it's only in the past six months that any information about it at all has emerged – from Krommer."

So it's only starting again now because the information was lost and now it's been found – or, at least, offered up? That makes sense. And Krommer had the original material.

"So what was the information you did see? What was the nature of it?"

Carey strides off down the road. I hurry after him. He stops in a cul-de-sac and sits on the low wall outside an office block. I join him, my body tense.

"It was just the information that Assadi gave when he defected. But the end of the file has never been decrypted. It looks like several people have tried but not managed to decode it."

He stares into the distance. More difficult words waiting to spill.

"For God's sake, Carey, spit it out. I already know Assadi's a nuclear physicist. I already know that this is about something terrible.

And I already know I'm on a morning flight to Iraq. So putting two and two together…"

"Yeah, because that's not bad enough. But the thing is, Kate, you were singled out. The last entry in the service file for this case was an instruction to recruit Kate Morden."

It all falls into place – why I was summoned. I'm not really surprised. That's the way it works at times.

"So? They wanted me to do the job. Why are you so surprised?"

"You don't understand. They wanted you because you're the only person who can do this job."

"Really? So you're saying that I was pre-selected even before I stumbled upon Krommer's missing fingerprints? That's not possible. I put in a call for assistance and that's when Karl called me in."

He's silent for a while. I hear a siren on the adjacent street and we both automatically look towards it. None of this makes sense. I'm good at my job but, admittedly, not the automatic choice in a case like this.

I think back to my initial conversation with Karl and his frustration about the missing data in Assadi's document, how he told me that finding it was my mission. And Professor Assadi withholding what he knew. His wife coming close but stopping short. Even Carey's holding something back now. I've known him long enough to know that. Eventually I sit next to him.

"Thanks for being concerned. I appreciate it. But I'm still going. It's my job, Carey."

The anger finally breaks out and he's almost shouting. When Carey's like this it touches the little girl deep inside me, the girl who listened to her mother and father arguing. It's a deep kind of alertness, unsure of an outcome, and it creeps up on me until I'm willing him to hurry up and finish what he has to say.

"You know what this is about, Kate. Everyone does but no one wants to say it. But I will. It's the question that hangs over everyone's heads. The big question. Did Iraq have weapons of mass destruction? It's the source of a million conspiracy theories online and it cost people their jobs and their lives. Was there or wasn't there? Only now, with more up to date information, the question is: is there or isn't there?"

"Come on, Carey. If they had, wouldn't they have used them? There've been two invasions and ongoing tension. If they had a nuclear trigger it would have been known by now. Uranium or plutonium would have shown up on surveillance. Then there are all the various terror groups out there, all the in-fighting. It would have had to get in or out somehow, and even a small amount would have been noticed. If anyone knew where they were…"

And it clicks. That's what this is. A hunt for something that's lain hidden for years. Something Assadi and his team know about. Something that was already there, before the first invasion. This isn't recent at all. It pre-dates 1991 and Desert Storm, quite separate from the WMD program mooted by Bush and Blair. And Krommer has reignited interest by trying to sell information about it to people who now want to wreak havoc with mass destruction. Terrorism.

Carey looks at me and shakes his head. "Took you long enough."

"I'm still going, Carey."

He puts his arm around me. It immediately reminds me of fresher's week at university when he tried to kiss me. I tense up and then relax. He's holding me tightly and resting his head against mine. Eventually he speaks. "You've got to understand that I'm only saying this in your best interests."

"I'll decide what's in my best interests."

He pulls away from me. "I know. Do you remember when we had that argument about me not telling you when that bloke you were seeing was cheating on you? That you'd rather know, have all the information so that you could make a decision based on the facts?"

I do remember. Fifteen years ago. Carey had kept it to himself to save my feelings. "Yes. And I still feel the same. That's why we're still friends, because I trust you to do that. But in this case, it's the opposite. All lies and secrecy from the people who are supposed to be on my side."

I see the concern in his dark brown eyes. Or is it more than concern? "Yeah. Right. The thing is Kate, it's worse than all this. It's worse than national security and it's worse than politics and war. Even worse than terrorism. A lot worse, because it involves you."

"But I have to do my job. It's what I'm born to do. You know that more than anyone."

"And that's the problem. I don't want to tell you this. Not just after Neil and the kids, because it'll shatter your world. But I promised you I'd never withhold information again. So I'll tell you. The code in the file. The encrypted data. It has a signature."

My heart beats a little faster and I steady myself on the wall with my hands. Suddenly, in the cold night, I feel alone. Part of being an intelligence agent is being able to pre-empt what someone is going to say. The ability to gather the evidence and create a set of probabilities to work on. So the odds are stacking. My father's meetings with Assadi. The way he died. The secret work in London.

"So you think my father coded it. So what? His codes have been revealed now. If his signature is on it, then they would have been able to read it. After all, you read it, didn't you? You read the data, Carey."

He looks directly at me. His eyes are glassy and reflect the pink light from the club sign. "I didn't read it, I couldn't, but I recognised the key. I seriously don't think anyone else has read it either. There's only one person who would be able to read that data. You, Kate. It's your signature on the encryption. I recognised it straight away. You coded that data."

Chapter 10

"That's impossible. I would have been a child when that data was coded."

But even as the words spill out I remember the long nights sitting in my father's study, him smoking with the window open. The smell of old leather mixed with tobacco. Me watching and learning, and working on my own projects that he gave me.

The bottom falls out of my world and sends me reeling back through time.

"It doesn't matter what the subject is, Katherine. You have to look deeper. Develop your own ways. That only you know. The key to secure encryption is where you anchor it in your own mind, as well as in the key. Layers and rotation."

Even back then the security services used computers to encrypt but any sensitive work was given to agents like my father to create a secure key. It was a key that only he would know, authored around a concept that he had either created or anchored it to. Words were interchangeable with other words in certain texts so that, even if the document was successfully decoded through the many levels, the final level could turn out to be a nursery rhyme or a traditional text.

Coders like my father create a story within a story. This helps them to remember their keys and creates an identity for them. This is known as their signature. The key can never be written down or told to another person.

The only reason Carey knows my signature is that we worked closely together in university, so closely that he began to understand exactly how I worked. He can't actually read it but he will always recognise my work. I have no doubt about that. I told him in order to teach him this unorthodox cryptography. Unorthodox, because despite today's highly mathematical methodologies, coders like me still use words and concepts.

Carey looks past me and up the road. He knows exactly what I am going through because he would have gone through the same realisation hours before. Disbelief and shock, numbing until it explodes in temper. My body slumps and sags in the cool night, the stuffing knocked out of me in a way even the suggestion of international terrorism couldn't achieve. He will have debated whether or not to tell me but because of our friendship and his loyalty he's chosen to. That doesn't stop the anger inside me. It's like a small stone hitting the windscreen of my childhood, the crack slowly spreading until what I thought was idyllic and solid is spider-cracked and about to shatter.

All the time my father was teaching me encryption, all those times we would 'get on' with our work, sitting for hours and hours, he was locking away information so that no matter how much he was interrogated it would be impossible for him to give anyone the key – because only I knew it. He used me. He intentionally primed me with what I thought were games and puzzles.

I would have been twelve. Twelve years old. My mother died in 1992 so it would have been while she was still alive. I thought back, searching my memory for any dissent from her about the hours I spent in the dark study. But there was none. She couldn't have known. I'd worked with him for years, creating hundreds, maybe thousands of codes, all designed to develop my signature; or so I thought.

I go further back, trying to pinpoint the work. Did I ever see anything remotely connected to the Middle East? No doubt he had already applied a first level of coding by the time I got to it, so I would have false memories of the text in any case. He went alone on business trips frequently, leaving me with distant aunts. To me, he was the ultimate hero, someone focused and interested in his job, a fabulous role model.

When he died and I found out what I thought was the extent of his work, I worshipped him even more. In fact, I began to emulate him. I was honouring his memory, wasn't I? But now. Now I'm beginning to see what he was doing. He was playing off one side against the other. As if his betrayal of me wasn't enough, another wave of realisation hits me. He was involved in weapons. Heavily involved, enough to code them. But not for us. Not for Britain. He was working for the other side. I know him well enough, still, to know he'd find it amusing. It would add excitement to his life. He was dedicated to his work, not his country. He would honour the job, not the client; this was just another way that he could earn money doing what he loved.

Probably the only thing he loved, it turns out. I reel with shock, my heart breaking, as I realise the danger he's put me in. All it would have needed was for someone to work out that I was the key. Years ago, when all this happened and I was a child, that was unlikely. How could anyone know my capabilities, my knowledge? But as I worked through university, as he realised that my career trajectory was going to be so similar to his own, he must have realised how dangerous it was for me. Yet he never mentioned it. Not once. He never even hinted at it. Why? Why would he fucking do that to me?

His mysterious death begins to make more sense; new probabilities slide into my consciousness. Someone wanted that information and he didn't give it to them. The problem for me, and what's going to be hardest to get my head around, is which side killed him – us or them? Who was he really working for - us? Them? Both?

And now. Now I am connected to a terrorist threat.

Carey is rubbing his eyes. It's chilly and he gets up. "So…"

"I can see why you think it's dangerous." I'm still too numb to argue, to show my deep anger.

He pushes his hands into the deep pockets of his coat. "It   is. You're the key. They're going to get that information one way or another, Kate. And when they realise it's you…"

It's true. He's right.

"But they'll know that I can't remember what it is. They must realise that he… he…"

Carey hugs me. It's a big bear hug, all-encompassing, and for a moment I feel safe. "Yes. They will. But that won't matter will it?"

"They're using me. He used me. Great. Just fucking great."

He lets me go suddenly. "Karl's trying to line you up with this information. They probably think that your father is the coder, and you might have greater insight because of that. They're sending you after a known threat in the hope that you're the one person who can unlock it. So, Kate, whoever gets the missing data in the end, either us or the fuckers harvesting the fingerprints, they need you whether they know it or not. And the way this thing has heated up lately, that need is critical. You don't have to do it. Call their bluff. Fade away."

But we both know the implications of that particular scenario. It would be the end of my career. I'd be farmed out to some government office, under heavy surveillance. I'd never be free. I think of Belinda and Zaki Assadi, hidden away in their little bunker. That would be my life, sneaking around, ducking and diving. My world would shrink. And I'd just escaped that particular situation with Neil.

I'd be the daughter of a traitor. Guilty by association. I'd be guarded day and night because, no matter what happens now, they believe I might have the key.

"Assadi knew, didn't he? About my father's involvement, at least?"

"Probably. He'd recognise the trigger, in any case."

"Yes. He said it's started. He said people would have already died. He said he knew it had started because I was there. I thought he meant because I was there as part of my job. Not because…"

But Carey's shaking his head. "Assadi has something to do with this but he's not integral. Not like Krommer, or whoever that is. Or the dead guy in Iraq. Assadi is just the messenger. Otherwise…"

"He'd be dead. Like my father."

We sit on the wall, shoulders touching, like we have a million times before in difficult situations.

"I'm so sorry. It must be a terrible shock."

It is a shock. It's like being dragged down the decades and forced to re-evaluate everything that I hold dear. I don't know him anymore. I didn't know my father. And how am I going to rationalise that? "It's the fact that he deceived me that hurts."

"And all the more reason that you shouldn't go to Iraq. It's personal, Kate. Personal. And that gets in the way."

He's right. Personal does get in the way. All the emotion and devastation reminds me of Neil's outburst after his ex-wife died. And how I've felt since I walked out yesterday. But I can't escape this. I could pretend I'd never had this conversation with Carey, cry off sick, but at some point someone would come for me. Isn't it better this way? Isn't it better that I have all the knowledge and make my own decisions? The fact that the service had even considered using me for this operation suggests that maybe they don't know as much as Carey suspects.

"So do you think they know it's me?"

He scratches his head and fake laughs. "Fuck me, no. I reckon they think it's your father or someone he knows. I think they're deploying you to make the connection with people, to get you into places. They know you have some connection and they're testing it. My God, if they knew it was you they'd have you locked up somewhere. There's only me and you that know, Kate, and I'm not saying anything. But if you go, and you interface with the information, you're facing a big decision. Before you decode it, you need to be absolutely sure that you're giving it to the right side. The thing is, now this is moving again, and moving fast, the odds are that someone eventually will make the connection and realise that you are the key. When it didn't matter, when it was dormant, no one really cared; it was stalemate. But not now."

"So I need to find the information and decode it for Karl before anyone realises?"

He looks defeated. "I was going to say just keep quiet about it. Keep safe."

"I can't do that. I'll be running forever, Carey."

"Your call. But please be careful. Please. Whoever is chasing the info is killing people. You could be next."

He walks away, leaving me sitting on the low wall. He doesn't look back until he reaches the end of Woburn Place. I watch as he disappears around the corner, then I go back to the flat and lie awake until dawn.

Chapter 11

When I wake all the emotion has solidified into a hard knot in my stomach. I think through my dilemma late into the night. The shock of my fractured childhood remains; I can't process my father's reasons for doing what he did, for putting me in the path of international terrorists. All I can think is that he must have known that someday it would come to this.

I call up the encrypted information that Carey alluded to, just to prove to myself that it is my coding. It is. And underneath it I see a glimpse of my father from beyond his treacherous grave, a snapshot of his technique that tells me that he was involved up to his eyes.

The last part of the data, the part we still have, explains that there had been no choice but to hide the weapons deep in the heart of Iraq. That very few people knew the full details of what and where it was. It alludes to the missing part of Assadi's document that is my mission target. It was clearly coded at the time of the rest of the information, back at our house. Yet the end of this sample was the only part coded by me, tagged onto the bottom of Assadi's file in the MI6 RIPA database. My father's Morden Codes were solved years before, and the base texts made public. But this isn't the Morden Code. Not Frank Morden, in any case. These are my codes.

The last line of the code is more difficult. It takes some thinking about and when it eventually emerges like a textual magic eye picture, my blood runs cold.

The last line says: *Take note, Katherine, for one day you will read this. I'm sorry. So sorry. A beautiful woman will precede Armageddon.*

Belinda Assadi's words – proof of the connection. There's no doubt now: I've been drawn in. Right in. The anger threatens to rise again. I'm hot and cold and pacing. It's a kind of craziness, a mad determination to put things right. Somehow my father was a traitor and now I have to take this mission to put it all back in place. I never trust myself when I'm like this. Level-headed calm is my agency signature, and I know that my very soul screaming at me to do the right thing, no matter what, is not a good start to the mission.

But I know that I will take it. Until this moment I've been only ninety-nine percent sure. Until I board the plane, I still have the chance to ring Karl and call it off. Yes. Make an excuse. Something personal had cropped up. Ha! It certainly has.

But I won't. Even through the madness, I grope at duty and make my mind up. No matter what that bastard had done, I'll go to Iraq and complete my mission. I'll find that information and locate the threat before anyone else.

So I head for the airport. As I arrive, I see the agent from the corner of my eye, following me into the departures lounge. I walk to the announcements board and check the flight times. The flight is eight hours with one stop, in Beirut. I walk over to a seating area and the agent sits beside me, checking his flight schedule, asking me the time. I reply with the case password and he leaves me with a packed laptop bag with travel stickers all over it.

I check the tag: Kate Lynch. I feel any lingering doubts slip away as I find a seat outside and look through the documents. Everything seems to be in order. I clear passport control easily and hang about by the gate until it's time. With a used mobile phone and a laptop full of Kate Lynch's life, I board the plane to Baghdad and prepare to use the flight time to familiarise myself with my life as a journalist.

It seems that I've been working on several projects in the UK and writing articles for a selection of minor publications on the role of women in politics. On arrival I'm scheduled to meet with a female academic called Farrah Amin, who will be my host for the visit. There's no information on Kaleef Ahmed.

It's quiet on the aircraft and it gives me time to think. I need to get everything straight in my mind from the beginning, because I feel completely alone. I run it through quickly. My father was given information by someone. I encoded it and it was returned to whoever employed my father. It was sent to a military base in 1991 but disappeared. Someone must have traced it back to him in 2001 and he was killed when he couldn't decode it. Or maybe they thought he had it still? Now someone knew where it was and needed the key to decode it. Possibly an IS cell. I know that key is me but I could only be part of it, because two people have died and are minus their fingerprints.

It suddenly occurs to me that no one has put the whole puzzle together. Are the fingerprints some kind of access key? Fingerprint verification biometrics were in their infancy in 1991 but if the people involved were academics like Assadi, maybe they were at the cutting edge. Were the fingerprints some kind of complex entry code? If so, then whoever needed them hadn't even seen the encoded data as yet. So they would know nothing about the signature.

I feel a rush of adrenaline. When Carey told me about what my father had done, I assumed that he had been assassinated by the enemy. Now, it seems, he may well have been eliminated by his employers. Because he knew too much. Because he had coded Iraqi papers. Because, to them, he was the enemy. But they are my employers too.

Real fear grips me. If they know all this about him, why are they so keen to have me on board? I remember his deep brown voice booming at me over the telephone as we laughed about him having fun in London: "Keep your enemies close, Katherine. Keep your enemies close."

And Assadi's advice as he grieved for his colleagues: "Honour your father, Miss Morden."

By the time the plane makes a descent into Beirut I wonder if I should just get off and go home and face Karl with the truth. But why should I? I'm making progress now, aren't I? Then there's the problem of someone finding out that I am the key. If my biometric fingerprint theory is correct, someone has begun collecting fingers. Once the collection is complete they'll have the data and they'll be looking for my father. When they find out it isn't his signature, which is locked deep in the data files of MI6, it won't take them long to work out it's mine.

It's a fucking mess. A dangerous mess. I'm heading to a foreign country where I will probably be in grave danger. My best friend has warned me not to go but I've gone anyway. I'm struggling to make sense of it and then I realise that I'm only here because I have nowhere else to go. Sadness rests on me. My life is empty. I've poured it all into Neil's life and it just didn't work out. While it was great to be back in London and see Carey again, I seriously doubt that I can live in that flat ever again; God knows what fucking treason went on there.

It feels dirty. It feels like I'm seeing everything through altered vision, a haze of naivety. No one could have prepared me for this. I've worked as a hardened spy for years. I've killed people in self-defence. But in my honey-drenched memory, my father was some kind of a hero and I was his protégée. Of course I know that people lie and cheat but that's everyone else, not him and me.

As the plane takes off on the final leg of this journey, I drift in and out of sleep and try to put the past to rest. But it won't lie down. I keep remembering strangers visiting our home, my mother making tea and taking me out somewhere. My father going off to work and her looking worried as he left with a big suitcase. The times they argued and my mother was crying, and afterwards he didn't go away for ages.

What had he been working on? Obviously intelligence matters; I've known that since I was at university and was approached by MI6. But I've never known the true nature of his projects. It never bothered me before but now I'm struggling to come to terms with the fact that he used me, his own daughter, when I was a child, for cover. I sink deeper into memories of me as a little girl with my Daddy; each memory is sullied and painful now. Everything seems to lead to his priming me to follow in his footsteps – but where does it all lead? Maybe he never thought it would come to this; but maybe he did.

It had occurred to me before that he was a little bit selfish. He never took my mother out. I knew other people's mothers and fathers went out to shows and to the pub. But he never went anywhere. When he was home he just sat in his study all the time and she brought meals and drinks to him – to us, whenever I joined him. She must have been so lonely after I defected to his side. She never complained, but she died alone. As alone as she had been in life. In truth, neither of us had been in her sickroom for days except to take *her* meals – which she didn't eat.

He must have cared once, because there were pictures of the two of them on their wedding day. Her in a cream, knee-length lace dress and short veil, him in his trademark dark suit and tie. They were laughing. Thinking back now, I never saw him laugh. I heard him laugh on the phone but he never laughed in the house. They chatted about world affairs and things on the radio but there was never any intimacy. Dredging my memories, I suddenly find one of me pushing the door of his study open very early in the morning and finding him asleep on the sofa with an old blanket over him.

I'd pulled it farther over him and he'd stirred. Later, when I went back, he was working at his computer, wearing the same shirt and trousers. I now realise that he slept in there. Did I always know this, or did I only realise in the light of his fallen hero status? I clearly remember his face, his mouth a thin line, his eyelashes short and stubby and, in the evenings, a light stubble on his ruddy skin. On Friday nights he'd drink a tot of whiskey with his hot milk and he'd let me smell it.

Of course, I still love him. He was my father. But the feeling that he's still with me has somehow almost left me. As the plane touches down at Baghdad airport and the safety belt lights clicks off, I wonder if this is what growing up is: realising that one of your parents is someone with different values to yourself. He had none of my loyalty and integrity. He was a different person to what I always thought. I realise that, apart from his parenting and the constancy of my childhood, I hardly know him in real-world terms.

One thing I'm sure of is that I need to complete my mission before whoever is collecting fingerprints gets to the missing information before me. I need to look after myself now, and that means damage limitation.

Chapter 12

It's red hot when I get off the plane and I catch my breath as the dust hits my throat. I clear passport control and follow the other passengers to the arrivals lobby and wait in line for the suitcase pick-up. The airport is busy; a football team is larking around while they wait for their bags. There's a perspex window separating the arrivals from the general public and I can see a woman standing behind a barrier holding a sign saying 'Lynch'. Game on. I know what I have to do.

I feel the adrenaline return and an excitement growing in the pit of my stomach. The conveyor belt starts and I watch out for Kate Lynch's bag. I smile to myself. Adventure or boredom? I could have been at Neil's house cooking chips and beans, or having a quiet night in. But the blood's running hot in my veins and I've got something to solve. Much as I hate him in this moment, I'm my father's daughter. I need a challenge and I definitely have one.

I grab my bag and hurry through customs. The woman with the sign spots me straight away and ushers me through the impressive lobby of Baghdad airport. Once outside, she shakes my hand.

"Farrah Amin. I'm your press contact for the university. You're here to look at our archives on Gertrude Bell?"

Shit. I was so busy thinking about my father and the bloody fingerprints that I hadn't read the file in depth. I look at Farrah. She's older than me, about forty-five. Her head is covered and she's wearing traditional Muslim dress. Her eyes are beautiful and full of joy.

"Yes. Kate Lynch. I've been writing about women's roles in politics. I'm hoping to get more information here. Thank you so much for seeing me, Professor Amin."

She laughs loudly. I can tell straight away that I'm going to like her. I look outside at the vista. It's much like any other Mediterranean or Middle Eastern city: low, sandy buildings on the city outskirts, progressing to taller sandy buildings in the centre of the city. I've travelled with Neil through Syria and Lebanon for work, and I've been to most of the Greek islands on holiday. Telegraph poles are always a major feature of the landscape, along with septic tanks the further you get out of the towns. I've done my homework. I've checked exactly which towns and cities IS has taken, and how near they are to Baghdad. I've read recent news reports and gauged the security of the area. They aren't here yet. But they aren't far away.

"You'll be staying on the campus, where I live. It's safer – probably one of the safest places for women. It's still not good for us here in Iraq."

I've covered my arms and my hair out of courtesy and so as to not attract attention. Farrah screeches out of the airport car park and drives at breakneck speed to the university.

"Welcome to my home!" She grabs my bags and carries them into what looks like student accommodation but is deserted. "Take your pick."

I choose a room closest to a suite of computers I see in the distance. "Will I have access to the computers, Farrah? I'd like to be able to check my email." On a college system. Perfect – an anonymous way to search the internet. No one knows I'm here and over eight hundred students will all be using the internet simultaneously. Absolutely perfect.

Farrah beams. "Everything here is at your disposal. Iraq gets such bad press. If we treat you well you will say good things about us."

She opens the door, shows me into the small apartment and leaves me alone. I seriously need to sleep after last night's deprivation but I also need to find out as much as I can about Kaleef Ahmed. I shower and read through the pack in more detail. Farrah's right: I'm here to look at the impact of Gertrude Bell's work on the Middle East.

Almost two hours later, Farrah knocks on my door. "Come and eat, Kate. You look like you could do with a good meal."

I join her and we go to the refectory. Although I still feel on high alert, Farrah's easy laughter puts me at ease. The food is the typical Middle Eastern fare of spicy meats and lemon-dressed salads, rich with chickpeas and lentils and tomatoes. I choose falafel and salad and flatbreads and reach for the local money that I found in the pack.

Farrah protests. "You're my guest! Eat, Kate, and tell me what you want to know."

She's lovely and vibrant and I completely take advantage of her generosity. "Well, first of all I'd like use of a desktop computer with access to your archives. I'd love to see what the university has on Gertrude Bell. I have my own laptop but it would be easier to be connected to the university network, if that's possible."

"Of course. As soon as we've finished our meal I'll show you."

We talk about her life in Iraq and how difficult it is for female academics. She talks about the fall of Saddam Hussein, the interim chaos and now the constant threat of IS. How there's a general feeling of discomfort over the future of Iraq. How at any moment there could be an attack on Baghdad and how her home city has already fallen to IS.

"Of course, I was educated in the UK. I was at Cambridge. I could have stayed in the UK but I felt I was needed here. There's a sense of danger here, a sense of something happening. It's constant. We've endured so much." Her eyes belie her easy smile.

"Are you afraid, Farrah?"

"It is pure terror we all feel when anyone mentions the invaders and the brutal violence. So I'm afraid. But that can't stop me doing what's right for me. And this is right. Working here and making sure that the education continues."

I grasp the opportunity. "Violence? What kind of violence?"

"The daily threat of unspeakable acts of terror. Crucifixions. Every day people are murdered and families are wiped out. It's happened elsewhere and it's coming closer. It's mainly people acting outside the law to take personal revenge. Sometimes it's driven by different cultures or religions, sometimes by arguments that can be centuries old. The police arrest the perpetrators where they can but communities often close ranks and no one gives information."

It's a sad state of affairs. But it's not what I'm here for – which is to find out about Kaleef Ahmed.

After dinner she leads me to the computer suite. When she logs me on with her username I see the university logo appear and Arabic text. She makes a few adjustments and suddenly I'm viewing in English. She touches my shoulder and turns to leave. "If you need anything just call me on 611. Let me know if you want to go anywhere. It's better that we travel together."

She leaves me and I watch as she disappears down the corridor. I look around the room; no obvious surveillance. I google Gertrude Bell and take half an hour to get an overview of the university archives. Then I reload the browser and type in *Kaleef Ahmed*. I hover the cursor over 'search' for a second and then click the mouse. A sense of dread comes over me. It always does in these situations. A sensation of being watched. The tick, tick, tick, of time running out. The tension of being found out.

The screen comes alive with news reports. The headlines roughly translate as *Man found in university library with hands missing*. I go on to read that he was thought to be a victim of an age-old tradition of cutting off a thief's hand. The third report in the search elaborates on this, revealing that Ahmed had an affair with a friend's wife several years earlier, speculating that the man's family might have taken revenge. No one has been arrested for the murder. There are no explanations for the apartment next door being blown up. His hands haven't been found.

He'd been working at the university for many years. He was forty-eight years old. He had a wife and children from whom he was separated. They live in his home town of Hit.

I scour the reports for details, for any sign that evidence was left at the scene or anything strange happened. Twenty-two reports in, I find it, in a linked blog. The author of the blog has linked Ahmed's murder to three similar incidents further afield, without mentioning the specifics of what these other incidents are. Krommer's murder is alluded to.

I search for UK reports of Krommer's murder and find some headlines but nothing that describes the removal of his fingertips.

The blog is run by a man called James Lewis. He describes himself as a conspiracy theorist and fantasist. He lists himself as living in downtown Baghdad. I search the local telephone directories and find him immediately. Fantasist or not, he's done part of my job for me. When I arrived here there was one victim, possibly two. If James

Lewis is correct, there are now five people who've might have had their fingerprints harvested.

Chapter 13

My heart is beating fast as I go back to my room and call Farrah. She answers at the first ring.

"Hi. I just thought I'd let you know that I'm going to sleep now. I've logged off the computer."

She laughs loudly, and it's a sound that somehow fills me with joy. Farrah's energy. "Sleep well, Kate. I'll see you in the morning and we'll visit the Bell archive. I've got lots to show you."

I replace the receiver and wait exactly ten minutes. Then I leave the student accommodation and hurry to the main road. I hail a taxi and, once inside, I ask the driver to take me to the nearest police station as they are expecting me. It's a failsafe method of getting somewhere as a woman alone in a taxi – tell the driver that the police know where you are.

First I transmit my location to Karl along with Lewis' name and details. Then I dial James Lewis' number.

He answers after two rings: "Hello. James Lewis."

I swallow hard. His voice gives me a chill. "Hi. I'm Kate Lynch. I'm a journalist working here on a project at the university. I'd like to interview you about a blog post I saw recently. May I come over?"

I hear the sound of papers rustling and a low hum in the background. "British?"

"Yes."

"Which publication?"

"*Telegraph.*"

"So if I call *The Telegraph* they'll have an employee called Kate Lynch?"

If Karl has done his job they will. "Yes. How about you call them and I'll come over. What's your address?"

He gives me the directions and I divert the taxi driver. In minutes we're outside a low building with mosquito screens over all the windows and doors, and a dusty yard outside edged by a grape vine. James Lewis is standing outside. He's about forty-five, greying and dressed in khaki trousers and a white T-shirt. He's smoking a cigarette and I see that he has CCTV camera on all four corners of the property. Beyond the house, further up the road, is a black sedan. Hopefully that will be my backup. He watches as I approach.

"Mr Lewis?"

"Come in, Miss Lynch. This way."

He watches as the taxi rounds the corner at the end of the street and then beckons me into the house. I sit, as directed, on a low sofa. I'm nervous because I am nowhere near the only exit to the room – which isn't good. The atmosphere is edgy and disturbing, thick with his cigarette smoke and it just makes me crave nicotine. His home is open plan and comfortable. The furniture is low budget but over in the far corner he has an expensive computer set-up. In the corner of the room a small CCTV camera twitches with every movement, its red light indicating that it's filming me. I look around and see another active camera in the opposite corner. I push the ashtray opposite me further away.

"I'm here researching the work of Gertrude Bell, Mr Lewis."

He looks mildly amused. "James, please. So your employers tell me."

"While I was using the university archive I thought I'd catch up on some local news and I stumbled across your blog. Any thoughts on the murders? Serial killer?"

He laughs, which unnerves me. "Serial killer? You've got to be fucking kidding me, Miss Lynch."

But I persist. "I noticed that you'd linked the circumstances with a recent case in the UK. Do you think there is a link?"

He pours coffee from a pot I hadn't noticed and hands me a cup. "OK, I've been here a while. After the first invasion there were lucrative contracts to be had. I came from South Africa, where I'd been working on infrastructure, and formed a company here. I know this place, Miss Lynch. I know the people. All that shit about traditional cutting-off of hands? It doesn't happen anymore, believe me. It's all Adidas and Man United, like every other capital city. Obviously there are still some influences left from the old regime, but not many."

"That's not what Farrah Amin told me. She said Baghdad was unsafe for women."

His grin is slightly manic. I hope that the CIA agent Karl promised has tracked me here. "Yet you still came alone?"

Touché. He isn't buying it. "I'm a journalist. It's my job. So the people who were killed – you were saying?"

"All I was trying to do is point out that this wasn't some traditionalist claptrap. That this sort of thing goes on worldwide. Like that case in the UK that I mentioned."

"And where did you get your information about that case?"

This isn't going to work. His face becomes a blank mask. I can feel my agency phone buzzing in my pocket but I can't answer it here.

"News reports."

"No. I checked them out. I'm familiar with the case but I didn't see anything about the similarities you claim. So I checked again about an hour ago, in case I missed something. But still nothing."

Silence. I can't read him. His eyes are set back and they mock me while his free hand gently strokes the arm of his chair. My phone is still buzzing. Over and over.

Finally he takes his turn. "I could have sworn I'd seen something somewhere about it. Maybe I'm mistaken."

"OK. So. What about IS? Living out here in Baghdad, on the outskirts. How has that affected you?"

He studies me again. "I thought you were here to write about Gertrude Bell. That's what your paper told me. So why do you want to know about IS?"

I nod. Fair question – if we wasn't grinning so manically. "As I said, women's safety. I was just going to ask how safe women are here in the shadow of IS."

He shakes his head and remains silent. He lights another cigarette and stares at me. My phone stops buzzing for a second and then starts again. I need to leave. "Thank you James. Sorry to have taken so much of your time. Here's my card in case you remember where you saw the report."

He doesn't take it from me so I drop it onto the bamboo table.

"Be careful, Miss Lynch. There are people around here who won't appreciate your questions. I'm OK. They've written me off as a crank and, like I say on my blog, a fantasist. No way would they harm me, though, because I have insurance. I'm on the right side. But you? You're much more credible. I'll call you a cab."

I wait on the porch while he makes the call. I glance at my phone. No fucking signal outside his house. When he comes outside he stands a little too close to me and I feel uncomfortable, my skin crawling.

"You're wondering how I got away with posting it, aren't you? How come I'm not lying in the morgue somewhere? They can't touch me, Miss Lynch. So I suggest if you need any more information you give me a call. You've already got my number."

The car arrives and he goes back inside.

Right fucking side? On the right side? Does he mean that he's part of IS, or that he's on the side of the Iraqi government? I'm losing track of the right side. I ask the driver to take me to the university and he drives very fast along a back road, making me wonder if I'll actually make it. I ask him to slow down and he stares at me in the rear-view mirror and drives at an exaggerated slow pace the rest of the way. As we near the campus I see a cordon and red and blue flashing lights. I stop the driver and pay him. There's still no signal on my phone. There's a clump of trees at the side of the road and I duck behind them, hoping to find a way in.

There is none. More police cars arrive and then two ambulances. Two middle-aged men rush out of the university speaking hysterically into their mobile phones. It strikes me that there might have been another murder. I keep checking my phone for a signal. It's crucial that I respond. Another victim with no fingerprints? Suddenly, among the alien Iraqi words I recognise a name: Farrah Amin.

I hurry forward towards one of the men but my mobile phone suddenly gets a signal and rings. It's Karl. My blood runs cold. He would never contact me unless there were a crisis.

"Kate. Pronto. Get out of there. Get to the British Embassy and ask them to get you to the airport. I've booked you on a flight to New York. Leave everything. Just go. Call me when you arrive."

I hurry towards the main road and summon a taxi. I arrive at the British Embassy and they are expecting me, as Kate Lynch. Even though I'm shaking inside, I calmly tell them that arrangements have been made and that I fear for my safety, and they arrange for a car to take me to the airport.

As we drive back past the university and out of town my anger rises as I think about Farrah, her vitality and life force. I swear, if she is dead, I won't let it be for nothing.

Then I think about James Lewis. He knew that this was about to happen. He was the trigger for this. For Farrah's death. When I arrive at the airport I stay close to passport control and go through as quickly as possible. At the gate I sip a bottle of water and wonder how long all this has been going on and how big it is. I quickly scan Sky News on my phone, looking for the news that I'm dreading. I let out a long breath: Britain is still safe. The world is still safe. So far.

Where does James Lewis fit in? He can't be part of IS, can he? I remember what Assadi said, that we are dealing with an unknown quantity. He unsettled me. But that's good. It means I was onto something. Onto him.

I watch as the air crew and pilots board the New York-bound airplane and the clerk opens the gate. As I stand to board I feel the phone buzz in my pocket – the unregistered phone with a private number. My personal Samsung S3, the one whose battery I'd just replaced so I could send a message to Carey. It's a text message and it fills me with horror: *Goodbye, Ms Morden. Come back soon. Jamie Lewis.*

He knows who I am. How? And if he knows, who else knows?

What the hell is happening here?

Part Two: Juliette Watson

The Truth Keepers

Chapter 14

Sometimes your life changes so completely that it's hard to locate the single second that the revolution took place. Wrapped up tightly in relationships and life and death of an everyday measure, a point in time almost too terrifying to recall can remain unspoken forever. Because who would believe you?

But I have to speak of this. Not out loud, because, like others who are outside the rigid boundaries of war, the uniforms and the bloody rituals, I'm not allowed to. Even if I did, I would not be believed. I'm just someone on the fringes looking in on something so awful that it defies explanation. My truth may be voiceless but it is not wordless. I believe now that a day will dawn when someone will want to listen, need to know, so here, tangled in the fusion of a thousand lies, my voice swims to the top and is heard.

I remember when it began: 17 January 1991. I was lying on the beach and life was so simple. So one-dimensional. Just me, Mark and my friends. My job and my family. I'd felt a movement beside me. I'd turned my head and Caroline Frazier had removed the foil sheet she usually held under her chin to catch the extra rays. She was pointing into the distance and shouting.

"What the fuck is THAT?"

I'd followed her finger to a point just above the horizon where a huge aircraft loomed larger and larger. We sat up, shaking the sand from our bodies, and stared. The first Hercules cargo aircraft roared above us and was followed by three more. I remember it so clearly because that was the first time I had ever felt really scared.

Everyone on the beach stopped what they were doing and turned to look. It was lunchtime and I even remember what Caroline and I had eaten: a mixed sandwich each. Unlike our Cypriot colleagues, who'd gone home to sleep in the shade, we'd embarked on our usual weekday top-up session. We were army wives. We both moved around with our husbands and, by then, we'd realised that it's best to make the most of the sunshine because at any time we could easily end up back in the UK on an army estate.

Unlike some of the other army wives, Caroline and I worked. We'd arrived within days of each other nine months ago and both our husbands were based at RAF Akrotiri. I'd taken to her immediately; God knows she seemed like a good laugh and that was what I badly needed. We'd soon secured temporary office work with Jenson's Ship Management Company. My hubby, Mark, worked long hours as an expert communications officer and Caroline's husband, Jimmy, was a cartographer. So we made the most of it and went shopping, sunbathing and sometimes drinking as often as we could.

I'd stared at the Hercules. Mark had been tense recently and I knew that something was going down. I'd been married to him six years by then, since I was nineteen, and I knew him inside-out. Or so I thought. When something was happening he went quiet and moody and sat outside smoking cheap cigarettes. His job wasn't easy and I completely understood but lately it had been constant.

Caroline rubbed on some more sun lotion and nodded at me. "Bringing stuff in. For that, you know, for the conflict."

Caroline and I didn't talk about such things. We were aware of the danger and had both managed to field worried phone calls from relatives who were concerned that British troops would invade Iraq at any time. The only thing we had done was to go and buy an atlas and to look at how close Iraq and Kuwait were to Cyprus. Sitting in my kitchen drinking brandy sours, we'd looked at each other when we realised that where we lived, in a tiny village half-way up the Troudos Mountains just outside Limassol, we were on the edge of a war zone.

It was terrifying. I remember my hands shaking as I turned the pages of the atlas. To cope with the terror, we drank more whisky sours and ouzo and stopped listening to the radio news. I bought more and more butterflies. They were my thing back then. I guess it was my teenage image: butterfly t-shirts. Butterfly jewellery. Butterfly hairbands. I was soft and feminine and my butterflies stood for that.

I'd brought the Manchester early-nineties culture with me, transporting the aura of the city I loved to a corner of a remote Cypriot village. In the early days Caroline and I blasted out the Stone Roses and The Charlatans, drinking and dancing, imprinting

Manchester onto the dusty quiet of the village. But the more scared I became, the more I purred around Mark when he was at home, hoping that he would protect me. And the more I faded into the village, blending in for protection. Camouflaging myself in the hope that it would keep me safe.

But we were stoic. No matter how bad we felt we silently acknowledged that we'd bought into this knowingly. I mentioned my fears to Mark but he'd just swirled his Nescafé and stared at me. He didn't divulge much about his work at the best of times but now he wouldn't even mention it. He's older than me, by nine years. He joined the army straight from school as a driver, trained as a secure communication operative, and then took officer exams.

When I met him he'd just returned from Germany. We dated for nine months and then he asked me to marry him. I wasn't too sure at first. Not because I didn't love him – I did. Now, in retrospect, when everything about me has changed so much, it's so difficult to remember how it felt, to locate that particular feeling. I really loved him, more than anything. Sometimes, now, it creeps up on me and catches me unawares, as if it's all I've got left of that time in my life. But most of the time it's buried deep down in my soul.

It was the army lifestyle that I wasn't sure about. But he won me round and we'd been all over the world.

Two years after we married, he told me that he wouldn't progress any further. He was tired of studying and said he was thinking of leaving the army.

Then the conflict started. The Middle East was always volatile and when Mark told me that we'd be going to Cyprus I knew something serious was going on. He suggested that I stay and live with my mum or my sister for a while but I couldn't bear the thought of Tesco bread and stewed tea, so we packed up our things and moved from our flat just outside Bristol. He rented a beautiful home in Parekklisia, a tiny village steeped in Cypriot history, and as soon as I saw it I fell in love. The first day we arrived, I sat on the back step and breathed in the sunshine and the smell of ground coffee. We lived next door to the coffee shop, a place where men went inside to watch football on a grainy black and white TV, the only one in the village. In the evenings the smell of *pougouri* and *keftelia* from the communal village clay ovens permeated the air.

I'd never seen an olive tree before, or seen snow on a mountain top and the sunlit seashore in the same vista. This place was all kinds of strange to my young eyes and I drank it in. There was an apricot tree in the back garden and I'd collected the ripe fruit and made four pies.

I took slices of pie to the neighbours but realised very soon that I wouldn't easily fit in. The women were all olive-skinned and dark-haired, heads, arms and legs covered. No plucked eyebrows or lipstick here. But their faces, natural as the dust and stone around them, were somehow very beautiful. The children hid behind their mothers' long skirts as they opened their doors a sliver for me, then slammed it in my face.

Across the road from our house was an ancient Greek Orthodox chapel, lined with icons cast out of pure gold. In Parekklisia life revolved around the church, not fashion or gossip. Here God-fearing really meant fear. Fear of the rain. Fear of the dark. Fear of breaking the rules. Fear of British women who would steal your husband. Fear of my bare legs against the almost white dust of the road as I stood in my neighbour's doorway with a slice of pie on a plate, the hot apricots spilling out onto the terracotta surface, still bubbling.

The doors were slammed in my face but I covered up and persisted. I cooked and cleaned and hung my sheets out when it rained. Just like them. I sat with the women and although I couldn't understand their language I ate their candied figs and drank their syrupy coffee and laughed when they did. In time they knocked on my door and called "Ela!" to summon me. I'd stroll through the narrow streets with them, my long skirt dragging up a cloud of dust behind me, and I'd run my hands across the rough stone walls and pretend that I belonged there and that I could stay for good. That they were my family.

Mark was away for days at a time as the problem in Kuwait went on, and I spent more and more time with Caroline. She'd stayed up at our house a few weekends and we'd walked around the village in the warm evenings and had kitchen discos later on. We spent the days feeling like rebels, watching the men play backgammon outside the coffee shops we weren't allowed inside and, in the sun-drenched early mornings, helping the local women pick the ripe watermelons from the fields behind my house.

Life was so simple for them. Everything in the village was done for the village. All the produce was grown locally and the animals slaughtered locally. It was so different from Manchester that it seemed like another world but I knew that I loved it. The tiny, functional village houses were flanked by larger family homes that generations had thrived in, their balconies heavy with five generations of villagers. No one seemed to leave, and who could blame them? Life was good and I was as happy as I could be so far away from home.

But that day on the beach signalled the start of something different. Caroline laid back down and replaced the foil card under her chin. I walked up to the edge of the water, the warm waves lapping my feet. I stared across the ocean that day, to where Syria and Lebanon's dark outlines loomed, and made a wish that Mark wouldn't be taken away from me. I loved him. Even though my mother hated him for taking me away from her, and my sister said that he was too 'pensive and serious', I loved him. If love is caring about someone so much that your young heart would be lost without them, then, oh God, I loved him with all my heart.

I waded into the waves on the beach and wondered what would happen to me if he was called away to war. I knew that I could go back to Manchester and my family, and that they'd welcome me with open arms. But I belonged with him. It seemed as if that belonging was under threat, and all I could do was wait to see what happened next. I stood in the sea and the motion of the waves gradually washed away the grains from around my feet, sinking, ever sinking me deeper into the sand. Then, as now, I liked to stand in the shallows, waiting until my feet were fully submerged and I was at risk of toppling over, at the mercy of the water.

And that's how I'd felt, I suppose. At the mercy of the inevitable. The world turning and all I could do was stare into the water and imagine Mark and I swimming out to the reef, snorkelling and holding hands as we watched the multi-coloured fish swim with us. Him smiling and grimacing and making me laugh through the snorkel. I know his face so well. Every tiny line and pit. The shades that signalled how he was physically and the expressions that told me how he was feeling.

I remember thinking, as I stood there in the sea, how I really loved him. *Really* loved him. It wasn't just a want or a need; we were attuned. I thought I knew about these things back then because I read philosophy in my spare time. One day I intended to go to university and get a degree and maybe even teach later on. I'd been reading something that said that true love involved attachment, attraction and attunement. I'd mentally ticked them off and closed the book, congratulating myself that Mark and I had all three.

But I was filled to the very top with fear. I remember feeling it beating in my temples and on the tips of my toes. Fear that I would lose Mark and fear that war was coming. Fear even for Jimmy and Caroline, and for my family back home. They, in turn, would be scared for me. I looked around the beach. It was the least warlike scene I could ever imagine, with children playing happily in the sand and couples holding hands as they walked across the beach. But the Hercules had been the first sign. Something had changed. Something was visible. But it would be all right, wouldn't it?

My feet were fully submerged in the water and sand and I swayed with the tide.

Caroline touched my shoulder and smiled. "Come on. Time to go back to work. Don't worry, Jules. It's not coming here. My Jimmy says it'll all be over in a flash, anyway."

I pulled one foot out of the sand and watched as the water filled the hole. In no time there was no trace of me ever having been there. I turned, half smiling, to Caroline. I expected her to be smiling back, her expression matching her reassuring words, but as I turned I saw her mouth quickly transform from a thin line into a fixed but false grin.

Chapter 15

If the beach was tense, you could have cut the atmosphere in the office with a blunt knife that day. There were fourteen of us and we had a tanker each to manage. We had to crew them, stock them and track their progress through the ports. As the precious cargo on board, which could range from chemicals to coffee, increased or decreased in value, we would adjust the capital account accordingly. It was exciting and interesting – and, now, dangerous.

None of us had to say it. We all knew what a devastating effect the Iraqi invasion of Kuwait had on our business. Limassol was a holiday centre and, until now, this wasn't something I'd had to consider. I'd been more about flip-flops and sarongs. But the Middle Eastern ports where our cargo ships were crewed and moored were now places of hostile tension; every vessel was thoroughly searched with suspicious eyes. In the months before 2 August 1990 I'd flown out to the ports and overseen some of the dealings but after that it wasn't safe to be an English woman travelling alone.

Everyone in Limassol was talking about it. The men in the coffee shops played chess and lay bets on when the bombing would begin, and where. When news of the Iraqi invasion of Kuwait reached Manchester there were a dozen telephone calls. My mother begged me to come home and my sister, Lorraine, blamed Mark.

"He's controlling you!" she shrieked at me down the international phone line, her three children squabbling in the background. I could picture them in their back-to-back terraced house, damp creeping up the back walls and the constant rain. "If it weren't for 'im you'd be home here with us. Safe."

As she shouted I looked around at the passion flowers and the olive trees, the bats flying here and there in the fading light, and remembered that she'd never been here. She'd never seen what a beautiful place this was, or seen how, in the evenings, Mark and I would walk up to the summit of a nearby hill and look out at the sea and stand there, arms around each other, swaying, swaying. She'd never seen me.

So while they all told me to come home, I was already home. That's how I felt. I belonged where he was, then – wherever my quiet, concerned husband did what he did best. With the greatest amount of conviction, I was there of my own free will. No one had forced me, least of all Mark. He was a good man; I knew this when he explained why he'd joined the army and didn't leave after the Falklands War.

I knew how much it all meant to him because I knew it had cost him what he wanted the most. I'd wanted children straight away but he'd shaken his head. "No, Juliette. No. This world isn't a place for children. I've seen things…"

I'd placed a finger over his lips. "It's OK. It's fine. We'll wait."

He watched me when my eyes followed a pram or a woman with a new baby down the hot streets, and eventually he had explained that he was afraid. "The things I've seen. I couldn't risk any son or daughter of mine seeing that. This world, Juliette, it's not meant for children. It's too cruel. You'll see. One day you'll know what I mean. I hope you don't but it's inevitable. Then you'll be glad."

It didn't stop me pining but life became busy and full of the village, Caroline and Mark. I put it to the back of my mind.

But that afternoon in the office I felt it acutely. I remember feeling an uneasy vibe threading through every conversation and I wondered whether, if I had a baby, I would feel differently – if I would be on the first plane back to Manchester and the grubby Arndale that I missed so much and saw every night in my dreams.

But it wasn't different. I was there and I had no baby. When the working day finished, I went to the market and bought pork chops and some salad. I went up to Parekklisia, where everyone was thankfully oblivious to the war-making in the almost visible distance. The women still pulled the sheets through a mangle and laughed, pulling their aprons over their heads. Because war wasn't women's concern, was it?

I stood in the darkened lounge of our home and watched them through the front window, shaping bread ready for the clay oven. In this village the streets had no names and mail was still collected from a wooden shed at the end of the road. All the women filed silently into my home on a Saturday night to watch the weekly lottery programme because I was the only one with a television, apart from the coffee shop that they were forbidden to enter. They would look sideways at Mark and nod at him, then look behind the TV set to try to see how it worked.

I was just twenty-five years old then but I knew that this was a serious situation, growing graver by the minute. I could feel it. I envied their innocence, their faith and most of all their children. It struck me that my life could have been so different if I hadn't chosen an army life and instead had settled for a Manchester lad. I loathed the insight because of my army knowledge and the way that Mark was the only person in the whole world who wouldn't talk about the danger that seemed to grow closer every day. No matter what I asked him, he just swirled his coffee and remain silent.

I was standing behind the blinds that evening, fingers parting the panels, watching the women stack the olive baskets, when I saw Mark's car in the distance, winding around the steep corners on the way up to the village. A trailing plume of red dust told me that he was in a hurry. He turned into the driveway and parked over a grid that he had painted with a 'no parking' sign. The women turned to watch as he got out, slammed the door and rushed inside the house.

He went straight past me and into the bedroom, where he started to pack a bag. I followed him and sat on the bed. "What's going on, love? Where are you going?"

He stopped momentarily and looked at me. "We have to go. I've booked a flight with a mate. Light aircraft. Pack some things."

"But why? Where we going? Come on, Mark! How long for?"

I didn't panic because he'd done something similar before – the visa run. Because I was an alien, as the immigration services of Cyprus put it, I had to leave every three months and return with a new passport stamp. We'd leave it until the last minute and then go on an adventure. We'd been to Egypt and Iran so far. So I'd assumed that this was more of the same.

Mark just looked at me and carried on packing. When he snapped the locks on the case shut, he held me by my shoulders. "Look, this is serious. We have to leave here. Tonight. And I'm not sure what's going to happen."

I'd felt my stomach turn over. "How d'you mean? Is it a visa run?"

He was more tense than usual and I felt the tips of his fingers digging into my arms. He stared hard at me. "Yeah. Visa run. So get your stuff together. You know that blue box you brought, with all your childhood stuff in it? Yeah? Leave it with one of them." He motioned towards the houses across the road.

I looked through the window, past the beautiful olive tree and the ornamental roses that he'd bought me to make it feel more like England. "Why?"

He grabbed the case and put it by the door. Then he packed a case for me and took them both out to the car.

"Why, Mark? My God, what's going on?"

He pushed the blue box into my shaking hands. I gripped it as I walked across the road to Maria's house. Her daughter had been to England knew a little English so I asked her to keep the box for me. As I dragged my feet through the dirt I felt like I was holding the last of my old life in my hands and that maybe things would never be the same again.

If only I'd known how right I was.

Chapter 16

Maria took the box as her daughter explained that I would be going away for a while and her gaze strayed to Mark and the car, whose engine he was impatiently revving. I could see in her eyes that my fears were infectious.

She took my arm. "Do not go, ma mou. Sto Kypros."

I'd never heard her speak a word of English before, and this was the first time I had fully understood anything she said. But no words were needed. She held me and patted my shoulder and watched with glassy eyes as I climbed into the car.

Once away from the village and winding down the mountain I spoke to Mark. This time more seriously. "So what's this about? Tell, me, yeah? Where are we really going?"

He was completely silent. I watched the dusty lane turn to tarmac as we eventually turned onto the coast road. I expected him to head for the airport but he drove through Limassol and into the old town, pulling into the driveway of a bungalow just two streets away from the harbour. The driveway was sheltered under several low-hanging olive trees and almost completely hidden from the road.

He pulled out our bags and put his arm around me. We walked to the harbour and stood gazing into the sea. I saw him look left and right, then overhead, then he pulled me close. "Look, Jules, I need you to do something for me. I've taken something from work. Something important. And I need to meet someone and give it to them. But I can't be found with it."

The thought of it now makes me sick with anxiety because as you grow older you know the world better. But then I felt scared but excited at the same time. When you're twenty-five your fear of risk isn't as morbidly vivid as it becomes years later; everything feels like an adventure.

"Right. So where are we going then?"

He pulled me closer and whispered in my ear, "I'll tell you when we get there. And when we do get there you need to take out your magazine and leave it where I tell you to."

"You're scaring me, Mark. Why are you doing this? What the hell is it for?"

He let me go and lit a cigarette. He pulled a speck of tobacco from his upper lip and then pointed at me. "You think you're scared? If you knew what was going on here you'd know what fear is. *I'm* scared, Jules. Scared what'll happen if anyone gets hold of this. Scared what'll happen if I get caught with it. What they'll do. But you know what? For once I can make a difference and I'm going to. No one of our lot needs to see it. Bad enough already without that."

He looked pale, almost haunted. I pushed my hands in my pockets and sighed. "Bloody hell."

"Yeah. So stick close to me and let's hope it all goes well. Just do everything I say and we'll be safe."

"Safe? What do you mean safe? What's going to happen?"

But it was too late. Seconds later a man appeared from a nearby boat and hurried us across a plank and into the cabin. He started the engine and in minutes we were heading out of the harbour and towards Lebanon.

Mark stared straight ahead and I sat on the hard wooden seat and looked inside the rucksack he'd packed for me. Sure enough, there was a magazine. I flicked through it and felt the difference in the texture of some of the pages to the rest of the magazine. But I was too scared to look.

When he saw what I was doing he snatched the rucksack and zipped it up again, fastening the buckles. He suddenly wasn't the man I'd fallen in love with. He was the edgy stranger who controlled my every move. His eyes pierced me and he frowned as if he'd never laid down with me.

I don't know how long it took us to cross the sea but it was pitch black when we arrived at the port. Shadowy figures moved in the darkness, the occasional flash of a cigarette tip exposing their faces. Even so, I recognised the place straight away. I'd been here before. It was Ghaziyeh.

I'd been here with one of the crewing vessels a couple of months ago. I remembered the entry to the port and the steps up to the arrival area. Once off the boat I made for the steps but the man beckoned us to a gate at the end of the dockyard. Mark grabbed my hand and we ran as fast as we could to a waiting car and, through my wheezing and tears, I saw guards with guns running after our car as it sped away.

"Mark..."

He squeezed my hand. "Don't forget. Do everything I say. Everything."

We didn't speak again until we were on a small aircraft, thousands of feet above the earth. Then he turned to me. "I'm sorry, Jules. So sorry. But I had to do it. One day you'll know why but for now just help me. Please."

Of course, I agreed. Back then I would have done anything for him. "Course I will. Course. But when can we go home?"

He hugged me tightly. "If it all goes well, soon."

"But if not? What then?"

Chapter 17

I felt sick. The plane rose and dipped in the darkness and all I knew was that we were flying even further away from Cyprus. Mark stared straight ahead and gripped the arms of the seat. Every now and then he adjusted his watch.

When we landed I staggered down the metal steps and ran as fast as I could to the waiting car, retching behind it. Mark pulled me into the car and it sped off, stopping at a dimly lit building after ten minutes, maybe more; I'd lost all sense of time by then. I just wanted to reach the final destination and sleep. We got out and watched as two sets of headlights approached. The driver of our car said something in frantic Arabic to Mark and Mark answered. I stared at him. I hadn't known he could speak Arabic. The driver disappeared into the night.

Alarm signals went off inside me. What else didn't I know? Mark was peering into the darkness, hands in pockets and I wondered if I knew him at all. All the secrecy, the silences. All the long working hours.

Suddenly the driver reappeared and Mark grabbed me. "I   want you to run. As fast as you can. Do not give that magazine to anyone. Do not tell anyone about it. Wait until I come to get you."

"Wait, where? Where, Mark, where? For God's sake. Where are we?"

"Just run, Jules. Run."

I turned around and saw the headlights coming closer. Two men rounded a corner and I ran as fast as I could into the darkness. I ran through the dust and stones, feeling my way up the road until it turned into a narrow, grassy pathway, then taller grass. Upward, upwards I went until I reached a rocky outcrop. I crouched down and made my breathing shallow. They mustn't find me here. In the distance I could see the faint outline of the buildings and the dim car headlights.

I heard shouting and then watched the cars drive away. I remember thinking that Mark wouldn't have driven away. He'd still be down there. He'd soon come up the hill calling out for me. Or he'd send the driver for me while he started the car and then we could start the long journey home. I could sleep all day tomorrow and then see Caroline in the evening.

A long time passed and finally I saw a band of light appear over a ridge above me. I could see that I was on the top of a hill, high above a valley where the road widened. The building below was a small derelict barn with a shed at the side of it. As it became lighter I saw two men standing beside the barn. I strained my eyes to see if one of them was Mark but all I saw were the men's semi-automatic rifles and khaki uniforms. There were no vehicles and the barn wasn't big enough to drive a car into.

The realisation was stark and it hardened me. It was the first real inkling that life wasn't what I thought it was. Mark had left me here. Mark wasn't down there at all. He'd driven away and left me.

I waited hours, until the sun told me that it was late morning. The men stood around watching the hills, occasionally drinking water and smoking. One of them moved along the road and peed at the side of the track, then resumed his watch. I was scared of moving but I would have to eventually. I looked up the road. The airport wasn't too far away but what if it wasn't an airport? I had got the sense that it wasn't exactly bustling with commuters by the way the car had been parked right beside the light plane – not to mention the lack of customs or immigration. What country was I even in?

The only other option was to go over the hill. I thought about what Mark had said, that I mustn't tell anyone about the magazine. That I should run and hide and wait for him. I'd felt scared and confused but I'd still done as he said. I brushed down my butterfly top, cleaning the dust from my clothes and trying to pat my hair straight, rubbing my grazed legs until they stung.

Then I set off. I followed the ridge across the top of the hill until I came to a strip of rubble. Tiny stones avalanched every time I made the slightest movement. I slid down the other side of the hill, trying not to raise too much dust that would draw attention to me.

As I came to a halt I saw that I needn't have worried. The landscape for miles was lush grass and stony outcrops. The land rose in steep inclines and fell into streams. Birds flew overhead and for a moment it looked like paradise. Then I remembered that I needed to eat. And drink. I scanned the whole of the vista for human habitation, houses, farms, maybe animals. But there was nothing. It was almost a full day since I had seen the Hercules fly over the beach and now I was in the middle of nowhere.

I turned back and scrabbled my way back up the rubble. Once at the top of the hill I peeped over and looked at the men below. They were two tiny dots from here so I raised my head over the summit and peered around. In the far distance I could make out the towers of mosques on the horizon. To the left was a mountain range and to the right flatlands. There were rough roads snaking a path through the land before me but no major motorways or anything that remotely resembled an airport.

My stomach hurt from hunger and my throat was dusty. I considered giving myself up to the two men. Surely they would make sure that I got back to Cyprus safely? Surely someone would be looking for me? Even if Mark was…

I turned away and dropped down the hill a little. Even if Mark was captured? Or kidnapped? He was scared of something and he didn't want me to be caught so he sent me off into the wilderness. But even if they had taken him somewhere it didn't mean that I would be in danger. I was a British citizen. I wasn't part of the army. Army wife, army life, sure, but that didn't mean I wouldn't be missed. So I decided. It took me a couple of minutes to pluck up the courage to climb back up the hill. But I did it.

I scrambled over the gravel, scraping my knees and the palms of my hands. Dust in my eyes, I stared down at the barn and the tiny figures, like toy soldiers against their toy jeep and my exit to freedom. I focused on them and took one step over the summit of the hill, then another. I thought about how this was all a big mistake, how Mark had been scared by something and had never meant for me to be left here. How could he? They'd take me to the nearest town or city in whatever country this was and I'd find the British Embassy. Tell them about Mark and how he'd been scared and run away from me.

The rucksack was heavy on my back, a constant reminder that however much I tried to tell myself that Mark hadn't meant this to happen, whatever I had in there was valuable to him. More valuable, it seemed, than me. I stood on the hill and stared out onto the horizon. I had to get home. I had to find out what was going on.

I took another step down the slope and felt the thunder through my body. You always hear fighter planes before you see them, and I'd been on enough RAF bases to know this. So when I heard that sound high on the hilltop I turned instinctively and saw them over my shoulder. They were above me in a moment and off into the distance, then there was silence before I saw the flash of light and the distant explosions.

My God. It's hard now to explain the terror that took over in that moment. Our bodies must have a mechanism that helps us to forget afterwards how bad things were at the time. The dust clouds, not quite a mushroom but arcing over the tower in the distance. Flashes of fire on the horizon, followed by echoes that vibrated through the airwaves and finally hit my ears several seconds after the initial impact. More thunder, more fighter jets, and the sudden shaking of the ground below me. I covered my head with my arms as I was knocked backwards, over the brink of the hill and into the rubble.

When I dared to look through the dusty atmosphere, over the hill and into the valley, the barn had gone and so had the two men. All that was left was a huge crater and a field of fire below me.

Chapter 18

It was horrific. I'd heard mess-house stories about the aftermath of explosions but I couldn't ever have imagined how it truly was. My world had shrunk. I could no longer see the horizon because dust hung in the air for what seemed like miles. The only sound I could hear was a high-pitched whirring. My left ear felt bassy and flat and I flexed my jaw to try to release the boom from it. My nose was running constantly and the first seemed like it was inside my head, churning. But the worst of it was the smell.

I could see the shape of the sun through the swirling dust, a dull disc against a grey sky. A sharp breeze carried waves of redness across the valley below and from time to time I glimpsed the crater where the barn used to be. But I could smell burning flesh. It was unmistakable. Hair and flesh. Like when you light the cooker and it burns the tiny hairs on the back of your hand, only times a thousand. I checked myself to make sure that I wasn't injured and then I slipped back down the rubble to the flat ground below. Incredibly, the layers of dust hadn't quite reached this low. The brunt of the explosions had been on the other side of the ridge.

So I ran. I ran and ran, Mark's voice echoing in my ear: "Run, Jules. Run." But his voice wasn't as loud as before. It was suddenly dull and didn't have the same impact. I wasn't running for him, even though I clutched the rucksack tightly. I was running for me. I kept running and breathing the fresh air until the dust was behind me and I reached a lush field. I could see another small ridge up ahead and I somehow climbed up to find an observation point. I desperately needed to find water.

As soon as I stopped moving I could hear explosions in the distance again. I climbed the ridge and pushed myself onto a small rock. My legs were weak but I managed to stand and survey my surroundings. I could see red dust clouds over the high ridge behind me; in front was a ravine with a stream at the bottom. To the left of the ravine was a small wooden dwelling.

"Thank God. Thank God."

But then came the roar of more fighters. Again, I heard them before I saw them and this time I doubled up and covered my ears. They flew low and, when I looked up again, I could see their vapour trails heading over the ridge behind me. I didn't wait around for more explosions.

I hurried downwards, downwards to the water and took off my shoes and socks. I was caked with a thick layer of dust and grime and I shook myself to dislodge it. My hearing hadn't returned properly and the trickling of the river was faint, even when I sat right beside it. I cupped my hands and scooped up the water, feeling it soothe the heat of my insides. The stream ran right up to the dwelling and I walked there barefoot.

As I approached it, I saw that it had shutters over the windows. The roof was made of dark wood and felt and moss grew up all the wooden walls. The grey dusty path that led up to it seemed settled, as if no one had used it lately.

I desperately needed to rest if I was going to try to make it to the town, and I needed shelter. No one would see me in there. So I turned the handle and pushed the door. It opened easily and I heard what sounded, to my dulled auditory senses, like the rustle of a bird's wing. I instinctively ducked but not fast enough to escape a broad plank of wood that glanced the side of my head.

I lost balance and fell over, even though the wood hadn't made full contact. I felt a dull pressure and opened my eyes to see a tall woman standing with one foot lightly balanced against my throat. She held a rifle and it was pointed at my forehead. I started to cry. Even to this day I cannot describe the fear I felt at that moment. I often wonder when I changed, exactly which moment made me a woman, and I think now that it was then. She held me there for minutes, and then she removed her foot but not the gun.

She motioned at me to get up by tossing her head back. I stumbled to my feet and held my hands up.

"English, yes?"

Her voice was deep and gravelly. Her long dark hair hung over her shoulder and her face looked sunken around her cheekbones.

"Yes. I'm sorry. I'm sorry. I didn't know you were here. I just needed to rest."

She eyed me suspiciously. "Kick the bag."

I kicked the rucksack towards her. She rustled through it and seemed satisfied. She pointed the gun towards some chairs arranged around a wooden table. "Sit."

I sat. The muscles in my legs were taut with lactic acid and I went to rub them.

"Do not move." She pointed the gun with one hand and poured me some coffee with the other. She handed me a steaming cup. I remember her fingernails, bitten to the nub, and the roughness of her skin. Her eyes, glassy and blank, reminded me of pain. Deep pain.

"Drink."

We sat in silence while I sipped the coffee. Eventually she spoke. 'Why you are here? You a soldier?'

I somehow managed to laugh. It was probably hysteria. Somewhere inside me, I could still see the funny side of things; some part of me was still the same Juliette as yesterday – twenty-five, carefree, in love with her husband. Selfless, naïve Juliette.

"No, no. No. I'm not a soldier. I don't know why I'm here. I'm lost. Lost."

Lost. Ain't that the truth, I thought. Lost, in more ways than one. Tears followed the hysteria.

She lowered her gun and looked genuinely concerned. "Lost? You do not know where you are?"

"No. I've no idea where I am. I don't know what this place is and I've just seen… I don't even know what it is. Explosions. Nearby. Just over there. Two men died."

I pointed to the door and she smiled. Her accent was Iraqi, like the Iraqi sailors I'd met on the crewing work who spoke broken English. But hers had an American twang to it. "Two men? I think you'll find it's more than two men. Who are you? Tell me."

She sat on the floor in front of me, listening carefully, and asking me to slow down when I talked too fast. I told her about the Hercules and the beach and Mark coming home and us coming here. She listened and thought. Then silence for a while.

"So he left you here? Alone? In a war zone?"

I stopped drinking my coffee. "War zone?"

"Yes. The explosions you hear are American air strikes. You're in Iraq. This is Iraq. A war zone now."

Of course it is. Of course. We all knew that this would happen sooner or later. Iraq had invaded Kuwait and the ongoing problems meant that air strikes were the inevitable outcome. I'd imagined, as most people did, that I would find out via a radio or a news report. I'd be at work and someone would say that it had begun. I'd feel a small excitement and I'd watch it on the television or listen to the World Service special news report. I'd discuss it with my relatives in England who would beg me to come home. I hadn't realised what it actually meant to be right there in the middle of it. The terror. The confusion.

I'd questioned Mark and was met with silence. I remember it vaguely crossing my mind that he must have known about this. He must have known it was going to happen. I remembered then about the magazine and the papers tucked inside it.

The woman fetched some bread and I ate it quickly. I felt better almost immediately.

"I'm Juliette. Juliette Watson."

I held my hand out but she didn't take it.

"Sanaa. Sanaa Pachachi. I worked as a professor at Baghdad University up to six months ago."

I was surprised but I managed not to show it. She didn't look like a professor. Until then I'd naively thought that she was some kind of wild woman who, for some reason, chose to live there. But I'd seen nothing of the desperation of war back then, the changes that it can create in a short time.

"OK. Sanaa. Nice to meet you. So what are you doing here?"

Her sighs told me that her heart was heavy. "It's a long, long story. I'll tell you tomorrow. But you need to wash and rest. Here." She handed me a towel and showed me a makeshift shower she had rigged up from a rainwater tank. It reminded me of my teenage years when mum and dad used to take us camping in the Lake District, and dad made a shower out of a hose pipe and a plastic bag. I'd called him barbaric and sulked for days. Ha, barbaric! I took a cold shower while Sanaa waited outside the door with the gun, guarding me. The way she looked at me now made me think she pitied me rather than considered me a threat. She was right, of course. As I scrubbed away at my hair and the caked–in dust I wondered what I would do next.

Maybe Sanaa would help me. Maybe she would show me the way to a town, perhaps to Baghdad where there would be a British Embassy. Where I could get safe passage back home… That made me think about Mark. As the cold rainwater cascaded over my head and mixed with my tears, I realised that he hadn't come after me. He really had left me here.

Chapter 19

I slept the deep sleep of exhaustion until my body clock ticked back to normality. I woke with a start as the ground shook and some tin cups on a low wooden table fell over. Sanaa sat facing the door, resting the rifle between her legs. As I sat up she looked over. Last night I'd been too brittle with fear to notice the details around me; I'd just been grateful for shelter and food. Now I could see that Sanaa looked very tired. She was around thirty-five years old with long, black hair that she wore loose. Her eyes gave away her exhaustion; they were almost slits in her face, swollen and red.

"Still going on." She stated it so matter of factly.

I got out of bed and stretched. "Well, it will, won't it? As long as the problem in Kuwait goes on."

After the initial shock, we both knew what this was. I'd already spotted a small radio that Sanaa kept under the table. That would allow her to keep up to date with what was going on in the world, even if it appeared that she hadn't left this hut for a long time. She turned her head slightly towards me.

"So he knew this and he still left you here?"

Of course he did. Of course he knew this was coming. He'd known there was a possibility of whatever he was planning going wrong. That's why he'd told me not to tell anyone about the magazine. That's why I hadn't told Sanaa. Yet. "He must have done."

"So what were you two doing out here? In the middle of Iraq?"

I swallowed hard. Visa run wasn't going to cut it here. "I'm not really sure but I think he was delivering something. Like some information. I don't know. But I still have it. Here." I patted my rucksack.

She shook her head. "He made you a mule?"

"Mule?"

"Mule. Drugs mule. You carry the goods. Do his dirty work."

Now she put it like that it was worse. "Yes. I suppose so. But it's not drugs. It's... well, I don't know what it is."

"Let me see it. Here."

I hesitated. I didn't know who this woman was. For all I knew she could have been exactly who Mark didn't want to get hold of whatever it was. But she had the gun so I unzipped the rucksack.

She started laughing as I worked slowly.

"You think I'm the enemy, huh? The way I see it, Juliette, we're in the same boat. Both stranded in the middle of a war zone having the shit bombed out of us. Don't show me if you don't want to. Suffer alone."

She went back to staring at the door. I got the magazine and flipped through it, pulling out the white sheets of paper. There were seven sheets with writing on both sides. Typed. I tried to read them but it was just random words. I stood up and passed it to Sanaa, who glanced through it quickly.

"Coded information. Who knows what it means?"

Mark, I thought. Mark knows what it means. "I don't know but it must be important for him to sacrifice me for it."

There it was. Hanging in the air. The words I knew were true. He'd dragged me into a situation that he knew was dangerous and he didn't care. He didn't care. I started to cry again but Sanaa was laughing.

"Same old story. Men get into trouble, women suffer. Same old story."

"Is that why you're here, Sanaa?"

She flexed her shoulders and fingered the gun. Then she came over and sat beside me. "My husband was working for the government. The regime. But he found things he didn't like, so he tried to change them. Then he met an Afghan guy and joined the Mujahideen. Not a thought for me. Not a thought for the danger we were in. We lived near the university in an apartment. Beautiful, I made it into our home. But he was never satisfied. Here and there with his rebel friends, all the time plotting and planning the downfall of the regime and their escape to Afghanistan. He told me nothing, I only found out by listening at doors. I worked at university, teaching the history of art. Mesopotamian art. I come from old Babylonia, I know this because when I was a child I found old treasure. My father sold it to the museum, and this is how I came to have an education.

So from then on I studied it. Old, beautiful times with beautiful things. But the truth is ugly."

She made more coffee and I dressed in a long black dress she had laid out for me. In the distance the loud rumbles told me that the bombing wouldn't stop anytime soon. My hands were still shaking from yesterday and I kept seeing the crater where the two men had been and smelling their death. My ear had recovered a little and was now throbbing but at least some of my hearing had returned.

I drunk the coffee and ate some of the bread she offered. All the time she held the gun, and I wondered what it was she was so scared of.

"So how long have you been here? In this hut?"

It was a loaded question and she knew it. "You are thinking how long you might be here. Six months. About. I came here in the summer. My husband was arrested and I think killed. I heard nothing about him. His last words to me were telling me to leave. To get as far away as possible. Go to Pakistan or Afghanistan. Find the Muj. You will be protected there by my brothers."

It sounded familiar.

"So I took what I could carry and I hurried out of the city and kept on walking toward what I thought was a village of my childhood, back to where I found the old charm. But I'm a city girl and I don't know the sun any more. When I visited other countries to study, I lost the position of the sun. I don't know the direction. So I walked through the small desert and over the hill and I see this place. They come after me to start with then they give up. Or maybe I don't matter. So I stay here."

"But how do you get food?"

She laughed again.

"I cover my face and walk to town. But it's many kilometres and I only go sometimes. I have no money so I have to steal coffee and bread so it's dangerous for me."

"So you've been living on coffee and bread for six months?"

She got up and opened the door to the cabin. "Come."

We went outside and she pointed to the roof at the back of the cabin. There were rabbits and what looked like large rats hanging in the shade. I stepped back, shocked for a moment.

Sanaa laughed. "I don't shoot. I trap. No need for unnecessary noise. Fish, too."

"How did you learn that?"

I realised that if I were alone out here I would have no chance. I barely knew how to fillet a bloody fish, let alone hunt and kill an animal.

"I watched my brothers. And when you see death it brings instinct to survive for yourself."

We sat in the dust in the shade for a while. Sanaa stared out at the horizon and I looked around for any way out of there. But there were no paths, just the stream. I looked up, waiting for the next roar of the fighter jets and the earth rumbles that followed but it seemed to have stopped for the time being.

After a while Sanaa pointed at the sun. "Midday. We listen."

She brought out the small battery-operated radio. It was tuned to the World Service and immediately told us what we needed to know.

Desert Storm, the allied initiative to win back Kuwait from Iraqi forces, has begun. Targets in Iraq have been bombed and the initiative will continue until Iraq surrenders Kuwait to the allies.

She switched it off.

"It will go on forever, then, because Saddam never gives up."

"So what will we do?"

She looked at me, her eyes bulging. "We? We? I'm staying here. I'm staying here forever. So whatever Saddam decides, it won't affect me. You? Do what you like. I'll show you the way to Baghdad, or to the village. But an English woman alone in Iraq?" She shook her head.

"Can't you take me?"

More head shaking. "I'll never leave here. I made a promise."

I was angry then. It had suddenly bubbled out of me, the pent up rage I'd felt since I left Cyprus with Mark. God knows where I found the courage to shout at someone with a gun. Someone like Sanaa, who looked a little crazed. Maybe I saw myself, and the fact that I was losing all sense of reality, reflected in her eyes. Why were we sitting here? Why were we not trying to get back to civilisation?

I stood up and shouted at her. "Promise? Who to, Sanaa? Who to? There's no one here. Just you and me. And we both know what promises mean. Mark promised to look after me but here I am."

I expected her to jump up and take the challenge but she sat still in the dust, rubbing her bare feet through the dirt and staring at the horizon. "I was pregnant when I came here, with a little boy. Riyadh and me, we see him on the scan. Little boy. We called him Shahid. I was here for twenty-three days before the soldier came. I saw him at the side of the stream one day, peeing into the water. Regime uniform. He spat on the ground and sat at the side of the water. I saw no vehicle so how did he get here? Then I understood. He was with a detail in this area, on foot. I know how they work. Central camp, then soldiers sent out to search the area. But he was alone, which means they expected no danger. So I hit him on the head and killed him. I buried him there."

She pointed to a pile of dry earth heaped slightly higher than the ground around it. My heart sank at the thought of death creeping closer and closer. So close that it was right in front of me. So that's how she got the khaki jacket hanging on the back of the door. That's how she got the gun.

"I took his clothes and his gun and buried him. Two days later they come looking for him. I hid downstream and took everything with me. They looked in the hut but then went away. Stupid. They didn't realise that pile of earth is his grave. They stood and smoked beside it, in the sunshine. They moved because of the flies. Even then they didn't realise. Then they went away."

"So didn't you think of leaving then? Trying to find your village?"

"I think, yes but then it began. The pain. The baby started to come. After two moons I went to sleep and didn't wake up until he was born. I lost consciousness." She swallowed hard and bit her lip. "Baby boy was there, and he was still alive. I tried to feed him but no milk came. He was weak and small. But he was my son and I'll never leave him."

I follow her gaze, past the soldier's grave, to a small heap of stones beyond.

Chapter 20

Neither of us cried. Instead, Sanaa stared out towards her son's grave as the wind whipped up the dust around us. I was still young then, and I felt a sharp anger pierce my sadness, as if all the injustice in the world were focused on the two of us.

Eventually I spoke. "You can't stay here, Sanaa. And neither can I."

It was as if something inside me had suddenly woken up. I was silently angry at all the waiting around for Mark to do this and Mark to do that, all that time wasted. I'd done what I'd done in the name of faith and love but now it didn't feel like that. He knew about the atrocity of war. He knew what happened. He'd told me that was the reason he didn't want children.

He knew about people like Sanaa and her son, a situation I was guessing wasn't so unfamiliar to him. Women left alone, after trusting that they would be cared for. Trusting that they wouldn't be harmed because, after all, what has war got to do with them? He knew all this and he still made me come with him – to Iraq. Just in time for the bombing to begin.

Sanaa shook her head. "No. I have to. I have nowhere to go. I can't return to Baghdad. I'll be imprisoned. Or worse."

"But what about your family? Where are they?"

She turned her head away. "No. I can't bring this to them. They'll look for me there."

"Can't they hide you? Just until all this dies down?"

She lay the gun down on the floor and rubbed her face. Her long hair streamed behind her and she looked so free. "Maybe. But I'll never leave. I can't."

"Because of your son? Because of Shahid? But he wouldn't want you to stay here to…"

"Not because of that. Not because of my son who I never knew." Her face crumpled and her chin, usually straight-facing and proud, fell to her chest. "I am afraid. I am afraid to die. That's why I killed the guard. I panicked. Everyone is a big person with a gun but I am one woman and Iraq is a big place. My town is many kilometres away, farther than Baqubah. I'm the only girl to ever go to study abroad. And now look."

Her lip trembled but she fought back the tears.

"I'll walk with you, Sanaa. I'll walk to Baghdad and you can make it from there."

She thought about this for a while. The stillness around us was broken only by the trickling of the stream and the dull thud of explosions which now seemed to come from another direction. I checked the makeshift net she had placed in the stream to catch fish, and the rabbit traps. All were empty. I checked her supplies. Plenty of coffee but hardly any bread left. When I returned she was still sitting by the gun.

"They speak about terror, Juliette. Terrorists. But this is real terror. Not knowing what will happen in the next second. Dead loved ones and no way to grieve. No way to feed yourself. I'm lucky to have clean water to drink. But this is terror. Me, just like you. Life is not what we thought it was. Not for you. Not for me. Even if we do go, I could never speak of this to anyone. There are no words. No one will believe."

I wasn't sure what she meant then but in retrospect I see that she was right. In the context of that day it all seemed plausible to me but later, when I recounted it, I wondered sometimes if I'd dreamed it. I've opened my mouth a hundred times to tell this story but it always sounded so far-fetched that I closed up again. But that's the nature of war and oppression, bringing horrors so terrible that no one believes that they really happened.

I touched her arm and she flinched. I'd started to think that she liked me but in that sudden movement I saw that even though we were out here, in the open air but imprisoned by our lack of knowledge about our own situations, we were still on opposite sides. Enemies.

"Too bloody right," I said. "I trusted my husband and look what he's bloody done – dumped me in the middle of a war zone. But he won't get the better of me. He won't. I'm going to walk to Baghdad. If I get killed on the way, tough luck for me but I'm going to get there. One way or the other."

I thought I saw the ghost of a smile cross her lips. "So what is the document he gave you? What is it? Let me see it again."

I went inside the hut and got the magazine out of my bag. We sat against the coolest wall of the hut in the afternoon shade and tried to make sense of it.

"It's code," she said. "We can't read it. Not for our eyes."

"Not for our eyes but it's all right for me to carry it to cover his ass. I bet he's drinking a nice cool beer now back home. Bastard."

She smiled again. "Maybe it's valuable. Maybe he wants to find you. Maybe he's looking right now."

"Nope. Not looking, mate. He knew exactly where to come to drop it off. He must have had co-ordinates or something. He's a bloody intelligence officer, for goodness sake. He'd know where I was, or the approximate vicinity. But he's not here, is he?"

"Maybe the bombs? Maybe he can't?"

I sat down very close to her. "If this was the other way round, I'd make sure that he was found. I'd find a way, because he was the most important thing in my life. I followed him all over the world. Just when I make a friend, we're away again. I try to keep in touch but I have no one. No one at all, not a single person. My family will be there for me and I love them but they're not friends. They're not Mark."

"Maybe he's sorry? Made a mistake?"

"What? Bringing me to the middle of a war zone and telling me to run into the desert? No. He was saving his own backside and sacrificing me in the process. But this is the last time. I wanted children and I've still got time. He was even selfish over that. He said the world was a bad place."

I realised after I said it that it was insensitive but she read my face and shrugged. "It's OK. It's happened. Good that you come here, you let me talk it out. Think it out. Instead of keeping it inside. Riyadh was not selfish. He was compromised. In a corner. Backed himself there and I watched him. I spoke to him but he said he needs to do it. That many people are involved. When I talk sense he tells me it's not women's business."

"So how did you come to be there with him at the university? Surely there aren't many women working there?"

She laughed loudly and the sound echoed through the hills and soothed my soul. "Oh yes. It's maybe not as bad as the western world believes. Women are allowed soft subjects. I left my town and travelled to America. To New York to study art. Very scary place, full of aggressive men. But Riyadh was not aggressive. He loved me. Or so he said. Not so sure now."

"Oh. Why?"

"Days before this happened I heard him talking to a friend he brought round. Sanaa, get bread. Sanaa, get drinks. He was kind when we were alone but when his friends were there he changed. Into someone I didn't like. If I didn't do as he said he wouldn't speak to me for days. Like punishment. I said to myself 'Sanaa, he's under pressure. Under stress.' But I was too, and he didn't care."

She picked up the gun and began to rub it with her shirt. "He put other things above my safety. I know what he was doing. Planning something. Hiding something. With the other men. Far too important for me to hear but I did and I understood. Do you know what they do to them? Torture. Slow killing. But all the time my heart cried and I felt hurt just by him and his actions." She spat on the ground and shook her head. "This love thing. All good when you have a roof over your head and food and all is well. But what now Juliette Watson? What is love now?"

What was love then? I remember feeling it in that moment. Not love for Mark or love for my parents, but a love of liberty – which was now lost. Love for a time when I could just go where I pleased and I was safe. I pined for it like I had pined for Mark when he was away for days, only much more. I wished it back and felt it in the first breaths before I opened my eyes and the dust invaded.

Things would never be the same for me again. I pushed the magazine back into the bag and hid the bag under the makeshift bed. Sanaa shared out some of the bread that was left and made some coffee. We drank it silently and although she never told me what she was thinking, I knew that she was wondering what the future held and what love meant to her.

Late at night we walked to the river. The moon lit our way and we checked the nets, finding two small fish. Sanaa gutted them and we ate them raw; it was too dangerous to light a fire. As we walked back to the cabin she brushed my arm.

"We are different, Juliette. In every way." I looked at her, a good five inches taller than me, statuesque and olive skinned to my five four blond paleness. "We'll go our separate ways soon but we'll always be friends, yes? Not like other friends, who leave you and you leave them. Always in our minds. We'll share all this, whatever happens. Then two people will know and remember Shahid."

Chapter 21

Early the next morning we drank coffee and ate the rest of the bread. Sanaa pulled out the radio and switched it on. We listened to the World Service telling us how the world around us was being destroyed, even as we heard a fresh round of explosions in the distance. Sanaa sighed.

"Not the best day to walk."

It was raining. I'd always thought that Iraq was a desert country but this area, so near to the stream, was lush. Dusty, yes, but I remember thinking that it would be easy to stay here and grow things to eat forever. Except I had no idea how to do that, and I didn't think Sanaa did either. Or she didn't want to.

I was just about to go outside and check the traps when a familiar voice drifted across the air: *We just want her back safe.*

My mum. Then a reporter. *Juliette Watson disappeared during a routine visa run five days ago on the eve of the Desert Storm campaign. Her husband Mark, a communications officer at the RAF base in Akrotiri accompanied Mrs Watson on her quarterly visa visit and appeals to anyone who has seen her to give her assistance.*

I switched the radio off quickly.

Sanaa snorted. "So, he's looking for you. Good. Now you'll be able to kick his ass. That's what they say in New York."

She carried on digging a hole in the earth, burying the tin pans and the dead soldier's clothes and, finally, the radio and the gun. I fumed in the corner. Brilliant. He'd got back home and told everyone it was a visa run. For a minute I even doubted myself and wondered if I'd got the wrong end of the stick and read too much into it. I looked at the magazine again, and the pages and pages of nonsense. Random words so precious to Mark that he'd lied.

After an hour the rain stopped and we went outside. Sanaa had packed a canvas shopping bag and slung it across her shoulder. I had my rucksack. We carried water. I'd tried to ask her where we were before but she'd been evasive. I had a rough knowledge of the major cities in Iraq from my job, but the distances between would be anyone's guess. So I tried another tactic.

"How long will we walk for, Sanaa?"

She'd taken great care to pack all her things together, with nothing of mine, and vice versa. I got the feeling that we wouldn't be staying together.

"Depends. On the weather and how we get on. How fast we walk, and if we have to hide. The best case is that we see a car on the road and they take you to Baghdad or Baqubah. Me, when we get to the road I'll walk the other way. To my town. If the government finds me they'll kill me. You, they're looking for you so you'll be found. I can't risk it."

"Road? There's a road near here? So why have you been eating bloody rabbits and fish?"

"Too dangerous. Silk road. The main thoroughfare through the Middle East since more than two thousand years. It's a main dual carriageway now. Everyone uses it. About ten miles away."

I knew about the silk road. I knew all about the trade route across the Middle East and somehow I knew the major cities on it. Probably because it was relevant to my job. The containers still followed the main port routes. I'd been to Aleppo, the Syrian port where the silk road met the silk sea route. Caroline and I had yawned our way through the history lesson given by a small Syrian woman, very serious and reverent, but some of it must have gone in.

"So when we get to the road there will be cars?"

"Yes. I'll take you to the road but then I'll walk back over the fields. Back towards Baqubah then I'll follow the sun. I know where I am then. My family is Sunni. Big problems with Shiite people. So we stay in our village, away from Baghdad. But I don't listen. I went to America. I went to Baghdad. I married Riyadh. He's Sunni too."

"Is that why he was killed?"

She swallowed hard. "No. He was part of a plot against the regime. He knew things. Like your Mark."

My Mark. My heart sang at the sound of these two words, even in the midst of my anger.

"What about you? Which are you? Sunni or Shiite?"

She stopped packing and securing and leaned against the cabin. "If anyone asks I'm Sunni. Like my family. But inside. Inside here,"

She dug her hands under her ribs. "In here I'm Sanaa. Stay safe. Be alone. No trust. Not even in God. Allah. Why, if he's so good, did this happen to Shahid? Why?"

I'd never been a religious person but I felt it too. The injustice. The pain.

She pulled the belt tight across the rucksack. "From now on I'm on my side. Just me. I'm just a normal woman like you. Cooking, cleaning, eating, washing. And you'd better do the same, Juliette Watson. Go home to England and look after yourself. Just you."

I knew that she was right. I could feel myself retracting and sealing my outer shell. Hearing my mother's voice had softened me and I felt bad that my family had to be involved, that they would be upset. My sister would be telling everyone how she'd predicted something would happen to me. Mum would be doing everything she could to get people to look for me. She was an action person, always on the go; she'd be badgering away at the officials.

But it was picturing Dad that broke my heart. Silent and helpless, he'd blame himself. He told me to go out and have an adventure but I think he meant in the next city, or even London, not in another country. I'd seen the dread pass over his face when I told him I was marrying Mark, and I knew it was because I would be permanently away and he'd never see me. Now he'd be sitting behind my mother, his eyes sad and his distress held just on the edge of his consciousness.

It had occurred to me, deep in the night when I woke to hear Sanaa's breath and the pattering of rain on the roof, that I could just disappear. Start again. I could have some time to recover from my clash with reality, the shattering of my romantic dreams. My growing up. Then I could resume life without all the complications I knew were ahead of me.

But that was before I heard the news report. Before I knew that there was a search on for me.

"What will you do, Sanaa? When you get home?"

"Hide. Work. I'll still do art. I'll maybe live in the fields. We'll see. Until they find me, then I'll go to jail. Or they'll kill me. What about you?"

"Not sure."

In fact, I did know. In a jumbled sort of way I did know. It was unthinkable that I could ever go back to the same life as before without addressing this with Mark. For all he knew I could be dead and it was his fault. All the anger inside me had ravelled into a tight ball of revenge and I suddenly knew exactly how I was going to play it. I began to unfasten my rucksack.

Sanaa rolled her eyes. "All packed. Why are you doing this? We need to go."

"I know. But I have to ask you to do something. You know how you trusted me with Shahid's memory? You said we were friends?"

Her eyes strayed involuntarily to the spot, the small pile of stones that we had avoided all morning.

"Yes. I buried him in the night, by the way. Deep. He's gone now. But we'll remember him. That he was there."

"Yes, Sanaa, we will. And I need you to do something for me." I took the magazine and the papers out of the rucksack and handed them to her. "I need you to keep these for me. Look after them. I'll come back for them one day, or ask you to send them to me. When you get to where you are going, call this number."

I ripped a page out of my address book. It was my friend Ellie in Salford. She'd take a message for me, and she was the only person I knew back then who had an answerphone.

"If she doesn't answer, try again. Just tell her where you are, the name of the town and maybe a number I can reach you. We need to think of a password so we both know it's real."

She thought for a while. Then she opened the side pocket of her own bag. She opened a plastic ID folder and shook her head. "OK. I have it. The name of the dead soldier. Saif Abed. Is that real enough, Juliette Watson? No one else knows. No one else can know."

It hadn't struck me that he was a real person. That he might have had a wife, definitely had a mother. But he was our secret, like little Shahid. I could see it in her eyes still: an eye for an eye. I nodded and memorised the name. All the while I wondered what the deep sense of foreboding was in my soul. A pulling at me, a sense of the unreal that started when I heard my mum's voice on the radio and heard the broadcaster spew Mark's lies. This was no visa run but I wondered who else knew what had happened and, when I returned to Cyprus, what kind of questions I would face.

Chapter 22

So we began the long journey back home. Both of us. For me, in the immediate future home meant Cyprus but I wasn't sure after that. My future with Mark hung in the balance. Half of me still wanted him to rush to meet me, swearing that it was all a big mistake, that nothing bad would ever happen again. The other half of me mocked these feelings, told me I was stupid, blind, screamed at me to see the truth and that it was hopeless to go on believing in Mark.

Sanaa had, at the last minute, dressed in the burqa and niqab. "It will make them not see me. Safer for me. Safer for you."

As we walked away from the cabin she looked towards Shahid's grave and then focused straight ahead. Even through the small slit in the veil I could see her eyes, glassy but tearless. She was determined; I could see that too. I hurried after her as she strode into the distance but soon she slowed down to my pace.

"How do we know which way, Sanaa? Do you even know where you're going?"

We scaled the hill that I originally slid down and stood just below the ledge where I had stood on that first night. In clear daylight the turrets of the distant mosques were visible – as were plumes of smoke on the horizon.

"That's Baghdad. Farther than it looks. A long way, Juliette. We'll make for the road and then you must stop a car and get a lift."

I knew she was right. We had plenty of water from the stream but no food at all. We'd eaten raw fish and rabbit before we set off but that wouldn't get us far. I was already weak and aching from my ordeal five days ago and only just recovering from dehydration.

"The bombing is not over. It looks like the city is on fire." She turned and looked towards the north. "My town is not on fire. Not yet. But we have to talk about this. You gave me the papers. What if something happens to me? What then?"

"Hide them somewhere. Leave a message on the number I gave you as soon as you have hidden them. My friend Caroline's husband said this will all be over in a flash. So hopefully I'll never need the papers. No one else knows about them. Only me, Mark, whoever he was meeting and you. And no one can possibly connect us. Even if the people who are looking for the papers happen to meet you they can't possibly know about us."

She looked down into the huge crater below us. "Our friendship. Our deal. No one ever needs to know. But I will tell you where I am and you tell me where you are, and we will still be friends."

She started to descend and I told her about the men with guns who were killed in the explosion.

"Checkpoint."

She stopped when we reached the remnants of the barn and the burned out Landrover farther up the road. She kicked around in the dust and flies swarmed and buzzed around us. She kicked at pieces of metal and burned wood but didn't find anything worth taking. So we carried on northwest. After an hour or so I saw a small dust cloud in the distance, travelling away from us.

Sanaa looked at the ground. "The road. You will find cars there. I'll walk with you until near."

We began to walk again and soon I felt rain on my face. The sky in the distance clouded dark with a storm and we hurried over to some trees to shelter.

We waited until the rain had almost stopped and then walked for more than an hour. It was so cold and I felt weak. The rain turned into a harsh wind that whipped dust against my face, making my skin feel raw. Still we pushed ahead. I wondered if we were going in the right direction but I followed Sanaa loyally, a tall, black figure that always preceded me. My feet hurt and both my heels had blisters. Eventually we rested.

"One more mile, then the road, I think. So you won't mention my name. Yes?"

I reached out and touched her wet clothing. "Of course. Nor you mine. I can't thank you enough for looking after me. Even though you nearly shot me."

She removed the veil and smiled at me. "I apologise. I was angry and confused. But you made me see sense. If you had not come I would still be there, grieving over my dead son forever. I would have died there. The soldiers would have returned or a bomb would have found me. This way, I may die in any case but I have more chance in my home town. Inshallah. So you will go and kick ass?"

I smiled back at her. I'd never been truly grateful for anything in my life before. But I was grateful for this woman and her courage. She was on the edge of starvation but she shared her food with me. She could easily have killed me, just like she killed Saif Abed. We hadn't spoken much in our days together but both of us had said enough.

"Yeah. I'm going to kick ass. Life's going to be very different from now on. Keep in touch, Sanaa. We'll see each other again. I just know it."

She laughed again. "I am glad you're so sure. I could be dead tomorrow. I don't think we'll see each other again. I think this chapter is over. But I'll never forget your pale skin and blue eyes, and strange translucent hair. I'll remember you and how you changed overnight from a little girl to a woman. Yes?"

"Yes. Yes."

We began to walk again and the storm passed. It was late afternoon and the light was fading. I'd always loved the golden light of dusk and, as we walked through a small clump of trees into some long grass, I thought how this could be any English field. It was cold and the trees had few leaves, and the long grass was a pale green and I wondered what this place would look like in summer. With each step I could feel the rumbling of the earth and, although I had grown accustomed to it in the last couple of days, the distant explosions made me nervous.

We trekked through two fields that were bordered by rows of stones and I instinctively knew that we were nearer to civilisation. I spotted an abandoned Adidas trainer at the side of the rough track I now realised we were following. The path narrowed into a small copse of trees and I stuck close to Sanaa. My foothold slipped on the wet tree roots and boughs that she had pushed aside sprang back at me as she passed through quickly.

Soon we reached a more defined roadway. It was still narrow but as I stepped out onto the hard concrete I knew I was on my way home. I looked down at my clothes and realised that I was a stranger in a strange country and that I would easily be identified as the missing British woman. Half of me wanted to go back and have another few days with Sanaa. Even though we had lived on the edge, waiting to be discovered and shot before any questions were asked, it had been a chance to realise just who I was. What my life was.

Here, in the harsh dusk, Sanaa had become another Muslim woman, in her dark robe and veil. No longer Sanaa with her jet black wild hair and her mad eyes, holding the rifle between her knees as she gutted a fish. She had become anonymous – which was exactly what she wanted.

She turned and began to walk up the road. As we reached the end, I saw a wide expanse of dusty concrete marking a crossroads, with an actual road sign. I was suddenly blinded by a pair of headlights and I stumbled backwards in the tail wind left by the speeding vehicle. I staggered back and turned around to ask Sanaa which way to go.

But of course, she was gone.

Chapter 23

I waited almost an hour for another car to come along and suddenly there was a long procession of vehicles, mostly saloons and open-back vans, all driving close to each other. The first few ignored my frantic waves and zoomed past me, so I stepped out onto the road.

I could see the confused faces of the drivers and the passengers pointing at me. Finally a Honda pickup slowed and stopped beside me. A middle-aged woman opened the car door and I rushed towards her.

"English?"

I laughed loudly. The relief flooded through my body as she smiled and moved over.

"Yes. Yes. I'm Juliette Watson. I need to go to Baghdad. To the police station."

The man looked at me, all tanned skin and bleached hair. "Ah. You're the missing woman. Soldier's wife?"

He spoke perfect English and I almost cried with joy. But not quite, because my paranoia was still at top notch and I was wary of these people even though they seemed to be the perfect ride to the city. I hesitated slightly, and the man noticed.

"It's OK. Juliette, isn't it? I expect you've been through a lot. We're on our way to Baghdad. Part of the peace keeping core." He flashed a badge and the woman flashed a similar one. "We mean you no harm. We'll take you wherever you want to go."

I remember the dizziness and the feeling that I was going to keel over. The woman passed me some juice and I almost snatched it out of her hand, relishing the sweetness as the liquid ran down my throat. She pushed the water bottle into her bag and handed me a pack of dried fruit. I ate it hungrily. The man jumped out of the pickup and pulled out a blanket from the back.

"Here, wrap yourself up in this. Take that wet coat off. And those shoes. Anya, you sit on the outside so she's near the heater."

They bundled me into the front and I sat there, the sugary food and drink seeping through my body, and I felt sleepy. He started the engine and introduced himself.

"I'm Andy. I'm an Italian aid worker and this is my colleague, Anya. Everyone's been searching for you, Juliette. Where have you been?"

I wanted to blurt out the whole story about Sanaa and her baby son, and the dead soldier, and how we were terrified, but I stopped myself.

"Where have I been? I don't know. I was lost. There was a hill and some sheep and a lot of explosions. It was very frightening. I got separated from my husband."

The word 'husband' stuck in my throat. A new wave of anger began to rise inside me and I clenched my fist. I'd have to face him soon and I didn't want to. I didn't want to hear his visa-run lies and his cover-up story. I'd already worked out what he was going to say: that it was all about his job and top secret. But that was bullshit. He'd been running away from his job and he didn't know if he was going back. That's the trouble with liars. They're only really lying to themselves, aren't they? Because they always trip up along the way.

But I was a liar now. In that second, when I replied to Andy the aid worker's question, I had set myself a precedent. I'd repeated his question first, to give myself time to think. Time to lie. Time to bend the truth until it was almost unrecognisable.

As I drifted off into a light sleep, the sound of the engine my lullaby, I knew that Mark would think that I would play along with him. That I'd just support his story and carry on as before. How wrong he was.

I woke up as the van shuddered to a halt, to find Anya gently shaking me.

"Oh, I'm so sorry. I haven't slept properly for ages. I don't know how long."

She looked sympathetic. "It must have been very frightening, being out there on your own."

Now I had to lie. But it was all in a good cause. "Frightening? Yes. I just wandered and wandered. For all I know I could have been going around in circles."

We got out of the van and she gave me my coat back. All the while I'd been clutching the rucksack to me, heavy with the weight of

Mark's secret. I could see my reflection in the van window. I still looked the same: small, blonde, soft. A butterfly on my shirt and a gold butterfly ring on my right hand, middle finger. Small and feminine. That didn't match how I felt inside, and I peered at myself for a second longer. I didn't know the woman in the reflection. She was the old Juliette.

"You're safe now. We're at the police station. We'll come in with you."

I followed them inside the low concrete building and waited by the door. I could hear Andy telling them how they picked me up on the road and that I was in shock. It took a while for an English-speaking police officer to arrive. He was about five feet six inches tall and stocky, with thick, black, wavy hair. He smiled at me but his eyes were dull.

"Mrs Watson. Would you come this way, please?"

I stood my ground. "I'm not going anywhere without a representative from the British Consulate or Embassy. Could you ring them, please?"

"I'm afraid the British Embassy closed on 12 January. But we will make sure that your country knows that you are safe."

I folded my arms. "I want to speak to my husband."

He moved towards me and I automatically backed away. Instinctively. There wasn't an ounce of trust left in me.

"Has something happened to you, Mrs Watson? You seem very upset. We just want to find out what has been going on and then someone will take you to the airport. We need to ask you a few questions. Is that all right?"

Andy stepped forward. "I'll stay with you if you like. Just to make sure nothing funny goes on."

The police officer shrugged. "As you like."

Andy and Anya followed me up a narrow passageway and into an interrogation room. I caught my reflection again and saw my cold eyes, not a trace of fear. Because I wasn't scared, just annoyed I'd wandered around the Iraqi countryside for days and now they wanted to ask me questions. But if it got me back to Cyprus, some dust-free clothes and my freedom, I'd get through it.

The police officer began. "I'm Arif Ibrahim. I'm a police officer with the Iraqi Police Department. Could we start from the beginning, Mrs Watson?"

"The beginning? Not much to tell. I got separated from my husband on the visa run we were on. I don't know how that happened. Then there were some explosions. Then it was morning and I was near some hills and some sheep. I slept under some bushes and just kept going. Then I saw the road. And here I am."

He wrote some notes and tutted. Clicked his teeth. Made me wait. "So you were near Baghdad International Airport when you became separated from your husband. What kind of aeroplane did you arrive in? Large? Small?"

I shrugged. I could see where he was going with this. "Aeroplane? I don't know. It was very dark. I'm no travel expert."

He looked up at me. "It says in your file that you work for a chemical container company. That you travel extensively with your job. And your husband works for the British Army."

"My file? What is this? We were just renewing my visa. It was left to the last minute as usual."

"So do you have your passport? Please?"

I remembered then that Mark had kept my passport. He had it. "No. I'm afraid my husband still has it. Look, I just want to see my husband again. And my family. Please."

"All in good time, Mrs Watson. I'm just trying to piece this together. So you've been in the north for five days yet you found water and food? Far away from the airport?"

"Food and water? No, I didn't. I drank from a river and ate some leaves which actually made me quite ill. So I slept and, to be honest, I'm quite weak. And a little bit delirious."

"What puzzles me is that at this time you chose to come to Iraq for the visa run. Why was that? Surely another destination would be better?"

Now he came to mention it, yes it was. Surely everyone could see that? Surely Mark's employers would think it was strange? My eyes narrowed as I realised that he would have probably blamed it on me.

All I could do was keep denying that I knew anything. I'd deal with it properly when I got home.

"Why? I don't know, Mr Ibrahim. I really don't know. My husband takes care of all that sort of thing. I just do what he says."

He looked irritated and I was even beginning to irritate myself now with my repeating of every question. But it was somehow out of my control. Liar, liar, my insides screamed at me. He shut his notebook and stared back at me. Andy and Anya sat silently behind me.

The policeman looked at me hard, searching my face. "Then that is all, Mrs Watson. I will call your government who I am sure will arrange transport. You may stay here until the car arrives that will no doubt take you to the airport. Let's hope that, in the meantime, no more of your bombs are dropped on our city, and your friends get in and out safely."

It was only then that I realised. The British Embassy had closed. I was the enemy. As I'd heard on Sanaa's radio, America and Britain were at war with Iraq. And I was in the middle of the capital city. No wonder the police officer seemed somehow edgy. Everyone was terrified of a bomb falling on their building. An allied forces bomb. What Caroline and I had dreaded had really begun. Sanaa had said that the city was on fire. Everyone was scared. Everyone except me.

Chapter 24

We sat around in the police station for hours. I guessed that it was around midnight when a car finally arrived. I didn't have the inclination to ask what time it was because I didn't really care. After my interview with Mr Ibrahim, it struck me that there would be some kind of a similar meeting on the other side as soon as I embarked.

Andy and Anya left as soon as the car arrived. I thanked them and we exchanged telephone numbers. I promised to let them know how I was and told them to be safe. Their eyebrows raised and lips pursed, then they cringed at the distant and sometimes not so distant explosions. As soon as they were gone I was escorted to the car.

Once at the airport, I was marched by armed guard to a waiting plane. A man wearing a British army uniform helped me up the steps.

"Welcome home, Mrs Watson. You'll soon be back on sovereign soil."

I settled into the narrow front seat I was shown to and shut my eyes immediately. I didn't drift off. I spent the flight time going over what had happened in my mind and wondering what had happened to Sanaa. Had she made it to her village? Would she really call me? As the plane touched down I wondered what the document was. Why was it so important? I remembered that Mark had said that he was trying to make a difference. I guess I'd never know now.

Once on the ground I was taken to a reception room. Three interviewers asked me almost the same questions that Mr Ibrahim had asked and I became more and more annoyed as I just repeated their questions back at them. My rucksack was taken away and searched, then returned to me. I denied any knowledge of anything and, after about an hour, Mark rushed in and hugged me, followed by my mum and my sister.

"Thank God. Thank God. we thought we'd lost you."

I pressed my face close to Mark's and felt his cool skin and his kiss on my cheek. Then my mum hugged me, and then my sister.

"We flew out when we heard." Mum was crying. I could see the relief on her face, the red flush of her cheeks. "What were you doing going out there on your own, you silly girl? Mark's been a hero. He's pulled out all the stops to find you."

To look for his precious papers, more like. Even now, as he handed my passport over to be stamped, he was eyeing my rucksack. Eventually it was time for us to leave and he picked it up.

I snatched it from him. "It's fine. I can carry that."

He stared at me, his steel blue eyes clinical. "OK. Just thought you might be tired, love."

We all got into a four by four and were driven from the Akrotiri air base back to Parekklisia. It was the middle of the night and the high moon glistened over the sea. I looked over the water and tried to imagine Sanaa arriving home and removing her veil and her parents' first glimpse of the daughter they must have thought was dead. How they would hide her until she felt safe. As we pulled up in front of our home, the driver patted Mark on the back and they shook hands.

My mother and Lorraine got out with us. Lorraine looked at me sheepishly.

"We've been staying here with Mark. I must say, Jules, I had him all wrong. Perfect gentleman. Worried out of his mind about you."

I was so tired that my temper was fraying. I could feel the heat rise in my throat. "Worried? Really?"

"Yeah. Phoning people, telling the papers. All the UK is behind you. Out there in that Godforsaken place. Who knows what could have happened? What were you thinking? You should have stayed close to him. He'd have looked after you."

I looked down at the polished wood floor. Looked after me? No. He hadn't looked after me. He hadn't even told me properly what was going on. I was sick of 'it's for your own good' and the half joking 'if I told you I'd have to kill you'. A shiver ran down my spine and I almost asked mum and Lorraine to stay with me. If he was capable of leaving me in the middle of a foreign country – a war zone, at that – what else was he capable of to save his own skin?

I glanced out onto the drive. Our car was there, as if we'd never made a dash for it six nights before. I could only assume that whatever he had done, he'd not been caught and he was able to backtrack. He must have flown back from Iraq, caught the boat back to Cyprus the same night, and picked up the car from the harbour before he reported me missing.

"My God, yes. Especially when the bombing started. We watched it live on Sky News. We were helpless, watching the bombing when you could have been out there. But I expect you found somewhere safe?"

Somewhere safe. Compared with this, my home, full of lies and deceit, I did find somewhere safe. Somewhere that was peaceful and allowed me to understand that whatever Mark had done and for whatever reason – which, on reflection, may have seemed noble to him at the time – he'd left me in the middle of a fucking war zone while he came home. My eyes felt like pits in my face as the anger rose and my throat flushed.

"Somewhere safe? Um, yes. I slept under some bushes. It was freezing. I just kept walking while it was light, then after a couple of days I saw the road."

Mark was making tea and listening to every word.

"There was a river and I drank water from it. I had to eat some leaves and they made me sick so I slept and slept."

Same old story, just like I had rehearsed in my head. I kept my eyes fixed on his back, burning the guilt into him. It would wait until tomorrow.

Mum chipped in now. "Well, Mark did very well to get it on the news. They didn't want to know, what with the trouble over there. Those Iraqis, they're getting what they deserve now. Good on our lads. I didn't want to say it before but I can now. Good on our lads. Good on you, Mark."

I was fuming. I couldn't help but ask – I needed to know how he'd got away with it, how he'd managed to make out it was a visa run. "Did very well? How do you mean? Wasn't anyone bothered?"

Mum carried on. "They were bothered but they seemed to think you were flighty or something. Gone on some kind of adventure. Didn't take it seriously at first. Thought you and Mark had a silly argument or something. And then there was all the confusion. You know, over the bombings. I'm afraid you weren't big news, love, not compared to that. But Mark insisted it was a visa run and you were lost. That you'd both taken a wrong turn or something." She touched my arm. "Easy to do love. Easy to do. But all's well that ends well. Eh, love?"

So that's what he'd done. Played dumb. Both of us lost. He couldn't find me so he raised the alarm. But he didn't try to find me at all. I'd watched as he ran away. Leaving me behind. And it had been conveniently smothered by the start of the bombing.

It suddenly struck me that he was probably hoping that I didn't reappear. That if I never turned up he would never have to explain me away. I'd simply be another casualty of war. I was shocked to the core.

Mum and Lorraine went to bed and I hurried into the bathroom. Once under the shower, I fixed my eyes on the door handle, waiting for it to turn and for him to come in and speak to me alone. Sure enough, after a few minutes he tried it. But I'd pushed the tarnished brass lock across to bolt it. We'd never used that lock once in all the time we had lived in the house but I didn't want him near me.

When I emerged he was in the bedroom. Checking through my clothes and my bag. I watched him through the slightly open door as he panicked his way through all my belongings, too afraid to ask me in case someone heard. And no one could hear this, could they? No one could hear the truth about what he had done. He was too ashamed to speak about it and I was the only other person who knew everything that had happened.

I watched him as he pulled out the blue suitcase from under the bed. He'd even got that back from Maria. I made a mental note to ask her when. He'd gone to great lengths to cover his tracks. Even though he'd watched me like a hawk since we entered the house, here he was rummaging through my memory box in case I'd somehow sneaked into our bedroom and deposited the magazine with its hidden pages in some secret place.

Finally he sat down hard on our spring mattress and held his head in his hands. I expected to feel a pang of hurt for him, the man I had married. Oh, I understood now that he thought he was acting for the common good. Whatever he had been so keen to hide away, to transport in uncertain times. So critical. So crucial. So desperately important that he had felt able to sacrifice me to it.

Sanaa was right. He'd used me. All it would have taken was for him to whisper 'sorry' and hold me tightly. To have shown an emotion and held my hand like he never wanted to let me go again. But he didn't because he knew. He knew exactly what the situation was. That only I knew how he had told me to run into the wilderness in order to save his neck from whoever was approaching at the checkpoint. He knew all right. He wasn't sorry. I could tell by the way he searched and searched for the papers that he was far more concerned about himself than his shell-shocked wife.

Chapter 25

I fell asleep on the sofa with one of the blankets Maria and I had crocheted around me. It was late afternoon when I woke, sensing Mark standing over me.

His voice, low and rough, permeated my senses. "Jules. Jules. We need to talk. They've gone to sort out their flights home. We need to talk while they're out."

I lay with my eyes closed for a moment but when he sat beside me on the sofa, his hand on my arm, they snapped open. In the moments after sleep I'd almost forgotten how I felt but his touch made it flood back and my heart was icy again.

"Talk?"

"Yeah. About what happened. We need to get some things clear. But not here."

I climbed out from the blanket and showered. I took my time, hoping Mum and Lorraine would come back, but they didn't. By the time I dressed, he'd made coffee. He was waiting for me at the breakfast bar.

"So what do you want to talk about Mark? How I am? Am I all right? Am I hurt? What happened to me in the six days I was missing? Anything like that?" I sipped the coffee and stared at him. "Or was it something else? Something you give more of a shit about?"

He looked surprised, then angry. He suddenly grabbed my arm and pulled me off my stool. My coffee spilled and, as he dragged me through the back door, I heard the cup smash on the kitchen floor. He hurried me to the end of our garden and through the apricot trees. When we reached an old, derelict building he stopped and spun me around to face him.

"Where is it?" He spat the words in my face, and I could feel globules of his saliva land on me.

"Oh. Now we're getting to it, aren't we? Where's what, Mark?"

His face reddened and I could see a vein in his forehead throbbing. "That magazine I gave you to look after. With the papers in it. Where is it?"

His grip on my arm tightened and I looked at his hand. "Where is it? I don't know."

He pulled me closer to the wall and his face was close to mine. "OK. I know you're pissed off but I need those papers. I put my neck on the line for them. You don't know how important this is, Juliette."

"Get your hands off me. Maybe if you'd told me I might have known. But you didn't, did you? You didn't tell me anything at all. Nothing. Not even where I was. You left me alone in a strange fucking country when you knew what was about to happen."

He let me go suddenly. I realised I'd been shouting into the Cypriot silence

"Jules. What's happened to you?"

I'd never spoken to him like that. I'd never cursed in front of him. But I'd never been this angry.

"What's happened to me? You mean apart from being lost in the dark, then nearly getting bombed? Then walking for days with no food or clean water? Then being interrogated by the Iraqi police and the British army? All because you didn't want to get caught? Well, it worked, didn't it? You were here, safe in our lovely home, and I was lost in a foreign war zone. Well done Mark, mission accomplished. Except for the fact that I came back. You didn't bet on that, did you?"

He stood back a little. "It wasn't like that. I didn't plan for that to happen. I just need those papers, Jules."

He looked desperate. The man I'd shared my life with for many years had changed beyond all recognition, and it crossed my mind that it had all been a lie, and this was the real Mark.

"The papers? I don't know where they are."

"Well, let's go through what happened and where you saw them last."

"Oh, no, it doesn't work like that. Only if we start from the beginning. Only if we're honest. But honesty isn't your strong point, is it?"

He grabbed me again, this time digging his fingers into my skin. "No. You can't know about that. Just tell me, Jules."

"Or else what?" I screamed at him. We'd had arguments in the past where we had both raised our voices but I'd never been so angry. "I can know about it, because if you don't tell me I'm going to go right back to the investigators and tell them what really happened. That it wasn't a visa run and that you nearly got caught doing whatever it was you were doing. And that you traded your wife for your own neck."

He held me away from him, still gripping my arms. "Who've you been talking to? Who's put this in your head?"

"Who? Fucking who? No one. Lots of time to think. You take me for some stupid little girl who's followed you around the world, who you can just throw away. Well, think again, Mark."

He let me go now and I stumbled backwards.

"No. No, I don't. It wasn't meant to happen like that. Look, I took the papers from work. I was supposed to archive them. Top security. I couldn't read them because they were coded. But then I opened the file they arrived in and saw what they were about. I'm sorry, Jules. I'm sorry. But I couldn't let them find out. I had to do something." He was crying now. He looked like a little boy and for a moment I wanted to forgive him and hold him, comfort him. "All those people. It would affect every single person on this earth. And all I had to do was give the papers back to the person they came from. Remove them from Allied eyes. Before it all started. Before they found whatever it was they were looking for. Before they decoded the document. I was just going to give it back. Then I saw the vehicles approaching. I didn't want you to get caught and that's why I told you to run. Not to save myself."

He paused to wipe his eyes, probably hoping that this would be enough, but I folded my arms and stared at him.

He continued. "But it was an American delegation at the checkpoint. I ran over to them and told them we'd been separated and we all searched for you. But you'd gone, and then the bombing started. I didn't want to leave but…"

"But you did."

"I had to. If they had suspected what I was really doing they would have arrested me. I flew home and raised the alarm. Told them it was a visa run. I did raise the alarm and people were looking for you. I swear, Jules, it was an accident."

"So where were you taking the papers? Who to?"

"Back to where they came from, to the people they belong to, the people who kept them safe – until someone among them sold out. I wanted to make sure the papers were kept safe by the people who have been looking after them until now. I had to try – before what's in them causes an international situation."

"Huh. International situation – isn't that a bit dramatic?"

"No. I can't tell you exactly what it's all about, but it's something you could never imagine, Jules. Something terrible."

It was just like before: I can't tell you. You wouldn't understand. It's my job. It would put you in danger.

I was tired of being treated like I was stupid and there seemed to be no point pursuing this now. He was never going to tell me.

I thought for a moment. "So what about work – hasn't anyone noticed that the papers are missing?"

"No. I replaced them with something else. You don't know how important this is. If those papers get into the wrong hands there'll be an international incident."

"Yes, so you keep saying. But what's to stop whoever gave them to you disclosing what's in them? Someone must have written the papers. Someone else must know about them."

"They were leaked to us. Sold. The people who wrote the papers were safeguarding a secret, something that could change mankind forever, according to the files. It's a fucking mess. Those papers hold the key to the secret. And right now, with Desert Storm going on, it's not the time for something so dangerous to be on the loose."

He had a good heart, deep down. I knew that. "But surely that's not your decision to make, is it?"

"Maybe not. But I've seen some bad things lately. You've no idea what's happening over there in Iraq. Innocent people being killed. Collateral damage. Whole villages wiped out. And information so damning and dangerous in the hands of people who don't give a fuck about children burning in their homes. That's why I took it. That's why, Jules. So for God's sake, where is it?"

But I was still back there on the innocent people. The villages and the children. Sanaa's face one morning when we had to chase the birds away from her son's makeshift grave and stack the stones back up. My terror reflected in her eyes.

"Where is it? Where are the papers? That's the fucking million dollar question, isn't it? It started raining. My bag got wet and the magazine was too heavy to carry. So I left it. It was destroyed. No one could have read it. Soaked."

"You left it? I thought I told you to keep hold of it?"

"You told me you loved me as well, and you told me you'd never let anything bad happen to me. But look." My arms had begun to bruise where he had gripped me hard. Small fingerprint-shaped bruises, punctuating my skin. Five-day-old grazes up my legs. "It keeps happening. You keep hurting me. I'm sorry about the papers. I'm sorry I didn't follow your instructions to the letter. But what are *you* sorry for, eh, Mark?"

He sat down hard on a stone wall behind him. "So we'll keep this between ourselves, yeah? Otherwise I'll lose my job and probably be arrested."

I was twenty-five at the time. Still young. Still relatively innocent to the realities of life, I realise now, even after my ordeal. But even in my shocked state, I knew that I didn't want more of this.

"Keep your precious job, Mark. Keep it. But you've lost me. You don't care about me. I'll always think that you're only staying with me to protect your secret now. And that's no reason."

This would have been the ideal time for him to hold me and kiss me and declare his undying love but he didn't. He just stared at me, his cold, steely eyes skimming my soul. I turned and went back into the house.

He followed me. "So what'll happen now?"

I started to clean up the pieces of the broken cup and mopped up the spilled coffee. "I'll go back to Manchester with Mum and Lorraine. We'll take it from there."

"And you won't tell anyone?"

Unbelievably, he was still focused on himself when our marriage was snapping apart.

"No. To be honest, Mark, I haven't got it in me. I need to recover. And you don't tell anyone either. Because if you do and this fucking secret is as dangerous as you claim, you're putting us both in danger. Not that you give a shit about that."

I put the dustpan and brush back in the cupboard and pulled on a cardigan over my dress. Once out of the house I rubbed my bruised arms and examined my bruised soul. In the beauty of this ancient village, with its depth of history and its dusty streets, I felt empty. Even after Mark's confession that everything he had done was for the greater good I still couldn't be with him. Not at the moment. All my love for him had drained and I needed to get away from him as soon as possible.

I walked through the village, through the huge purple passion flowers and the beautiful stonework that suddenly felt spoiled and shabby, to the shed that doubled as a post office. The man behind the counter hugged me and told me, in Cypriot, with tears in his eyes, how the whole village had prayed for me and how happy he was that I was safe. I thanked him and asked to use his telephone. He showed me into a back room and I dialled the international code for the UK, then Ellie's number. She answered after two rings.

"Hi Ellie. It's Juliette. I'm just ringing people to tell them I'm safe."

"Thank God. I saw it on the news. Thank God you're safe."

Then silence. I willed her to have checked her messages, or to remember any for me that might have come through.

Finally, she spoke. "Oh, someone called for you. A woman said she had a message from Saif Abed. Is that right? Sounded foreign. Told me to tell you Buhriz 925635. That make any sense, Jules?"

"Make sense? Yes, yes it does, just a woman out here who's interested in keeping in touch once I get back."

"Oh, you coming back?"

"Yes. Yes, I'm coming back."

The lying just came. I'd started to cover it with constant questions, and I was changing. Changing into a liar. But even so, my heart leaped. Sanaa had made it, and she'd done as she promised.

I walked back towards the house but stopped in the little chapel at the centre of Parekklisia. It was thousands of years old and packed to the brim with gold icons of the saints. I wasn't a religious person but I remember thinking that there would be no harm in backing my odds both ways, so I lit a candle for Shahid and Sanaa and sat for a while considering my options.

Part Three: Kate Morden

The Truth Keepers

Chapter 26

As soon as the plane hits the runway at JFK I text Carey. I use my own phone even though it's probably unsecure, because only Carey and I will know what the message means. We have a set of children's stories from which we remove all coding concepts. The codes are from various stories in a particular order, with several possible combinations. Our idea of fun at university wasn't all-night parties but making cyphers and working out the mathematical statistics of them ever being discovered. I invoke the strongest.

"Hi Carey. How's the cat? Did you feed him?"

This will alert Carey to the correct set of codes and the precise variable. I wait, tapping the edge of the seat. I'm still numb from the realisation that whoever Jamie Lewis is, he has access to my personal details. And that Farrah is dead. In this line of work you're trained to kill, and on some cases it's the only form of self-defence that will get you out of a situation alive. But I'm still human. I still cried at the half-alive mouse in a trap at Neil's house. I still hid it from Sammy and Leo. Farrah's death was unnecessary – and connected to me in some way.

My resolve to find out why strengthens inside me. The plane taxies towards the gate where I will disembark and be immediately confronted by my opposite numbers in the US security forces.

Carey replies within seconds: "Cat's fine. Eating well."

I type the code quickly, knowing that there are probably several agencies monitoring my phone by now. Carey will be able to translate it as: *Great. Wait near a phone. I am almost in New York and I need a secure contact line sent. I need information on Jeremy Lewis. I'll call you from a public payphone.*

I'm doubtful that he will get information about Lewis. If he was a cell, it won't be recorded anywhere. Terrorists don't work like that. Terrorism is organised using technology, and he certainly had some at his disposal if he knew my private phone number.

Carey responds immediately. I sift through the words, quickly matching them to the selected transcript in the correct order. I breathe in sharply as message comes together: *Karl's waiting for you in New*

York. He flew out this morning. They know that someone has breached top level but they don't know who.

I switch off the phone and remove the battery and SIM. It's only a matter of time before someone notices that the files have been read. Carey won't have left a trail but the opening of the file and the corresponding date will alert Karl and his superiors to the possibility that their own security has been breached. I've seen this before. Rather than exclude the American service and risk them breaching, they'll join with the CIA. Particularly in cases that involve intelligence against a common enemy. In this case, the harvesters. Then there will be less people to suspect.

That's why Karl is already in New York, to forge that relationship.

The plane door opens and I make my way to the front. The sixteen-hour flight with one stop in Istanbul has taken its toll and, even though I slept for a good proportion of it, my legs are wobbly. As I descend, two agents step forward at the foot of the stairs and guide me to the left, away from the gate and to a waiting travel cart. We sit silently in the back until we reach the main airport building.

Once inside, one of the agents makes a call. "Target received."

The other one walks me into an office and we wait for a moment, then a door opposite opens and we leave. A black limousine is waiting for us and, once inside, one of the agents smiles, even though the atmosphere is tense.

"Miss Lynch. Could we see your documents, please?"

I hand him my passport and we go through what we both know is the farcical identification procedure. He doesn't ask for my real passport and I don't offer it.

After driving for about half an hour we arrive at Broome Street, between Lower Manhattan and Chinatown. Even in the darkness the buildings, all concrete and trademark iron fire escapes are instantly recognisable to me. I stayed around this area with Neil in the early days of our relationship and the memories come flooding back.

We stop outside a lively bar and go through a small burgundy door at the side, which leads up a narrow staircase to the first floor, then take the lift to the third.

We step out and there are a series of doors leading to apartments. The agents lead me to the third door and one of them knocks.

A tall, thin man answers. "Ah. Here you are. OK. Come right in, Katherine."

I'm tired and disorientated, fading quickly, and I look for a clock.

"Two AM, Katherine."

That's when I remember that, just as I am reading the situation, I'm being read. He's scanning me for any sign of fear or panic. All he sees is jet lag. I'm good. Yes. I'm good at hiding my feelings. And right now those feelings are raging inside me. Even so, I remember that American surveillance often doesn't stop at observation and can stretch to biometrics such as heart rate and perspiration monitors.

"Thanks. It's been a long journey."

"Tom Caines, by the way. I'll be looking after you while you're here."

He's a good-looking guy. Well dressed but not too smart. Certainly not trademark Secret Service. You can usually tell a mile off. But Tom's different. There's a spark in his eye and, although he's monitoring me, he's still friendly. I shake his hand and his skin is cool and smooth.

He continues. "Look, Kate, sorry to do this straight off the plane but we need to debrief, and then there's a meeting just through here."

"Great. I slept on the plane so I'm OK. Just need some clothes. I had to leave my case in Baghdad."

He fixes his eyes on me and my body temperature increases just a fraction.

"I'm sure I don't need to ask you this but anything critical in that case?"

"No. Just Ms Lynch's personal effects and some notes about Gertrude Bell. Oh, and a laptop."

"Used for the web search?"

He clearly doesn't know the full details of my trip. He's stabbing in the dark, which doesn't make me feel any more secure. Where had the US agents been? How had they let this happen?

"No. I used the university system."

"Ah. Using the username Farrah Amin? Which explains why…"

"Yes."

"Unfortunate. Very unfortunate. It seems like there were a lot of unknowns in that situation. And several facts have come to light in the hours you were in the air. I think the best thing is that we join the meeting. You can get up to speed."

I turn towards the meeting room and he guides me with his hand on the small of my back. I check out his left hand for a wedding ring then stop myself. He's an attractive man but this isn't the time or the place.

As the door opens I see a large, ornate room with an oval mahogany table. At the other end of the room is a huge video screen. The air is thick with tension. Karl is standing by the window talking to another man in a suit. No smile. He doesn't make his way over. I turn my attention to Tom.

"So, when is this meeting due to start?"

He gestures towards the screen.

"Waiting for your Foreign Secretary to join. And our Chief of Staff."

I take a glass of orange juice from a nearby tray. Then add some ice. "So it really has escalated?"

He takes my arm and pulls me into a corner. "So what do you think this is then? WMD?"

I don't know how much he knows. I get the usual squirm in the pit of my stomach that I hide so well when I'm in an awkward situation.

He puts my mind at rest. "All information has been shared. Including your report on Assadi. And Krommer. My God, Kate. May I call you Kate? God only knows what would have happened if you hadn't noticed the fingerprints and connected with the ice tray. That's gotta be the key to all this. It's gotta be. So. Nuclear weapons? Trigger, maybe? More sophisticated weaponry? Even cyber threats?"

"I'm not sure. Not sure at all. I still don't think there were WMD in Iraq. None have ever surfaced. No components have ever been identified. A nuclear trigger would need plans. Engineering. People. Given the politics around it, someone would have spilled by now. And this case doesn't seem connected to that. Wrong kind of science.

And earlier. There's so much information going back so far in so many different places that I'm wondering if we've got a complete picture. I'm wondering if WMD is even the right terminology."

He suddenly looks confused. "Oh. OK. I guess no one told you. That's what we'll be doing. You, mainly. Collating the information. Analysis. Then making recommendations for investigation."

It's news to me and I blink at him. I specifically requested no partnering. Karl knows my feelings on this and I see him, out of the corner of my eye, watching for my reaction. I click my glass against Tom's. No point protesting now. I'll discuss it with Karl after the meeting.

Everyone takes their seat and I sit next to Tom, as near to the door as I can get, with Karl facing me. He's still monitoring me but I simply smile at him. The man he's talking to, well-built, middle-aged and, by the sounds of his accent, born and bred in New York, calls the meeting to order.

"Welcome to New York. I'm Joe Newman, Director of Investigations. I'd like to particularly welcome our British friends, Karl Ronson and Kate Morden." There's a ripple of murmurs around the ten people in the room. "That's right. Kate is Frank Morden's daughter. Kate, we're honoured to have you here. We hold your father in great esteem. OK. As you know, the situation vis-a-vis the men who have been targeted for their fingerprints has worsened. We now have six victims with very little evidence to link them. For my part, on behalf of the US Government, and solely because one of the suspected victims is a US citizen, we've put one of our best operatives, Tom Caines, to work with Kate Morden to assimilate all the current shared information. But before we start work, we have someone here who would like to brief you on the current situation. We'll be joined by the British Foreign Secretary and the US Chief of Staff to hear this."

Chapter 27

The screens flicker to life and the two men appear. Tom is sitting fairly close to me on my left, and I look to my right. I hear Tom's sharp intake of breath and his slow exhale as Donald Winger walks into the room. I feel Karl's eyes on me but I turn to look straight ahead. There's complete silence as Donald takes up a position at the head of the table.

Donald Winger is almost a legend, probably the only person alive who can truly remember the Cold War. I've seen him before, a younger version of him, at my home with my father; back then he was part of the inner circle of code-breakers, like my father.

He's old now, his face weathered, but his eyes are still bright blue and lively. He scans the table and his eyes rest on me. I wonder, for a second, if he knows that I coded whatever we are looking for, and that I am the key. But his look is cold rather than accusatory. He knows about my father.

He addresses the table. "Good evening. I've been seconded by the UK government, who take this matter very seriously, to build a team of top investigators to deal with this critical situation. In this room we have the most experienced agents holding knowledge about this case. We have Lauren Gaynor, the top CIA cryptographer, and of course, as Joe said, Kate Morden, Lauren's opposite number in the UK. This is particularly important in this case as, from the sample information, everything is encoded. We know that the code is very similar to those generated by Kate's father and my once very good friend, Frank Morden. The Morden Codes. So we're hoping that once we have the missing information Kate can help us out."

I don't flinch. All eyes are on me and I smile slightly. They don't know. Thank God. They have no idea that it's me who coded that information. He's playing the game and keeping what he knows about my father to himself.

He continues. "We now believe that the twelve pieces of information we don't have refer to twelve people, six of whom are dead and have had either their fingerprints or their hands removed. For what reason we can only guess at this point. This case has layers and layers of information going back to the early nineties, and cases such as this are notorious for being tangled and inaccessible. But we have to solve it."

He becomes suddenly more intense and leans forward. His voice, heavy with a received accent, booms out in the room. "What's your biggest fear? Not war. War has rules. War has conventions – yes, they're sometimes broken, but on the whole we all know where we are with war. Natural disasters? We fear them but somehow accept them because they're not within human control. Our biggest fear, therefore, is that someone will do something so evil that it affects the entire human race. We live our whole lives worrying about it and relying on people to have a conscience. But not everyone has. Something has lain hidden for decades. And someone seems hell bent on letting it loose."

His breathing is heavy and panics me a little. "The worst part is that we don't know what we are dealing with. We strongly suspect this is the work of a terrorist group. Maybe IS. Maybe Al Qaeda. Maybe cells that have been activated after laying dormant for years. We've had full teams both here and in the UK, investigating all the links. Every loophole has been tied up and all we are left with is six bodies and some code that we can't decipher yet. But like I said, this goes back a long way. Tom Caines and Kate Morden, you'll be investigating the historical aspects of the case but first you need to find out who the last victim was. John Jones. Age forty-two. Lived here in New York, on Lafayette, Brooklyn with his mother. We know that four of the deceased had connections with Baghdad University in the late eighties and early nineties. But Jones and Krommer had no obvious links."

Tom raises his hand and Joe points at him.

"Dr Winger, I'm Tom Caines. Having reviewed the information, is it safe to assume that we are searching for a weapon of some kind?"

Joe answers the question. His expression is deadly serious and his face greyed. My heart sinks. "Yes. This is a weapon, for sure. But we have intelligence that all the uranium that was shipped to Iraq has been accounted for. Whatever this is, it seems that there's been a careful conspiracy of silence around it since it was first created. At various points along the way someone has recognised its financial value and tried to sell it. Luckily it's always been intercepted by someone else with more integrity. Whatever it is, no one that knows anything about it ever speaks of it – that's how potentially threatening this thing is. One thing's for sure. The basic information is out there again, and it's in the hands of someone who's prepared to kill to get it. I have to stress, though, at this point this is mere speculation. We have no evidence at all to link the deaths – except the missing fingerprints."

Donald interrupts. "On the contrary. This is not; I repeat not just an assumption. We've decoded all the available information that we can, and it indicates that we're looking for an organisation that is several steps ahead of us in the hunt for this weapon, and one that has breached our top-level security. They've obtained access to all our information and will no doubt be trying to decode it. But we have the advantage. We believe that someone who trained with Frank Morden coded those documents, and we have the next best thing. We have Kate. And Lauren, of course, who is an expert in post-war cryptography, and a specialist in the Morden Codes. This is a race: a race to find out exactly what we are dealing with, and to find it before anyone else does. You'll find all the information you need on a dedicated networked server."

It's an awkward exchange. Clearly, our American friends are not as committed as we are. Winger turns now and looks at the screen. The US Chief of Staff, Mark Davies, nods and begins to speak.

"I'm here to represent the President who unfortunately cannot attend but gives full consent to the joint working relationship between the US and the UK on this matter. Once the evidence is confirmed and links are established."

The Secretary of State, John King, nods his approval. "Good luck."

The screen fades and Karl sighs. He looks across the table at me now, bemused, and this doesn't reassure me. The US government is stalling until they are sure. I can't blame them.

Joe says, "OK. Any questions?"

I raise my hand. "Has anyone identified Krommer?"

Karl answers. "We've got the autopsy report back and we're trying to trace who he is. Not Krommer, we know that for sure. The other victims were academics at Baghdad University but John Jones has no connections whatsoever. So until we know who Krommer is, we need to find out what the angle is with Jones."

"OK. So who's James Lewis?"

A silence hangs over the room. Joe and Donald look at each other.

"James Lewis is a bounty hunter." There is a hint of disgust in Joe's voice and he stares at the oak table. "He's a mercenary. Unpredictable. Difficult to pin down the people he works with. He plays mind games and he's not to be trusted."

I suddenly realise that I'm lucky to be alive. Or valuable enough that he let me live.

"I saw his blog and went to meet him. He knows who I am."

Joe's face says it all. He's furious. This is turning into a roller coaster. "Yeah. We heard you'd been to see him. And we know about the blog. We considered his involvement with whoever is after this information but we think that he's working alone, as usual. But he'll work with whichever side pays him most, and in the meantime, find out as much as he can and make it public knowledge. That's how he gets contracts, and that's how he's playing this."

Tom raises his hand again. "So what are we dealing with here? Ballpark?"

Direct. Just the way I like it.

Donald stands again. "We've spoken to various informants who entered the UK and US in 1991 to escape from the invasion of Kuwait. Anyone who exchanged information. Several people in this room have met with at least one of these people. In every single case the informant was scared and either would not divulge or did not know the end game. But in every case they uttered the same word: Armageddon."

I think of my conversation with the Assadis. And the decoded section of the top secret file that no one else knows about except Carey. My heart rate raises and I fume at the danger my father has put me in. I'm still thinking about the scale of this when a small voice from the corner of the room seeps through.

"Armageddon? Isn't that a little bit dramatic, Joe?"

I haven't particularly noticed him before – a tall, lithe man dressed in a light grey suit, sitting apart from us on a folding chair with his ankles crossed. I try to remember, and can't, if he was already in the room or if he entered during the meeting.

Joe smiles. "Elliot. We'd be grateful for anything you have to offer."

I feel my heartbeat quicken some more. Elliot Brady. So legendary that no one truly believed he existed.

"Thank you, Joe. I've reviewed the file and I agree that this is something other than regular warfare. We're looking at something that was developed for a particular purpose, and then whoever developed it had an attack of…" – he looks around the room and then speaks the word so softly that we hardly hear it – "conscience."

His presence has a strange effect on everyone, including me. Calming, almost, and the room is still.

"Collective conscience. I would wager that of the twelve people whose names are listed in the missing information, those whose integrity failed them are now dead. Which makes it progressively harder to find the others, because they have been silent for a quarter of a century or more. So we either have to find the perpetrators who killed the six dead victims, or find the information Krommer was selling the remaining six people. Unless they speak – and then they will be no use to us as they'll be dead too. Luckily, our opposition has the same dilemma. Unluckily for us they seem to have a lot more luck tracking them down. My best guess is that, like us, they need the code to find the location but unlike us, they are halfway to finding the biometric key. And until they do there will be no Armageddon."

He flicks some pages in his notebook. I glance at Tom, who is transfixed. Finally, Elliot Brady finds the correct page and holds it up. "So my recommendation is that the names are the critical item and should be prioritised over tracking the opposition. Of course, once we have that we will need the coding key."

The room erupts into enthusiastic agreement but when I break away from Karl's firm handshake, Elliot Brady is staring directly at me.

Chapter 28

The meeting is clearly over. Karl manages to leave before I get the chance to speak to him privately. Tom escorts me out of the building and we are soon on the cool New York Street. He guides me right.

"I'll walk you home. Well, I have no choice as we're staying in the same apartment. Separate rooms, of course."

I might have been offended if another stranger had said this to me but Tom seems easy to get on with. His natural charm is a dangerous weapon because it makes him difficult to resist. I see immediately that he's the kind of person who puts others in a position where they would do anything for him, and would be too embarrassed to object. But my awareness of this puts me slightly on my guard.

"Of course. There's the small matter of my clothes…"

"Ah. We had one of our operatives pick out a wardrobe for you." He looks me up and down. "I think it will suit."

We walk up Broome Street in the direction of the Holland Tunnel. Although New York is famous, even notorious for violence and more recently terror attacks, I always feel strangely at home when I'm here. I've had reason to visit many times, with Neil and alone, and stepping out onto the pavements and seeing the grafittied walls as we walk block by block towards Soho, I settle a little. Tom walks beside me and for the entire world we look like a couple returning from a late-night party.

We cross Delancy Street and stop beside a pizzeria on the corner. Tom unlocks a red door tucked behind two wide concrete pillars and we go inside. We take the lift which, unlike some of the lifts I've been in when staying in this area, doesn't smell of piss and vomit. The apartment is on the second floor and he has a key card. On the inside the door clicks locked when it shuts; we'll need Tom's key card to get out, too. He doesn't give a key card to me and I feel myself panic a little. But I hold off for now. I keep it under control. I have to.

"This is it. Home for the duration."

It's a beautiful apartment. The furniture is dark wood and it's what anyone who has ever watched American sitcoms would imagine a New York apartment to look like. Leather sofas and a widescreen TV. A set of bonsai plants on the pristine surfaces. It's the perfect hidey hole for us, suspended two floors up above a New York street, with a clear view to both sides, and a security door. There's the vague sound of people talking in adjoining apartments, along with televisions. I remind myself that it's the middle of the night but it's true, New York never sleeps.

I'm not tired either. Tom points out my room and I look at the clothes that have been provided. As I run my hands across the fabrics I realise that whoever chose them must have had access to the wardrobe in my flat. It's almost identical. Black jeans, black T-shirts. Smart flat pumps and a pair of ankle boots. A short, smart-casual leather jacket and a business suit. Two dresses, both suitable for daywear. I check the garments to see if they are actually the ones from my own wardrobe but most of them still have the price tags on them.

Fear stabs at me again. Ever since I discovered that James Lewis knows who I am I've felt more afraid. Afraid that my father's secret will be discovered and that people will blame me. I mentally risk-assess my flat but the likelihood of anyone finding anything to identify me as the coder is non-existent. I stopped keeping diaries long ago. So I shower and change into an identical outfit of black jeans and T-shirt. I pull on a hooded jacket, tie up my curly red hair and then go to the kitchen. The whole place smells of fresh bread, and I lean against the worktops to wait for the kettle to boil. I sense Tom behind me, watching me.

"We even got English breakfast tea for you."

I open the cupboards and see that I've been well provided for. Lots of my favourite items: Marmite, strawberry jam, even a selection of teas. Again, I picture my flat in London and wonder if whoever's been in there found the panel in the bathroom. Although it's what I do for a living, encroaching on other people's lives, it feels odd to think that I'm public property. Eerie, somehow. Carey's right: I can never go back from this.

"Yeah. I'm not tired yet, Tom. It might take me a day or so to get rid of the jet lag."

He pours himself a coffee while I brew my tea. I perch on a high stool at the worktop and he leans on the island in the centre.

"OK. So we've got a situation."

"Yeah. We have. I definitely wasn't expecting to see Elliot Brady there. Or Donald Winger."

"So serious. We need to act fast. I'd like to hit the Jones case in a couple of hours, as soon as it's light. Then we need to pull the involvement list together. We need to know what the other names are, what they've been doing. Jobs, locations. Although I'm tempted to chase the fucking terrorists."

"Of course. Only natural. So what do we know about Jones?"

"Not much. No background that's obvious. Unknown to us. Fairly sure that John Jones is his real name."

Krommer's identity is bugging him as much as it is me.

"So we need to establish his movements around 1991," I say.

Tom shows a reaction. Until now he's been in control but the gaps in his knowledge about this case are showing. "How so?"

"Because whatever we are looking at, it started then. Just before the invasion of Iraq by the coalition. Around the time Assadi defected. The twelve names were supposed to be given to him but weren't. We need to establish how the six dead men are linked and we have our path. That was my original mission, Tom, to find those names. It still is."

Basic stuff but Tom still looks confused. "What I don't understand is if someone already has this information, how has it not surfaced before now? It's the human condition. Greed. Nothing for all those years, then all of a sudden... boom."

"Mmm. We know Krommer was offering the information. And as Elliot Brady said, they're probably dead because at some point they have offered it. One thing's for sure, whoever our target is, whether it's IS or not, is ruthless. I saw Krommer and the injuries sustained. Brutal. They sent a clear message."

Tom's pulse in his temple has changed speed. He's getting fired up now. "Message. OK. Shoot."

"In my opinion, they're after one thing only. The data and the biometrics, then the prize. They don't want us or anyone else. They'd prepped Krommer's place quite clinically and, as far as I can see, there is no collateral damage."

"Agreed. John Jones lives with his mother. She was in the next room when her son was killed and she didn't hear a thing. And she wasn't harmed."

I look out of the window. A ribbon of sunlight is breaking across the New York skyline. Poor woman. I can imagine her waking and looking forward to a new day and then, in a second, her world falling apart.

"OK. That's our first port of call. I'll be in my room. Give me a shout when it's time."

He turns then turns back. "Oh. Before I forget. Here's a phone for you. Better use this one. Charged up and works on the US networks."

He hands the phone to me and our eyes meet briefly. There's no trace of humour in his eyes now. This is an agency phone and he's been instructed that I use it so that I can be monitored. But what the hell? The only person I'll be calling is Carey and that wouldn't be flagged as an unusual communication.

"Thanks, Tom. That's useful. I can leave these in my bag now."

I make a show of bundling Kate Lynch's mobile and my own mobile into my handbag and wait for him to ask me for them. He doesn't, which is just as well because I wasn't going to hand them over.

In my room I take out the case file and flick through my own reports, pausing at Tom's background report. He's thirty-eight. I would have put him a few years younger, around my own age. Born and bred in Old Brookville on Cedar Swamp. Mother and father still living. Unmarried – I was right. Attended great schools. Straight A student right through college. Joined the CIA sixteen ago. I search through the document for his specialism. And there it is: he's a trained killer. He'd gone through bodyguard training at the highest level.

I read on and he's easily on a par with me, assignment wise. There are even photographs of him with high profile politicians. Chief of staff. The President. He's even looked after the Pope. I flick through a little further. No record of him contributing to major investigations, although he's been on plenty.

My jet-lagged brain takes a moment to home in on the fact that his assignment is to keep me safe.

The last page of the file contains CCTV pictures of me at Baghdad airport, and some grainy pictures of James Lewis. I read through the briefing; HQ was a step ahead of me. They were tracking Kate Lynch's mobile and got jumpy when I arrived at James Lewis' address. I stare at the last paragraph of the report. It details how John Jones' time of death was estimated to be at the same time as Farrah Amin's. I was an open target, yet they killed Farrah as a warning shot. They didn't kill me.

Chapter 29

I'm so incensed that I'm entangled in this mess that I end up banging on Tom's bedroom door at seven fifteen. He emerges immediately, looking as if he hasn't slept at all. I stand in front of him.

"May I have a key card for the front door, please?"

He looks confused for a moment, and then rallies. "I thought we were going together. To see Mrs Jones?"

I'm fuming inside but I know that on the exterior I appear calm and collected. "Yes, we are, Tom. But maybe I'll want pizza. Or just want to go for a walk to clear my head. So, key please."

He isn't ready to crack yet but I'm going nowhere until we both know why we're here. "I'll have to get one made. We only have one."

"Oh. So that means that we'll have to go everywhere together? Yes?"

"Yes. For the time being."

I go over to the door and turn the handle. It's locked, of course. "I need some toothpaste. I'd like to go to the shop. Please could you unlock the door?"

Tom's lapse is exactly the same over-long gap as Nathan's on the roof that time. Brain ticking over. Not fast enough. I'm not supposed to challenge what the department has arranged. I'm supposed to play the game. And, under normal circumstances, I would. But none of this is normal.

He sits down and rubs his forehead. I wait for his answer. Eventually, it comes.

"Look. It's for your own good."

"Is it? Why's that, Tom?"

He thinks for a moment longer. "I'm under orders. I'm under orders to look after you. Protect you, because of your father. You're an asset, Kate. We can't risk anything happening to you. Because when we do find the data you'll be heading up the cryptography team. It can only be you because of your father's work. Don't act like you don't know that. You know it's best."

"OK. What about Lauren Gaynor?'

"She's a notable expert on the Morden Codes. She'll be assisting you."

I can feel my temper rising. It's still all about my father. My feelings for that situation are like the tides, constantly retreating so that I think I'm recovering from the hurt but then more debris washes up with every mention of his name.

There's no point pursuing this with Tom. He's assigned to me and I can't shake him.

"OK. Let's go then."

He looks surprised. His iceberg front melts away gradually. I'm wearing him down. "Is that it? No more questions?"

"No. Just unlock the door. Some things you have to accept. But we're doing it my way."

He unlocks the door and we descend to street level and hail a taxi. In fifteen minutes we're on Lafayette between two towering apartment blocks. It's early but when we ring Mrs Jones' buzzer she answers immediately. I look up at the apartment block. Tom pre-empts me.

"Third floor. Lift and stairs. Buzzer security system on the doors."

The door mechanism clicks and we're in. The lift doesn't work. I sprint up the dark red painted stair case with Tom close behind me. Whoever killed John Jones had only one way in. I check for alarms and cameras and, apart from across the street at the junction of Lafayette and Nostrand, there are none. It's a basic downtown block, just the bare minimum. Concrete stairs and rough metal handrails. The smell of stale cooking odours is overwhelming the farther up the stairs we get and then, suddenly, it's replaced by a laundry smell.

The door's open when we reach the top of the stairs. The hallway of Mrs Jones' apartment is a deep contrast to the red of the stairs – it's completely white – and the terracotta floor tiles are scrubbed scrupulously clean. Mrs Jones is sitting in the lounge in her nightgown. There are pictures of a man on the mantle, some of them from his teenage years and some more recent. Mrs Jones is in her late sixties. I peer round the corner of the hallway into a spacious kitchen with three washing machines and a large dryer installed.

When we reach her, Mrs Jones turns her head slightly. "I've already told them everything."

Tom checks out the rest of the apartment. I know from the notes in the file that John Jones was manually strangled. His mother found him soon after his death. The ends of his fingers were bleeding. I can only imagine what this woman has been through.

"I'm sorry, Mrs Jones. Very sorry for your loss. But we need to ask more questions."

I follow her gaze to one of two white doors off the lounge.

"Agnes. I'm Agnes. He was John. My son. My boy."

"Thank you, Agnes. I'm Kate. Kate Morden. We're investigators. We'll do everything we can to find out who did this."

Poor Agnes. I open the bedroom door and see that it hasn't been touched since the scene-of-crime people did their worst. There are seams of blood on the wall above the headboard and on the sides of the bed. They cut off the ends of his fingers before strangling him.

Agnes reminds me that it's been several days since John was killed. "They told me not to touch anything in there. That someone else would be along."

I look around the room. It's been stripped of most of its contents. I saw the evidence list in the file. Books, a laptop. Clothes. All the everyday remnants of John Jones' life have been collected and stored. The room looks unlived in now. Devoid of his effects.

I turn back to Agnes. "You didn't hear anything?"

Tom, breaking away from his examination of the locks on the front door, joins us.

"Not a thing. Nothing."

"And you've seen no strangers in the building?"

"No. I have my regular customers for laundry. I don't see no one else. Except John."

John had been working for a glass company in the city. Driving stock around, loading up trucks. In his spare time he'd drink in a local bar and go to the movies. Alone, or with friends, all of whom have been questioned. I go through to the kitchen and open the fridge freezer. I grab a kitchen towel and pull out the ice tray. The freezer is a Traulsen G-Series. The more expensive model. I take the ice tray through to Agnes.

"Agnes. I wonder if you can help me? Is this your ice tray?"

She looks at the generic white tray. The ice is already melting in the hot room and dripping onto the tiles. Splash, splash, splash. Her brow furrows and she gets out of her chair with difficulty and hurries through to the kitchen. Poking around in the freezer, she pulls open drawers and cupboards.

"Hey, that isn't mine. Where's my tray? Where did you get that from? Maybe John put that in there but it ain't mine. Mine came with the product."

I move closer to her. "Agnes. It's really important that you tell me if anyone you don't know has been in your apartment recently."

My eyes meet hers. I recognise that pain. Visceral. Searing.

'No one. Not a single person. Just my regular laundry people. The postman. John. That's all."

I touch her arm gently.

"Thank you, thank you so much. We'll just take another look in John's room and then we'll leave you. I'll need to take your ice tray."

She walks slowly back to her chair and sits down. I know that grief. I remember it so well – the smell of the gun and the uncertainty over what happened to my father. Now Agnes has to face that someone came into her home and killed her son. I push the ice-cube tray into a plastic bag that Tom hands to me, follow Tom into the bedroom and shut the door.

He shakes his head. "I read the file. No break and enter. The door was still locked when she found him. I just checked the locks. No auto devices. No sign of tampering. The CCTV outside shows that no one entered the building for hours before John was killed. And no one left."

I look out of the bedroom window. It's a sheer drop of three floors onto an open road with CCTV at the junction. Just like the front.

"So the fire escape's at the front, is it?" I lean over and look right and left. "OK. That means that the killer lives in this block. This is exactly the same as Krommer. Same MO. We're finally getting somewhere."

I pull out the new mobile and dial Carey's number. He answers immediately.

"Hi Carey. It's me. Can you do me a favour?"

"Of course. Everything OK?" It's good to hear his voice.

I don't miss a beat. I don't want him embarking on a top-level conversation on an agency phone. Too risky. And I can't really tell him what's going on until I shake off Tom. "Fine. Look, I need you to get a full list of residents for the building Krommer lived in. There's a similar case here and I think that the plans for these murders have been well laid."

"You mean the killers lived in the apartments for some time? Befriended the victims? Jesus. Looks like Assadi's cell theory was right."

"Maybe. But there's no forced entry here and no one entering or leaving anytime around the time of death. While you're at it, can you get me a list of everyone who attended or worked at Baghdad University between 1989 and 1991? Including research students and lab assistants."

"I'll give it a go. Do you want me to act on any information about Krommer?"

I think for a moment. I can't act alone here. I'd need to share anything I have with Tom at least. "No. Just let me have the information to start with. I'll fill you in later."

Something is wrong his end. I can tell by his strained tone. "Kate…"

"I'm sorry, Carey. I have to go. I'll be in touch later."

I turn off the phone. Tom is standing very close to me.

"Who's that?"

I smile widely. "Carey Morrison. My right-hand man. It's OK. He's service authorised. Let's go. We need to take the tray in and find out who lives in this building."

We leave the bedroom and I look at Agnes, lost in her own thoughts about her dead son. Probably wondering what all this is about. Not realising that somehow, in some way, he is part of a biometric key that could unlock something deadly.

"We're leaving now, Agnes. Before we go, could you tell me if you've had any new neighbours recently? Anyone who came here who lives in the building? In the last year?"

She stares at me, grief contorting her features. "Yes, of course. There was Asiya. Asiya Siddique. Lovely girl. Brought me pie every other Sunday. And Joe and Phyllis Swift. Old couple, stuck up there on fourth when the lift is broken. Bring their laundry and I'm glad of it. Other than that, no one else."

"Thank you. Where does Asiya live?"

She pointed upward. "Right up there. Right above us. Quiet as a mouse, she is. No trouble at all."

Chapter 30

We leave the apartment and Tom phones the information in. Agnes' next-door neighbour, Don Thompson, a forty-two-year-old mechanic who was interviewed at the scene of crime, tells us that they've just gone out.

"Down the stairs. First time they've been out in a week. Lift's broken."

I look at Tom. He doesn't click on to the relevance at all.

"Restricting movement around the scene of crime. So whoever this is knows the building really well."

It's beginning to irritate me. It's as if he's just a bystander, no comment or agreement, hardly any input at all. We leave the building and stand on the street outside the apartment block. He's looking up the road for a taxi and I can't help but question the investigation so far.

"What I don't get is why no one looked for the ice tray? It's exactly the same as Krommer's killing. Fingerprints removed from the scene in ice. Did anyone read the file?"

"Yeah. Good point. I guess some of our guys aren't as convinced by British methods."

His own contribution so far hasn't been exactly outstanding.

"Really. Any better ideas?" I hold out my hand and a taxi pulls in. "Or any ideas at all?"

We get into the taxi. He's really pissing me off. It's strained now and I look out of the window to avoid his gaze.

"I'm not here to give my opinion. I'm here to help you. To keep you safe."

"But you're an agent, Tom. I saw your file."

"Yeah. True. But my assignment isn't to investigate. Let's just say that there's some division over how this case should be run. Our government wasn't happy with you on the loose in Baghdad, or being accused of hacking British top-level security. It's only because of the seriousness of this case…"

I laugh out loud. "Great. I was nearly killed in Baghdad. I wasn't on the loose, I was on a mission. To investigate a similar case. But I didn't get very far, because it all went to shit."

"I heard. I also heard that our guys were also out there monitoring the Lewis guy and you just went ahead and strolled right in."

I turn to face him abruptly and he jumps back. "Not my fucking problem, Tom. If there was a little more working cohesion, then it wouldn't have happened. But even now there's a fucking standoff. That's a terror cell in there. God knows how many more there are. We're on the brink of cracking something big. Lives are at risk and they still can't play fucking nice?"

His countenance remains calm but he can't hide the fire in his eyes. "Nothing will happen to you while I'm here, Kate. No one will harm you. Everyone agrees that you're an important player in this case. Integral."

I feel the anger burning inside me. "I can look after myself."

"No doubt but just look at me as a little extra insurance, huh?"

He gives the driver the address for the Broome Street HQ and we head back.

Four blocks away, I call Karl. "Karl. Kate. Get me Elliot Brady and get your ass up here. Pronto."

He breathes down the line. "What's the problem, Kate?"

I look out of the window at the everyday people going to work, pushing prams and bicycles. All those innocent people who are at the mercy of a ticking time bomb. Six dead, six to go. We need to push the case on now.

"We've got our link. All I need are some forensics to establish that Jones's murder is the same MO as Krommer's. I'll explain when I see you. But this isn't just some opportunist plot. This has been precision planned, possibly for years."

"OK. I'll meet you in fifteen. I'll call Brady."

When we reach Broome Street Karl is already there. He's sitting alone in the meeting room talking on his phone. He ends the call when he sees me.

"Kate…"

"Karl. Thanks for filling me in. I had to find out from Tom here that we're playing silly fuckers."

He's prickly because he knows that I've worked out exactly what he did to get me there. I can tell and it infuriates me.

"Look, it wasn't my idea. I swear I didn't know anything when I assigned you. Anything at all. This has escalated in fast time."

"Right. It's escalated. But if we're so eager to find out who's doing this, why is an old woman sitting in an apartment with her son's blood still all over the bed? And why is the US Secret Service being so divisive? What's the fucking problem, Karl? Why haven't all the residents been interviewed? That should have been the first task."

"There's a difference of opinion. Joe Newman feels that this is something that has only just been planned. Very recently. He's personally interrogated the intelligence and there was not one single suggestion that there was something about to happen. No cell. No intercepted social media. No telephone intelligence. No informants. No chatter. Nothing tangible to link the victims. Nothing to suggest that something like this would happen right under his nose in New York. In his own words, he's pulling this together just in case it blows up in our face. He's lukewarm. Lots of gesturing, as you saw earlier, not much action."

"But we had no British intelligence either. Not until Krommer made the data offer. From what Assadi said, this was a cold case. It seems that only those people around at the beginning ever expected it to re-emerge."

Then it hits me. The apartment upstairs.

"Karl. The apartments around Agnes. They have been searched, haven't they? For explosives. You know, like…"

"Joe thought there was no need. There was no explosion straight afterwards like the others. Another reason he thinks it isn't linked."

A quiet voice from the back of the room confirms my fears. "That was the plan. That it would be forgotten and never rear its ugly head again. Lost to the world. But unfortunately as long as there are people alive who know about it there is a risk of it coming to light. An increasingly probable risk, what with the new push to control Iraq."

Elliot Brady has arrived. He's sitting in a corner with a tablet.

162

I turn to face him. "So which side of the fence do you fall on, Mr Brady?"

He smiles a little and tilts his head to one side. It makes him look more quirky than usual. "Like you, Miss Morden, I'm on my own side. But, for the record, I agree that this is probably a terror cell, planning and waiting, waiting for the right time, for the signal."

Great. At last. Someone who's clued up.

"Finally. So, we need to act quickly. Get the apartments next to the Joneses searched. Evacuate that building. After speaking to Professor Assadi I feel that this has gone on since the early nineties. I'd like to have access to all information, including top level about the origins of our knowledge of this. I'd like to go right back to basics and find out exactly where this started, and with whom. I'll take that task and I'd like everyone else to focus on the links between Krommer's death and Jones's. We can take a look at the Iraqi murders but I doubt that they will yield anything." I look at the time on my phone. "It's ten now. I'd like a full collated file to present to Joe Newman at five this evening."

Karl stares me down. "But this could take a while. We need resources."

"We don't have a while, Karl. Whatever this is, it was worth someone planting perpetrators in sleeper cells for a long time. There are six more cells somewhere, just waiting for the signal. I suspect that my looking into Kaleef Ahmed's case triggered Jones's murder. What's to say that us finding out about Krommer and escalating that didn't trigger Kaleef Ahmed's and the other three? Get the resources, Karl. If our American friends won't spare them, fly them over."

Brady weighs in now. "She's right. Completely right."

I'm tired. Jet-lagged and out of sorts from my realisation about my father. I'm also acutely aware that I took this mission and assured Karl that I'd be unaffected by personal issues. I feel like calling the shots, telling them that I'm out unless they hurry up and pull together to progress this case. But I manage to rein it in. Just.

"With respect, Mr Brady, I don't need your approval. I asked you to be here because I respect you and I know your expertise in analysis. I need you to help me re-analyse this from the beginning. Revisualise, because this is something we haven't known before. Like

Donald Winger said, it's outside the rules of war, outside the battle lines. The stakes are high."

Karl stares at me, for once lost for words. Tom looks surprised and Brady breaks out a slow hand clap.

"Bravo, Kate. Bravo. I must admit, I thought you'd never ask. By coincidence, I've had the CIA bring over some computer equipment and had you authorised at the highest level." He turns to Karl. "I take it I will be granted the same privilege by British intelligence?"

Karl smiles. "Great minds think alike, Kate. Great minds think alike."

Chapter 31

In half an hour I'm on a secure line to Carey. "All systems go, Carey. I've finally got them on side."

Again, there's a pause. He wants to tell me something but he can't. And Tom's still hanging around, making sure I don't have a moment alone. Annoying the hell out of me.

"OK. What's the instruction? I got the list by the way, from the university. Some familiar names are on it. Kaleef Ahmed. Assadi."

"Great. The other guys, the ones who were killed in Iraq. Mohammed Aslam. Sahid Ahmed. Peter Sidiquee?"

I hear him tapping away on his laptop.

"Peter Sidiquee. Lecturer in Chemistry. Left the university 1991. I'll check out his whereabouts now. The others, no. Not obviously. They could have been on secondment from another university, who knows?"

I think for a moment. "We need to find out who Krommer is. Can you look for a match on the list? What department did Kaleef Ahmed and Peter Sidiquee work in? Were there any similarities? Commonalities? Maybe I should speak to Assadi again?"

I need to find a pattern. There must be something. Carey pauses again. It's Assadi. Something's happened.

"That might be difficult. I wasn't going to say anything until I was sure but Assadi's flown the nest."

Carey could only know this if he's been monitoring top-level files, and we are dangerously close to crossing a line here.

"Oh. "

"Yes. I called his office and they told me that he had left. Just after you visited, and he hasn't been back."

We both know that Carey hasn't called his office. I log onto the system and bring up Assadi's file. Two agents have been monitoring his movements from inside Cambridge University, alerted by my report. He hasn't been seen since yesterday. The Assadis didn't own a car and they didn't leave by taxi. They haven't taken a train. From the report, they've just disappeared into thin air.

"OK. Thanks. Keep working on the list, Carey. Let me know if you get anything else."

Elliot Brady sits beside me. Tom on the other side. Tom has been arranging for Mrs Jones's home to be put back in order and for all the residents to be interviewed. An email pings into my inbox from Carey and I open it. No message, just the list. Hundreds of names, with just two highlighted. I scroll up and down the list and my heart sinks. It's going to be almost impossible to go any further with this unless we go to the university. Even then it will be unlikely that we'd get permission to look at their files. We'd have to go undercover and, with the sixteen hour flight, it would be an impossibility.

But I know the key lies there. Way back in the archives there will be some connection between the dead men, and the names of the others. If I've learned anything from looking back in time, it's that data from before a critical event is rarely as protected as data from after the event, because no one can know its importance ahead of time. It's what intelligence services often rely on.

I stare at the screen. I think about making the trip, leaving Elliot here and travelling with Tom – his silence and non-co-operation bugging me the whole way. The nerve-wracking passport control process, made worse by my mistrust of his ability not to make a mistake. Passport control. I have a mental picture of the last time I was there, at Baghdad airport. Of Farrah holding her sign. I feel a strong wave of regret and tears at the back of my throat but then realise that I still have her login to the university computer system.

I work quickly. Last time someone was monitoring my search and it led to Farrah's death. There may still be a tag on it – or not – but in any case, I'm speedy to avoid being traced. Even though our IP addresses are protected, there are people more adept than us who can hack them. I bring up the university welcome screen, select 'staff' and then log in.

The screen is the same as when Farah logged me in, and I select the English option. My heart thumps. I quickly locate the 'search all' option and type in Aslam, Ahmed, Ahmed, Sidiquee and Jones. Not Krommer, because we don't know his true identity. This search has

166

no doubt already been conducted in all the public search engines by Carey and Elliot but...

The university servers chug through the search – and suddenly I find it. A document from 1989 authored by all the victims except Kaleef Ahmed, and also by four others: Hamid Talibani, Stuart Pearson, Peter Beresford and Kazi Ifani, and John Jones. I look down the search list; there are several other papers written by various combinations of these same authors.

But the main paper isn't in the public archive. It's part of a presentation given at a conference in Basra. The quality tells me that that it's been scanned in as part of an archive; which means it's a graphic – which means it isn't searchable. The title of the paper is 'Genetic engineering: Can we engineer Genesis?' I quickly save the pdf and log off. I read the affiliations of the victims: chemists. Biologists. Physicists. John Jones is listed as a genetics researcher at Yale. I check his background reports; nothing of this is mentioned in the police files.

There's an eerie silence in the room, as if suddenly everything has stopped. Then I realise that it is my whole world standing still while I contemplate what I've just discovered. All the victims were involved in genetic engineering. The paper itself reveals nothing of significance but I already know from their background files that for years before they were killed each of these academics worked outside academia, in everyday jobs.

They'd run from whatever they discovered.

I turn to Elliot. "I've found it."

He looks at me over horn-rimmed tortoiseshell glasses. I share my screen with him.

He's compact and cool but even he lets out a little whistle. "OK. We have our connection. So what was Professor Jones doing working for a glass manufacturer?"

I grab my coat and run for the door. "Elliot, could you follow up with the other people mentioned in this paper? One of them may be Krommer."

Tom follows me and in fifteen minutes we're back outside Agnes Jones' apartment block. A police car is stationed outside and the scene-of-crime team is carrying items out. Agnes is sitting in a police car around the corner. I crouch in front of her at the car window.

"Agnes. Sorry to bother you again. But could you tell me why you didn't tell the police that your son went to Yale? About his academic career?"

She looks at me, eyes blank with sadness. "He was a good boy. Good at school. Went to university. He told me he didn't want to speak about it. So we never did. He's just a regular boy."

"Thank you. Thank you, Agnes. Did he keep any of his university stuff? Books? Photographs? Anything, Agnes. We need to know who did this."

"He did have some things. Years ago. When he came home, his father helped him bundle them up and move them."

"Where did he move them to? Can you remember?"

Her eyes fill with tears. "Jimmy would know. He loved Johnny. Loved him. But I don't remember. Just that he moved it all. Not to the trash. Jimmy took it in his van. He worked for the glass company too. They weren't gone long. Johnny didn't like it there, you know, where he was. Over there. He was glad to come back here."

Her voice is shaky and full of emotion.

"How long? How long were they gone, Agnes?"

"Maybe fifteen minutes. Jimmy said it was all taken care of and Johnny didn't have to worry no more. All locked away."

"Locked away?"

"Yeah. Locked away, he said."

I take hold of her hand. "Thank you Agnes. Thank you so much."

She tries to smile but it's too soon yet. Tom chats to the police officers who are carrying potential evidence and the blood-stained bed covers. Agnes's washing machines might still be churning and her life, on the surface, would continue. But it would never be the same again.

I quickly risk-assess her situation. Someone in this building was involved in this crime. I find Tom leaning on a street lamp in deep conversation with a uniformed officer.

"Tom, could you please arrange round-the-clock protection for Agnes Jones? Get someone into that apartment upstairs. This building needs securing and until it is she's not at risk."

"Should we move her to a safe house?"

I look at him. Top of his field in protection but not a sentimental bone in his body. "No. Look at her. Her son's just been murdered practically in front of her. She needs to be near her own things. Make that search quick and until then put her up in a hotel. On my budget if need be. From the sounds of it, there's no one left except her."

I feel tears prick my eyes and realise that I could easily be talking about myself.

I call Karl. "We've got the link. You need to talk to Elliot. And I need you to authorise a search of all storage facilities within a ten-minute radius of the Jones apartment, including his place of work. Looking for documents relating to his time at Yale and in Iraq."

"Will do. This should change Joe Newman's mind. His problem was that there was no US link apart from the fingerprints. We should get full co-operation now."

"OK. I still want a meeting with him at 5pm. We have new information. New names. We'll need whoever both countries have on the ground in Iraq."

Chapter 32

A car picks us up and we head back to Broome Street. We're almost there when Karl calls me.

"Another one. Peter Sidiquee. One of the US contacts close to the Iraqi police heard about it. Same MO. Hands cut off this time."

Peter Sidiquee is listed on the paper as a geneticist too. When the car comes to a stop I hurl myself out and rush up to HQ where Elliot is sitting calmly.

Carey calls me as soon as I reach my screen. "Kate. Turns out Peter Beresford was working at City University in London."

"Great. Thanks, Carey. I'll get Karl to locate him. So we have all the names except one now. And one of them is Krommer."

"Yeah. No trace of Ifani, Talabani or Pearson, though."

"Right. We just found Sidiquee. Like the others."

Carey's silent, which I know isn't a good sign. "Five to go, two identified. That puts a different slant on things. Almost unbalanced."

I sit up straight. Slant on things. Unbalanced. Those are red alert words between myself and Carey. There's something here that he needs me to know that can't be said in public.

I don't miss a beat. "Yeah. I see what you're saying. I wonder if it would be worth talking to Assadi again?"

He answers immediately. And it isn't what I want to hear. "I'm not sure. I don't think I have the time."

I know what this means. He's trying to tell me that he still hasn't found them. The situation is critical. I look around the room. Tom is hanging about around the door. Elliot is busy researching the document's origin.

"OK. I'll do my best to arrange something then. But it's not too likely."

He will know now that he needs to somehow transmit the information he has in code. I go through the decoding scenario in my mind, grappling with my reasons for not speaking up about it. After all, it isn't my fault that my father made me do it. I was a child. But then I smell the gunsmoke again, and feel the empty space in my heart. He was a traitor. I'm so entangled with him that my own life would disintegrate if any of my colleagues knew what had happened.

Then there's the question of the information. Once decoded, it will be available for whichever power has it to use it. How do I know that it would be used for the common good, and not for destruction?

I suddenly get an insight into why the information has been hidden for so long, why the twelve names on the list were hell-bent on keeping it under wraps, even at the cost of their own careers; because whatever this was, it was dangerous. If everything goes to plan, once I find it and decode it, perhaps I can make sure it's safe?

If our opposition gets there first, who knows what will happen? They appear to be hell bent on getting their own way and killing anyone in their path. Terror mongers. They might be well on the way to having the biometric key but they'll need me to decode it.

I am suddenly thankful for Tom. It's suddenly clear to me that his role in keeping me safe is much more important than anyone knows. I'm working all this out in my head and reading the paper again when Tom whoops.

"Found Jones's papers. In a small safe at the glass company. On their way up with them."

A few minutes later a uniformed officer appears with a bank box full of documents. We sort through them, sifting academic papers from travel documents. Jones travelled to Baghdad as a young research assistant in 1987 and worked under Sahid Ahmed. He left in 1991 and returned to Yale for a short time.

The box contains souvenirs from his travels and makes me think that this is all that is left of a man's life. All his mother has to remind her of him. This is what I've been waiting for, the place where the real patterns lie, embedded in people's lives. I sort through the items, pulling on some white rubber gloves that Tom hands to me. There are souvenirs from Iraq and Syria, and one from London. I pick up a cast-iron model of the Empire State Building and wonder why he would have collected this when he could have travelled a short distance through the New York streets to see it. He probably passed it every day.

Then I realise. All the items have significance. They trace his travel destinations after he left Baghdad and before he went to Yale.

I flick quickly through a pile of postcards that are fastened together with an old rubber band. It pings away as I mentally place the destinations on a map. He travelled the Silk Road. Then he deviated from it and travelled through southern Iraq. On 18 January 1991 he stopped at a small village around ten miles off the Silk Road. He starred this in a diary that accompanied his journey. After that, he doubled back and caught a plane to New York.

I pin his travel map onto a whiteboard.

"Something happened on 18 January. Something that involved Jones and this case. He hasn't hidden this for nothing. Yet, apart from the big deal he's made of going to this village and the fact that all these souvenirs relate loosely to the locations of the people on the list, there's nothing of interest."

I flick through the papers. Plenty of complex work on genetic engineering. I give the papers to Tom. "Get someone in the know about this stuff to have a look through, see if there's anything unusual, new discoveries, unpublished work. From what I can see they're all from published journals."

I look through the souvenirs again. Four from Iraq – Ahmed, Ahmed, Aslam and Ifani. Two from Iran – Hamid Talabani and Ali Hashemi. Two from Syria – Peter Sidiquee and Yousef al-Sharaa. One from New York – Jones himself. And three from the UK – Peter Beresford, Stuart Pearson and an unknown. And one of them is Krommer and dead. That narrows it down. According to this, the unknown was British.

I load the whiteboard with all the information. As I draw a red line through Jones's route, Elliot looks up. I can see him studying me out of the corner of my eye.

Eventually he speaks. "The two Ahmeds. They were brothers. Here's how I see it. The group was working on something, obviously something to do with genetics. It all came to a head and they got an attack of conscience. None of them have the knowledge to hide the information securely. We can see that by Jones's crude attempt at hiding his own information. So they get Kaleef Ahmed's rock-expert brother, Sahid, to help."

He stands up and for the first time I notice that he's a good six inches taller than my five ten. I would have put him much shorter. He extends a skinny arm to the white board and circles an area east of Baghdad.

"They wouldn't have the means to carry something far, and certainly not out of the country. None of them originates from the north, so they would choose a place close to home. Sahid Ahmed was an expert in sedimentary rock formations and would have known the protective criteria of encasing the item. Mohamed Aslam was a biologist specialising in biometrics. He could have constructed a biometric key with all their fingerprints. All sworn to secrecy and bound by their consciences. Including your friend Assadi, who probably knows the basics because he was on the outskirts of this team."

He shows me an archived copy of department materials dockets signed off by Assadi and Ahmed.

"All makes sense Elliot but I thought you were concentrating on the document and its source."

He sits again. "OK. We had the document but something happened. It went missing. It was handed to British intelligence on 17 January 1991, encoded. By the next day all traces of it had been removed from the records and it had been replaced by gobbledegook. Because no one had the expertise back then to recognise the coding differences, it wasn't noticed until much later on."

"So who had it? What happened? Was there an investigation?"

'Laughable, really. The substitute document was logged as the actual document and dismissed as a fake. It was only later, and I mean years later, when one of the original receiving comms guys checked the file, that he noticed that the context file that he had written was missing. The transaction reports were checked and they found out it had been replaced. They'd been trying to crack a code which was nonsense for years."

I check my phone. It's one o'clock US time and I'm flagging. I need to sleep but I have to keep going.

Elliot swings one long leg over another. I watch as he presses keys and, finally, a US driver's licence photograph of a middle-aged woman, blonde with sad eyes, appears on the screen.

"And this is what I've come up with. Juliette Sanderson. Forty-eight years old. Formerly married to Mark Watson, communications officer in the Royal Air Force. Based at Akrotiri in 1991. Both of them went missing on 18 January 1991. He told officials they had gone on a visa run and she'd got lost. Six days later she turned up at a Baghdad police station looking like shit. Said she'd been walking through the desert. Problem was, there were no consulate services and the bombing had just started so no one took too much notice. He stayed in Cyprus and she went home to Manchester, UK."

I look at the whiteboard.

"So where did she go missing?"

Elliot gets up and points to the centre of the red circle he's drawn on the map.

"Says she was around here. Coincidentally, at the same time as John Jones, it seems. And luckily she's living right here in New Jersey so we can go ask her ourselves."

Chapter 33

I know that when Elliot says 'we', he means me. As far as I know he hasn't left the office yet. We all have our strengths and his seems to be focusing on digital inquiry.

I make a note of the address on Elliot's screen. Grabbing my jacket from the back of my chair I run for the door and the lift but Tom spots me and runs after me. He says nothing but his expression says, 'You don't get away that easily, Missy,' and it's patronising. I feel my temper rise but push it back down again as I walk out into the New York mid-afternoon.

We've been afforded our own car now we have earned our American keep by providing more solid justification for the case. It's a predictable shiny black saloon that has Federal Investigator written all over it. Tom automatically assumes that he's driving and I don't argue because, after all, he knows the city better than I do. I jump in the passenger seat.

"Make it snappy, Tom. I need something by five."

He starts the engine. "She may not even be home."

I'm slowly getting used to his casual pessimism and I just ignore him. I watch the New York streets flash by and suddenly realise why I feel so at home here. Like Britain, this is an island. You're guaranteed to see water at the edges if you drive for less than a day. Today we take the Hudson Bridge and follow 18th towards Main Street. Then we take Sinatra Drive. As we pull up I feel my phone buzz in my pocket. It's a text from Carey. I pull out my phone and Tom leans over.

"Anything interesting?"

I know he is on the same case as me but he's so irritatingly nosy. "I'm sure you'd get a text too if it was anything crucial."

"Yeah. I guess I would."

I read the text. Coded as usual but roughly translated as: *We need to talk. Securely.*

Tom's craning his neck to see so I switch off the phone. I need to find a way to contact Carey, away from Tom and away from the agency tracking my mobile signal. I need to find a public phone box.

We're outside Walter Barry Independent Court. There's a huge apartment building but the view of downtown Manhattan from here is the stuff of legends. I've seen this vista in photographs and in films. I'm surprised to see it now, as I turn and look across the Hudson River.

It makes me think that Juliette Sanderson has done well for herself. Elliot's note told me that her husband, George Sanderson, was big in shipping. Originating from New England, he met Juliette in London in 1999 and they moved to New York with his company. She divorced Mark Watson in 1997. A divorce petition was filed earlier but had remained unanswered by him, so she'd had to wait the full five years.

Tom's phone rings and I see his face change. A trace of terror, similar to the trace in my own heart, flashes across it. He ends the call. "The apartment above John Jones. The Sidiquee woman. It was booby-trapped. Two guys injured in the explosion. One critically. Joe's going ballistic."

I steady myself. No time for gloating that I was right, but at least they'll take me seriously now. Poor Agnes. She won't be going back home for a while. Collateral damage. That's what her emotions are. Her grief. The victims in this are mounting. Agnes. The policemen who have been injured. Their families. Everyone affected by the murders. Collateral damage, to be written off.

There's a buzzer system and we wait a few moments until someone comes out of the main door and lets us slip in; people are less prepared that way. We take the lift and we're soon outside Juliette Sanderson's door.

I look at Tom. "Leave this to me."

He sighs and rolls his eyes. "Of course. You're the boss."

It doesn't feel like it. He's everywhere, even waiting outside the bathroom when I take a pee. I shrug and knock on the oversized oak door.

After about thirty seconds a small blonde woman appears. "Yes? Can I help?"

Her accent contains my own low vowels and those of Neil's family and, for a moment, I am reminded of him.

"I'm Kate Morden and this is Tom Caines. I'm working with the British Intelligence Services and Tom's with the Central Intelligence Agency. May we talk to you? Inside?"

Her expression hardens and I see a trace of a smirk and the narrowing of her eyes, all of which puts me on edge straight away. She steps aside and we enter.

Her apartment is luxurious and adorned with all kinds of coloured glass, ornaments and lamps. We follow her up a wide hallway, past a large kitchen and dining room and through to a huge lounge. The room has floor to ceiling windows and a fabulous view of Manhattan. Even Tom looks impressed. I take in all the sightseeing landmarks, the Statue of Liberty, Empire State Building, and Central Park. It's a few moments until my heart ceases to soar, and when I turn around Juliette Sanderson is sitting on the sofa. As usual, I sit near the door.

"Can I get you anything to drink?" She's still on the verge of a smile. She definitely doesn't look forty-eight. I would have put her around forty, maximum. Her eyes are cold and alert, and she is very focused on me. Tom picks up a picture of a boat and studies it carefully.

"No thanks. We'd just like to talk to you about something important that has cropped up."

She crosses her legs. Immediately defensive. "Cropped up? OK, go ahead. I'm all ears."

Tom's still looking at the photographs.

I pull out a file from my bag. "We've had some occurrences lately that have made us look back to your husband's movements in 1991."

She cuts in quickly. "I expect you mean my ex-husband, Mark Watson. I've remarried."

"Yes. Sorry. Ex-husband. So, we're trying to find out more information about a trip you both took to Iraq on the eve of Desert Storm on 17 January 1991. Could you tell me the purpose of that trip, Mrs Sanderson?"

She sighs. "Isn't it in my file? The one you have there?"

I turn over the pages. "Yes. It says you went on a visa run. Is that correct?"

Her eyes penetrate me. Her focus is complete. I assess that she's had a lot of practice at explaining this over the years. But it's more than that. She has a coldness about her that unnerves me.

"Yes, it is. We went on a visa run and we got separated. He found his way back and alerted the authorities. I wandered around for days and then found my way back. That's it."

I look at the file. That's more or less what it says. She's never deviated from her story, and neither has he.

"So do you have any contact with your ex-husband?"

"Ex-husband? No. Haven't seen him. As you probably know, I had to wait a while for a divorce from him as he couldn't be contacted."

"Mmm. So you travelled to Iraq, to Baghdad airport. You became separated and you were wandering around the area near the airport?"

"Airport? Yes."

"But weren't you picked up on Omar Bin Al Khatab Street, about ten miles from Baghdad? And you say you heard the fighter planes approaching and were scared by them? So you must have been southeast of the road at some point to wander around in what you described as an isolated land and desert in order to reach Omar Bin Al Khatab Street?"

"Southeast? I've no idea. I just don't know. I was very young then, and confused. My husband made all the arrangements. I just went along with him because it was me who had to go in and out of Cyprus to get my visa stamp."

I turn another few pages. I'm not yet convinced that Juliette Sanderson is part of this investigation. We often chase dead ends, open loopholes from the past that mean nothing. But, in the file, I suddenly catch sight of copies of her passport. Each page has been photocopied, up to her passing back through passport control in Cyprus on 22 January 1991. The corresponding departure stamp is missing; this was flagged up by the service at the time. She's been asked about it and, as before, has always answered that her husband took care of everything.

"So where did you leave from when you flew from Iraq?"

A trace of a frown. She touches a tiny doll hanging around her neck on a leather cord. No one has ever asked her this before.

"Fly? Oh. Larnaca airport I guess. Some airport. I don't know."

"And they didn't stamp your passport?"

She visibly relaxes. Back down the same old questioning route. "My passport? That's what the authorities said when I got back. Neither mine nor Mark's. But I don't know why. Mark took care of everything. I just followed him."

It's there right in front of me. I savour the moment for longer than I should, knowing that this is my way in.

"Thank you, Mrs Sanderson. There's just one other thing confusing me. It says here, on your visa records, you'd been on a trip with your company to Beirut a couple of weeks before your visa run with your husband."

The pulse in her temple quickens and she blinks slightly faster. "Yes but I've been asked about this too. I may have been an experienced traveller but..."

I hold my hand up so quickly that she stops speaking and Tom spins to look at me.

"OK. OK. I read all that, Mrs Sanderson. But if you'd recently visited Beirut and had your passport stamped on the way out and back in again, then why go on another visa run just a few weeks later?"

Her skin colour flushes ever so slightly. Her pupils recede and her breathing quickens a little. "Beirut? Oh. I don't know. Mark thought it was necessary so I went with him. I really don't know.'

I'm tempted then to ask her about the stolen document, ask her if she or her husband knew about it, but I can't. It would be disclosure, and she may really have been innocent. But I seriously doubt it. She's dying to get away from us.

"Are you sure I can't get you a drink?" She stands and goes to the kitchen to get a glass of water for herself. I look around the apartment. The ornaments she has look vaguely ancient and have a commonality to them. Right here in the middle of New York, in her opulent and ultra-modern surroundings, she is preoccupied with something else. She returns and sits.

179

"No, thank you. We'll be going now.'

She suddenly looks uncertain.

"Is there something else, Mrs Sanderson?"

She places the glass carefully on the table. "I just wondered why, after all this time, you're here, asking me all these questions. Has something happened?"

"Like what? What could happen?"

She swallows hard. "I don't know. I wondered if there was some kind of trouble. Or maybe something has happened to... to bring this up again."

I stay blank. I need her to open this up. "Not as far as we know."

"OK. So why me? Now?"

Tom stands. "We'd better get going. It's three thirty and we have a five o'clock meeting. Let's go, Kate."

But I stay rooted to the spot, staring at Juliette. I look at her for a good two minutes, which is a long time in a silent room.

"It'd be better if you told us everything, you know."

An almost indiscernible movement of her eyes towards Tom tells me everything I need to know. *Not with him here.* And her cold stare tells me that even with Tom gone I'll have to be totally up front with her for her to trust me.

There is more to this than what she is telling.

Chapter 34

Tom and I leave quickly. As the door closes he shakes his head.

"How didn't they pick that up at the time? About the visa dates?"

"Retrospective investigation. The passport pages weren't added to the file until she renewed her passport. No one really suspected anything at the time because no one knew the data was missing until later on. From the looks of it, the case was temporarily reopened around the time they discovered the missing data but closed again when they couldn't find Mark Watson, and Juliette Watson had no new information. They've been out to interview her regularly."

We travel a half-hour journey in an hour through the rush-hour traffic. Tom drives while I read further into Juliette Sanderson's file. According to her travel record she hasn't left New York since she arrived, but I recall seeing in her apartment a photograph of her and an older woman, probably her mother, in London – sightseeing shots. Pictures of her and three Middle Eastern women, also in London. Her and a slightly older man in Paris – her husband perhaps, George Sanderson. She didn't mention him once. She was totally focused on her well-rehearsed script from the minute she saw us.

Her apartment was decorated with lots of exotic ornaments. Pots, pictures, all quite out of place in the minimalist setting of an expensive New York penthouse. Quite a stretch for someone who claims to remember almost nothing about her experience and has put it behind her. I return to the file and focus in on her relationship with an Iraqi artist. Sanaa Yazid. It's been followed up but there's more here. I can feel it. The patterns of Juliette Sanderson's lives are punctuated with Saana Yazid's shadow.

We reach Broome Street dead on five o'clock. I stand outside and prepare myself for my meeting with Joe Newman, Tom loitering nearby. He's actually kicking at some stones and I watch him. He's the nearest thing I've ever seen to a perfect depiction of a TV stereotype. His whole mannerism shouts New York and, although professionally he annoys and irritates the hell out of me, I suddenly think that it would be good to sleep with him.

The thought shocks me for a moment, until I realise that one of his best assets is, indeed, his visceral attraction. He's an attractive person and I am clearly rubbing him up the wrong way with my indifference. I need to get him to relax.

I go through my routine of deep breathing and gathering my thoughts. Then, as I walk into the building, I give Tom a smile. He look confused at first but then he breaks out his bright white teeth and smiles back. We get into the lift and I see his reflection in the chrome, smoothing down his dark hair. I brush against him as we walk out and slow down to walk beside him.

My phone vibrates again in my pocket and I know instinctively that it's Carey. I duck into the ladies room and Tom waits outside, graciously opening the door for me. Once inside, I sit in a stall and check the message. To anyone else it would be a string of random letters. I'm even more alert now, wondering why Carey has risked sending code. It's like shouting, 'I'm sending something secret to Kate!'

When I read it I see why immediately: *For God's sake, Kate, ring me. On my old Vodaphone. And don't say another word out there. There's some new information on the file. They're changing the focus. They're going after IS instead of trying to find the other names or the document. Reckon it will stem it at the source.*

It doesn't really surprise me. It's the wrong thing to do but it doesn't surprise me. Not after what I've learned about my father. I sit completely still listening to water drip somewhere in the plumbing. I know from past missions that the focus of a case can change like the wind. I reckon it is Joe Newman's doing. There's only one thing for it now.

I flush and wash my hands. I can see that the ladies room door is slightly open and that Tom is watching me. I make a show of patting my hair down and wiping around my eyes, rubbing off the excess mascara. I go in my bag and get some lipstick. Then I straighten my clothes. He'll think it's for him. As I exit I look at him from under my lashes and he looks pleased with himself. His hand is on the small of my back again, like the first time I met him, and I don't hurry to avoid contact.

He guides me into the same room. Joe Newman is heading the conference table and Karl sits beside him. Lauren Gaynor is also there and she immediately looks at Tom. I sit beside him and point my body language at him. Karl's eyebrows rise as he sees my display, and I monitor Tom's reaction. His pulse quickens and he moves his hand closer to mine on the oak table top.

Joe Newman starts the meeting. Elliot is lurking in the corner of the room. He gives me a salute and I can't help but smile at him. Joe stands and walks towards the whiteboard.

"So, Kate, this is what we have so far. Good work. I understand from Elliot that you took control of the situation and, as a result, we now have firm links between the victims. And as one of them is undeniably a US citizen we have just cause to intervene. So, after consulting with the President, I can now grant full operational involvement. So, have we made any more progress?"

I stand. Tom pushes back his chair to give me space. I've finally got him singing to my tune.

"We went to see Juliette Sanderson. I don't think she has anything else. I believe that we have to find Mark Watson if we want to know more about the missing document."

Tom looks a little surprised and I pre-empt any comment he might make. "She may have more but she's been in no-comment mode for the better part of a quarter of a century, so she's in no rush. Bearing in mind the ticking clock, we should concentrate on finding Watson."

Joe Newman nods in agreement. A deep but insincere movement. I can sense his detachment. But he has to agree. For now, I'm goading him to reveal the real focus of the investigation – the changed focus.

"OK," he says. "That's the main focus."

Elliot speaks up now. "That's the document taken care of. We've made a lot of progress on the list. We have eleven names. We need the twelfth man. We also need the location and the biological key. So, at this point, it's crucial to find out who the enemy is. The terrorists at large in our city."

So there it is. Out in the open. I can't work that way. Elliot fills Joe in with the names and affiliations on the list and I concentrate on Tom. I move my foot so that it's almost touching his as I reach for a glass of water, then giggle when I almost spill it. He grabs it in a 'here, let me get that for you' way and steadies my elbow.

As Joe finishes with Elliot and prepares to go, he barks out orders. "Kate, you find Mark Watson with Elliot and Tom. Karl, can you cover all the bases on John Jones and the others on the list, and plot out possible locations. Lauren, keep interrogating the data we do have, and stand by for when we locate the document. Good luck, everyone."

I know in that moment that Joe will have every available agent and security officer in NYC looking for terrorists. Even though it's futile, because whoever killed John Jones is long gone. It's the source we need to find. But he doesn't see it that way. I can't work like this. No. It's dangerous.

He strides away and Karl rushes over to me. "So what happened with Juliette Sanderson?"

I shrug at him and lean towards Tom so that he can share the conversation. "Not much, did it Tom?"

I stare deep into his eyes.

The pause that I fear, the vulnerability that stops me from working with a partner, is there but this time it's going to work in my favour. Eventually he speaks. "No. I mean, yeah, she may have been holding back but no one's broke her yet."

"Maybe we should bring her in?"

I defer to Tom again. When he sees I'm not going to answer, he jumps in. "Like Kate said, it's probably a waste of time. She's going to hold back as long as she can, that's if she does have anything."

Karl is persistent. "So you didn't notice anything in her apartment? Anything suspicious?"

I take my turn now. "No. Apart from one of the best views in the world, which I have to admit was quite distracting, she just had a load of junk ornaments and some family pictures. Nothing unusual at all. Was there, Tom?"

There was nothing unusual, except that she only answered questions; there was nothing forthcoming from her. She was closed in. Rehearsed. And I could see in her eyes that something terrible had happened to her.

"I sure didn't see anything, Kate."

Karl sighs. "Another door closes. Someone must know what happened to that data. There was only Mark Watson and his colleague Jimmy Summers on duty that night. Jimmy's dead and in any case, he has a solid alibi. Mark Watson went off duty early and then the rest is history. It stinks. We're going all out to see what's happened to Mark Watson."

I get up to go, grabbing my bag. "Well, if anyone can do it, Elliot can. I'm going to grab some sleep and something to eat. Jetlag's catching up with me.' I turn to Tom. 'Are you ready? Shall we get a steak or something?"

He isn't a stupid man. He wouldn't be where he is now if he were. But right at this moment he looks like he has won a prize.

Karl rolls his eyes. "OK Kate. Get some sleep. But don't sleep too long. We need to find the twelfth man."

Chapter 35

I walk to the lift with Tom. The knife turns deeper and I begin to understand that this is exactly what my father was doing – just like me, he was ploughing his own furrow. Going his own way. I suddenly remember him laughing with some unknown visitor, one of the times when my mother and I sat in the kitchen listening to the radio while he entertained. We could still hear him, and he didn't care.

"All's fair in love and war, Jim. The thing is: to truly understand what's going on you have to look at the beast from all angles. Turn it around in your brain; see it from their point of view. And that's when the lines start to blur, Jimmy. When you start to see what they believe in, why they are fighting. Never clear cut. Never."

I'd asked my mother what he meant and when she just turned away and began to roll out the pastry for a pie, I tried to work it out for myself. Surely it *was* clear cut – we hate the enemy, they hate us? Otherwise, why kill each other? To a child's brain, it really was that simple. But as I grew older I started to grudgingly admit that things can get foggy. I was around fourteen years old when the concept of collateral damage was explained to me. It seemed like the most unfair thing I had ever heard, the killing of innocents.

Now the world I lived in was often foggy. In the middle of espionage and trickery it's easy to lose sight of your own moral stance, to become desensitised to what really matters. To why you're here.

Suddenly it comes into sharp focus. I know what I have to do. We are racing towards a ticking timebomb – Armageddon – and that will, at the very least, involve mass collateral damage. Through my anger I'm starting to see why my father struck out on his own: in times like this, it can look like every man for himself.

We reach the lift and Tom presses the button. I look behind me.

"Oh. My jacket. Just wait there. Hold the lift."

I walk as casually as I can, through the swing doors, not even looking back to see if he's waited or if he's following me. The conference room is empty now and I grab my jacket. I knock over some chairs and the glass of water at my place on the table and leave a trail of destruction in my wake. I hurry over to the adjoining doors, four in total, and choose the one by which I watched Karl exit. He was leaving for his hotel, which implies there is another way out of the building.

The door opens into another room, with another door at the far end. I hurry over, checking for cameras, and open the door onto a corridor. We're on the third floor so I can't exit through any of the windows that face me. I know I am at the back of the building, exactly where I want to be. I rush towards a fire exit and push it open. The alarm bells begin to ring and I double back, watching as the wind catches the door and slams it against the wall, the metal bar ringing against the rusty fire escape.

I double back and duck into a room halfway up the corridor. In a second I hear Tom's voice and hurried footsteps.

"Yeah. She went to get her coat. Looks like there's been a struggle. They got out through the fire exit at the rear. On third. I'll go on foot. Get a car to Broome St on Delancey. Now."

I immediately hurry back up the corridor, retracing my steps until I get to the lift, then I take the stairs down. I check the main entrance and wait until there is no one in sight. Then I leave and duck right next door into the pizza house. I hurry to the back of the building and sit at a table in the back bar.

The waiter hurries over. "Can I get you a drink, Miss?"

I smile sweetly. "Yes. Yes. May I have a glass of tap water?"

I take the menu from him and watch as Tom and another agent stand on the street outside, looking left and then right, talking into their phones. A black limousine pulls up and they get in. I duck behind the waiter as the car passes the picture window. Then they are gone.

I look at the menu. "Actually, I'll just use the ladies room, and then I can choose."

"Sure, I'll leave this right here. Behind you and left."

In the ladies room I pick the lock to the tampon machine and empty the quarters into my bag. Same with the condom machine. I lock them both neatly, flush and leave. I take out my phone and pretend to talk, signalling to the waiter that I need to go outside to take the call. He barely acknowledges me.

Outside I survey the street. It's quiet. No one I recognise. I take my agency phone and bring up the Uber app. I choose my destination on the map, Central Park, and summon a cab.

It arrives almost immediately. I smile as I think how the fare will be charged to the agency and eventually they will pay for their own mistake. They thought that they could cage me but I truly am my father's daughter. I push the agency phone down the back of the seat. I feel a tiny pang of guilt as I look at the back of the driver's head and imagine him surrounded by federal agents later on today, but he'll be released when they realise he isn't involved. I book another cab from Central Park back to Broome Street and see it register on his small screen.

He'd probably remember a woman in her thirties, going to Central Park alone, who got out halfway. But when they suggest that she wasn't alone he won't know for sure, because he hasn't even looked at me. He's focused on the traffic and on his satnav, his money maker for the day; thanks to his automated systems, he isn't paying attention to his customers. We turn onto 6th Avenue and I spot a payphone on the corner of W 3rd.

"Hi. Excuse me. May we get out here? If you carry on to the Central Park entrance as arranged your next customer will be waiting."

I drop my head to pick up my bag as he tries to catch my eye in his rear view mirror. He releases the door and I'm out. I stand on 6th Avenue, momentarily breathing in my freedom while I watch the taxi continue on its designated route, and then I head for the phone box. I push in quarters and dial Carey's Vodaphone number. He answers in half a ring.

Chapter 36

"Carey. Thank God. Thank God. Call me back."

I hang up and I'm breathless, hand on telephone receiver, waiting for it to ring. When it does, I grab it in a second. "Hello? Carey?"

"Yes. Kate. Are you all right?"

I take a deep breath in. "I am now. I've been under constant surveillance since I arrived. Look, I've broken out. I'm on my own. I need to get back to the UK."

I can picture him sitting at a table in some East End café, anonymous and cool, whispering into his vintage mobile.

"Yes. I see. I know someone. I'll call him and get some ID sorted out for you. Do you need cash?"

"Yes. I left with just my handbag. This has really escalated, Carey. It's out of control. I have no clue which way this will go but we'll find out soon enough. And I can't be part of it if they don't chase the document. What about your end?"

"My theory is this. A mobile phone was tracked to the apartment above Krommer's when we investigated the harvester cell. It turns out to be a woman called Sarah Kay, who disappeared as soon as Krommer was killed. Exactly the same as Asiya Siddique."

"Shit, Carey. Anything else? Anymore?"

"No. But there's activity on that log to and from Iraq also. I'll keep looking." People on the inside. Terrorists in our midst. There's a short silence as he enters the system. "OK. I'm into the level one mainframe, watching all the logs on this case. They think that you've been abducted by the perps. They think they want you because you could assist with the decoding, as they put it. I don't think they know you are the key."

"Right. And the Assadis? Is their disappearance connected?"

"No. Nothing on the file to suggest that. Just a note saying that an agent went to see them two days running but no one was there. So they looked for them leaving but nothing. I checked the CCTV myself. No sign of them. I put feelers out and again, nothing. It's as if they've disappeared into thin air."

I think for a moment. Assadi must have got scared. He must have known that the biometric key was close to being complete.

"OK. Look Carey, can your friend sort a phone out, too? I'm going underground. Chances are when they realise what's happened they'll be all over you."

He laughs gently. "If they can find me, which I very much doubt. You're not the only one who's running. I sensed that someone was watching me, following me, so I took off. Best I don't tell you where, Kate. Just in case."

This isn't a good situation. This is the last situation I wanted to put Carey in. "Sorry. Sorry you're involved. You did warn me."

"I make my own decisions, like you. I only do what's worth it. And this is worth it. I saw the paper you filed. Genetic engineering. Do you know what that could involve? That would be so precious?"

I backtrack to that morning. Things had moved so fast that I hadn't even considered it. I just took it for granted that this set of experts had made something so powerful and dangerous that we had to find it and destroy it. And that our opposition was hell bent on finding it too, but their motives might be less ethical.

"Yes. Yes, I do."

Of course I do. This stuff has been my lifeblood for years. The possibilities, the variables of war, the potential for total annihilation – I've always known, always been alert to it. But I've always hoped that no one hates the world or their fellow man sufficiently to do the unthinkable.

I can hear Carey's breath down the phone, short and shallow. He's scared. Carey's scared.

"I'm not saying I'm right, not for definite but – these guys were working on engineering cells. Human cells."

I feel a rush of blood. A random set of scenarios flickers through my brain. "Human experiments?"

"There probably were. Their work was originally around the sequencing of the human genome and working on ways to fight common diseases that were obviously down to genetics. For the good. But it can also be used for the bad."

Standing on 6th Avenue in the middle of New York, talking to Carey as he probably sat on a similarly random London street, I finally realise the gravity of this situation. I feel in my soul the reason why my father changed sides. Why he coded some secret for a bunch of academics who wanted to lock away something terrible for the rest of time. Was I his legacy? Was I the guardian after he had gone? Was that his thinking?

"Oh God, Carey. This is potentially catastrophic."

His tone is suddenly harsh. "Think the worst, Kate. Think the experiments the Nazis carried out. Think ethnic cleansing. Think being able to choose who lives or who dies, and breeding things in and out through generations. Maybe they coded for a weak artery, for an unstable hormone. Maybe for a disease. Genocide, Kate. That's the scale we're dealing with."

I can't speak. Why would someone want to let this kind of information loose now, after all these years?

Carey pre-empts my question. "Money and power are the drivers. That's what's involved. So far, whatever this Armageddon is, it's been avoided only through the goodness of the people who discovered it and realised it must never see the light of day. And when it did threaten to break free, those who received it immediately returned it. Good people, Kate, that's what it relies on. Good people."

We listen to each other's reverent silence for a while. Then I realise that it's time for me to go and push forward with this. Follow my instincts.

"OK. OK. I need to get back to London. I need to deal with this now."

Carey sounds choked. "Yes. Of course. I'll meet you back here and sort us out a place to stay. If that's OK? Where are you? I'll get my pal Roy Beesley to order you a cab to his place. He's over on 24th. He'll give you papers and some cash and a phone. His number will be on the phone and he'll book your flights when you are ready."

"Thanks Carey. I'm on 6th at the corner of W 3rd. I owe you one. I know you said not to do this…"

"Yeah, but just as well you did. Otherwise we'd be none the wiser and who knows what would happen in the future? Like Assadi said, this has the potential to change the course of mankind. Better go, Kate. A taxi will be along in a short while."

"Thanks Carey. I'll check in as soon as I'm ready to leave New York. Bye."

He's gone. I sit on the low seat in the pay booth. Change the course of mankind. Those words ring a bell and it takes me a moment to remember who had uttered them recently. Belinda Assadi. She'd pushed me towards the nuclear defence argument. Towards WMD. Her husband was a physicist but his more recent work was in defence, so who's to say that he hadn't been consulted on how to use their discovery?

I shudder. The Assadis have probably gone into hiding. If the security services had them it would be in a file somewhere and Carey would have found it. More likely that they've made their own decisions.

I look up and down 6th Avenue, at the men and women hurrying home from their jobs, hurrying to meet people for dinner. Children with their parents in cars, just returning from visiting relatives. All blissfully unaware of what could, in a matter of days, or even hours, be unleashed. I tense and pace about, looking up the road for a slowing taxi. It takes another eight minutes for it to arrive. Every minute seems precious now as time ticks towards the final outcome – winning or losing the race to find the genetic time bomb.

The cab driver leans out of the window. "Beesley?"

I get in and we set off up 6th. As we turn up West 24th the streets become shabbier, with black refuse bags piled up against lamp posts. We slow as we pass the Hampton Inn and pull up outside an apartment block that isn't unlike the one on Broome Street. The retail units on the ground floor are to let, and I search for a way in. Before I find the door a small, slightly built man appears. He's wearing a yellow polo shirt and blue dungarees with splashes of paint on them. For a moment I wonder if this is Carey's contact, or if it's a trap.

"Kate? Hi, I'm Bees. Carey's friend. Went to college together. Then he went to Oxford and I went to Cambridge. You know how it is." He laughs and I immediately feel relaxed. I follow him around to the side of the building and up to the second floor.

Once inside, he opens a small rucksack. "Everything's in here. You're Sandra Lees for the duration. Phone registered to you. Passport. Papers. There's some cash in there, and a credit card. But don't go mad! My number and Carey's number are on the phone under Tom and Jerry. I'm Tom by the way, and if you want anything booking online, flights, cars, anything, let me know. Now, do you want a coffee?"

I take the bag and feel the shape of the gun inside. So it has come to this. I flash back to the day I was passed my father's gun and I'd wondered why the hell he had it, how he had used it. Now I know. How many people have been here before me and not succeeded? My father, for one. But not me. Not me.

Bees watches the question in my eyes. "This is America. Dog eat dog. Need to start on an equal footing, yeah?"

It would be hard not to like Bees. I look around his apartment and it's loaded with computer equipment and screens. I have people like this in the UK, people who can find out almost anything. Carey's one of them. I know that, should I ever need him again, Bees will be there for me. I get the info and assistance; he gets compensated plus twenty percent. That's how it usually works.

"I'm fine, thanks. I need to get home." I take my passport out of my handbag and give the bag to Bees. "Could you send this to Carey, please? Minus the quarters. There's a phone in there. Can you send that on a dead-end journey, just in case someone's tracking it?"

"Home being London? Yeah, sure, I'll take care of it. Well, give my regards to Carey. Good guy. The best. Puts a lot of work my way. Sounded pissed off when I spoke to him. This must be some big cheese. He's not the pissed-off kind."

I smile at his accent, which I immediately place midway between Bristol and London. "Mmm. We'll see. But thanks, Bees. I'll be in touch. Today and maybe in the future."

He looks satisfied, like someone who has just landed a big business deal. "Right. Thanks, Kate. Or Sandra." He punches me a little too hard on the shoulder.

I leave and I'm on the street again. I attempt to flag a taxi but step back onto the pavement as Carey rings me. It's four in the morning in London so I know it's critical.

Chapter 37

I press the answer button and he has no time for pleasantries.

"OK. Listen carefully. Ali Hashemi and Hamid Talibani are dead, both in northern Iraq. Yousef al-Sharaa is dead – he's the tenth person on the list. Karl still thinks you've been abducted and he's got an all-forces alert out for you in New York. They tracked your phone and they've got the taxi driver but the file says he's unhelpful. They're activating all their IS intelligence leads but it's going nowhere. They're panicking now because they believe that their opposite number has the document and is working his way through the biometric. They think they're almost there."

Carey sounds afraid. This case is veering off in completely the wrong direction, driven by fear and speculation. I think for a moment. Cutting through the fear, I realise it's time for action. Time to finish this.

"OK. Carey, can you make a fake demand from the terrorists? Directly to Karl? Using the service comms, so they think they've got someone on the inside? Make them think that they have me for sure?"

"I can but it's a dangerous game to play. It means that they'll increase their activity to find you at a time when you need to make it home."

He's right but it's a risk I have to take.

"I know. But the stakes are high, Carey, and I have a plan. How did al-Sharaa die?"

"Manual strangulation, fingerprints removed. He was living in a flat in Central London. The tabloid press are mooting a serial killer; they made the connection between Krommer and al-Sharaa. Seems like Krommer was Peter Beresford."

Ten sets of fingerprints. Only two more to go.

"OK. So they'll all be looking for the document now. Because the likelihood is that, apart from the eleventh and twelfth people on the list, and whoever took it from Akrotiri in 1991, no one has ever seen it."

Carey pauses. Never a good sign.

"Get back here, Kate. Leave them to it. I know that's not what you're about but you could just turn up somewhere with a kidnap story."

It has crossed my mind. While Karl still believes that I'm captive it's a viable option. Apart from one thing.

"True. Except that I'm the key."

"Yeah, you're the key. So no one will ever be able to decode it. Or use it."

"Until someone works out that I'm the key. Someone Like Lauren Gaynor. Or Elliot Brady. Then I'm fucked."

I end the call and grab a takeaway coffee to keep me awake. I'm stuck in the middle. I'm the asset that everyone wants, even though they don't know it yet. Like Carey said, there's still a way out. There usually is – another option, unthinkable at the time but later on glaring at you accusingly from the past.

I flag a taxi and tell the driver my destination. I sit in the back seat sorting through the bag that is now my new life. Sandra Lees. British passport with my picture on it. A thousand dollars in different denominations, and five hundred British pounds in twenties. Some paper, receipts and a credit card, and a hand gun. No doubt Sandra has a history, either real or constructed, that can be checked out easily.

I think about the taxi driver from earlier, probably detained. They'd have found my mobile and thought it was a signal from me, carefully planned to expose my abductors. I feel vaguely sorry for Tom: "I only let her out of my sight for a second." Proving that I am valuable, that I have something the other side needs. The small doubts in his mind would crop up over the next couple of hours or days. Did she trick me? Was she playing me? Did she run? But it will be too late by then. I'll be back in the UK, with Carey, well on my way to solving this case. One way or another.

I think about my father and wonder if he had the same resolve as me. Is that where I get it from? If so, is that what got him killed? I smell the gunsmoke again and remember the coldness in Winger's stare. They must have worked out what he did. What did he do that was so bad? Work for the enemy? Yes but now it's not so clear cut.

The 'enemy' were the ones who wanted to keep it safe, hide it away so no one could use it. He was working for them for the common good.

So if they were the common good, what were his employers – my employers – planning?

Karl hasn't told me what the endgame is. Neither has Joe Newman or Donald Winger. Just to recover the target. As it became clearer what we were searching for we focused on the detail and not on the wider issue – the issue of what the US and British alliance would do with it. What if neither side is playing for the common good this time?

So many questions. I check my phone again. No doubt Carey would text me if Karl had realised that I had run. I think about Elliot and wish that he was on my side. He's clever. Like me, he's one step ahead of the game. One thing I know for sure is that he'll pull out all the stops to find me. His reputation as a man at the top of his game was hard won. I'm completely certain of who I'm dealing with – the best agents in the world. Karl, Elliot, Tom, Lauren. All chosen for this mission on merit. Unlike me, who was chosen because of my connection to my father. But I know for sure that by the end of this I'll have proven that I'm a force to be dealt with in my own right.

We're nearly there. I pull my leather jacket around me and watch the sun set over the Hudson River, dipping behind the towering buildings of New York. I feel my blood pump through my veins as I pay the taxi driver. My adrenaline builds as I enter the building and knock on the door.

She answers quickly, as if she was standing in the hallway waiting for me.

"Hello, Juliette."

She looks behind me and up the hallway, searching for my backup. When she sees no one she smiles. "Kate. We don't have much time. Come with me."

Part Four: Juliette Sanderson

Jacqueline Ward

Chapter 38

After the trauma subsides, our lives wind back around themselves, a tight twist, the uncertainty and hurt bent around itself until it is so small that we think it has disappeared. But it's still there, running through our blood and waiting, waiting for the trigger that will resurrect the sleepless nights, the cold sweats, the realisation that there might have been something we could have done differently, or better.

For me, the trigger came at 8.46am in the morning on 11 September 2001. I'd been out of bed for at least two hours, drinking coffee, writing an article, to and fro between the computer in my writing office and our lounge overlooking the Hudson River and, in the distance, lower Manhattan. I'd been talking to my friend Joan on the telephone, discussing what my godson Alec would do on his birthday in two weeks' time. He was nine. A difficult age.

Joan had asked what I thought and as I turned and automatically looked out of the huge plate glass windows, I saw the plane fly into the tower. It didn't register at first but then the background television commentary filtered through my shock and it was confirmed that it was true. I had just seen it. I hadn't imagined it.

Joan lived farther inland and a little up the coast but she too had a good view of the city. I almost whispered down the phone: "Did you just see that?"

I needed another witness. I needed someone to tell me that I wasn't mad. As the North Tower of the World Trade Centre began to bellow smoke from a gaping hole, I listened to the silence between myself and Joan as we stared into the distance from our ivory towers.

"Yes. Oh my God. Oh my God. Alec. I need to get Alec."

The line went dead but I still held the receiver to my ear. I could see my own reflection in the window glass, frozen with fear, holding the phone, unable to drag myself away from the spectre in front of me. I don't know how long I stood there. Seconds. Minutes. Half an hour. My mobile phone rang. It was Sandy, my husband.

"Julie. Oh my God. Julie. Are you OK?"

I nodded and I saw my reflection nod. "I just saw…"

"I know. I saw it on the news. It was just announced. Are you OK?"

Sandy was in London. He often worked away. I was used to it. I loved our life in New York. He sounded almost hysterical, which I remember thinking was quite out of character for him.

"Yes. But I just saw…"

I felt puzzled. Puzzled by what I'd seen. The scene in front of me just didn't compute. Yet strangely, it brought to mind another impossible situation ten years earlier and held it just behind my consciousness. I bent my body rigid and covered my eyes, smelling the sulphurous explosives on the edge of my reality. Shaking, shaking. Not yet, Juliette. Don't think about that yet. Push it away, Juliette. This is too important.

"Get out of there. Get out, Julie. Go over to Joanie's. Anywhere away from the island. Just get out of that building."

It was then that I realised. Like all the people in the North Tower, I was suspended in the sky in a concrete box. I suddenly felt exposed and worried.

Even so, my rational self kicked in. "But it's contained, Sandy. Look."

I looked at the TV screen and back at the burning tower in front of me. In the years since I left Cyprus I'd grown a thick shell, a barrier between me and the world so that it couldn't get in and I couldn't let the secrets I held, and my tears, out. I felt it melting around me now as I watched people run out on to the road in front of my home, up the jetty to the water's edge, pointing and running frantically up and down. Sandy was silent at the other end of the line. We just listened to each other breathe for a long time, sharing this moment like we had shared so many others. Minutes ticked by. Sandy started to sob. More minutes. I wished I could hold him, shield him in some way. I knew that he would be watching similar footage to me, and I felt sorry for him, a native New Yorker, watching this happen to his beloved city.

"Please, Julie, please get out of there. Get to somewhere safe."

I looked at the huge fireball on the side of the tower and the plume of black smoke heading for our neighbourhood. More people rushing to the waterside, rubbernecking the unfolding horror.

"I think I may be safer here. I really do. The smoke. I don't really want to go out in…"

Then the second plane hit the South Tower. I could hear people screaming on the TV footage and the sound matched the shapes of the mouths of the people at the waterside, those standing along the jetty. I heard Sandy make a low, inhuman moan, something visceral, then the sound of sobbing.

"Julie. Get out. For God's sake. As far away as you can. Don't think about anyone else. Help yourself. Hurry, Julie…"

The line dropped. I hoped for the landline to ring, desperately tried to call Sandy's mobile but there was a constant unavailable tone. All the while I breathed in the fresh air, instinctive deep breaths as I watched the dust and grime bellow out, the smoke drift towards me and consume my building until the view was hazy. I peered through it and, when it became too thick, I looked at the TV screen broadcasting almost the same view as I had but from a slightly different angle. Helicopters came into view now and I realised that the world would be watching this from every angle.

It felt voyeuristic, somehow wrong. I tried to turn away and answer the landline that was now ringing out urgently but I was mesmerised, hooked on the unfolding of something I couldn't even comprehend. listening to eyewitness accounts of what had happened and wild speculation as I watched live.

Finally I answered the landline. It was my father.

"Juliette. Are you OK?"

Everyone has a guardian angel, someone who silently stands behind them and supports them with the lightest touch of the palms, just below their shoulder blades, gently pushing them forward into life, whispering, "Don't be afraid." My father had never once asked me what happened in Iraq but I knew from the pain in his eyes that he knew it wasn't good.

I was a small child again, fallen off my bike with blood streaming out of my knees. Upside-down as he dislodged a Spangle stuck in my throat. Crying at the kitchen table over first love gone wrong.

"OK? Yes, Dad. I am. I am."

I didn't really know if I was but I did know that this wasn't about me. It was about pulling together and helping. It wasn't about running the other way like Sandy wanted me to, although I understood his reasoning. I would run towards the danger. I had my reasons.

"Thank God. Come home for a bit. Come home. It's not good out there."

"Come home? I can't Dad. This is my home, with Sandy. It'll be all right. It'll have to be."

Dad had seen my brand of all right. He'd watched me fall to pieces after I left Cyprus and quietly gathered those fragments and kept them until I was ready to be put back together. I didn't speak for weeks. I couldn't. I knew that he was scared it would happen again, I would crumble and revert to innocent, naive Juliette who was a pushover. But he didn't know that, at the core, I'd put everything into keeping my secret. Keeping it wrapped up tight so that it wouldn't spill out of my sticky-toffee exterior in a fit of anger. He didn't know how strong I really was.

Of course, there was something wrong with me. Almost straight away. The nightmares. The panic and the sweating. The shaking and the slow simmering of it all, deep, deep below. From time to time I'd watch myself going about my business as if I were separate from my body. It didn't get any better but I got better at hiding it.

"OK love. But let us know you are all right. Terrible business."

I could hear his TV on in the background. It would be late afternoon in Manchester, whereas here in New York a whole terrible day loomed before this injured city. I pulled on my shoes and my hooded jacket and scooped my now long blonde hair into a loose ponytail. Ready for action. My heart beat fast and I limbered up for what I already knew was fight and not flight. Fight for Sandy and Joanie and Alec and all the other New Yorkers who had accepted me wholeheartedly.

I had a plan. I'd go down to the water's edge with the others and try to find out if the ferry was going to run over so that we could go to help those poor people. The people. It gradually sunk into my soul that those people weren't anonymous disaster-movie actors, victims with unfamiliar faces. Some of them were my neighbours who commuted every day to lower Manhattan.

I'd been in both the North and South Towers myself, and look at them now; smoking burning wrecks. I went to the bathroom and splashed my face with water. My hands were shaking but my resolve was strong. I hurried back into the lounge and grabbed my phone and that's when I heard it for the first time: "I think we can now be certain that what is happening today in New York is no accident. It is an act of terrorism. So terrible, it will affect the whole of mankind."

Chapter 39

I stopped in the hallway and rewound. The whole of mankind. Wasn't that what Mark said would happen? I'd dismissed it as ass-saving drama and turned my back on his words. But somewhere inside, deeper than my heart, I held them there. What did he mean? How bad could it actually be?

Looking at the scenes now on the TV, I began to realise. For the second time in my life I was directly experiencing something that most people only experience vicariously courtesy of Sky News. And there it was, the question I had avoided for all that time: was this my fault? I'd lied to everyone when I said I had no idea where the papers were. I'd lied to Mark. Even after I left Cyprus he used to call me. My family thought he was pursuing me, that the long telephone calls were romantic gestures.

I knew differently. They were lengthy, tensely silent battles. He wanted answers. I would not give them. Eventually he gave up but I knew from the desperation in his voice that he wasn't fooled. With every call he became increasingly distant and erratic. When they stopped I considered calling his employers to check that he was all right. But by then I had met Sandy and petitioned for divorce. Mark was the past and I was determined to put it behind me.

Inside, though, tied up in my guts, was the guilt. And now it was rushing toward my throat as I tasted bile. Was this my fault? Was this what was in those coded documents? Because this was certainly on the catastrophic scale that Mark had spoken about.

I pushed the thought down as far as I could but the panic had already gripped me.

On shock autopilot, I opened my front door and suddenly it became less about me and more about a community joining together. People from my building were running down the stairwell carrying blankets and first-aid kits, out onto the street and towards the small harbour. The towers still smoked in the distance and the air had an acrid smell that I immediately recognised. It was the smell of burning debris, the smell of explosion and combustion.

Down at the harbour I met Kit Dawson, one of Sandy's crew. He held me by the shoulders. "Julie. Is Sandy safe?"

"Yes. He's in London."

We both knew that he could easily have been in the city.

"Thank God. Look, there will be a lot of people needing to get out. I'm taking my boat over in a convoy to pick them up. D'you think it would be OK to take Sandy's?"

"Of course. Of course. Take it. What can I do, Kit?"

"Wait here. This'll take some time to organise but when we bring people in from the island they'll need water and food. Blankets. Maybe some of those emergency blankets."

My organisational skills kicked in. I knew the neighbourhood shops well. I'd been working as a jobbing writer but because of Sandy's standing in the Jersey community I was expected to do fundraisers and organise events for the homeless. I'd used my own brand of all right, my rough-edged, I've-been-there persuasion to elicit all kinds of donations from people who otherwise would have turned away.

"Right. I'll set up a donation station right over there, Kit. Can you direct anyone who isn't going to sail over to me and I'll map out a grid of retailers who can donate."

He hurried off. I dragged over two barrels from the harbour side, pulled down a sign from the hire shop as a makeshift table top, and tried my mobile. There was an erratic signal. I called all my contacts, demanding that they bring supplies. There was no time to think about Mark now but all the while my guilt nagged at me and I cursed myself and my inability back then to see how important those papers must have been.

My mind twisted itself into a knot as I faced up to what I'd been denying for over a decade – the possibility that Mark had been acting in good faith. True, he had sacrificed me and run away, leaving me stranded. But what if it was for the greater good? What if this awful attack on New York was the end product, the awful outcome that he was trying to avoid? What if I, by obsessing over myself and my love life, had ruined everything? Just to spite Mark.

I was in the middle of what would later be known as the 9/11 boatlift but all I could think about was the wrong I had done. Why had I given those papers to Sanaa? Just so that Mark couldn't have them. I berated myself for knowing so little of the world. For my inability to imagine what Mark had meant about it affecting all mankind. For not understanding how bad things could get, even after my experience in Iraq.

This was different. The scene before me now was like end times. Supplies were arriving thick and fast and someone had set up a radio so that we could hear what was going on and when we could expect the first boats to come in. The first crates of water arrived and I coordinated them onto the vessels that were about to sail over the Hudson River. Then the North Tower collapsed. It crumbled and disappeared into a huge bellow of thick, dark smoke and people around me dropped to the floor, tears making tracks through the thick dust on their faces. Time stopped as we watched the smoke and dust bellow through the familiar landscape towards the river. Then everyone ran for the boats.

I watched as Kit's crew sailed Sandy's boat out of Jersey Port, then stood by the edge of the water as it returned, handing water to people who, although shaken and dirty with ash and smoke, were smiling. Mothers holding children. Injured firemen. Grown businessmen holding each other tightly for comfort over lost colleagues. They were lucky to be alive, I realised.

Lucky to be alive. Unlike the poor souls who had lost their lives today. Because of you, Juliette. Because of you, whispered my conscience.

I carried on organising into the night, breaking off only when my mobile rang, to give Sandy updates.

"I'll be home as soon as I can, Julie. Stay safe. I love you."

"I love you too, Sand, I love you too."

It's what people were suddenly saying to each other. My neighbours, who had a long-running dispute over a water pipe, suddenly hugging and saying they loved each other. Strangers fresh off the boats saying they loved me as I handed them water. Looking back at their devastated city, they embraced life and embraced me.

Nights turned into days and days turned into a week. Sandy still hadn't returned from London, his telephone calls heartbreaking reminders that he still had to face his city on its new, devastating terms. My nights were punctuated by nightmares in which I was in the hut with Sanaa in the middle of Manhattan and all the buildings around us collapsed. I repeatedly woke in a cold sweat and ran to look at myself in the bathroom mirror.

My reflection was always the same. The same soft features, blonde hair and pink cheeks. But the light in my eyes had changed. If Iraq had battered the fear out of me, then New York had reminded me what terror was. And they were two very different animals. My days were anxiety ridden as I wondered if I could put this right; if I could muster up the strength to face it. I had never told anyone what happened with Sanaa, or really what happened with Mark. Although it was the soundtrack to my life, and louder over the past week, I realised that no one actually knew the full story. Except Sanaa.

I couldn't wait for Sandy to return. Our relationship was built on mutual trust, on knowing that, however far either of us went around the globe, we'd always return to the other. Until now I had rested easy in my skin, living happily alone when he was away, writing or watching TV or visiting our friends. Now, I could hardly sleep. The nightmares were getting worse and I had a constant feeling of doom.

I talked to Joan about it. "I don't know, Joanie. I can't sleep. I just feel like it'll all be better when Sandy comes home."

She tilted her head to one side. "Not back yet then?"

"No. He's not looking forward to it. He says his heart is broken. I told him all about what Kit did with the boats and how over three hundred thousand people were rescued on the river and he cried like a baby."

Joan is a very understanding woman. She's older than me and even more laid back than I usually am.

"Ah. He'll come home when he's hungry. Tragedy affects people in different ways. Some guys I know won't even talk about it. Like it never happened. Some of them won't stop talking about it. Anyways. That's what'll be wrong with you, girl. Delayed shock. It's a terrible thing that's happened."

More terrible by the day, as it turned out. We were only just beginning to discover that many of our close friends had either lost someone in the attack or their place of work was destroyed.

"Yeah. I suppose."

How could she help? She didn't know the full story. She didn't know what I was preoccupied with day and night. So I went about my business.

Nine days later, when I'd returned after popping out to buy some paper for my printer, my heart lifted as I saw a familiar figure standing in the stairwell of our building. I'd know that shape anywhere, the person I've spent so many days and nights with, almost a muscle memory. It was etched on my memory. I hurried through the glass doors, a sliver of happiness piercing the guilt and remorse and terror, and touched his shoulder.

"Sandy."

But it wasn't Sandy. It was Mark.

Chapter 40

It was Mark. His eyes were the same piercing blue. But more about him had changed. He was unshaven and his hair long and curly on his shoulders. His clothes were khaki and he wore army boots but not standard issue; more like the kind you might pick up in a charity shop. His skin was deeply tanned and his hands wrinkled.

"Mark. My God. How are you?"

It was a stupid question but under the circumstances it was all I could think of. He stared at me and I suddenly felt exposed.

"Is there somewhere we can talk?"

I followed his gaze to the lift doors but it didn't feel right.

"My husband will be home soon. So here's probably not the best place. There's a coffee shop just down a block. Would that be OK?"

It was then I saw it. He didn't have the same poise, the same surety that he'd had when I last saw him. He'd been worried back then but now he looked desperate. He had a hunched look about him.

We walked along the block to Joe's Coffee Shop and he chose a table near the door. The shop was nearly empty but he glanced around nervously. "OK. Look. I know some things happened between us and well…"

He picked up a salt cellar and was turning it over between his fingers. I watched as small grains of salt spilled onto the table.

"Was this what it was about, Mark? Was this what the documents were about? Is that why you were so worried?"

I felt myself slip back into the liar I was inside. Covering with questions. Giving myself time to think.

He turned his head quickly towards Manhattan. Then put the cellar down carefully. "No. It wasn't."

My heart soared. I wasn't to blame. It wasn't my fault that all those people died and that Sandy couldn't face his own home.

Mark was still talking. "It was something else. Something that's in danger of emerging again. Something worse." He took my hands in his, gripping them a little too hard, and I remembered that day behind our house and the tiny bruises up and down my arms. "So you have to tell me, Jules, you have to tell me. What happened to it?"

I tried to pull my hands away but he held onto them, curling his fingers around mine. I kept my nerve. I'd made a promise and I wouldn't break it unless it was absolutely necessary.

I leaned forward, my face close to his across the table, my voice a hissing whisper. "What happened? Like I said before, you tell me what it's all about. It's up to you, Mark. It's up to you."

He spoke to me now through gritted teeth. "Stop fucking around, Jules. This is serious. You've seen now what they are capable of. You've seen all this. And you saw what happened in Iraq. Well, it's going to happen again. It never really stopped."

I finally pulled my hands away. "What's it to you, anyway? I'm guessing you're not still in the army from the state of you."

He didn't wince at this. The old Mark would have been hurt if anyone critiqued his appearance but he just shook his head. "Yeah. Well. I had to get out. They were going to find out sooner or later that it was me who took it. There'd already been more questions. So I ran. Out of sight. But now I need to know where that information is."

"Why? What's it to you?"

He sipped his coffee slowly and then swept away the salt with the side of his hand. "Well, for one thing, I know what it is. I know how dangerous it is. But that information's no good without the document. I know the ballpark. That information is the ball."

"So you want to sell it now?"

"Yep. I'll split it with you."

"I don't need your dirty money, Mark. I don't need it. And how do I know you aren't going to sell it to someone like… like…"

He laughed loudly. A little too loudly. A woman sitting at the back of the café looked up from her newspaper.

"Like who blew up New York? Nah. I'll be selling it back to the people who sent it. I've got a contact." He sniggered to himself. "Once again, for the common good."

His sarcasm bit into my soul.

"You're a liar, Mark. I don't believe you."

"It doesn't matter if you believe me or not. Because there's something out there that's worse than what happened here. Yes.

Worse. Can you imagine that, Jules? Worse than anything anyone's been through before."

"But how do you know? How do you know if you don't know what it is?"

He thought for a moment. His eyes searched the room and settled back on me. "I saw the file. The part that wasn't coded. It said that a team had developed a genetic defect that could affect populations. The whole of mankind, I think it said. There were no specifics. No location, no names, not even a delivery method. No real details. They were all in the document. All it said was that the product was in a bio-locked canister in a secret location somewhere in Iraq. Only a handful of people knew the details and they were the team who made it. One of them had sold out and sent the data to us, and I was the person who intercepted it. The rest of the file was encrypted, the part I gave to you."

He stared at me and became much more agitated. "So I just want it back, Jules. It's the only copy. The other members of the team just disappeared. But I want to get it back where it belongs before it all kicks off again."

"And what makes you think it's going to? Kick off again?"

He looked left and right. "President Bush will appear tonight in an address to the nation. There are plans to invade Iraq again. Which means that, wherever this product is, it's in danger. I don't know if it's some kind of airborne chemical weapon or something else but I'd like to see the people who want to keep it safe, secure in the knowledge that the data isn't on the loose out there. So, I'll ask you one last time, where is it?"

"Where is it? For the last time, I don't fucking know."

He heaped a teaspoon of sugar into his half empty cup. "Have it your way. But eventually someone will come looking for you. When they find out that the data was substituted, they'll come. You can say you don't know where it is forever, Jules, but every time you see a child killed or hear about problems out there, you'll wonder if it was your fault. Been sleeping badly lately, have you? Looking a bit tired."

"Fuck off."

"I will. But you can tell me now and be free."

"Tell you? Tell you? I don't know where it is. But even if I did, I wouldn't tell you so that you could make a quick buck."

He laughed loudly again and the woman shifted in her seat. "Everyone's got a price, love. I've got a price for my info and you've got a price for yourself. Married to that Sanderson guy. Boatyard owner. Millionaire. Nice work, Jules. Nice work."

My anger rose and almost spewed out of my mouth in words I would regret. "I love Sandy. He's an honest man. Not a liar. Tells me the truth. You know? The truth."

"Yeah. I know the truth. And I know you're lying. I knew it from the day you came back from Iraq. That's why I'm here, Jules. To get to the bottom of it. Because if I don't, there'll be a long queue when the people who want this product realise that the shit's about to hit the fan."

I took a deep breath. It would have been so easy to just tell him and have done with it. But there was something about him that was even more untrustworthy than before, an almost sneering attitude.

"Truth? You would know the truth if it kicked you in the balls. I don't know where it is. It got wet and I ditched it. It was unreadable. I tried to read it but it was just a jumble of words. The ink ran and it was ruined. I don't have any ties with Iraq. I just want to forget the whole thing."

He finished his coffee in one gulp. "OK. Have it your way. But sleep well, Jules, because if you're not telling the truth, I feel sorry for you. You've already had a taste of guilt by the look of you."

He stood up and walked out of the café. I watched him walk back down the block towards my apartment. I needed to find out where he was. Just in case I changed my mind. I gave him ten minutes, in which time I called Sandy's lawyer Jack Grove with some story about needing to find my ex-husband because of some property issue that had cropped up.

Within minutes Jack had called me back. "I'm sorry to tell you that Mark's deceased, Juliette. His body was found in a quarry in southern Iraq six years ago."

Chapter 41

I hurried out of the cafe and looked up the road but he was gone. The terror that I'd felt for almost two weeks, the underlying guilt, was now replaced by confusion and doubt. I knew that I'd just spoken to Mark, but according to the records he was dead.

And how did he know that the president would address the nation shortly, or what he would say?

It all sounded like Mark's usual bullshit, a vague announcement followed by utter secrecy, that I had grown tired of. But he had a point, because I was lying. I had never severed my ties with Iraq because I had kept in touch with Sanaa. As soon as I'd arrived in Manchester from Cyprus I'd written to her to find out if she was all right. There was no response at first, which had contributed to my sense of hopelessness.

Then I received the first letter. They would arrive every few weeks thereafter, but the first one was the catalyst that ended my brooding depression over what had happened. She had a way about her, Sanaa, one that I hadn't really got to see when we were alone in Iraq. Her letters cheered me up.

She didn't mention Shahid at first, just her situation.

Dear Juliette Watson

I arrived here with my parents and there was great joy that I was still alive. They had heard about my husband and thought that I too had been arrested and sent to an unknown fate.

My mother and my sisters are so happy, and I am working with them in the fields. Already my father has set me a small area for my art. I have been in contact with some of my former colleagues and while they advise against coming back, they are working on a collection of Mesopotamian art that they want me to curate. Keep safe. No one has been to look for me. It seems that, for the time being, I am safe. But as a precaution, I have changed my name back to my unmarried name – Yazid.

This means that I might travel, Juliette Watson, to America or even to England where you stay. We shall meet again but never speak of how we met. I keep your secret safe and you keep mine.

The letter went on to talk about the village her parents lived in and how it was so beautiful, about her sisters Fatima and Farhana, each with two daughters. How her mother crept into her room every night when she thought Sanaa was asleep, to stroke her hair and thank Allah for her daughter's life. How her father encouraged her to continue with her search for knowledge, and accompanied her on small excavations where they found ancient fragments of pottery and animal bone.

She ended her first letter with the words, *'My dearest friend, I am earnest in my friendship and always thinking of you. Sanaa.'*

I'd never had a real friend before. Not someone who was thinking of me. Not someone who held a secret in their hands like a butterfly and never let it go. So I wrote back to the address in Buhriz and waited patiently. Six weeks later I received a parcel containing a small pot, delicately crafted with a frieze of two women at opposite sides of the circle, their hands held together forming a complete ring around it. The women were tiny but the details were clear. It was me and Sanaa. And there was a note in Sanaa's handwriting.

For you, Juliette, to empty the secrets of your heart into and shut the lid when they become too vivid.

Somehow, through all the pain, it gave me a glimpse of hope. Over the next few years my trauma was dissolved by gestures of kindness and lots of letters and notes from Sanaa about her success and how her exhibition was going from strength to strength. And tiny figures, ranging from detailed dioramas carved into stones, to figures of animals and people. I looked them up in a book at the library and they were exactly like the ones in Sanaa's ancient collections, except they were decorated with modern day scenes. So January 1991 had been buried in the past, underneath the bonds of my friendship with a woman far, far away.

Until today.

Mark had brought 1991 careening back into the forefront of my mind. After I searched Sinatra Drive I rushed back to my apartment and grabbed Sanaa's letters. No one must find them. No one must read about our private business. About her dead son and the fact that she had killed a man. But most of all, no one must know that she had the documents. Not that these were ever mentioned but wasn't a link to her enough?

I stuffed all the letters into my bag and hurried to the ferry. I needed to be somewhere I could think, somewhere Mark couldn't follow me. Where no one could follow me. I needed to decide what I was going to do next.

I hadn't been to Manhattan since the week before 11 September and a terrible sight met me. I travelled by bus – any form of transport that would allow me to see if Mark was following me – right to the place that would later be known as Ground Zero, where so many people had lost their lives. Where so many people were still searching.

The rails around the destruction were lined with photographs of the victims and I stood, awestruck, gazing at the twisted metal and the harrowed expressions of the people around me. Surely this was the worst thing that could happen? Surely this was enough for me to own up, if not to Mark them to the authorities? Tell them that secret information was on the loose.

Sanaa had told me in one of her letters what she had done with the papers.

Your heart, Juliette Watson, is safe. It is safe in my father's home, underneath the tree that grows tall beside the oven in our garden. I will never tell a soul, never, or ever write of it again. It will never be found as it lies unmarked, so destroy this letter to make sure that only you and I know.

I had destroyed the letter but not the others she sent me. I could end it all now. Tell them where the documents were. Tell them about Mark. Tell them that I hadn't meant to lie. I stared at a young woman for a while, tears rolling down her cheeks, which she wiped away with the sleeve of her cardigan that was pulled over her thumb. Then at the buildings around me, scared and partial now, a circle of ever-decreasing dereliction, like ripples.

I had meant to lie. I had. To teach Mark a lesson at first. Then to save the world from something I knew nothing about. In too deep. When I was young, back then, I was surer that I knew everything, that I could take good care of my secret. But with age comes uncertainty, ever-creeping in the form of small events that rubbed against the crumbling of that confident youth.

I realised then that I was straddling a void, with the past pulling me in one direction and the present in another. Just for a second I had an insight into the constant nightmares and the noise; fear rose out of nowhere and I no longer knew where I was.

The shock of seeing Mark again, then hearing that he was dead, had all but eroded my false bravery. Standing at Ground Zero, seeing the grief and the horror, and knowing that something worse was possible, clawed at my sanity. I should tell. I should go straight away to the nearest police department and shed it.

But what about Sanaa? What about her son and Saif Abed? Her past was forgotten now but what would happen to her if I told the full story?

My mobile rang and shattered the terror in my heart. I answered it immediately with shaking hands.

"Were you sitting on your phone?" A familiar voice, full of laughter, strange in this place full of sadness, broke the spell.

"Sandy."

"Where are you? Home?"

"Home? No. Downtown. Had to see it for myself."

A short pause. "Are you OK? Jack just told me the bad news. About Mark Watson. He reckoned you sounded upset."

I focussed on a couple holding hands, holding each other in the shadow of the desperation of New York. "OK? Yes, I'm OK. It was just a shock."

"Yeah. Jack said there were some property problems? Do you want me to…?"

"Do I want you to deal with it? Um. No. No, thanks. It was just my blue memory box. I never knew what happened to it, where it was. I was thinking about visiting Cyprus again and wondered if Mark knew where I had left it. If it had been there when he packed up and left. I asked Jack if he could find out about Mark. Contact him on my behalf."

More lies. Lie upon lie upon lie. Question upon question to cover myself. I pictured the blue box in my mind's eye, in the attic in my mother's house in Manchester.

"Right. And that's when he told you?"

"Yeah. Yeah. That Mark's dead."

My relationship with Sandy had been built on trust. I'd never needed to lie to him before, mainly because he'd never asked me what happened in Iraq. So I knew that the silence at the other end of the line was the run-up to kindness and love – which made me feel guiltier.

"I'm on my way home. I've avoided the city for too long. You're more important than that, Julie. I need to face it. We need to face this together. I'll be back tomorrow."

He ended the call and I sat for another three hours reading Sanaa's letters. Scouring every page for any damning evidence. The letters themselves were damning enough but I'd always planned to say I met her in Cyprus and kept in touch, if anyone ever asked. Now, in the shadow of this wreckage, I see more clearly the tenuous links I made to cover my own tracks.

Of course someone would find out Mark took the papers. As he said, it was only a matter of time. Of course someone would put it together and check me out. Then they would find the letters and connect me with Sanaa.

I thought long and hard on my new perspective and decided that instead of cutting all ties with Sanaa and pretending it had never happened, I might as well see it through. Lie to the end. If they did come with their questions, I'd just repeat what I had said before; I'd lie that Sanaa was just a friend I'd met along the way.

Eventually I walked away from Lower Manhattan and returned to our apartment. I turned on the TV to find President Bush addressing the nation. He talked about a new kind of war against a terrorist organisation in Afghanistan called Al Qaida, and specifically a man named Osama Bin Laden.

I remember smiling to myself. Because Mark had got it wrong – there was no mention of Iraq. Because my secret was still safe. Sanaa was still safe.

Chapter 42

Sandy returned home the next day and we slipped into the routine of everyday life. Visiting bars and restaurants with our friends, skirting the perimeter of Ground Zero until Sandy was ready to talk about it. He was haunted. Haunted by every speck of dust in the city, every wind that carried the still-acrid smell. I could see it in him, a diminishment of his spirt as he mourned for the people on the wind. He returned to his business dealings and I developed my work as a writer and illustrator.

Two months later, in November 2001, I received an excited telephone call from Sanaa. I'd given her my mobile number but never expected her to call or text – she never had until now. But suddenly I heard her voice on the line.

"Juliette Watson? Yes?"

"Sanaa? How are you?"

She laughed loudly on the other end of the line. "Very good. Very good. I'm calling from Baqubah. To ask a favour."

I had to smile at her excitement. She sounded so vital, so alive. "OK. Fire away."

"I'm coming to London! The exhibition is being sent to London. I can see you there."

Silence. I suddenly realised that she didn't know that I lived in New York now. After Sandy and I married, we'd moved here almost immediately, and it was my home. But Sanaa still sent her letters and gifts to my mother's address in Manchester; my mother forwarded them on.

"But I live in New York. In America."

Silence again.

"America? You didn't tell me. In your letters. You didn't tell me." She suddenly sounded full of suspicion. Panic. Almost fear.

"Didn't tell you? Didn't I? I must have forgotten. I get all my mail forwarded. I guess I never looked at the address." More silence. I needed to make this right. "But I can easily fly to London to see you."

Laughter again. I relaxed.

"And my sisters. My sisters are coming. You won't believe it. London is the new home for the treasures. Ancient treasure, more than thousands of years old. Lots of pieces. A collector has paid a lot to get it out of Iraq."

I felt the hairs on the back of my neck stand on end. "Why? Why does it have to leave Iraq?"

Sanaa became serious now. "You must see the news. America and Britain want to start trouble here again. That's the rumour. So we need to get the precious things out. Not like last time."

I swallowed hard. It couldn't be true. "But Al Qaeda has nothing to do with Iraq, do they? So why trouble there?"

"I know this and you know this but try telling the Americans. Anyone is fair game. They want the blood of Saddam. Anyway. Enough. You are coming to London? I'll send the dates to you."

"Yes. I'll come. It might take a lot of arranging but I'll come. And Sanaa, it's lovely to speak to you."

Her voice choked and I could hear the emotion. "Yes, you too, my friend. And nothing has changed. Nothing."

I knew what she meant. No more words were needed. "Thank you. Thank you. I can't wait to see you."

She rang off. I honestly couldn't wait to see her.

She emailed me her details and I arranged the flights for the next week. I explained to Sandy that I was going to meet old friends in London and to see my parents. He's a good man. He never batted an eyelid, taking my word as the gospel truth. All the while I was wondering if I should ask Sanaa to bring the document. At least then I would know where it was. But then I would have all the responsibility. At least this way it seemed distanced, far away from me. It wasn't right in front of me, slowly burning a ragged hole in my consciousness.

So I went to London. Sandy booked a suite at the Ritz for us, as a surprise, and I met Sanaa and her sisters at Green Park tube station. I caught sight of her before she saw me and I was shocked. Still beautiful, her face was lined and her eyes dark with lack of sleep. She wore a long black robe and a loose hijab and her body was fuller than when I last saw her more than ten years ago. The front of her hair was still jet black and I could see a long twist of thick black hair outlined against her back. Her sisters looked very similar to her, except a little younger, and they were all laughing together.

I touched her on the shoulder and she turned. Her eyes met mine and I saw that the pain, while reduced, was still present. It was understandable. After all, I represented that terrible time and the death of her only child.

She held me for a long moment, and then let go of me. "Juliette Watson. Hardly any older! These are my sisters."

Fatima and Farhana shook my hand and we hurried to the hotel. Sandy had been generous, and each woman had a bedroom off a huge suite. The whole layout was beautiful, in gold and cream, and quietly serene. We ordered room service immediately.

I caught Sanaa watching me and went to sit with her. "It's been a long time. I didn't think we would meet again."

"Yes. It didn't seem impossible. But my life became successful and many things I thought were impossible have happened. Except children."

It was so sudden that it shocked me. For a second I dived down into the depths and I saw the pile of stones and the birds peck peck pecking and tasted the dust in my throat. Sanaa's dead eyes as she stared into her son's grave, building up the stones each morning.

"Oh. I didn't think you wanted to talk about..."

Her eyes warned me not to say what I was about to. "I never had a child."

"Of course. Of course." There had been no need to speak it but I guessed that she felt she had to warn me. Her sisters obviously had no idea what she had been through. "Me neither. I remarried but no children."

She tapped the table. "So what happened to your husband?"

"What happened to Mark? Oh. He died."

Deeper into the tangled web of lies. But he was officially dead. No need to worry Sanaa with the details. And I sometimes wondered if I had imagined his visit.

"So nothing ever happened when you got back?"

It was a shock to actually talk about it. It was only in that moment that I realised that I had not spoken to another living soul about how I knew Sanaa and why I was in Iraq in the first place. I'd only ever had conversations with myself, reasoning out why I did it, and why I was still doing it.

"Well, there were questions but I just told them I knew nothing."

"And you never found out what the important information was?"

Had I told her about it? I couldn't remember. I'd blocked out most of those days of death and fear. I must have told her.

"No. Why?"

Sanaa looked very serious. Not like the angry woman I knew back then. And not like the woman with the deep belly laugh whom I had come to know in our telephone conversation. This Sanaa was bitter and serious. "Sometimes, just between sleep and awake, I wonder what those words mean and why your husband held them more precious than you. We spoke it back then in the angry words of failed love but in the cold light of day I worry. Why he would risk such a thing at the beginning of Desert Storm?"

She met my eyes again. I couldn't tell if her look was accusing or pitying.

"Mmm. I don't know. Saving his own skin, maybe?"

She ignored my question. "It must have been very important. But not for our eyes, yes? We're women, what can we know about war? We sit on the sidelines and weep. We have no voice. I am deeply worried about my country and what will happen if America attacks us again. Deeply worried. But I have no voice, no volume to say it. I use my art, of course. But it makes no difference."

"What are you getting at, Sanaa?"

"Nothing. I just observe that just as I have no voice in my country, you have none in yours. You have something so precious that you nearly died for it, yet you don't know what it is or what it means. And no way of finding out without looking like a liar. So we are the same. We make small talk about our family and this room and the weather but in the background we have big truths that we cannot say."

The decade of tension suddenly released itself and I was on my feet. "So you think I should have admitted it, do you? And then they'd have come after you?"

"No. You misunderstand. I am merely saying that we have no route to our voices without sacrificing ourselves." She leaned forward. "Saif Abed. If a man had killed him, it would considered an act of war, a battle. If I kill him it is murder and I hang. I see his face, and that of his wife and child, every night in my dreams."

I turned away and looked out of the window. I watched the shoppers, the hustle and bustle of commuters. "Did you know that I watched the aeroplanes hit the Twin Towers only a few weeks ago, Sanaa? I live just across the river from there. I helped with the evacuation."

She shook her head. Her expression changed. Now she was guarded. "No. And I am very sorry."

"Yeah. I believed it was my fault. That the information in the document was somehow related to the attack. That I had caused it by not giving it back."

Sanaa shrugged.

I went on. "It turned out that someone else was responsible, not me. But for a while I thought that blood was on my hands. So yes, I do know how you feel."

"But who did you tell? Your husband? The authorities? No. Just me and you know this. And about Saif Abed. Everyone understands the rules of war, that people get killed, and soldiers know that is their job. Even your husband. So why do we feel so guilty for protecting ourselves?"

I didn't know then and I still don't know now. Sanaa rose and changed. When she returned, Fatima and Farhana were telling me about their village and how Sanaa has made a memorial garden for anyone who had a child killed in conflict, to remember them. Sanaa shushed them and lowered her eyes when I smiled widely.

"We tell in many ways, Juliette Watson, even if we do not speak the story."

We stayed in London a week. Sanaa took us to see her exhibits at the Royal Academy, just up the road from the Ritz, at the Museum of

Natural History and at the British Museum. I hadn't really understood what she did before this but when I saw the pieces, and her excitement, I realised her investment in her country. There were friezes from long ago and tablets of writing from several different eras of Iraqi history. Sanaa explained that this was real history; I could tell from her animation that this was her deep passion.

There were pots, much like the one that Sanaa had sent me with the first letter, and statues and tablets. But the things that struck me most were the amulets. Tiny chunks of agate and stone, metals and onyx, all representing something beyond words, something that these ancient people had needed to communicate. About who they were, how they lived, what was precious to them. I turned to Sanaa and asked her what her amulets meant.

She pursed her lips. "My heart. My soul. The things I cannot tell. I make them the same as my people made them. Same techniques. Same spirit. Something hard to explain. Important to me. You have to understand that I love my country, an attachment that is deep and wide. We belong to each other."

With age Sanaa had grown more serious. She wasn't light and airy like her letters. She was preoccupied with politics and, in particular, with America and the threat of war. She'd explained to me that the whole purpose of her visit was to relocate this collection permanently, because so many artefacts had already been lost. Her lip curled when she mentioned the war against terror and, eventually, I challenged her on it.

"But don't you want to see Saddam removed? Wouldn't that be better for everyone?"

She laughed and shook her head. "At what price? Of course, it would be the ideal situation if we did not have a dictator. But at what cost? You saw with your own eyes what happens in war. You saw it. What it does to us. To me. To you. Don't pretend you aren't affected."

She was right. Time had changed me. It had changed my life into an ongoing lie, a continuous battle to hide the truth about who I was and what I had done. But instead of telling her this, I just shrugged.

"So for it to happen again is unthinkable," she went on. "I am nothing to do with Al Qaeda. Nothing. Nor my family. I had not heard this name until this year and the terrible attacks on the city where you live. So I am not to blame but I will suffer. How is that fair? Men will kill each other, the innocent will die and, in the end, for what? What do you think will happen when Saddam is deposed?"

"Democracy?" I said it in a quiet voice, because I knew how she felt about the West.

"No. Not true democracy. Because someone always wants the power and people are evil."

I wanted to shout at her, scream that people are not evil, that some people are good. But I knew deep down that she was right. I'd seen enough close-up terror to know that evil exists. It was in that moment that I nearly told her what Mark had said. About the document and what it meant. What he knew about it. Genetic engineering. Something more terrible than 9/11.

But somehow it felt elitist. If I told her I would be saying, "Here Sanaa, take this information back to your country and deal with it. I'm handing it over to you." Yes, I'd feel better, but I had no idea what she would do. Most probably hand the document over to the authorities.

So I nearly told her. But not quite.

Chapter 43

It was time for her to leave. I went to the airport with them and held her tightly. She hugged me back and I could feel her love for me. Her trust. Even then I thought of telling her but I couldn't burden her. Fatima and Farhana went on ahead, waving and crying a little.

Sanaa hung back. "I thought you would ask me for it."

I pulled back a little. "What? Ask you for what?"

"The papers. I thought you would ask me to bring them." Her tone was earnest but her eyes mocked me.

"Did you? No. If they're safe then leave them where they are. Where they're doing no one any harm."

"But what if someone comes to you for them, and connects with me? What then? Will you still keep my secret?"

"Just deny everything, Sanaa. It's the past. Gone. We can't change it now."

She leaned on a pillar in the airport lounge. Her cheeks flushed a little. "But I deal with the past. The past is my business. It always comes back to haunt us."

I could feel the anger rising in my chest. "OK. OK. FedEx them to me, if you feel like it. FedEx them."

She smiled and touched my arm. "No. We had a deal. If you think they are safe, hidden away, then I'll keep them. But I brought them anyway, just in case you asked. I had them with me all the time."

My gaze strayed to her hand luggage but she shook her head.

"No. The papers are still under the tree. The words are here." She pointed at her temple. "I memorised them. I gave them my voice. So no matter what happens to me, you will be able to find them."

"No matter what happens to you? Why? Are you in danger?"

She shook her head and moved closer to me. "I've always been in danger. Iraq is a dangerous place for me. But I have to stay."

I couldn't let her go back to that life. That half awareness of someone watching, someone listening. Someone coming for you. God knows I knew what that was like.

"Come home with me. Come to New York. Stay with me for a while."

I expected her to be pleased, to welcome the sanctuary but her expression was disgust bordering on hatred. It took me aback and made my heart thump.

"America? No. Never. My homeland is the beat of my heart. I will die without it. I could never live in that land. Never. It is not my home and it isn't yours either. But thank you."

She touched her head and her heart and turned away for a moment. When she turned back her anger was gone. We hugged again and she walked towards passport control, looking behind her all the way.

I stood in the viewing lounge and watched her plane soar high and realised how traumatic my life had become. It had never occurred to me that Sanaa might think she was a hostage to me. But then again, isn't that what all relationships are built on? Expectations? Why should ours be any different?

I spent some time with my parents before returning to New York. Once home again, I changed the forwarding address for UK mail from our apartment to a postal box. Just to be safe. I asked Sandy to rent me a studio in the city where I could do my illustrations. In truth, I hardly went there, save to read and store any mail from Iraq.

For a while I successfully managed to separate my life with Sandy from my neurosis over my past. But it was temporary.

On 29 September 2002 Sandy and I were getting dressed to go to a gallery opening. Sandy switched on the TV. President Bush was partway through his State of the Union address and Sandy listened intently.

I went to brush my hair in the hallway mirror, out of his view, because although I had learned to control my panicked facial expressions into a mask of inconsequence, I had started to feel faint and nauseous whenever Iraq was mentioned in the ever-expanding war politics of the day.

Sanaa's letters were increasingly political, going into great depth about the fear in Iraq. There was an underlying accusation in her tone which made me feel somehow responsible, as if I was the enemy. Which I suppose I was. I suppose, by this point, everyone was an enemy to Sanaa. Every time I left the apartment my stomach lurched;

I expected to see Mark standing across the road, or walking towards me, or in some bar where Sandy and I were enjoying a burger.

That evening, as I listened carefully to President Bush's measured tones, the bottom fell out of my world. I felt my foothold falter as the term 'axis of evil' punctured my consciousness and filtered through to meaning.

States like these, and their terrorist allies, constitute an axis of evil, arming to threaten the peace of the world. By seeking weapons of mass destruction, these regimes pose a grave and growing danger. They could provide these arms to terrorists, giving them the means to match their hatred. They could attack our allies or attempt to blackmail the United States. In any of these cases, the price of indifference would be catastrophic.

Catastrophic. Indifference. Panic surged through me, waves and waves until I felt like I was choking. I brushed my long blonde hair harder and harder and thought about what Sanaa had said about silence. I could hear Sandy commenting on the address, cheering at the defence budget – and then it was over. I felt like I'd been on a bumpy rollercoaster ride but actually I was still brushing my hair in the hallway and my scalp was bleeding. Sandy's head was bobbing up and down, the way it did when he was silently celebrating something. His coarse hair was combed down.

I wanted to rush into the room and slap him, tell him that this wasn't a good thing. That people would die; people I know. That he was celebrating death. Catastrophe upon catastrophe. But Sandy was a patriot. He'd defend his position with 9/11 and the collateral damage argument. I felt like asking him if he felt that his friend who'd died in the second tower was collateral damage too? If he knew what danger we might be in?

But I didn't. It wasn't because I was a coward, but because I suddenly realised what the last twelve years had done to me. I was heading for forty and I had no children. We'd tried, but not too hard. I'd adopted Mark's stance, that the world was too difficult a place for children. But deep down, I knew the real reason was that all my focus had been on keeping my lies safe. Safe in case anyone asked, and especially safe from Sandy.

Constant lack of sleep and deliberation over what I should do, what the papers were about, whether Mark would turn up or not, whether someone else would turn up – all these things had occupied my mind and filled that part of me that could have developed into something. Mark had his boats. Joanie had her children and her watercolours. Even Sanaa had her passion for her history. But I had nothing.

My writing and illustrations were mediocre, just a means to an end, although I was grateful for them and the chance to immerse myself in something. Of course, I realised that none of this was directly my fault. I didn't make Mark take the papers, or hide the dangerous items in Iraq. I had no part in Sanaa's hate for Americans or the Americans' decision to go to war. I didn't even know what the papers were, except for what Mark told me, and God knows he could be lying. I'd become obsessed.

"Ready, Julie? We're going to be late."

I looked in the mirror. Was I ready? Was I ready to give this secret up? Could I do it without involving Sanaa?

Just do it, Juliette, I told myself. Just do it.

But I didn't. I couldn't. I was hedging my bets, hoping that Mark was lying and that the papers were as meaningless as I thought they were. After all, no one had asked me anything relevant for twelve years, so how important could they be?

I quickly dabbed away the red pinpricks of blood from my scalp and put up my hair, and Sandy and I went out for dinner. I held his hand and smiled for all I was worth as we discussed the State of the Union address with his colleagues and their wives. We'd been married ten years that week. I'd watched him age from mid-thirties to mid-forties. His hair had greyed and his smooth skin had begun to crinkle around the eyes. We'd honoured each other's space and respected each other's busy lives, and this had suited me. To speak up now, to evoke Sanaa and my first marriage might damage us.

He'd mentioned Mark's death more than once, questioning my feelings for him and my reaction. Each time I'd lied and told him that I'd had no contact with Mark, and his death was therefore a soft blow. In fact, Mark's fabricated death was the one piece of the jigsaw that made me doubt that Mark was lying and worry that he was deadly serious about what had happened in Cyprus, that he wasn't over-dramatising it as I'd suspected at the time.

So I smiled and laughed and ate and drank and pushed Mark and Sanaa to the bottom of my mind. I visited the studio less and less and looked around for something, anything, to occupy me.

I found it in Sanaa's art. The pieces she had sent me. I began to read about Ancient Babylon and all it entailed, its demise and how the area between the Euphrates and the Tigris Rivers. I read day and night, and soon Sanaa's art woke up for me, the symbols and the colours making some kind of sense, becoming somehow familiar, rooting themselves in my home.

I read articles about the destruction of ancient artefacts, both by the coalition bombs in 1990 and by rival religious factions. As the pieces she sent piled up in my spare room, I began to register that Sanaa was sending me priceless pieces of Iraqi history. The less valuable stuff she sent to the museums but she was sending original pieces to me, mixed in with her own art.

She sent me more pieces, some of them original and some of them modelled on ancient artefacts but with a modern twist. Every piece told its own story, with its frieze and its date and its vibrancy. I looked closely at them, drank in the precision of the work both ancient and modern, and marvelled at the pieces made by Sanaa's own hand. There were scenes from her own village; one pot even depicted our six-day stay in the Iraqi wilderness, complete with craters and the texture of red dust. Sanaa had also modelled the New York skyline in several of the pieces, each time a little differently.

Our letters became suddenly more frequent as I enthused in ever-longer tomes about my new-found fascination in her country's history. Sanaa filled in the details that the books left out, and gave me a feel for the land. No need to hide these letters, because their content and tone had changed; we were now two women on different continents discussing art. That was all. No undertones, no agenda, no politics. Just a shared delight.

But all that was about to change, so soon after it had begun.

Chapter 44

I'd been exchanging gifts and letters with Sanaa frequently. We talked on the phone about some of the pieces she sent me, continuing our conversations by email but then deciding that email wasn't private enough, that it left a permanent link between us.

Both of us were still uneasy about the past but I really felt that I had it under control. The less Sanaa said about Iraq and the problems there, the easier I felt. I even admitted to myself that by maintaining my obsession with Mesopotamian art I was side-lining all the issues that fired my fear.

Months passed and by Christmas I was feeling much better. My anxiety had subsided and I'd begun to think about the holidays, putting up holly boughs around our apartment. Sandy had been home since September. I knew that he was worried about me, keeping an eye out for me. I'd catch myself spending long periods staring into space, and he would nudge me and ask me if everything was OK. Finally, the week before Christmas 2002, he sat down opposite me at our solid oak table.

We didn't have heart to hearts. We didn't argue. Sandy and I had met and married within six months. It's funny, looking back, the first things people talk about. Unusual. The first thing he said to me was that he was born on the same day Martin Luther King died. I'd warmed to him there and then and I'd known that he would be good to me. We'd met while I was working at the UK branch of the ship management company I worked for in Cyprus. Sandy had recognised me from the news reports he had seen when I was missing, and gently asked me if I was OK. He was the first person outside my immediate family to do that. Most people wanted to know what happened to me when I was lost and what happened to me and Mark. But Sandy had focused on me.

Our marriage had been very successful. I loved him and he loved me. Apart from the millstone of guilt that hung around my neck from lying to him, all was well. We were wealthy and privileged and I was thankful for it every day.

Today, though, he looked serious. He took a deep breath and clasped his hands in front of him.

"Julie. I need to ask you something."

I worried that the tap, tap, tap of my rapid heartbeat would give me away. "Oh. What?"

He pushed his hand into his pocket and pulled out a foil wrapper. "I found these. In our room. On the floor beside the bed."

I focused in and saw a strip of my contraceptive pills in his hand.

"I thought you didn't take these?" he said.

His face was contorted and his eyes shiny. I decided there and then that one lie was enough. I had to be truthful about this. In any case, it was connected.

"Yes. I know. But I wasn't ready. I told you how I feel."

He rubbed his forehead. "Yes, ten years ago maybe that was valid. Understandable even. But now? I wondered why it had never happened. I thought it was because I was away a lot."

I felt like crying but my hard shell stayed put. "No. No. It's me, Sandy. I just think this world isn't a good place for children." I looked out of the window towards the shattered city, still overflowing with grief and anger. "What if that happened again?"

He looked pained. Distraught, even. "But I want a family, Julie. You always knew that. You always knew."

It was true. Before we married, we had both dreamed about a boy and a girl, maybe more. Initially I'd thought it would happen once we settled in New York but I quickly realised, by watching the women around me, that children take away your freedom. Sure, there were the rewards, but there was plenty of time, wasn't there? Plenty of time to make Sandy's family. I'd worked out that a baby would tie me, make me unable to go to my studio and to write long letters to Sanaa. To care about the artefacts she had entrusted me with. To sit worrying and fretting about Mark and the consequences of my actions.

More than once I'd thought it might be a good thing but then something would surface and shake me to my senses. So I'd kept taking my pill. Just another month, I told myself, and then I'll stop. But now I was thirty-seven.

"I'm sorry Sandy. I just wasn't ready then."

I saw the ray of hope flit over him. "Then?"

"Then? Oh. Yes. I stopped taking them a while ago. That's an old packet. It must have fallen out of my holdall when I was cleaning out the closet. I stopped taking them last year when I came back from London."

It was too easy to lie again, against my best intentions. And at thirty-seven it would be difficult to conceive, wouldn't it?

He walked around the table and took my hands in his. "Thank God. I was so worried with all that business over Mark and then you didn't seem yourself. Maybe it was the change in your hormones?"

"Hormones? Oh, I don't think…"

He placed his finger over my lips. "Never say never. You never know, Jules. You never know. Oh my God. I might be a father yet."

I hugged him tightly but stared at the packet of pills on the table. I hadn't taken one today, and that was my last packet. Today was Saturday and Tuesday was Christmas Eve. Wednesday Christmas Day, Thursday Boxing Day. If he put those pills back in his pocket I would need to get a new packet Monday latest. Our regular doctor's office would be open holiday hours.

Finally he released me and walked back around the table. He picked up the pills. There were about ten left in the packet. I could feel the crimson heat spreading from my neck to my face.

"I knew there'd be some explanation. I knew it. I knew you had your doubts but I promise I'll be there for you. I promise. Our life can take a new turn now, Julie. You and me. And a little one. I love you so much."

He pushed the pill packet into his pocket; I felt all hope disintegrate in that moment.

Later I went through his clothes in a vain attempt to try to find the pills. I searched through my bags hoping to find a stray packet. My replenish wasn't due until the New Year and, because of my age, my doctor wouldn't give me them without taking my blood pressure and weighing me. It was an impossible situation but I crossed my fingers and hoped for the best.

We spent the holidays making love, with Sandy limiting my alcohol intake 'just in case'. I didn't make it to the doctor, because that year there was a heavy snowfall in New York, starting just before Christmas and ending in the New Year. It was almost as if fate was against me. Sandy began to watch me like a hawk. Of course, his intentions were honourable and he showed me the deepest love and care. But I'd preferred our relationship how it was when we could both come and go as we pleased. Now he insisted that we go everywhere together. He even cancelled his business trips for the first quarter.

We spent long hours lovemaking, as if getting pregnant was another project he meant to be successful at. He spoke to my parents and hinted at a baby. We couldn't visit his parents in New England because of the storm but I heard him confiding in his mother : "We're trying, Mom. Juliette's as keen as I am."

I suppose I was, in a way. And when I missed my period mid-January, then again mid-February, I did feel a tingle of joy. I took a pregnancy test alone, before I told Sandy. Naturally, it was positive.

I sat down heavily on the plush toilet seat in my luxury home and felt completely broken. A baby. Half of me was lost in wonder that Sandy and I would actually have a real family of our own. The other half settled on a grey cloud of despair: someone would eventually come knocking on the apartment door, I would be found out, and my child would be used against me to force out the truth.

I told Sandy that evening. The next day we took a trip to the doctor's office and had a formal test – which was positive. He was overjoyed. I phoned my parents and he held me the whole time I told them, stroking my hair. Then we went over to his parents for the weekend and told them. In many ways I was lost in the occasion but it felt like another woman, a blonde doll of me, who was walking through the happiness, the joy. The real me was overwhelmed.

Work began immediately on the nursery. He did it all himself, in pale yellow and white. We ordered the furniture together and went for an ultrasound scan. Sandy cried when he saw the little bean-like creature squirming around inside me, its heartbeat strong. I was mesmerised. And in love. Until then it hadn't seemed real but suddenly the restrictive voice in my head was silenced. Rather than something to beat me with, this would make me stronger, give me something to protect. Yes, this was what was missing. This was the future.

My only reluctance was telling Sanaa. When I'd met her in London I told her that I'd not had children, as if it were final. As if the end point to that particular adventure had already come and gone. But here I was, eight weeks pregnant. I'd received several letters from her, and two pots that she asked me to store. These weren't any old pots but the real deal – ancient pieces that told me it was no longer safe where Sanaa was, that it had become so dangerous that she had sent them to America, even though she had sworn never to have any of her personal pieces, ones that she had excavated herself, here. But I felt like this deserved more than a letter. Written words would be too casual, an affront to everything that happened to us. After what she had been through, I needed to talk to her.

On 19 March 2003 I rang her home. "Sanaa, please?"

Fatima went to fetch her.

"Yes? Juliette? Is that you? Has something happened?"

I paused. Yes, it had. "I'm pregnant. I just thought I should tell you in person. Not in a letter."

There was a long silence. I listened for her sobs, any indication of tears but there were none.

"Good. That's good.' Her voice was strained. "When will this be?"

"Around September. I have no due date yet."

Her voice was soft now. "Good. I will love your child like you love mine. I will be an honorary Aunt."

I blurted out laughter. "Yes, of course. Like your sisters' children."

"You are my sister, Juliette Watson."

It was a special moment. Everything I felt for Sanaa fell into place. Yes, she was my sister. We shared the same kind of soul and the light in our eyes was similarly dimmed with pain.

"Thank you, Sanaa. Thank you. I must go now. I'll write."

I heard the receiver click as she ended the call. Through the night and into the next morning I wondered if she had gone to the fields and thought about Shahid and what might have been, or prayed for him. But when I got up in the morning and switched on Sky News I knew she would have had no time for that. Because on 20 March 2003 the allied forces, led by America and the UK, attacked Iraq in Operation Shock and Awe.

Chapter 45

I watched it on Sky News. Sandy stood in the lounge and stared his way through the bombing, only stopping to grab a beer from the kitchen. I looked on, horrified. Once again, my body tried to mould itself into a tight ball to protect me. I felt my hands go to my ears as I felt each explosion ripple through my body. The smell, the smell invading my lungs. I resisted but only just. I couldn't let Sandy see my flashback, my connection with this.

I'd known that he was patriotic but his attitude towards the axis of evil was bordering on obsession. Of course, I understood why. Like Iraq was Sanaa's, America was Sandy's. It was visceral for him, a deep belonging that lived with him every day.

He still went to Ground Zero every Saturday and, along with hundreds of other Americans, stared into the wreckage and quietly shook hands with the construction workers who were clearing. His patriotism was quiet and brooding, haunted and weighty. He mourned for the city he loved.

For me, Operation Shock and Awe was just that. It seemed strange watching it on television. As if the little person growing inside me was already creating a barrier between me and the world.

Sandy stayed home and I had a model pregnancy. I'd never felt healthier physically, and I was determined to put my family life first and not to worry about Sanaa. The little boxes that she sent still arrived, albeit more spasmodically, and as well as the beautiful pots and sculptures that I so looked forward to, she sent baby clothes.

These were no ordinary baby clothes. There were sewn by Fatima and Farhana with gold thread. They were beautiful but some gut instinct told me not to let Sandy see them. He'd started to look more closely at my art collection, questioning its origins. The cuneiform seals, the tablets, winged animals, the tableaux, the gods and the goddesses, all mixed in with modern scenarios. He's an intelligent man, and he knew what my description of Babylonian really meant. I saw the slight narrowing of his eyes and the pursing of his lips. But he kept quiet.

Then, in July, Sanaa emailed me. It was a bolt from the blue and I opened the email on my studio computer with trepidation. We'd agreed only to email in emergencies and she only had a hotmail address that was registered anonymously. I held my hand on my ever-growing stomach and wished for her to be alright.

And she was. Or, at least, she wasn't harmed. The email was emotional and I could picture her tossing her hair, her eyes flashing as she wrote it.

Dear Juliette Watson

I'm sorry to write like this and to upset you in your condition but I have bad news. My father's house has been destroyed. I am no longer in Buhriz. I am staying with my cousin in Baghdad. My sister's daughter Anna was injured in the attack and we are all here together.

This is the way of war and I am not surprised. The American allies don't care about us. Collateral damage. Anna will never walk again. She was hit in the back with shrapnel, fracturing vertebrae and trapping nerves. A seeping wound in her thigh and pelvis means she will never bear children. But the bombs come and the soldiers come and more people die. But you know all this, Juliette Watson.

Worse, our secret place has gone. The tree was destroyed and the bombs blow up the ground, making a big crater. I tried to find the papers but they were gone.

The shock cascaded through me. Poor Anna. Poor Farhana. Poor Sanaa. I gulped in breaths and tried to stay calm. Then, suddenly, I felt elated. It was gone. The secret was gone. Destroyed. No one had ever come for it. No one had followed up and Mark was obviously talking bullshit. And even if they did, I truly no longer knew where they were.

But do not worry. As I said, I have memorised it. I know all the words, I recite them day and night to keep it safe. We will stay here now until it is safe to go back to the village. Only then will I be able to resume our letters. In an emergency call my mobile, or I will call yours. For the time being I am in great danger.

I closed the email and deleted it. I felt myself spiralling into panic but just about holding myself on the edge. My worst fears about the conflict, those that kept me awake at night, were now true. Sanaa was in danger. It was like a replay of 1991 but this time I couldn't run and hide. I had to stay here and produce a child. I had to stay calm. I had to convince Sandy that everything was fine. I walked back to the apartment, still numb with shock and full to the brim with the novelty of this new information.

Once back inside my life with Sandy, I pushed it to the back of my mind and refused to watch anything related to the war on the TV, claiming it upset me. It was true. It disturbed me so much, made me feel so helpless, that I was afraid it would harm our child. Our child who was winning the competition for my attention. From moment to moment, I was glad. Glad of the distraction and glad of Sandy. He was the absolute perfect, doting father-to-be.

Until the beginning of August.

It was a normal Wednesday afternoon. I'd been to my antenatal appointment and my due date was 30 September. All was well and, to celebrate, I brought home a bag of fruit.

Sandy took it from me at the lift. "You shouldn't be carrying that!"

He was full of smiles. Even though I was insanely worried about the situation in Iraq, which seemed to have no end in sight, and some kind of catastrophe being unleashed on mankind, I was beginning to understand why women with children were cocooned. Why they formed self-sufficient units, buffered against the world. Sanaa's letters had taken a political and sometimes desperate turn, with vivid descriptions of the battle and how indiscriminate it was. How soldiers came and took what they wanted; some of them were good men but some of them looked behind them as they closed the door and entered houses full of women, helping themselves. How men were taken away and tortured and returned unable to speak or walk. How scared she was for her family.

Each angry paragraph ended with, "Of course, you know exactly what I mean." I was worried, more than worried, but my immediate quest was self-preservation. I needed to be OK for this baby. Sandy's and my baby. I replied with baby news and hopes that the conflict would end soon but I was less worried than I had anticipated. Until the doorbell rang that day.

We wondered who it was, because no one really visited from outside. Most of our daytime callers lived in the building and would simply knock. Sandy answered. He went to the buzzer plate and I watched as his handsome face turned into a perplexed frown.

He stood in front of me, hands on hips. "CIA. Want to see you. I told them to come up."

I knew immediately: this was it. They'd come for me.

If there had been time, Sandy would have asked me what it was about, but they were already at the front door. He opened it slowly and two tall men in grey suits, who I immediately thought looked more like accountants than government investigators, came in.

"So what's this about?" asked Sandy. "As you can see, my wife is pregnant. Our first child."

They introduced themselves as Jack Turner and Sam Black. Jack did all the talking. Sam looked around the room.

"We'll get right to the point, Mrs Sanderson. We're investigating an incident in 1991 which involved your husband."

"Ex-husband." I grabbed Sandy's hand. Maybe a little too tightly.

"Yes. Ex-husband. Mark Watson. He was working on Akrotiri base in Cyprus when some information went missing. Around that time you and he travelled to Iraq. Your husband returned without you. You returned six days later."

I could see he had a file. My heart was beating fast. I could feel the delaying questions rise up in me, clearing a space to think. I'd tried so hard not to lie for so long. I didn't want my baby to hear the lies. But they came anyway.

"Iraq? Yes. I know. I was there."

"So you know about the missing information?"

Shit.

"Missing information? No. No, I didn't. How is that connected?"

"That's what we're here to find out. We need to ask you if your husband ever passed any information on to you? Or asked you to conceal any such information?"

"Passed me information? Um. No. Not at all."

"OK. So we've gone over the time you were away. In Iraq. You've been interviewed many times about this, Mrs Sanderson. You say that you were separated from your husband after travelling there on a visa run and you wandered for days before finding a road. We won't go over all that again but we'd like to know if you met or spoke to anyone in that time?"

I could feel the sweat running down my back. "Met anyone? No. Not until I was picked up by the aid workers."

"So you didn't speak to a single person?"

I swallowed hard. This would be the ideal time to tell them. Tell them everything. But I still felt I had to protect Sanaa. I don't know if it was my pregnancy hormones kicking in, or just my natural instinct but I had to protect her. She was almost family.

"Speak to anyone? No."

Jack sighed. I could see Sam out of the corner of my eye, fingering my precious pots and paintings. Picking up the picture of me and Sanaa and her sisters in London.

"So how do you know Sanaa Yazid?"

This was it. The moment I had been dreading for more than a decade. Sandy's expression changed from concern to suspicion in a second. I knew I had to hold it together.

"Sanaa? I met her in Cyprus. She's remained a good friend ever since. We share a love of Middle Eastern art."

I monitored myself. Yes, I sounded convincing. I felt my hand sweep the room, pointing at the artefacts.

"And you met Dr Yazid in London recently? What was the purpose of that visit?"

"Purpose of the visit? Leisure. Dr Yazid has an exhibition in London and I attended the launch."

It was more than Sandy could take. "Who is this Yazid woman? You said you were with friends? Who is she?"

I turned to him, my breathing shallow and my pulse racing. "Who is she? She is a friend. A long-time friend, Sandy. You know who she is. Her picture's over there."

He was red in the face, more angry than I'd ever seen him. "I didn't know she was from there. From *there*. I thought she was some Greek woman you knew." He turned to Jack now. "So what's your interest in her?"

Jack lowered his eyes. "Dr Yazid is known to us. She's outspoken on her anti-US stance. And with her having an international platform and having lived in New York…"

Shit. She had. I'd forgotten about that. She'd studied in New York.

Sandy exploded. "She's a fucking terrorist. How could you, Julie?" He pointed at me. Then pointed towards Ground Zero. "Is she involved in this?"

Jack was shaking his head. "There's no evidence that Dr Yazid is a threat. None whatsoever. We're just investigating the missing information. It's integral to national security that we find out what happened to it. Mr Watson is now deceased so we need to know everything, Mrs Sanderson."

"Know everything? Well, I have some letters from Dr Yazid. You can have those if you like."

"Do you have her address?"

"Address? Yes. On the letters."

"And you're sure that Mr Watson didn't pass any information to you or ask you to deliver anything? Anything at all?"

I got up and pulled the letters from the writing desk. Just the long letters about art. Everything else was hidden behind a ceiling tile in the studio downtown. I handed them to Jack.

"Deliver anything? No. Nothing. I was comprehensively questioned at the time."

They began to leave. Jack handed a card to me. "If you remember anything please get in touch."

Sandy fumed in the corner. "What about that woman? The Iraqi?" He spat out the words like venom.

Sam spoke now. "Nothing to worry about. We just needed to check things out. We'll carry out further investigations. Thank you both. Thank you for your co-operation."

They left but everything had changed now. Doting Sandy, suddenly armed with new knowledge, was hostile and spiky. "Why didn't you tell me you were friends with an *Iraqi*?"

He was incandescent with rage. I'd never seen him like this before. I froze but not with fear. I realized in that moment that I had never been scared since I sat in that tiny hut with Sanaa in Iraq. Anxious, yes, but not scared. It was different. One of Sandy's favourite saying was "don't sweat the small stuff" – and that's the difference. Why be afraid of what's in front of you when you know that out there something much, much worse could happen? After years of deliberating, I knew it was true.

Another popular theory is "don't worry, it might never happen". But it had happened to me. Twice. So I was the expert on terror.

Just then, as Sandy stared at me, a strange thought struck me and I half smiled.

He moved closer. "Oh. Think it's funny, do you? Huddling up with people hell bent on destroying our country?"

No. Not funny. I was smiling at the irony of what I had just realised. Both times I had been caught up in terror it had been a similar feeling but provoked by a different source. The first time by America, the very country I lived in now, and the second time by the Middle Eastern enemy. Was that why I couldn't take sides? Why I couldn't stand in bars, waving the American flag, or discuss Sanaa's hatred of America with her? Or was it because, as Sanaa had said, I was on my own side, protecting me.

I stood up and faced Sandy. "Destroying our country? Don't patronise me, Sandy. I'm not stupid. Sanaa is a friend and that's all. She's a nice person, an artist, and, like me and you, entitled to her views. Not that she's ever done anything about them. Like you haven't. So I'll be friends with whom I like, thank you very much."

He sat down, head in hands. "You've brought the CIA to our door."

"CIA?" I couldn't seem to stop using those delaying tactics, repeating phrases as questions, and that panicked me more and more. "No I haven't. Mark Watson has. You knew all about this. And I'm glad they came, because if you are right about Sanaa, and she is part of some terrorist plot, I'll never speak to her again. I'm glad they are investigating. I hope that they find her and conduct a full investigation." Not that they would. Because the address I gave them was the one for her father's house, the place that had been bombed to oblivion. "Because then we'll find out the truth."

I hadn't realised that I was shouting. The room was suddenly silent. I could hear Sandy breathing heavily. I stood there for a long minute while he considered what I had said.

Finally, he got to his feet. "You do what you like. But I don't want that fucking murderer anywhere near my child. Do you hear?"

Chapter 46

Sandy became the proponent of everything pro-US war and anti-Iraq. He quietly sponsored the names of victims of 9/11 on the side of bombs that would decimate Iraqi villages. He attended the funerals of soldiers killed in battle. In a matter of days he had signed up for everything pro-war he could find and this seemed to allow him to come to terms with my friendship with Sanaa.

He didn't mention her at all. He barely spoke to me and slept in a spare room, allegedly to give me more space but, in reality, I knew, because he couldn't bear to be near me. He spent a lot of time in the nursery and I watched him through the crack of the door, spinning, spinning the nursery mobile hanging above the crib.

Just one week after the CIA had called he sat down beside me and held my hand. "So, did Mark force you to carry that information for him? Is that what this is about? Does that woman have something on you?"

I shook my head. I didn't want to lie to him but how could I tell him the truth? He already hated Sanaa. How would he feel if I told him about Saif Abed and Shahid? About my giving the papers to her and her hiding them? About my lies for all this time?

"Did Mark force me? No. No, he didn't. But it wouldn't surprise me if he had done it. He wasn't a nice person, Sandy."

His eyes betrayed his love for me, still intact. "Did he hurt you?"

I could see where this was going. He was trying to lay the blame elsewhere.

"Hurt me? He bruised my arm." I rubbed my left arm, chubby now with my pregnancy. It was true. He had bruised me. But I was making it sound a lot worse than it had been.

He kept hold of my hand. "Look, Julie. I won't lie. This has hurt me. I can't come to terms with it. I thought everything was good for us, perfect, with the baby and all. But this, I just…"

I squeezed his hand tight. "Can't come to terms with what? Nothing's changed. Nothing. I haven't done anything wrong. All these things existed before those CIA guys turned up. They just need to do their job. We'll be fine."

I tried to look into his eyes. The gesture that had bound us for so long that I had taken it for granted. But he avoided my gaze.

"I don't know, Julie. I don't know. Something's changed."

He broke free and left. He didn't come home that night. He called me the next day and muttered something about drinking with Ted Phillips and that he was taking a trip west but would only be an hour away. The unspoken "in case the baby comes" hung between us.

If only he had stayed; two days later, just six weeks before my due date, I felt my first labour pain. I waited and waited, and then I phoned my midwife.

She told me to write down every time I had a pain on a piece of paper, along with the time. When she arrived at the apartment two hours later I greeted her with a blank piece of paper and doubled up in pain.

"Where's your husband? You need to go to the hospital."

I called Sandy. He didn't answer his mobile and I left a voicemail. I called his office and they promised to forward a message. I optimistically picked up the bag we had prepared so early for the birth, and watched the midwife's sad gaze as I carried it to her car. She drove in silence and I kept my hand on the top of my stomach ready to report that the pains had stopped, that we should turn back.

But the pain was ceaseless. I was rushed to the ultrasound scan room where a doctor was waiting. He asked me if I wanted to wait for my husband for the results. I checked my phone but Sandy hadn't called.

"No. I can face it myself."

I could because I already knew, somehow. The baby seemed fine. But it was very small, which was confusing because my stomach was so big. It wriggled and squirmed like on the other ultrasound, and I saw the shadow of its face on the screen. A tiny hand, waving at me from inside me.

The staff looked at each other, uncertain how to proceed.

"He's out of town. I've left a message. I'm sure he will be here as soon as possible."

Their expressions shifted from uncertainty to pity. They probably assumed that I had been left alone. A single parent with just a token father. But I wasn't, was I? I struggled to make sense of it. A feeling of being lucky enough to be granted a child came over me, a sense that everything that had gone before led up to this event. I needed to get on with it. I didn't know what would happen next. Sure, I knew about women who had premature babies but everything was up in the air. How small was small? How worried were the doctors?

"What happens now?"

The doctor stepped forward. "We'll need to carry on with your labour, I'm afraid. Your waters have broken. There's no turning back now. But I need to warn you, Mrs Sanderson, the baby is very small. We'll move you to the labour ward."

They took me in a wheelchair. I was wheeled through a corridor where people were giving birth on each side. Giving birth to live, full-term babies. There was crying and women screaming. I'd prepared myself fully for this but now I'd been cheated of it. I let my hands drift to the sides of the wheelchair, afraid to touch my swollen stomach.

Eventually they took me into a dark room and left me there.

I got out of bed and reached for my mobile phone. Still no calls. I needed to speak to someone. Anyone. I dialled Sandy's number again but he still didn't answer. I left no message this time, because I didn't know what to say. He'd listen to the first message and understand.

The pain became worse very quickly and before long they gave me gas and air. I was too far gone to have pethidine and, in any case, they were worried about what effect any drugs would have on the tiny mite inside me. Two midwives delivered my tiny son, and laid him in an incubator. He was just a little bit bigger than my hand as I touched him through the slots that caught your arms as you reached through.

They worked fast and within minutes he was wired up to a monitor and a respirator. I held his tiny hand as he squirmed a little. He didn't open his eyes or even wince as they hooked him up to a saline drip but he gripped my finger hard. Then they left us alone.

I stared hard at his chest, making sure that every breath in was followed by a breath out. I was completely exhausted but I stared at the heart monitor, its regular beep, beep, beep reassurance that life was still here. My son was alive.

I talked to him, told him about me and about Sandy and about his room and what our lives would be. I hardly noticed Sandy come into the room, and hardly felt his arms around me and his tears dripping onto my face as he kissed my forehead.

"I'm sorry, Julie. I'm sorry. I've been a fool. I never thought…"

I turned to him and smiled. "He's here. Our son. He's here."

But I could see it reflected in his face. He tried to be joyous, tried to celebrate, but he was shadowed by deep concern. As was I. Our son. So small. So perfect.

"How much did he weigh?" He almost mouthed it, as if he was afraid to ask.

"Two pounds one ounce."

"I've heard of that before and… and…"

"They survived."

"Yes."

But we both knew that it was in the balance. We both knew.

Chapter 47

When I woke up, at one minute to four the following morning, I instinctively ran to the special care baby unit. The nurses at the entry station ushered me through and I found him pale and listless, his tiny belly artificially inflated by the respirator but his veins blue and his skin so very white. He was different from last night. Even smaller, if that was possible.

Sandy had gone home to have a shower and get some things, so I sat for a while. I touched him and talked to him. I told him about everything that had happened to me, almost. That I loved him and that he would always be a part of my heart. About my family. That his father was a good man. The best. I knew he could hear me and I'd almost expected it. As I finished speaking the heart monitor alarm sounded. I hammered on the buzzer and the crash team rushed in and surrounded him, giants working on a tiny scrap of flesh.

He was gone.

I was allowed to hold him then. I held him tight and studied his perfect face. So peaceful. I held him against my heart, willing it to share its beat, correct this gross mistake. I held his hand but now he didn't grip my finger back. Eventually I gave him over to Sandy, who had arrived moments too late. He held him and cried and cried, then held me as well and sobbed his apologies into my hair as I stared in disbelief at our dead son. Dead. I hadn't thought of it so finally until that moment. I let out a little gasp.

They took him away. I watched as they placed him in a crib that was far too big for him and wheeled him down the corridor forever. Sandy and I were escorted back to my room, where we talked for hours. We planned another baby. We planned a tribute for our son. We even talked about us, how we were strong and nothing could separate us. But both of us knew that we were on the brink of the end, that if our son hadn't arrived early, if he had thrived, if this disaster hadn't arisen to overshadow our differences, chances are we would have parted.

In the event, Sandy thought that this was his fault, that he had been unfair to me. He left at 10am to let his parents know what had happened. Then he would collect me later. I knew we would have to deal with the nursery and the early gifts from friends. The tiny new baby clothes and my deflated stomach. I sat on the bed and thought how it wasn't fair. How even though I hadn't wanted a baby, I loved my son like nothing else. Had the universe sensed it? Did the world make a mistake and get it wrong? Never see my regret and loss of freedom replaced by becoming a mother?

I phoned my mother. It would be late in Manchester. When she didn't answer, I imagined her and Dad sound asleep, safe from this for the time being.

So I rang Sanaa. I hesitated at first, in case the CIA had bugged my phone. But this was an emergency.

She answered on one ring. "Dr Sanaa Yazid. Who is speaking?"

"It's me Sanaa. Juliette." I heard the silent counting of weeks and months as she worked out if this was good or bad news. "Don't say where you are or who you are with. I just needed someone."

Her voice softened. "I'm here, Juliette Watson. I'm here."

"The baby came early. Very early. And small… he… he… died. He's dead, Sanaa."

I could hear my own voice, hysterical, but it felt detached from me somehow. As if someone else was talking too loud and fast, and I was just numb, inside and out.

She paused. "How? How did this happen?"

"I don't know. I don't know. My labour started this morning."

"Oh, Juliette. I'm so sorry. But listen. It's not the end. Your son will be in Jannah with my son, Shahid. Shahid will care for him until we arrive. All is not lost."

I didn't know so much about heaven, or hell. I'd never really considered it before. But Sanaa's words comforted me a little. I stared out of the window. A murmuration of starlings flew overhead and I tracked them over the horizon and back again. A couple settled on the lawn outside in the midday light, puffing up their feathers and fighting over some orange peel. All is not lost. All is not lost.

"Thank you Sanaa. Thank you. I never knew how you felt before. I never knew what made you do it."

I pictured her, mad eyed and wild, and now I knew what that was. I caught my reflection in the hospital window. I looked neat and tidy. But inside I was flailing and whirling like a dervish.

"Your boy, Juliette. He is Ibni. My son. Your son. I'll take some of your grief, Juliette, like you carried mine. I never forget."

"Ibni. Yes. Yes."

The line went dead and a nurse entered.

"What did you call him?" She stood in the doorway with a tag and a pen, waiting to write down his name.

Sandy and I had talked about names. "Samuel   Charles   Ibni Sanderson."

She paused after Charles. "Ibni?"

"Yes. My son. My son. Ibni."

I saw her eyebrows raise and she shrugged slightly.

We never saw him again. Somehow I'd expected there to be a viewing or identification. Expected or hoped, because I missed him, or the idea of him. There was a short service at the hospital and my parents flew over for it, and then flew back immediately. It was all too sad.

Sandy and I – well, we just slipped back into the constant groove of life, caring for each other like the good friends we were. We scattered Ibni's ashes in the Hudson River. As all that was left of my tiny son floated away on the wind, dropped into the fast-flowing water, rested for a second, then dissolved, I fully understood why Sanaa hadn't wanted to leave Shahid. I would never leave New York now.

We tried for another child – we even tried IVF – but it never happened. Sandy never mentioned Ibni, or the fact that I referred to him by that name. He called him Sam, if anyone asked. We never talked about Sanaa again, not even when another trinket arrived – a tiny amulet of a woman with a very serious face and arms outstretched to heaven. It came with an even smaller figure of a baby, made from terracotta-coloured clay with a thin leather cord threaded through a loop, and a photograph of Sanaa wearing an identical white figure on a cord around her neck. The note she sent read: *We look after our own* in ancient Babylonian.

I often pictured my baby with her son, friends, like we were. She wrote seldom. When she did, it was to outline the troubles and tell me how Anna was faring. How, as the days passed, she grew more bitter. How she had been on a trip to carry more art out of Iraq. She told me that the family had returned to the village and was rebuilding her father's house but she had stayed in Baghdad.

Ibni's fate was another layer on my outer shell, and when the CIA returned and asked me the same questions, I gave them the same answers. Sandy didn't back me up; he merely listened. Three times they came in three years. Each time the questioning became more desperate and each time I became more frightened that whatever was in those papers was posing a real danger. Each time I came close to telling all, telling them that Sanaa had memorised them and that she was at her cousin's house in Baghdad. But I couldn't do it to her. I just couldn't. I couldn't banish the image that constantly ran through my head, of our sons together in a better place, protecting each other. The world might be falling apart but our two little boys were united in love and paid no heed. Giving up Sanaa would be giving up the little bit of sanity I held onto.

Then there was a terror attack in London. On 7 July 2005 – the same day that a small, handmade pot arrived from Sanaa, with a map scratched into the sandstone – I was settling down to dinner when the news flashed onto the TV screen: London had been bombed. My own territorial heart sunk. Now I knew what it was like to hurt over my home, to become defensive over something I had no control over. Fifty-two people died and hundreds were injured.

As events developed and the images lit up my TV screen, I walked through the Victorian tube stations in my mind and reeled, reeling with shock at the thought of a blown-up carriage and what that meant. I walked up Tavistock Square in my imagination and hurt for a whole nation – my nation, this time. It fuelled my confusion and heightened my sense of how unfair war was – because I clearly saw this as a war, albeit with different goalposts for the opposing sides. It was driving me mad.

I sat quietly through discussions among Sandy's friends, listening to them speculating over who had committed this atrocity and how they should be caught. None of them had set foot in Iraq. Many had never been outside America. I knew I had the advantage, if you could call it that, of not only experiencing atrocities but having Sanaa's accounts. Sandwiched in the middle of all the territorial posturing and opposing views was the psychopathy of terrorism, the desire to kill and maim to make a point.

My city. My London. In some way all previous events had been impersonal to me, even when I was caught in the middle of them. Throughout my life England had been my safe haven, a childhood innocence that I could return to, to assess the damage, lick my wounds. Now that was sullied and it made me a million times more paranoid.

By the end of 2006 I had become obsessed with news reports from Baghdad, and terrified that something terrible would happen, that the 'genetic defect' Mark had alluded to had been released and that millions were suffering because of it. I scoured the news for reports of symptoms of chemical warfare or anything that might vaguely suggest that there was a problem.

I found none. But I did find this:

BAQUBAH, 16 January 2007 (IRIN) - Hundreds of people have been trying to flee the eastern Iraqi province of Diyala, close to the Iraqi-Iranian border, following a recent offensive by US and Iraqi troops in the area. Although the offensive has ended, scores of families in rural villages were said to be hiding in their houses for fear that air strikes might start again.

"During the past week, US forces have been attacking rural areas near Baqubah trying to flush out insurgents. Their air strikes have killed about 14 civilians and led to the capture of dozens of insurgents. But these attacks have caused many people to suffer because of lack of assistance and difficulties in getting to health centres," said Salah Ahmed, media officer for Diyala provincial council.

The most affected areas are villages east of Baqubah, a city some 40km west of the Iraqi-Iranian border. Very few families managed to leave the area before the attacks started on 5 January. The closures of entry and exit points in the vicinity forced hundreds of families to stay inside their homes.

"We were informed [by locals and volunteers] that approximately 110 families were without water and food supplies because there was no prior

announcement about the offensive and those families were either unprepared or could not leave the area," Ahmed said.

"Theoretically, the offensive has ended but many areas near the villages are still occupied by US and Iraqi troops who are preventing people from leaving their homes. Officials there have told us that [some] houses have been destroyed with people in them. Most of these were in rural areas."

I knew that this was where Sanaa was. She'd sent me a terrain map of her village when she was trying to explain the irrigation that she and her father were funding. I knew where Buhriz was. Right in the centre of the offensive. And when no more letters arrived, I feared that Sanaa was somehow caught up in it.

Chapter 48

Months, then a year went by and I heard nothing from Sanaa. I checked with the exhibitions in London; they confirmed that they had received no additional pieces or correspondence for over a year. I even checked with my parents to make sure the post hadn't arrived there and not been forwarded.

But there was nothing. Her mobile went straight to voicemail. I rang Baghdad University but no one had seen her; they assumed that, because of the ongoing military situation, she was lying low in her village, like so many others. No one wanted to be near the areas of conflict and many people were simply too scared to leave their families. I emailed her and wrote letters but I never got a response.

My paranoia had reached new levels. I checked news reports every day for any small snippet of information about Buhriz or reports of genetic engineering mishaps. When Sandy was at work I watched Al Jazeera continuously, adding a basic knowledge of Arabic to the ancient Mesopotamian and Babylonian languages that Sanaa had helped me to read on the artefacts she sent me. I was beginning to understand the pain Sanaa had gone through, the images she had fashioned reflecting her innermost torture at the events that had unfolded around the world.

Worse still, I didn't speak to anyone. I closed myself in, speaking only to Sandy when he was present, on a kind of autopilot. It was as if speaking about anything that had happened in the past destabilised my fragile core and sent me reeling into somewhere dark. So I just didn't speak. I knew that everyone took it for granted that I was like this "because of the baby". And I played on that. Because I just couldn't talk about the baby or anything else. I just couldn't.

I began to map-catalogue Sanaa's art and to describe it, which grew into a story in itself with a timeline not unlike my own story. But Sanaa's images were sometimes too difficult for me to read, too abstract. Or, as I now realise, too glaringly obvious and near to the truth. I imagined them to be the internal workings of her own mind, which made me all the more interested. I was a willing student to whatever she wanted me to know, accepting her cathartic offerings willingly.

Then one day in early, early in 2011, just over four years since I had found the report about Sanaa's village, there was a knock on the door. I'd spent practically the whole four years alone, except for when Sandy returned home and I slipped back into wife mode. So I stood behind the door and listened. There was another knock. I knew that it must be someone from inside the building. A neighbour.

I opened it a fraction. It was a small woman, around thirty-five years old, holding a plant. She smiled through the narrow gap.

"Hi. I'm Louise. Louise Turvey. I've moved in upstairs. I just wanted to meet my neighbours."

She pushed the plant forward. I had no choice. I had to interrupt my daily routine and ask her in.

"Oh. I see. Please come in. Could I get you a drink?"

She smiled wider. "Ah. You're English? What a delightful accent. I'd love a coffee, please."

She was like a breath of fresh air wafting through the apartment and into my life. We had coffee and talked about how she had moved here from Florida to work as a graphic designer. She worked at home and was keen to meet other people in the block to share lunch and coffee with. I was unsure at first but when she looked at the TV set, muted now, she recognised the channel and commented immediately.

"Ah. Like to see both sides, do you? You know, so many Americans are blinkered. No idea what is going on over there. Of course, after what happened here…"

I talked quickly for over an hour, outpouring everything that happened to me on 9/11 and the time afterwards. She watched me silently, blinking and sipping her coffee. I realised that this was the first time I had spoken about it in full to anyone. It was such a relief.

When I had finished, she placed her cup on a coaster. "You know we should join together and do something. Like maybe a memorial book or article? Something we can work on together? I just know we're going to get on."

Her cheeriness and positivity was irrepressible and, I guessed, normal. Who was I to know normal, with the turmoil going on inside my brain, the world I had imagined for myself where Sanaa was hurt and couldn't contact me or worse? I had recurring dreams about her, Shahid and Ibni sitting peacefully in a field, Sanaa with her hair loose and her legs bare…

I even wondered if Sandy had employed Louise to befriend me, to make me give Sanaa up and occupy my days better.

But despite all this, I knew that Louise was going to be part of my life. She came down every day to have coffee at what she referred to as her break time – which often turned into hours. She invited me to her flat and I spent evenings looking at her work and admiring her new furniture. I even started to go down to the studio again and wrote some articles. Sometimes I'd bump into Louise on the way back to the ferry, and she'd tell me that she had been visiting an agency for work or seeing a friend for coffee.

I bought it for nearly a year. I never questioned her constant presence in my life. Sandy was delighted with my new American friend. He openly praised her and fixed her up on dates with his colleagues. Louise and I had an open dialogue on the war in Iraq, especially as it came to an end and American troops were scheduled to leave. My concern over Sanaa was pushed deeper inside, and my new friendship meant I now had only limited time to search for her remotely.

Mid-June Louise invited me to a benefit concert for the children of soldiers who died in Iraq during the war. I figured that I could make some contacts with people who knew what was really going on there and perhaps raise the question of what had happened in Buhriz. I dressed up for the occasion and had my hair trimmed and highlighted. Sandy had bought me a pair of expensive Jimmy Choos, and hugged me tightly as I left home that Saturday lunchtime.

Louise suggested a brisk walk through Central Park, followed by afternoon tea before the benefit started. It was to be held at the Ritz-Carlton on Central Park South and I found myself excitedly hurrying through the park, linking arms with Louise and laughing, Jimmy Choos in hand and flat pumps on feet. She threw back her head, her short blonde bob bouncing in the breeze. We both wore smart suits and she was about the same build as me, small and slender.

"All the rooms have telescopes!" She sounded delighted at this small detail.

I'd never stayed at the Ritz-Carlton but I knew many people that had. "Oh. Have you stayed there?"

She laughed loudly. "Yes. Before my apartment was ready. I visited all the museums. I never saw any of your friend's work there, though."

I'd told Louise about Sanaa's exhibitions in London when she had examined the pieces in my home so carefully, and with full appreciation. I told her the standard scripted version of how Sanaa and I met, which I was coming to believe.

"Saw her work there? No. I don't think she would like her work to be exhibited here. She's quite anti-American. And who can blame her?"

Louise mimicked me. "Yeah. Who can blame her? Heard from her yet?"

"Heard from her? No. I guess she's rebuilding her life after it was bombed to pieces." I heard the bitterness in my own voice, contrasted against Louise's sunny disposition. I needed to lighten the mood. "I'm sure she'll be in touch when she's ready. Anyway, you never told me how your date with Steve went."

She laughed again. "Yeah. Well. What can I say? I'm not the marrying kind. What with my mom and her three husbands and you with first Mark then Sandy."

I almost stopped dead. I'd never mentioned Mark to her. I was absolutely sure of it. I'd never once talked about him. It took every ounce of my nerve to keep it together.

I gave a fake laugh. "Hmm. Not ideal. Not ideal at all but I'm happy now."

She turned to me and took my hands in hers. We were outside the hotel now, its shadow cooling the winter sunshine. "It must have been very hard on you. Alone for all that time on your own in a strange country."

I relaxed a little. It was public knowledge that I was *that* woman. The poor army wife who was separated from her husband on a visa run.

Louise went on: "Worried out of your mind. Have you ever thought about reconstructing your journey, you know, through art? Writing? A map, perhaps."

Too obvious. I barely knew what was real anymore but this was just too transparent. But I played the game because if this was what I thought it was, I was in danger.

"A map? That's a great idea. Why don't we do it together? You know, I've always thought about writing a book about it." I stared at her. Challenging her to walk away, leave it alone.

But she didn't. "Fabulous. I can draw the map for you! You just need to tell me the route and what you did along the way."

"What I did? How do you mean, what I did?"

"Well, who you met and where you went."

Once again, I trotted out the scripted story I'd told every single person who had ever asked me. "Where I went? Well, you've clearly read the articles on this and it was mainly walking. Trying to find the road. I was sick for a couple of days but I didn't really meet anyone."

She didn't miss a beat. "Articles? No, you told me, silly. Don't you remember, about six months ago? When we talked about your friend and the Babylonian art. You told me then. You told me what happened." She linked my arm again. "Come on. Those scones won't butter themselves. And we need to change our shoes!"

Chapter 49

I sipped my champagne at the benefit and ate dinner, laughing and nodding, but inside I was petrified. Louise wasn't who she said she was. I knew for sure that I had definitely never mentioned Mark. Of course, she could have looked it all up. It was widely reported. But her insistence that I had told her about my time in Iraq troubled me more. I absolutely, definitely hadn't. And her searching questions smacked of a set-up. She was a better liar than me but I still hugged her when we parted on my landing.

"Thanks, Louise. I had a wonderful time."

Sandy had joined us on the landing and he put his arm around me.

"I really can't wait to get started on our little project. You give me a knock first thing in the morning," she said, touching my arm. I almost flinched.

"Project? Yes. I'm excited too. We can start in the morning. You could make some notes to help you remember?"

She headed for the door to the stairway. One more flight up to her flat, which was directly above ours.

I shuddered and Sandy hugged me closer. "You cold, darling? And what's this about a project?"

"Cold? Oh, no, I'm not cold. Just felt like someone walked over my grave. And, well. Yeah. Louise has this idea about us writing something about when I was stuck in Iraq, with a map. She thinks it would be good to do it together."

Sandy winced. "Really? Do you want to go over all that again?" He looked genuinely concerned, which kind of reassured me that this was nothing to do with him.

"Nothing to go over. And I really don't know how I'll draw a map of what I don't know. I was genuinely lost."

At least that wasn't a lie. He closed the door behind us and hurried into my office.

The apartment was on one floor that covered one side of the building. There were two bedrooms, a bathroom, a lounge, a dining room, a large kitchen, and a third small bedroom that I had made into my home office when I first moved in. I looked along the ceiling to see if there were any obvious alterations, any drilled holes for wires or microphones, but I really had no idea what I was looking for. Then I did the same in all the other rooms, while Sandy talked on the phone to his mother. I found nothing. Nothing that I could recognise, anyway.

We went to bed early but I hardly slept. I kept going over and over everything I had told Louise. It was just everyday talk, even about Sanaa. It just brushed the surface. But now I thought about it, she had delved deeper in some areas. She had looked at my passport photograph and then flicked through my passport, pointing out that I had no visits abroad, and then glancing at the picture of me and Sanaa and her sisters in London.

I wasn't about to tell her that I had two passports, one in my current married name and one in my first married name. It had been a mistake when I applied for a new passport in the name of Sanderson. They had sent it to my New York address as requested but sent the old one back to my mother's house, which she sent on to me. I'd simply used the old one when I'd travelled to London. That way the authorities had no way of linking me and Sanaa to my New York address.

Then there was the time when Louise questioned me closely about Cyprus. Asked me where the airports were and about my visa runs. But more closely about what happened after I landed in Iraq. When Mark and I parted ways, as she put it. I remembered thinking that it was more like an interrogation than a cosy chat. But never, at any point, did I mention Sanaa in that context, and I certainly never mentioned anything about what happened between us.

I was trapped. I had nowhere to run. Louise was intent on getting information out of me and all I could do was play along with her.

The next day we met up and I spent time drawing a map of Diayla province and a fake trail of where I went, starting at Baghdad airport. She asked all the right questions and I gave all the right answers.

Then, early in 2012, I got my annual CIA visit. I buzzed them up and as I opened the door I saw Louise in the stairwell beyond my apartment. Our eyes met and she covered by motioning, "Who are they? Do you need me?"

I shook my head and showed them in. They also asked the usual questions, more panicked than usual, and I was so close to telling them. Sandy went into his study and I was glad. It made me tense when he sat in silence.

When the routine questions had been posed, the taller of the two sat down on the coffee table directly in front of me.

"Mrs Sanderson. We need to ask you some questions about Sanaa Yazid." He handed me some photographs of her. Some of them were from our London visit and some were clearly of New York. She looked younger in the New York pictures, and older in some later pictures, her eyes dark and heavy. "Is this Sanaa Yazid?"

I nodded. I assumed they were just going to go over the same old questions. But the agent turned the pictures over and placed them on the table. There were dates on the back of them.

"So, Dr Yazid visited New York in late August, early September 2001. And then, as you know, she visited London with you in November 2001."

I shook my head. I felt confused and hurt. "New York? No. She hasn't been to New York. She would have visited me. No. Not possible."

He continued. "So, she visited New York again in 2003, and then London again in June 2005."

"2003? 2005? Not possible. If she had been in New York in 2003 she would have come to see me. We're friends and it was a bad time for me. She would have come. Definitely."

He ignored me. His colleague, short and stocky, handled the pictures of me and Sanaa and snapped them on his mobile phone. The tall guy handed me copies of Sanaa's entry papers. "So,   why would she be in New York and London? If it wasn't to see friends?"

"If not to see friends? Art. She was probably bringing her pieces to the museum or a collector."

"But Dr Yazid has no pieces in New York."

"No pieces? Maybe she has another friend here. Who knows?"

But I knew. I knew she hated America and would never come here without telling me unless... unless there was a reason. I looked at the dates and the reason began to take shape. Her angry letters. Her bitterness.

No. Sanaa would never be a part of something so evil.

The agent stood. "OK, Mrs Sanderson. OK. We have a problem here. We need your help. Did Sanaa Yazid ever discuss terrorism with you? Did she even hint at it?"

"Terrorism? No. Sanaa would never hurt anyone. Never. She's a good person." Yet, through the mist of my anger I saw Saif Abed's face, smiling from his ID. Sanaa's mad eyes as she held his gun. "We talk about art. Just art. We're friends."

He stared at me for a full minute. "Then why didn't she visit you when she was in New York? Mrs Sanderson, did Sanaa Yazid ever mention her husband, Riyadh Pachachi?"

I swallowed hard. Riyadh. I quickly considered that, as my friend, of course she would have mentioned her husband. "Yes of course. She told me that she hadn't seen him since the early nineties. She thought he was dead."

They looked at each other. "He isn't dead, Mrs Sanderson. He's a veteran in terrorism. Fled to Afghanistan and then returned as a Jaish al-Mujahideen fighter in 2004." He placed a photograph in front of me on the table. "This is a picture of Pachachi and Sanaa Yazid taken in Baghdad in 2006."

I felt numb. She'd lied about Riyadh. Well, not lied. Omitted to mention. Like I did about my meeting with Mark. I was confused. I knew what they were suggesting and I couldn't deny that it was strange that she wouldn't visit me while she was here. And that she had never, ever mentioned Riyadh's reappearance.

Then again, I recalled that she had been surprised, even shocked to find I was living in New York. And shocked when I told her about my proximity to 9/11...

Could they really think that she was involved in terrorism? Could I? And if she was, how come she had kept my secret and never disclosed the documents?

No. They'd got it wrong.

They left and I added their suggestions to the bubbling mass of anxiety that simmered just below my conscious mind. I thought about calling them back, telling them what I knew. In fact, I probably would have if I hadn't believed that Louise was upstairs listening. And what would I tell them now? That the information they wanted had been memorised by a woman whose location was hazy at best, a woman who they believed was a terrorist?

In any case, I had something urgent to deal with: Louise. When she came down to the apartment later she fouled again. Almost immediately.

"Who were those men?" She looked innocent enough, with her notebook and her bright eyes.

"CIA. Wanted to ask me some questions." I'd prepared well this time, not leaving anything to chance. I'd mentioned Mark to them. I'd mused on whether, in my young, dazed, confused, state, I'd really understood what happened. I'd said, just to whet her appetite and scare the shit out of Mark, who, by now, I was sure she was working for, that I kind of remembered a checkpoint and a crater and the rest was a blank. Now I explained to her what I had said to them, word for word: "I expect I've buried the details underneath everything." Implying that the truth might yet come out.

She sat down on the coffee table in front of me, unconsciously mimicking the CIA agent who'd just left, and took my hands in hers. "Juliette. Have you ever heard of false memory syndrome? You should be careful what you tell those people. I'm sure that you would have mentioned the two guards before if they were there."

I just stared at her. But I wanted to scream that I hadn't mentioned any guards to them. I'd only mentioned a checkpoint. She added the guards.

She was still staring at me earnestly. "But if there is anything else you remember, even now, you can tell me. Anything about your friend. I'll be your confidante. I'll write everything down and keep witness for you."

So I worked with her every day on the project, feeding her new lies, because, after all, that's what I'm good at. It's all I've ever done. Almost a career choice.

But in the early mornings I was busy writing the truth. I wrote this account in case anything happens to me. Right from the beginning, when I felt the first stab of fear, back on that Cypriot beach in 1991, when I was still a girl.

I know I am playing a dangerous game. I am an "interesting party" now and although the CIA can't make me tell them anything, they will never go away. I want someone to know the true version of my story, the one that I can't speak out loud for fear of ruining lives and unleashing the evil that was waiting somewhere deep in the memories of that, hell bent on locating it. Eventually I'll give this story to someone who I know is on the right side. Someone who I trust and respect. Someone who will protect me and Sanaa.

But in reality, if you're reading this, you're probably one of Mark's employees, or someone from the CIA. You're probably wondering why I took some of the decisions I did, why I didn't just tell someone in authority. But the power of terror goes hand in hand with the prison of silence, and although you may judge me or think I am weak, I'm just an everyday woman with a big secret. I don't have a bargaining chip, because I've no one to bargain with. I'm on my own side, just like Sanaa.

I don't know where the information is. Not now. I don't know exactly. But as of last week, although my soul caved in on itself, I have a pretty good idea. And when I hand you this account and you have read it and borne witness to my story, then you will find out too and everyone will have said their piece. Everyone will have a voice. Even Sanaa, it turns out.

Part Five: Kate Morden

The Truth Keepers

Chapter 50

I open my mouth to ask her where we are going but she puts her finger to her lips. She gently pulls the door closed behind her and hauls her satchel over her head and across her body. We head for the stairway.

Juliette Sanderson is small and light and she skips down the stairs. I hurry behind her until she stops abruptly about halfway down and turns to me. "I'm in danger. This woman, Louise. Well, when you read this you'll understand. She'll appear outside on the street just after we do. I'll acknowledge her and you hail a taxi." She presses a document, hole-punched and held together with treasury tags, into my hands. "This is everything. Don't say anything until you've read it. I've booked a room at a hotel. We need to hurry."

I follow her down the remaining flights of stairs. We step out into the New York sunlight and walk towards Sinatra Drive. Sure enough, a woman jogs past us, followed closely by a man, and Juliette greets her.

"Louise! Out for a run?"

Louise is dressed in running gear, as is her companion. Both carry fairly large backpacks.

"Hi Juliette. Yeah. Just off training. You going anywhere nice?"

I assess Louise. Slight, fit, approaching forty. Clearly alert to me: she knows exactly who I am. She's pulling her legs behind her, one after another. Her companion doesn't speak but scans my face, committing it to memory. A pulse in his forehead tells me that he is on high alert.

"I wouldn't call it nice. My friend Pamela is visiting and I'm just going to show her Ground Zero."

They both nod. "Yeah. Vital on a visit to New York. OK. See you later."

I get a distinct feeling that we'll be seeing them sooner than later. I raise my hand to hail a taxi. Louise and her friend follow me with their gaze, assessing me in the same way that I'm assessing them. Sizing me up. A taxi stops and we get in. I watch them as they watch me, and then they start running again.

Juliette shakes her head. "They'll be right behind us in the next taxi. We need to lose them." She pushes a fifty dollar bill into the driver's hand. "Just pull up around the corner on the right. When we get out head for the bridge and drive to Ground Zero."

In a second we're on a Jersey backstreet, ducking into the back doors of a bar.

"I do this all the time to lose her. She usually finds me in the end. Ten minutes and we should be clear." She sits on a steel beer barrel and rubs her eyes. "I've booked us into a hotel so that you can read what I've written. Everything you need to know is in there." She points at my backpack, which now contains the document.

I take it out. For a moment I think, or rather hope, that it will be the code. The words I coded when I was a child. But that would have been too easy. As I read the first line I know exactly what this is: Juliette's testimony. Starting with her life in Cyprus and ending yesterday.

I continue reading in the taxi and while Juliette checks us into the Varsity Price Inn. She leads us up to the room, a fifth floor louse-infested pit with a window that barely shuts. She sits on the bed and stares at me as I finish reading and close the folder.

Fuck. It's worse than I thought.

"Why now, Juliette? Why now after all these years?"

She shrugs. Her eyes are more than sad and now I know why. "Because I'm worried something will happen to me. I found Louise in my bathroom the other day. She said Sandy popped home and let her in. I'd told her he was at his parents but he was really in Paris. So he would have had to pop back a long way."

It's a lot to take in but we don't have much time. "Juliette, I need to know where Sanaa is. I need to find that document, or find out what it says."

Her face changes. Her blonde good looks can't hide the grief. She reaches into her satchel and pulls out another package. Brown paper, tied around with string. I see the unfamiliar postmarks first and my heart beats fast.

"This arrived a week ago." She hands it to me and I untie it. There are two letters. A scanned picture marked "Ibni" and a photograph of a younger Juliette and Sanaa together outside the Ritz in London. An ID wallet of a soldier, dark and young: Saif Abed. Inside, a picture of a young woman smiling, and two small children. And a small clay figure, a bleached white baby, identical to the one Juliette is wearing around her neck, except for the colour.

Juliette has covered her face with her hands now. There are several pages covered with what looks like cuneiform writing and symbols, along with translations, photocopied lesson sheets. I read the first letter.

Dear Juliette

I'm sorry that I could not write before. A terrible thing had happened and all my family has been killed. It was five years ago now but I could not write to you because I was hiding in another village and I needed to go back to my father's house for our things.

I will tell you about Sanaa. One night soldiers came. You may think now – whose soldiers? Were they American or British or Iraqi? But we don't know. We just know they came and they shot my father and Fatima's husband in front of us. I was hiding in Sanaa's studio, below the tree. But I saw. I saw what they did to her and to Anna and to Fatima. They raped them and then killed them. They left Sanaa until last. They shot my sisters and Anna. They made the other children watch and then shot them. My children. They shot my children in front of me. Then they dug a hole, quite far from the house, and threw in all the bodies.

I played dead. I was not found but after two days, when they left, I ran and ran. I ran to another village and told them but no one believed me. I told them to go and see. But everyone was too scared to go out of the village. So no one ever saw. I stayed in that village until two months ago, when I walked back over the abandoned fields to the place where our village used to be. Everything was the same, except there were no people. I looked around for where my family had been buried but the grass had grown thick.

My father's house had been plundered. But Sanaa's studio had been left exactly as it was. I took as much as I could carry and went to her friends in Baghdad. There I looked through her things and found a letter to you, which had a note asking whoever found it to post it. I also found pictures of you and your unborn child.

271

Sanaa is dead. I am sorry to bring this news. I will see you again one day Insha'Allah.

Farhana Yazid

I look up at Juliette. She shakes her head.

"She was an extraordinary person. A great artist. And now she's forgotten. Raped and thrown into a hole. No roll call for Sanaa. No plaque. No remembrance. All that life. It must mean something. It must."

I choke back the emotion. My God. Juliette has lived all this.

"So her secret died with her?"

Juliette snorts and rolls her eyes. "Yeah. Sorry. I forgot that's all you're interested in. The fucking code."

"No. That's not true. I do care. But I have to do my job. What I'm here for. I need to find it. I can't tell you why but it's critical, Juliette. A lot has happened in the past week and it's crucial that I know where it is."

She was still holding the other letter. Turning it around in her fingers, pressing the open flaps together.

I hold my hand out. "You can trust me. I'm trying to do what's right. I'm not going to give the details to anyone who wants to do harm. Let me see the letter. Please."

She hands it to me. It's from Sanaa.

Dear Juliette Watson

If you are reading this then I am probably dead. It was inevitable. I am greatly surprised that it hasn't happened before now. You can read the details of the war between our countries anywhere. The operations, the battle plans, the strategy, the military devices. But you can never know the price individual people pay. You know me better than anyone and you know my grief. What I did. How I paid for it, with a life of no tears. Too sad to cry. My heart too dry. Yours too, I know.

But even now, before my death, I and other women have been reduced to animals, starving and scratching for food. Fatima had to kill her pets to feed her children. Can you imagine it? We have no clean water. Somehow we are now bargaining chips in the men's battle. I, Sanaa, with my university education and my art displayed all over the world. I am reduced to nothing.

Somewhere inside my heart I had a flicker of this, that it would happen to me and my family. A terror, raising its head at night. When my father's house was bombed I knew that this was the beginning and I hid all my precious things in museums and in the university.

You know exactly what I have done, even though I have not said the words. I need you to know that everything I did was to protect my beloved country but I kept your secret safe in a corner of my heart, the only peaceful corner left.

And I hid your precious thing in my mind. I memorised the words and recited them as much as the men recite their prayers. In my anger and blind rage at the Americans and British for what they do to my country I decided to play the perfect trick. I would never betray you, Juliette Watson, but I would betray them. I would shout from the rooftops that I have what they want. What better than to put what they want right before their eyes?

It has been there all the time. You could have seen it any day you pleased. You looked at it when you were in London with me. We saw it together but you had no idea. It was my joke, my way to have a revenge on the bastards. Did I feel better? Did any of the dead innocents make me feel better? A little. But it was no substitute for peace.

Now, when my life has gone, you should have what is yours. Even now I cannot bear to write where it is in case this letter falls into the wrong hands. But it is on public display. It is for everyone to see. It is where we once were, where we stood together. You will find it from these things that only you and I know.

So, for now, goodbye. When I arrive in glory and embrace Shahid I will go to Ibni like he is my son and tell him his mother is a loyal and wonderful friend, who defended me to the last, at her own peril. I know you have been under pressure to tell but I thank you forever for keeping my secret, as I kept yours. As a last request I ask that you find a way to let Saif Abed's family know where he is. Then everyone in this terrible circle will know where their loved ones lie. I cannot rest until this is done.

I will see you in Jannah, Juliette Watson, for that is surely where you belong.

We talked that time about what love is. How little we knew the world then. But I know what love is now: loyalty, care, longevity, dedication, perseverance. I love you, Juliette Watson.

Your friend

Sanaa

I hand the letter back to her. "I'm so sorry. That's terrible. I'm so sorry. I can take care of letting Saif Abed's family know. I have a route to do that for you, anonymously."

But the larger question hangs over us. Her eyes catches mine and their dull pain belies her calm exterior.

I take her hands. "I promise, promise that I will feed this into the system and it will be dealt with. I'll make sure that this becomes known and is properly investigated."

She rolls her eyes but then stares intently at me. "Will you? Really? Without mentioning my name? You'll really help me? And Sanaa?"

"Yes. There are ways I can flag it up anonymously. I absolutely promise you that when this is over I will do that."

I push the ID deep into my backpack. As I do this she hangs the tiny figure around her neck beside the other one she is already wearing. I know what it represents: her dead son. Sanaa knew what was about to happen and made sure that Juliette got back what was hers. I falter for a split second, thinking about Sammy and Leo and the child I never had. The choices I made. How I decided that I'm not a natural mother. For a moment I doubt that decision as I feel Juliette's grief and understand that her love for her son, and Sanaa's love for hers, transcends whatever their worldly decisions had them do.

Suddenly Juliette snaps out of it. "Yeah. Terrible. It's a terrible fucking world, isn't it? I'm guessing that you want to know where it is then?"

I need all my strength and experience to do this. But I have to. It's a lot to ask of her after what she's been through but I have to. "Yes. I do."

"London. It's in London."

I call Bees. "Hi, Sandra Lees here. Two flights to London ASAP. Me and Juliette..." I look at her.

"Watson. Juliette Watson."

The flights are at 9.45pm and we'll be in London by sunrise. Bees gives me all the details and I write them down. He tells me to drop the gun and anything else I can't take on the plane in a waste bin just before passport control. When I look up Juliette is reading Sanaa's letter again.

The optical red dot that searches her face tells me that Louise has found us.

Chapter 51

My training kicks in and I quickly pull the door open.

"Move slowly, Juliette. Just get up very slowly, pick up your bag. Turn around and walk out of the door."

Her face is pale and puzzled. But she does what I tell her. She moves slowly but purposefully towards the door. I reach into my rucksack and retrieve my gun as I watch the red dot waver, then fix on the back of the door, then drop. We're outside the room and she looks at me, panicked.

"OK. We need to run, up to the next floor."

We rush to the far window and look down. It's a sheer drop of five floors with no fire escape. So we take the stairs. First up, wait a while at the lift until we see it descend, stop then rise to the floor below us. I press the button immediately but run to the stairs. We hurry down, listening all the time for footsteps above us.

They come when we're just reaching the second floor. I know that there are two of them; probably one of them is waiting outside for us. There's a loud crack and a bullet whistles past my ear and misses Juliette, who runs faster, taking two steps at a time.

We finally reach the exit, which leads directly out onto the lobby. It's crowded with Japanese tourists, and I usher Juliette into the lounge. We sit down in the middle, surrounded by other guests. No one is going to take a pot-shot here. I see Louise's friend exit the stairs door and glance at us as he leaves the building. No doubt they'll be holed up outside.

I call Bees. "The situation has worsened. I need a car to pull up right outside. There are two possible shooters and the risk is high. But I need to get to the airport, so I have no choice."

"No problem, Sandra. Ten minutes. I'll ring as it approaches. Be ready. Good luck."

Juliette taps her fingers on the table. She's ghostly white but bearing up well, looking more irritated than scared. I've been trained to be patient but right now the threat is so high that I can feel the panic rising.

"Where's your husband, Juliette?"

She rolls her eyes again. I'm getting accustomed to her external boredom. But she doesn't fool me. In her eyes is a flash of panic or regret.

"Canada. For three weeks. Won't even notice I'm gone."

"OK. I'm going to put protection on your apartment. And get someone to round Louise up."

Our eyes meet.

"Will I ever be able to go back there? How long will this go on for? What's going to happen to me?"

I'm scanning the room as I answer her, avoiding her eyes. But I have to tell her.

"I don't know. Like you said, we're in great danger. Are you absolutely sure about Mark Watson? Are you certain it was him?"

"Yes. Yes. It was years ago now but it was him. Of course it was. I'd know him better than anyone wouldn't I?"

I look around for the laser dot. My eyes are drawn to the outer door of the crumby hotel, where I see Louise loitering on the pavement, talking into a mobile phone. Suddenly my own phone beeps, sooner than I thought. I press the answer button, keeping my eyes on the door.

Bees' voice, chirpy as ever, talks to me. "Black limo, passenger about to cause a big scene. Lots of people. There right now."

The call ends and I see the car. A woman opens the back door before the concierge gets to it, pushing his hand away. A suited man follows her and she begins to scream at him: "Get your hands off me!"

He's pulling her this way and that. "Get in there, you fucking whore."

The tourists move towards the door to see what's going on and the car edges forward. I grab Juliette's arms and we push through the crowd, our heads low. As we reach the door I can only just see Louise through the ever-thickening audience. I manoeuvre behind the suction from the mob and towards the door. I push Juliette in and Louise spots me. I'm in the car before the first bullet rings out on the pavement and everyone starts to scream.

Juliette is crouched on the seat beside me, rigid. She flinches when I touch her. She's in a bad way, scared, but there's no time. I'll address it with her later. I breathe a sigh of relief.

The car screeches off and heads for Brooklyn, leaving downtown behind quickly and keeping off the main routes. I ring Carey. It rings a few times, and then I hear his familiar voice.

"Carey."

"Jesus, Kate. Where are you?"

"New York still. On my way back. I need you to meet me at Heathrow with my laptop. I've got Juliette Watson with me and we need a safe house. I need you to do a few things for me."

He laughs, a short but relieved sound that tells me that we're back on course. "OK, shoot."

"Right. I need you to keep sending ransom demands to Karl. Keep up the pretence that I'm captive. It's essential for my plan to work. I need you to tip off Elliot Brady about Louise Turvey. She's living above Juliette Watson at her Jersey apartment. Same set-up as John Jones and the others. A cell."

"It's a big risk, Kate. A big risk. They're all out there looking for you. Even getting through Heathrow will be tricky."

"Yeah, I know. But I'm nearly there."

Silence. I know that he's working through the possibilities. Sifting and sorting until he rests on the end game. "Not…?"

"Yeah. There's a good chance that I'll find it before they do."

"Right. I have to tell you, though: Stuart Pearson is dead. The penultimate fingerprints. There's only the twelfth man now."

"OK. So when I arrive, I need all the details of everything found in the apartments of the dead men. Everything. Documents. Photos. Everything. And I need a full background on Mark Watson."

"Already done, Kate. He's dead."

"No, he isn't Carey. No, he isn't. I need a full background on him, anything that might have been missed. Any intelligence. Same with James Lewis."

"You don't think…?"

"I don't know. But I need to find out as soon as I get back. We're close, Carey, so close. But it's going to be very dangerous."

I can hear his breath and imagine his eyes flickering as he processes the information. "It is. But I'm in. All the way."

I swallow hard, pushing back the deep emotion over this camaraderie when the chips are down. He has always been there for me.

"So what about Assadi? Any news there?"

"No, he hasn't been seen for days. They've had a presence at his address but that's been eased off since Pearson. They've been concentrating their efforts around there. Same scenario – manual strangulation. Abandoned apartment above. Investigation ongoing. Press in a frenzy about a serial killer stealing fingerprints. At least they're not mooting terrorism. Not yet anyway. Karl thinks it's him. Assadi. The twelfth man. So do you know what it is?"

The question takes me by surprise. I'd been pushing the end game to the back of my mind, trying not to speculate. In another way I'm excited. Anxious about it. Getting Juliette to wherever it is and finally, finally seeing my prize. It would be like finding an old exercise book in the loft and reading essays from when you were fifteen. I'd see my best work, guided by my father. I'd be back in our cottage with the smell of tobacco and whiskey and my mother's baking. I wouldn't be able to avoid it.

Part of me wonders now if this has been driving me on. Then I remember what Mark Watson told Juliette: a genetic defect that could change populations. The whole of mankind. I think about Neil and Leo and Sammy and wonder how they are. I think about how I'm the key and how the whole weight of the world is on me, silently urging me to forge on.

And I'm ready. I know I have to do this, no matter what it costs me. It's clear now that whoever wants the data wants it bad. They've spent years holed up in cells in cities all over the world, watching, waiting until the time was right. That time is here and I'm going to beat them to it even if it kills me. I feel my lips involuntarily curl with anger at the injustice that anything like this exists. I don't know the details yet but I have a feeling that it can only get worse. I automatically put my hand to my pocket and feel the outline of the gun. Then it occurs to me. Is this what my father was doing? Is this how he died, protecting this secret?

I bring my attention back to Carey and his question. "Not   now. Not until I'm absolutely sure and I have it in my hands."

I can't articulate it. I suddenly know exactly what Sanaa meant – that some things are unspeakable. Why Juliette kept it all to herself. It was almost as if any words that tumbled out of my mouth would somehow become unbelievable on the way to Carey's ears, and sound like some fabulous imagined plot. But it isn't. It's real. And I have to keep it inside, safe, until the puzzle is complete.

"OK. I'll be waiting at the airport. I'll wait until you're through and I'll have a car. It'll be tricky, Kate. They'll have someone there, I expect."

I'm not sure who "they" are any more. I'm not sure if he means Mark, Louise, Karl or Tom, or the terrorists, or someone else entirely. But it doesn't matter. I want to stay on the phone a little longer, talk to Carey some more. But we're approaching the airport. I end the call and as we get out the driver hands us a suitcase each.

Juliette looks puzzled so I explain: "Looks suspicious if we both have just hand luggage. We don't want to draw attention."

She looks back at New York. We walk through JFK, mingling with the tourists and business commuters, and find our gate. No one and everyone could be our tail. I watch for the tell-tale signs of agents or terror wreakers but I don't see any. I quickly pop my gun into the waste paper bins before the gate, and pull my suitcase along. Juliette smiles at me and we assume the role of excited tourists, returning from a trip. She's good. But then again, she's been lying all her adult life so she should be.

Chapter 52

We clear passport control without a hitch, which is slightly worrying in the current high security climate. I look around and wonder which other passengers might not be who they say they are. We wait for only minutes until the flight is called and when we board we discover that we are flying Club Class. The attendant asks us if we are on business or leisure and Juliette smiles.

"Leisure. On holiday."

We eat, then sleep – well, Juliette sleeps and I pretend to. In eight and a half hours we land in London. I stretch and crick my neck. Juliette is disorientated and, as the plane taxies, I put my hand on her arm.

She frowns at me. "All looks different in the cold light of day, doesn't it? I bet you think I'm weak. For not telling anyone."

I think for a moment. Weak isn't the correct word for what I think of Juliette. On the surface she seems as if she's afraid. Her decisions, on one level, might indicate that she's terrified. But on another familiar and more complex level I guess she's just like me. It's a balancing act, keeping it all together. Never knowing who's good and who's bad.

"No. Not weak. You've been through a lot." And you're going to go through more, I think.

She shakes her head. "Sometimes I wish I'd just agreed with Mark in the beginning. Told him what happened. Or not given the papers to Sanaa. But once I'd lied the first time it was hard to stop. I had to protect myself. And her."

The tone of her voice is even and she's calm. Either she really isn't fazed by this or she is very good at hiding it.

"None of that matters now. What matters is that we find whatever Sanaa has left for you to see. That's our priority."

That and finding the twelfth man. Whoever is chasing the same prize is very near. It occurred to me, in the shitty hotel in New York, that the only reason Juliette is still alive is that they are using her as bait. To get to me. Knowing that eventually someone involved in all this would attract the key.

As soon as the plane halts and the seat belt lights turn off I switch my phone on and call Carey.

It's 6am and he sounds sleepy. "Landed?"

"Yes. We'll likely be another hour."

"It's OK. I'm nearby. I'll be waiting."

"Thanks Carey. In the meantime, can you feed Elliot some more information? The suggestion that every person involved in the data exchanges pre and up to 1991, and still alive, will have a tail just like Jones, Pearson and Juliette Watson. These people are in it for the long game. They're taking no chances, or prisoners. That means Assadi also. So someone close to him has to be part of the cell. Disrupt that cell and we'll find our enemy."

I can hear him tapping away at his keyboard. "Done. But he knows it's you, Kate."

I involuntarily breathe in sharply. How does Elliot know it's me feeding him the information?

"He sent a message saying, 'Thanks Kate. Good luck.'"

Of course, Elliot is the same calibre as me. I guess he's known from the beginning but, like any good freelancer, he'll keep his peace until it goes wrong. For the greater good.

"Hmm. Well still send him the info. Privately, not via the service system. I don't want whoever is snitching to have access to this."

"Done. OK, I'll see you soon. I've set up a safe house and a car. I've brought your laptop. Be careful, Kate."

The call ends and we disembark. We hurry through Heathrow with the rest of the bleary-eyed passengers and miraculously encounter no problems. I spot Carey standing at the front of the crowd.

The woman next to me points at a sign saying, 'luggage collect': "You'll want to get your bags?"

She's looking at Juliette, who is picking at her nails.

"I was behind you in the queue for the check in. You'll want to get your bags."

I look her in the eye. Of course, we'll wait for the bags while you size us up and verify our ID. "Someone's getting them for us. That guy over there. My friend's husband."

There's confusion on her face as she turns to see a man reaching for some bags. I turn quickly and walk the other way, gripping Juliette's arm. We hurry through the 'no return' doors and through the 'nothing to declare' exit.

The woman hurries after us, a tall, lean man in her wake. Once clear of the security exits we run towards Carey, who sees us, and sprints ahead.

He gets into the front of a car at the pick-up point and pushes the rear door open. The car starts to move and as it levels with us I push Juliette into the back seat and jump on top of her, pulling the door shut. The car does a screeching u-turn and leaves our pursuant standing in the road.

"Move!" I'm shouting, bellowing at the driver who follows my instructions and speeds away from the airport. "My God, if that didn't attract fucking attention, nothing would. Take the back streets."

Carey looks serious. He passes me a small case containing a Sony notebook. I grab it and feel its familiarity, its shape making me feel like I'm home again. Juliette is still crouched in the back seat and I suddenly realise that she isn't one of us and is unused to the panic situations we often find ourselves in.

"Juliette. Meet Carey. And Jim." Jim was Carey's driver. He turned round and smiled at us, then focused back on the road.

Ten minutes later we stop on some spare land. Carey and Juliette get out of the car with me. "OK. We don't have much time. Juliette knows where the data is and she's going to take me to it."

Juliette interrupts. "I don't know exactly where it is. It could be one of three places. We went to three places."

I stare at her, willing her to think. "The letter said that you would know where it was. That you carry it with you. Think, Juliette. Think. What do you carry with you? What would it remind you of most? Somewhere you went with Sanaa."

She bites her lip and turns away. She takes out the letter and reads it again and her hand goes to her throat, to the tiny glazed figures dangling from the necklace around her neck. She turns back to us and looks very serious.

"I know where it is. What it is. Oh my God. It's there. For everyone to see." She's deathly pale.

I step forward. "What? In public? And everyone can read it?"

She shakes her head, still dazed by the realisation. "No. It's in an ancient language. But anyone with a basic knowledge of ancient Babylonian could decipher it. It's in the British Museum."

We hurry to the car and get back in. Jim speeds off.

"Drop us on Euston Road, Jim. Whoever's after us will be looking for this car."

We're completely silent. Juliette fingers the talismans and reads the letter yet again. In ten minutes we're on Euston Road.

Carey gets out with us. "I'll drop behind. Just in case." He hands me a leather pouch and I extract the pistol. "You'll need this. Bees told me what happened in New York. The department is on high alert. They think you're still captive so they haven't issued facial recognition yet. But they're thinking the strategy is to take you to the data and decode it. So if they see you…"

If they see me they'll think Juliette is the enemy. I push the gun deep into my pocket. I hope I won't need it. We walk up Woburn Place towards the Museum. The contrasts between here and New York hit me straight away. The familiarity, the aged buildings and the majesty is completely at odds with New York's modernity and anonymity. I glance left towards my flat and pine for normality.

It's Friday morning and the crowds are thin yet; at 10am the workers are in their offices and tourists are just leaving the hotels.

We hurry along, trying not to be too conspicuous but aware that time is of the essence. I guide Juliette across Russell Square and then she knows where she is. She knows the pillared grandeur of the museum entrance and the amazing transition to a glass-ceilinged entrance hall. We pause and Carey catches up with us.

Juliette is already looking upwards and straight ahead. "Room 56. That's where her exhibition is."

I whip a floor plan from the rack and open it as we hurry up the stairs. "Room 56. Mesopotamian Period. But it's not Sanaa's exhibition. Ray Adami."

Juliette looks distraught. She hasn't broken over Sanaa's death. Hasn't grieved.

"That's what it says. They couldn't contact her. She was no longer a pull, so they put another big name on it. Famous painter. Conveniently living in the Netherlands. Still alive. Not raped and thrown into a pit."

Carey's eyebrows raise.

"I'll explain later."

We enter room 56. There are two entrances so Carey stands between them, vigilant. Juliette walks around the room, examining each exhibit. Ancient tablets inscribed with various texts for different eras. Fragments of pottery and jewellery, some of them still labelled as recovered by Professor Sanaa Yazid, Baghdad University.

Finally Juliette comes to a halt. She moves closer, ever closer to the thick glass plate and her lips move as she reads the cuneiform writing which, even to me, looks alien.

"Here it is. My God, I never thought I'd see it again. But here it is."

Chapter 53

Juliette takes a notepad and pencil out of her bag and works quickly, crossing out mistakes and adding letters to form words. I stare at the huge stone tablet inscribed with Sanaa's code in tiny cuneiform symbols. The label reads 'F.2250 Late Old Babylonia Tablet 16th Century BC. Excavated by Prof. S Yazid 2005'.

"So this is a fake? She's just put this in the middle of the exhibition and no one's noticed?"

Juliette smiles a little. "Mmm. The beginning is a list of materials. No doubt a translation of it is in the archive, saving anyone the trouble of having to translate it again. But she's slotted the code into the middle of it. Here."

She points to the twelfth line of the text and I see a familiar symbol: the shape of a tiny doll baby, exactly the same as the one Juliette wears around her neck. I scan the stone and see the same symbol much farther down. Their sons. The children they lost because of all this.

She continues scribbling words, one after another, then looks up and hands it to me. I take it from her, my vision blurred with all that the words hold. On the one hand, the secret that everyone wants. But, to me, it was like a rainy weekend decades ago when my father used me to cover his treacherous tracks. My hands are shaking and Carey puts an arm round me.

"OK, Kate? It's OK."

Of course it is. In many ways, I realise now, this is what my life had been leading to. This is why I have my gift.

We move through the Near East Exhibitions to the Egyptian rooms and further into the museum, to the Japanese exhibits. I know this place so well; how appropriate. It's steeped in childhood memories, a perfect setting for me in which to decode the words I've worked so hard to find.

I particularly remember a small annex at the back of the Japanese exhibits, a dimly lit room with an ancient manuscript in a glass case. I lead Juliette and Carey there and take out my notebook, plugging it into a power point. I quickly type in the words from Juliette's pencil scrawl and save the document. As they materialise on the page a deeper memory springs to life.

My father hurrying me along. My mother pouring tea in the kitchen. There's a woman with her, and a child. A little girl. I want to play with her but my father wants me to work. No laughter, just solemn talking while my father chivvies me along. I try to look back through the years and see who the woman is but I can only hear her voice, and my mother's. My father's thumb tapping his pipe on the fire grate and the smell of burned tobacco and the hot cinnamon milk that my mother would bring me from time to time.

Then the snatching away of my work and the "well done, well done" without making eye contact. The clicking of the door as the woman and the girl leave and my mother and father staring at each other silently for what seems like an eon as I watch through the hinge of the kitchen door. Then the shouting and crying.

The coder deciphers them in a second and, as I'd thought, there's another layer. I open a different program, one that I see now was written by Lauren Gaynor, and I cut and paste the next layer in. Then the next. Then another layer of disjointed words that mean nothing until they are matched with a complex cypher system and the set of texts my father used to build the codes in the first place. Minutes seem like hours and Carey stands by the entrance while, on each pass, I hope for coherent language on the page.

It takes seven passes, and then the eighth is mine again. Something inside me knows this is the final pass, some inherent recognition that I can't quite place. And it is. I press the button and almost instantaneously the text is there, in front of me on the screen. I turn and stare at Carey, almost afraid to read it. Our eyes meet and he smiles a little. Then my eyes drift to the screen and the terrible words in front of me.

Author: John Jones
Location: Al Qurnah 31.008152, 47.437295 31°00'29.4"N 47°26'14.3"E
Canister material: titanium alloy
Depth: 200ft
Guardians and Order of Biolock:
PB

SP
BL
JJ
KA
SA
MA
KA
PS
YAS
HT
AH

Key: Bio information fingerprinting from guardians

Contents:

Background:

A team of scientists was tasked with developing a form of contraception that would help to control a population. The aim was to develop a contraception that could be introduced via food source or water and that was a temporary measure to prevent the spread of disease and starvation. The effects should be completely reversible. The product would be tested around the Omo Valley region of Ethiopia at Omo Kibish. This site was chosen because of the suggestion that the L genotype originated from this area.

Outcome:

The project was completed in May 1990 and a contraceptive produced but never licensed due to international ethical concerns. A by-product of the research was the production of a synthetic gene that could be introduced into a population to stem fertility. The carrier for the gene is the homogametic XX chromosomes.

The delivery method investigated for is germline therapy. The germ would be introduced by piggybacking the modifying gene onto an infection, which is introduced to the population. The original contraceptive product would have been combined with a vaccination program carried out on a population, designed to temporarily stem fertility in recently delivered mothers. The synthetic genetic modification would be delivered the same way but would be permanent. It would also be passed down through the children who inherited the gene.

Because of the irreversible nature of the gene therapy the by-product, which was referred to within the team as 'Ea', was put aside in a sealed container and is buried at the place where the Tigris and the Euphrates converge.

The potentials for this modification, when reviewed, are immense and destructive. At a final review meeting the team tabled the proposal that, because the product could easily be used in eugenics to wipe out a specific population, largely unnoticed over several generations, it must never be used. Further, accidental (or intentional) release into a population would carry a certainty of widespread infertility and thereby amount to an alternative method to conventional warfare to control nations.

Storage of excess materials: Failed attempts were made to destroy the genetic material but in order to be absolutely certain that it was secure the team entered a pact that combined their own genetic material in the form of a bio lock so that in order to release the information all twelve would have to be present and consenting.

The product is stored in the delivery agent virus. Therefore, should the canister be opened without completing the bio lock sequence, the product will be released into the local area and will inevitably contaminate all present.

Trait expressed: Infertility in female gene carrier and in all female descendants by whom the active gene is inherited.

Juliette looks around the room, mesmerised by the gentle light and the beautiful Japanese prints.

Carey's gaze is fixed on me, his eyes questioning as I raise my head. "Is it what we thought it was?"

It's worse. Now that I know exactly what it is, the definitive object, I'm overtaken by a sense of dread. No wonder Mark Watson panicked and ran. No wonder he gave the papers to Juliette rather than let them fall into enemy hands. No wonder he ultimately realised the value of them and chased them back through time.

No wonder Karl and Donald Winger want to get their hands on them, and Joe Newman. Suddenly everyone's rationale came into focus. Everyone wants a weapon that can be activated remotely and left to take its course. No blame. No obvious cause, just a devastating, gradual effect. No wonder Assadi didn't want to tell me what it was. The fewer people who know about it the better.

"Yes. Yes, it is. But even worse."

I turn the laptop screen towards him, hiding the top section of the document so he can't see the location, and he reads. When his eyes leave the screen he's clearly ejected into the potential horrors that the product promises. A way to control any population. A way to silently wipe out a whole race. Finally he runs his fingers through his hair and sits on the bench opposite me.

A couple enter the adjacent room and spend time looking at the Japanese prints, then leave. We sit in silence. The only sound is Juliette's soft footsteps as she paces around, eager to return to her friend's legacy.

Eventually, Carey speaks. "Is that even possible? An airborne virus that affects a whole population?"

"That's what the common cold is, Carey. But we've got immunity to that, to an extent. This is the same. Infects with the bacteria then drops the piggybacked load into the system. Highly specialised genetic engineering. Definitely possible."

I can see that he's asking the same questions as me: who would do that deliberately?

"So, what now?"

I think for a moment. About how my father must have known about this, and how he probably died protecting it. How twelve other people, the team who discovered it, knew, and one of them was a Judas. One of them sold out. Eleven were dead. Mark Watson knew the basic details but not the location, just like Juliette and Assadi.

The only ones who know the full details are the twelfth man. And me.

"This needs to be contained. We need to find the twelfth man."

Carey shakes his head in disbelief. "You mean it doesn't say who it is? Who the twelfth man is?"

"It lists the guardians by initials. We're looking for someone with the initials BL. Fourth in the bio lock sequence. They can't execute the sequence without their fingerprints. They have all the other fingerprints now."

I delete the document from my laptop and backtrack the code, finally deleting all traces of the program. I tear up Juliette's transcription into tiny confetti pieces and drop them into a duct behind the glass cabinet with the Japanese manuscript in it. I set my laptop to wipe the white space so that no one can easily retrieve the information.

Juliette is sitting at the end of a far bench and I go to her.

"All this, Juliette. You need to never speak of it. To anyone. No matter what."

She snorts. "I'm good at that. I've never once spoken of my time in Iraq or what happened afterwards. Never. No matter what. I couldn't. So what is it? Is it very bad? Would it really affect the world like Mark said? You know, all mankind?"

I debate with myself now. She's been through a lot and I want to spare her from knowing any more: the evil that is possible. The fact that people are capable of depriving others of an existence proves that evil exists in the world, that it hovers around in the sinister power dynamics of those hell bent on destroying other people.

But wasn't that what she'd put up with all her life? Other people deciding what was best for her? How much she should know? How much she could say? How much she would be believed before she was dismissed as collateral damage? It's something I personally despise, that false protection, not granting people the knowledge they are entitled to. So I tell her.

"Yes. Yes, it is. Mark was right. It's genetic engineering aimed at mass destruction of races. But not in the way you thought. Not what you've endured. No explosions or war planes. No tanks or guns. It's much simpler than that."

Juliette isn't stupid. The horror crosses her face before I finish speaking. Her hand goes to her mouth and her pupils shrink to pinpricks. "No! Not poor innocents. Not that. How? How, Kate?"

"It's almost unimaginable. They could introduce a gene modification by infecting a population. It would render the women infertile."

"Infertile? Oh my God."

"Yeah. The gene would then be passed down to anyone who escaped the first generation, and so on, until eventually everyone in a given population was affected. It was meant to be controlled, an experiment in contraception, but if it gets into the wrong hands, who knows?"

She shakes her head. Her hands clutch her backpack and her knuckles are white. "The cruellest blow. Women unable to reproduce. To not have a child. To know something is wrong but be unable to find the answer. To have no choice. It's would be a slow torture."

Chapter 54

The implications floor us into a long silence. Then as more people flow into the Japanese art room, we have no option but to move on. We return to the Mesopotamian room, where Carey takes photographs of the tablet and other artefacts. As we leave I see Juliette mouth the word 'goodbye' and I feel deeply sorry for the loss of her friend.

Carey phones ahead and, by the time we reach the gates of the museum, Jim is waiting in a blue Volvo. We get in and Carey gives him an address in Camden. When we arrive Jim pulls into a back alleyway and opens a garage adjoining a semi-detached house. We enter through a side door in the garage and it look like someone is living there and has just nipped out to the shops. The TV is on Sky News Channel and I immediately tune into the report.

Kay Burley is explaining that a serial killer is murdering people around the London area. I listen carefully for any reference to the missing fingerprints but there is none. Juliette makes some tea and I load up the evidence data on Carey's laptop. I can see that he's logged in anonymously to the service databank and I smile. He's good. Very good. But works entirely within RIPA.

I flick through the photographs of the bodies and of the evidence from the cases I have already reviewed, hungry for any links between them. People are careless. They love to keep little mementos of things that are important to them, as if letting them go will somehow dissolve the memory, while holding them tight will keep it there, safe in their memory bank, for instant recall.

This is often how I find patterns. This is what I'm an expert at: looking at the personal effects, finding the small pieces of people's lives that point to a commonality with someone else. So far the only link is John Jones's photograph, the one he tried to hide in his employer's safe. And, obviously, the fingerprints. What if the twelfth man lived in Alaska and is lying dead right now, his fingers leaking blood, but no one has found him? All the other victims had removed themselves from academia and were living isolated lives in normal jobs, striving to go unnoticed. What if the twelfth man was so isolated that he was completely alone and no one really cared if he was dead or not?

I flick through the evidence files. Trinkets, wedding rings, clothes, contact lenses, cigarette lighters. Blood groups, DNA, medical histories, dental records, eye colour. I flick backwards and forwards, more quickly now, hoping that something will jump out at me.

It isn't until I make a mistake and flick too far forward into Stuart Pearson's file, which has been tagged onto the end of the others recently. A comprehensive catalogued record collection, suggesting that he's been living in London a while. DNA evidence, hairs from his pillows, belonging to him and to a woman who has been identified as his on/off girlfriend. Photographs of an ex-wife and children. Photographs of his parents and his two brothers, and of him at university. All catalogued into chronological order. It seems that Pearson liked order, and this bodes well for me.

And there it is. Right after his university collection and his official master's degree shot. A picture of a group of people in front of a whitewashed building, which I recognise from John Jones's picture as Baghdad University. I scan the photograph and it's almost the same picture: thirteen people with everyone I recognised from the other picture – except Assadi. Of course. He was in the last picture, because someone else must have been taking it. And now he's swapped places and the other person stands at the end of the line. A woman. Belinda Assadi.

I shout Carey in from the kitchen. "Assadi. Where is he? Does anyone know?"

He shakes his head. "No, he hasn't reappeared yet. He could have skipped the country."

"I need to find him."

I quickly go through our meeting, reliving it and focusing on Belinda. The tears in her eyes, the fear, the solemnness. The card she pressed into my hand as I left. I rummage through my wallet and, incredibly, it's still there. Belinda Lindon-Assadi. I'd dismissed the Assadis long ago as major players. I only hope that everyone else had.

I dial her number. The tone rings out seven, eight times, and then the answerphone clicks in.

"Belinda. It's Kate Morden. I need to see you. Immediately. I know, Belinda. I know. And I can help you."

I end the call and place the phone on the table, hoping she will call back.

Carey's eyes widen. "So Assadi is the twelfth man?"

I look at him. Caught in the same trap as me. Probability. Proximity. Of course it always looked like it was going to be him. Because that's how he made it look.

"No. Not Assadi. His wife, Belinda."

We research her background. A gifted geneticist, working in America in the late 80s, then at universities across the world. Her research project was part of the HapMap project, where haplogroups of DNA are tested and plotted across the world. Yes. That would tie in with why the Ea product was to be tested in the Omo Valley; it's where man is thought to have originated. She returned to the UK in the early nineties and met Assadi when he defected.

That's the official story. But the photographs tell a different story. They'd already met by the time he defected. She'd told him enough about Ea for him to know the potential for the slow Armageddon of entire populations, and he feared that it was his people who would be the target if it got into the wrong hands. So he came here and turned informer. Yet he left out the key piece of information, because she had never told him. She had stayed true and not even told her husband the full terror of the slow elimination of an entire race.

I remember how she'd put me off the scent by suggesting an alternative, altogether more immediate catastrophe: a nuclear Armageddon. Designed to put me on immediate high alert, to drive me to look in the wrong direction.

Carey whistles into the air. "Belinda? But how? How haven't they found her?"

"Because she had the perfect foil. Her husband was a suspect but she was clearly a bystander and, given the logistics, couldn't possibly be involved. She strengthened the illusion by warning off anyone who asked, on the pretext that he was sensitive – diverting the attention back onto him. Genius. And it would have completely worked if it hadn't been for a few sentimental mementoes. The human condition has a lot to answer for."

We wait. And wait. I close my eyes and allow myself to relax a little but my mind floods with memories. I pace. The coding, my mother, her sadness. My father's study and the smell of the leather chair that carried an imprint of his shape. The long days immersed in my task, my father watching and prompting. I find my way back to the coding of the document and the woman. Was it Belinda? Was it?

The phone rings and it's an unknown number. Carey rushes in.

I answer. "Hello, Belinda?"

There's a silence. A long decision as to whether this is the right thing. Then an unmistakable voice. "Not Belinda. Zaki Assadi. Can we meet, Miss Morden?"

"Of course. Where are you, Professor Assadi?"

He thinks for a moment. "I'll meet you at the Dorchester. In the reception. In two hours."

He ends the call and Carey picks up the car keys.

"No, Carey. I have to go alone. You need to stay here with Juliette. I'm going to take the tube. No."

"Too risky. The CCTV will have face recognition activated by now. They'll spot you and then game's up. They've got people everywhere. The longer we can make them think that you're in New York, the better. I'd like to drive you. Jim can stay here with Juliette."

He's right, of course, but I'm not about to put them in any more danger. It's highly unlikely that Carey and Juliette would be tracked here, to an anonymous house in Camden. The car is hidden. Carey's well aware of anything that could be tracked – phones, computers – and he's protected them. The odds are astronomical.

"No. I'm going alone. But could you find somewhere safe for the Assadis to go? Somewhere they can stay for a while and not be found. Text me when you've found somewhere. It's imperative that whoever is behind this doesn't find them."

I look at Jim. I don't trust anyone now, except Carey. The world is suddenly even more complex than I thought it was, with loyalties and duties ever switching. Double-crossing and lying – everyone claiming it was for 'the common good'. I only know that I'm alone in this now. I can't divulge what I've learned and that terrible secret I shared with Carey and Juliette. But I'm still the only one here who knows the location. The only two people with that knowledge are me and Belinda Assadi, and I need to get to her before anyone else does.

Chapter 55

In the end I decide to walk to Euston. I buy an 'I Love London' cap from a shop on the next corner and push on some oversized sunglasses as an afterthought. I need to avoid CCTV as much as possible and pulling my hair underneath my black jacket will help to disguise me.

I know how facial recognition works. It picks out a best-fit and the more I do to cover my bone structure, the better. The last thing I need now is Karl on my tail, slowing me down. I hurry through the back streets of Camden Town towards Euston. When I reach the station I turn left up Euston Road and hurry towards Kings Cross.

Everything is bigger and gothic-charismatic now I'm central, from the spires of St Pancras Hotel to St Pancras Church opposite the station. The trees, I notice, as I grab a takeaway coffee at the Espresso Bar by the library, are trimmed, their branches stunted in their growth making their black tips stark against the chalky skies.

I jump onto a 205 bus and flash Sandra Lee's Oyster card over the reader. It's a risk, because whoever accosted me at the airport will have had the passenger list for the flight and could be monitoring for Sandra Lee. But I have to balance two needs: reaching Belinda and Assadi, and staying unrecognised. I don't want to use a taxi in case it too is monitored, or there is a description of me in circulation.

CCTV everywhere. I scan the people around me through dark glasses and continue towards the station. There's a young woman and a man. That's how they seem to operate. A woman on the case with male backup. That was also their design fault: a pattern. Something that jumps out at me to expose them. I move off but they don't. Then, again, out of the corner of my eye, I see something familiar. Then it's gone. I'm in a hurry, too busy to investigate, but it slightly unnerves me.

So I sit on the bus, cap pulled down, watching for any small sign that someone is watching me. A glance, a lingering look. I change to an 82 bus, alight before the hotel and walk the rest of the way. As I approach the hotel I stop on a corner and pretend to look in my bag. I take out my phone and faux-selfie against the backdrop of the hotel. I scan the horizon but all I see is moving cars and tourists eager to see the sights.

So I go in. All the while I consider my game plan. How I will persuade Belinda and Assadi to come with me. How I will get them to the safe house.

I'm early and I call Carey from the lobby as I wait. "I'm here. I'm about to meet them. I'll call you when I need you to pick us up."

"OK. Be careful. I've got a house. Very remote. I've rented it for six months with an option to extend the lease."

I pull off the sunglasses. "Good work, Carey. Good work. OK. I'll call soon."

I can tell he's concerned and, for the first time, wonder if he's in too deep. Not with the case. No. He's fully engaged and competent. With me. A feather-like realisation touches my consciousness as I register Carey's concern for my wellbeing. But the spell is broken as my mobile rings. It's Assadi.

"Miss Morden. Suite 25."

I'm suddenly hyper alert. This wasn't the plan. Meeting in a room is never good. It gives the occupant time to set up whatever they have in store for you. Before I have time to object he's hung up. I have no choice. I take the lift and move along the corridor. It's quiet and serene and I can hear my own heart beating. I knock. He answers and steps aside.

I look inside the room. It's empty except for a small suitcase, Assadi's ornate cigar box, the one I first saw on his table at the university, and some of the ornate pieces from his study. Even though it's been less than a week since I last saw him he looks older. His skin is pallid and he stoops. Out of the context of his study, away from the books and the rugs, he looks oddly unkempt. He sits down heavily on a Chesterfield sofa behind a marble coffee table.

I stand in front of him. "Why now, Professor? Why me?"

He doesn't smile. Closer now, his eyes are reddened and heavy.

I continue. "You know that half of the secret service is looking for you. So why respond to me?" I look around the room for Belinda.

He opens the box and fingers a Cuban cigar. "Because you know the truth. You've worked it out. Your father always said that you were a smart girl. I knew when you visited me that it would only be a matter of time. Only a matter of time until we both know the truth."

I pass over this. I don't want to think about my father right now. There's no time for sentimentality. "Look, I need to get you both to a safe place. I've arranged for someone to take you there. I swear that you'll be safe, you and your wife. Away from anyone who wants to kill her."

He smiles. "Oh, I don't doubt it. I trust you implicitly, Miss Morden. Unlike your father."

He's persisting and I realise that if I want to get them out of here I'll have to play the game. "My father?"

"Yes. If you know of Belinda's involvement and you have had that confirmed by the document, which I assume you have, you obviously know what happened. Your father never wanted to involve you. But he had no choice."

"I don't want to discuss it. I just want to get you and your wife to somewhere we can keep you safe. She's the only person now who…"

"Knows the location. Yes. You and her. Even I don't know the details or the location. Some secret, eh? Kept for decades, then, well, someone got greedy. Someone sold out."

I sit down. He wants to tell me what happened and I have to humour him. I listen for any sounds from the adjoining rooms. Where the hell is she? Where is Belinda?

"All those years ago. They knew what they had found. They knew. At first they were excited, passionate. Today engineering genetics are an everyday, simple procedure. Back then, this was revolutionary. They found a way to deliver the gene modification in a virus. It was revolutionary. The potential for good was enormous. But once they had made it, they couldn't destroy it. It was like the common cold. And that's why it's so dangerous now, because there still no antidote to the infection that carries the infertility modification. Their antidote didn't work. It was tested on humans." He wipes a tear away. "It was tested on Belinda."

I wait for the reality of this to sink in. So not only was she part of the biological key, she also carries the modification gene. She's a walking time bomb. Assadi continues.

"But don't worry, she can't pass it on. She can't infect others. Hers was not the final batch. The one that could spread across populations and infect everyone it came into contact with. That's what is in the canister, Miss Morden. That's what would have been unleashed."

"It still could. That's why we have to go now. To make sure that whoever is looking for this, and obviously knows about the bio lock, never finds her. And me."

But he's shaking his head and crying now. His hands are shaking as he ignores the 'no smoking' sign and lights his cigar. "Your father, Miss Morden. Do you know how he died?"

I sigh. No time. But I indulge him. "No. I don't. Obviously I know the official version. But I don't know for sure. I expect it is something to do with the encryption. Someone suspected it was him and killed him."

He smiles through his sobs. "But how do you explain that I am still alive? It took only one look at the security files to see that I am an informer, a refugee from my own country who knows a great deal about this subject. That's why you came to see me and that's why I'm still alive, because I'm more valuable alive than dead. So why would anyone kill your father? If they suspected that he was the key, surely they would keep him on their side. Keep him safe?"

Like they have with me – that's what he means. They've manoeuvred me into a position where they can keep an eye on me. When the time came I'd be an asset. Yes. He is right. I am more valuable alive than dead. Unlike the eleven people who, once their purpose had been harvested, were killed, because they knew that the key is the document. That's why I am alive. That's why Assadi is alive. But according to that particular logic my father should be alive too. So why did they kill him? Why?

I know Assadi is leading me towards something. Something just beyond my comprehension. His eyes will me to complete the journey.

And suddenly I do. "You don't mean...?"

He sits forward on the edge of the Chesterfield, leaning forward and pointing at me. "Your father wasn't an honourable man. Not to me. But he did the right thing. He did it at the right time. He was on the brink of being captured. The net was closing in and he could never be sure that he wouldn't betray the thing he cared about most."

"No. No. He wouldn't. He would never do that. Not for a piece of paper. For any code. He was a trained agent. He would never have shot himself. Never. Not for that."

Assadi sighs. "Not for the document, Miss Morden. For you. For you."

I stare at him. My head is spinning with this new information, a new perspective on something I've built terrible scenarios on for so long. Through it my instincts tell me to lock in on Assadi, watch him for any sense of mocking untruth. Is it a trap, a way to destabilise me? To capture me when I am at my weakest?

But he's beyond any of this. He's crumbled and shaken. Destroyed. He sags and wheezes, all the time holding onto the corner of the sofa to protect himself. I'm reeling but I still need to do my job. I can deal with this later. Later, when Belinda is safe.

I steady myself. "It was a long time ago. In a different era. But the reason remains, and I need to get you and Belinda to safety. Please, Professor Assadi. Please get Belinda and come with me. We can talk more on the way."

He starts to cry again. He leans further forward and puts his hand on an ornate box, studded with golden knots and exotic fretwork.

"But she's already safe, Kate. She's already safe."

Chapter 56

The awful reality hits me hard. Of course I'd heard rumours that people had died rather than given up vital information. But wasn't that before? Wasn't that in the Cold War, in the World Wars? Was that what really happened to my father – he shot himself rather than risk betraying me?

Assadi picks up the box and comes to sit beside me. "She   always knew it might come to this. She worked hard to lay a false trail but she knew that eventually it would all tumble down. She knew when you came that it had started. She wanted to tell you but I wouldn't let her. I still held hope that it wasn't the end, but Belinda knew."

How was it possible? How could she have done it? Or had he done it?

"But wouldn't there have to be an inquest?"

"No. She knew a way. She had some chemical that would make it look like a heart attack. That was her first love, chemistry. She had heart problems in any case. So she took it. She took it." His voice breaks and he wipes his eyes. "I watched her till the end. We had cover in place. She was declared dead and taken to the morgue. She had a living will and it was all arranged. Belinda knew the right people."

He picks up the box and holds it against him.

"There was a short ceremony at the crematorium. It all happened so fast. But like everything Belinda did, it all went exactly as planned. And now, like you, I am alone. I was denied a son by that fucking experiment. She was barren afterwards. She sacrificed everything."

I put my hand on his arm. It's almost unbelievable but the box and his grief are the proof. "I'm sorry. I'm so sorry."

He laughs again through his tears. "Don't be sorry. She was the last. They can never safely open the canister now. Never. She thought of everything. She was committed to never giving up the secret. She was a pacifist but she knew the potential catastrophic harm that Ea could do. The suffering. Against everything moral. And Belinda was a moral person. But now, Kate, you need to decide what you will do. Where will you go?"

I know exactly where I'm going now. I know exactly what I will do. "Already have. Come on. Let's get you to somewhere safe."

I try to take his arm but he pulls away. "I won't go with you. I've lived as a prisoner for years. I can't see the future without Belinda but I have no choice. I'm not as brave as her. I tried, but I couldn't do it. But then again, I don't have as much at stake. No, Kate, I'm going back to Iraq. Back to my home."

"But it's too dangerous. With IS and the air strikes. It's too dangerous. The whole area is at risk. Terrible things are happening there."

I think about Farhana's letter and the horror on Juliette's face. How Sanaa, a respected, educated woman had been slaughtered and thrown into a hole like an animal, and for what? The world was a poorer place without her. It's no different now in Iraq. Farrah had confirmed that before she died. And the world would be poorer without Assadi. He'd protected Belinda and protected her secret.

His was a balancing act. He saw the threat to his country and his colleagues and he saw a way to bring it to the attention of governments. Yet he still managed to safeguard his wife. I think back to the data, to his file, and to the twelve missing names. Then to the photographs. He knew all along whose the names were but he kept it to himself for fear of triggering exactly what happened. He knew Belinda would be hunted down.

And he knew about the document. He knew my father had coded it, and he knew my part in it. He'd hedged his bets both ways and calculated the astronomical odds on every secret being revealed at the same time. He took a chance and it paid off – he had a life with Belinda. His calculation began when he defected and gave the information. He knew exactly how much to give to be convincing yet not involved.

"I must go back. There is nothing here for me now. I have a brother in Basra and I can stay with him. I need to help people. I failed in my original task to help in 1991, because the need to hide Belinda's secret was greater. But now the Iraqi civilian body count is in double figures every day. I need to do what I can to make sure these people did not die in vain. There will always be someone to fight. Al Qaida, ISIL, Iraqi army, coalition. Belinda said there must be a better way. A human way. I need to recover. I need to decide if I can go on."

I'm standing in front of him. I can't leave him like this. I just can't.

He senses it and takes my hand. "Go, Kate. Go and have your life. Forget about all this now. They can never open the canister even if they find out where it is. It's too dangerous. If they ever decode the document, even after you and I are gone, then they will see how dangerous it is. You might think that people's greatest fear is nuclear war or mass murder but real Armageddon is the extermination of all humanity. The greatest fear of all is that we can't live on. That we can't reproduce ourselves. Believe me, I've lived it."

"I'll never forget about it. And I'll never forget about you or Belinda. Are you sure you'll be all right?"

He stands up and walks towards the door. "I've got a flight booked for this evening. I leave with nothing. First, I will take Belinda to her final resting place." He shakes his head. "She loved the Serpentine. We used to walk there when we first met."

I touch the door handle but there are too many questions. "My father. Are you sure?"

"I didn't see but it was the only way for him. He did it to protect you. He wished he'd never made you do it but he was desperate. It was your mother's idea. She said that no one would ever believe that he would use a child to code a national secret. When we came to collect it she was so proud of you. So proud. They both were. But neither of them had another full night's sleep after we took the document."

"So where did you take it? Who was the traitor?"

"Belinda and I met up with the team just before we disbanded. No one had an appetite for the destruction of the human race and we were all scared. Each had his own path to follow. The document was placed in a safe in Baghdad. Only the crucial part was coded because, after all, there were twelve people with in-depth knowledge who could have disclosed it at any time. But everyone would have to be together to open the canister. Or so we thought. Even we never dreamed that there would one day be a way to harvest fingerprints."

He sighs deeply. It's obvious that this is very difficult for him but he's determined to tell me everything.

"But I knew that one of the twelve tried to sell the information. Just after I defected I was contacted by Mark Watson, an intelligence officer who had intercepted the data and wanted to give it back. I arranged for John Jones to meet him at a checkpoint but we did not know that it was the eve of Desert Storm. He was intercepted and questioned but released. It was too late. And the document was lost. From that day we knew that it would one day reappear. And I knew that you would inevitably be involved, Kate. As I told you, Armageddon would be preceded by a beautiful woman."

I turn the door handle and leave. My father. My father. And Belinda. I lean against the wall beside the door and collect my senses. Assadi's testimony wove the final part of the story for me, and helped me make my decision. Like my father and Belinda, I'd never tell. I'd keep it to myself and never disclose the information. I'd uphold the code they kept and bury it deep inside me for the rest of my career, whatever the cost.

As I get out of the hotel lift I call Carey. "Cancel the accommodation. I'll be back in an hour."

"Why? What's happened? Are they with you? Did you find them? Are you OK, Kate?"

I sniff loudly and two older women in the lift give me dirty looks. "'No. They're not with me. I'll explain later. Send Jim to the Dorchester to pick me up."

I enter the hotel lobby and walk toward the sliding doors. I get about halfway there before I see a familiar figure sitting alone in the corner beside a potted palm plant.

Elliot Brady.

Chapter 57

"Elliot."

I sit beside him. I realise that I am still carrying the 'I love London' cap and the sunglasses. He's wearing a light cotton checked suit and reading a newspaper.

He looks up. "Kate."

"How did you find me?"

His face softens a little, a trace of a smile flitting across it. "You did exactly what I would have done. I guess you're either a team player or you're not. I knew you'd go get the Sanderson woman. I lost you just after that. But I also knew you'd go for Assadi. He checked in here under his real name. My associates found him."

I check him for an anxious tick or a bead of sweat but he's perfectly relaxed. Unlike me.

'"So, what now?'"

"'Where are they? The Assadis? My next move would be to take them to a safe haven somewhere in the British countryside but…"

He doesn't know. He knows Assadi has the basic details but he doesn't know about Belinda.

I think quickly. "Yeah. But they won't come with me. They want to do it their way. They've already left. And since they have no real information that we aren't already aware of…"

He stares at me, scanning my face. For once I'm absolutely sure that I won't give myself away with a muscle tremble or uneven breathing because I'm numb with shock and grief. In the background of my life is the suggestion that my father was a hero after all. That he ended his life to save anyone revealing his lack of judgement in making me code the secret. I push it backwards into my soul. I need to solve my current dilemma first, and Elliot has just thrown a spanner in the works.

"Yeah. At least I've found you now. It was only a matter of time."

"But why were you looking for me, Elliot? For them? Surely you must realise why I did this? Why I ran with Juliette Sanderson?"

He leans forward, exaggerating his height. "Yes, I do. I know that you are the most likely person to be able to decipher the data. When it's found. And that the probability is that Mark Watson gave it to his wife. That it's crucial that it's found before it falls into the wrong hands – the IS terrorists who are chasing it. You know that Asiya, the girl above John Jones's flat, has confessed that she went to Syria for training? But that's not what you are asking me, is it?"

"No. No, it isn't."

"OK. I'm not working on behalf of the security services. I'm concerned for the same reasons you are. That's how I work. That's how you work. We're not so different, Kate. I realised that when I received a message regarding Louise Turvey, who, by the way, has been dealt with: American citizen radicalised. The line of enquiry involving the terrorist cells in the victims' place of residence is coming along nicely, FYI. You know it too. That's why you chose me."

He's right. Except he's missed the crucial point: I'm better than he is. I realise that he hasn't solved this case at all. He's followed my lead and waited at the pivotal point to hang onto my hard work.

"Mmm. So, again, Elliot. What happens now? Are you going to bust me? Tell them what I've done?"

I stare at him but out of the corner of my eye I watch Assadi exit the lift and walk behind him. He looks at me but doesn't smile. He's carrying the box. Elliot is preoccupied, focused on me.

"No. I'm not on their side. I'm not on anyone's side. I work with them, not for them. The priority is to find the document and to stop the opposition before they harvest their final victim's fingerprints. So I would suggest that you are suddenly released. That you walk back to them and work with them. Not for them. As I said, it's always worked for me. Then everyone can concentrate on the task ahead."

I feel my pulse slow and relaxation ebb through me. It's nowhere near as bad as I thought. He knows almost nothing. He still thinks that I'm just here because my father was involved in the original case. Time to kick in with the damage limitation.

"Yes. You're right Elliot. That's what I'll do. And what will you do?"

He settles back in his seat and pushes his gold-rimmed glasses up his nose. "I suggest that we work together, Kate. Pool our excellent resources. Works for me."

He isn't looking directly at me and I can see the cost to him in this statement.

"Let me get back into the real world first. Then I'll be in touch."

I get up to leave. With Assadi gone, there is no reason for me to be here. Elliot has lost the trail now. He stands with me and hands me a business card. I almost smile. We both know that there are other ways I could contact him, as proven by my anonymous tips about Louise. But this is an acknowledgement of his respect for me, something tangible.

"I'll look forward to it, Kate. Until then, be safe."

I walk away and don't look back until I'm in the car with Jim. Then I peer through the revolving doors to the Dorchester and Elliot is gone.

We arrive back at the safe house quickly. Carey rushes to meet me at the door. "What happened? Where are they?"

I shake my head and gave him a 'not here' look. So we walk through the garage and into the alleyway behind the house.

"OK," I say. "The direct threat to Juliette has been dealt with."

"Yeah. She's had a text saying her husband is due home in three days. She'd like to get back there by then."

"OK. Make that happen, Carey, and make sure she has some kind of protection for the foreseeable. Bees can arrange?"

Carey laughs. "Thankfully Bees can arrange anything."

I take his arm and guide him farther away from the house. "Look, I'll cut to the chase. Belinda is dead. There is no further risk. The harvesters have failed in their mission and the canister can never be opened safely now."

He's silent for a moment. His eyes widen and his pupils dilate as he understands the implications. "Dead? How? You didn't…"

"No. Not me. It doesn't matter how. Assadi is flying back to Iraq to disappear. Elliot followed me to the hotel but he doesn't know it's over."

Carey flushes red, and then pales. "It's over. It's over, Kate."

"Not quite. The problem is that I can't reveal that it's over. If I come clean, then Juliette will be hounded for the rest of her life and so will Assadi. They'll know I faked my kidnap and I'll never work again. But most importantly, they'll stop looking for the terrorists. No one except me, you and Assadi know the implications Belinda's death brings, so let's keep it that way. The canister is still out there and whoever wants to find it won't stop until they do."

Carey thinks for a moment. "Or, just to throw this out there, you could tell them. You're the only one who knows the location now Belinda and the others are dead."

"No. I can't trust any of them. I can't trust them not to use it for genocide."

Carey looks shocked. He's a Queen and Country man and hasn't got as far along this trajectory in his thinking as I have. "Let's face it, Carey, no one wants to solve the secret so that they can destroy it. It'll just be another threat against another country. In this case, against innocent people who have no part in war. I'm not handing it to them. Never."

For a split second I wonder if this is where Carey and I part ways. Where our ideology is too different to work closely.

But he rallies. And he says one word. "Sanaa."

"Yes. Sanaa. Fatima. Anna. Belinda. All of them. Wonderful human beings destroyed for nothing. And if the contents of this canister are released on a population, it would be mass genocide." He's coming around to my way of thinking. "So here's my plan. Juliette goes back to New York. She doesn't know the location and I'll arrange to get that exhibit in the British Museum removed."

"Already done. It's currently being removed and shipped to an address in Inverness."

"Great. You're always one step ahead. You send an anonymous message to Karl telling him where he can find me. I'll weave a story about how I was kept in a darkened room and the search for the fingerprint harvesters and the twelfth man will continue. But obviously never be solved. Once they realise that there is no twelfth victim the case stays live but eventually become inactive. And let's face it, even if we found the IS cell responsible for the murders and fingerprint harvesting, another one would spring up and replace it, or some other fucking terrorist organisation. This way they can't even access the threat, whoever they are."

"OK. Consider it done. But the thing that puzzles me is how did the harvesters know who the twelve men were? If they hadn't seen the document? They couldn't have found the photographs until just before we did and there's no evidence to say they did find them. They knew in advance. But not about Belinda."

I think hard. He's right. My money is on Mark Watson to be the harvesters' ringleader. He couldn't have known who the team was from the original coded data, or from the uncoded snippet. Whoever knew who the team was hasn't read the document or they would have gone for Belinda. I flit through the possibilities and land on Jamie Lewis.

Someone knew that Farrah's account at the university had been accessed. I'd thought that her murder had been a direct result of this, that someone had decided it was her looking at the blog. And when I arrived at his home, Jamie Lewis already knew who I was and had my personal phone number.

"Carey, could you access the files relating to Farrah Amin's murder?"

We hurry into the lounge and he taps away at his computer. In seconds we have the report on the screen. I read through it quickly, halting at the part that explains the location.

"She was killed in one of the dormitory rooms. Not her own room."

Carey loads the case pictures. There is poor Farrah lying in her own blood. In the background I see Kate Lynch's rucksack and laptop, set up on the table exactly as I left them.

"They thought she was me. That's why she was killed. They thought she was me."

The blog suddenly made sense. I'd always questioned why Lewis would put up such sensitive information, right there online. And Newman's explanation hadn't rung true, that Lewis was some kind of kooky mercenary. But now I saw clearly that it was bait – bait to get me to Lewis. If Lewis knew I had logged in as Farrah and had tracked me, he had access to the Baghdad University computer system.

And the academic paper the team had written.

I scan the files and zoom in on a familiar mobile number on Lewis's call log. It's mine. But another number leaps out at me. It's the same number as the one linked to the woman living above Krommer's flat, Sarah Kay. I compare the two files on the screen and it's an exact match.

It's becoming clear that Lewis is like Elliot and me. Self-motivated, one step ahead, always planning and thinking. But on the opposite side. He'd found the team members in exactly the same way I had. He'd used all the facilities at his disposal. But the difference was, he didn't have the key to the document. His attempts to lure me had failed; no doubt when his henchmen realised that Farrah wasn't me, they'd shot her.

"Lewis. Carey, get a picture of Mark Watson on the screen. Along with Jamie Lewis."

I call Juliette from the kitchen. She hurries in to join us.

"OK. Is this Mark?" Pictures of Jamie Lewis appear on one half of the screen.

She shakes her head. She studies the pictures for a long moment. Then her eyes widen. "That's not Mark, but I know him. Bloody hell. What happened to him?"

I turn to her. "Who is it, Juliette? Who is it?"

"It's Jimmy Frazier. My friend Caroline's husband. Ex-husband. He was on Akrotiri with Mark. A cartographer, he was."

Chapter 58

Carey rubs his forehead. "So he got your personal agency number off someone in the service?"

We look at each other. Carey closes his eyes and pinches the bridge of his nose.

"I don't fucking know. Probably. And at the time it was secondary to getting the hell out of there. Karl knew about Farrah almost immediately so it would have been logged on the file then. But Lewis, or Frazier, texted me on that number as I was boarding the plane."

"When he knew that it wasn't you they killed. But the good news is that if they were going to kill you, they don't know that you are the key."

He's right. Carey's always right. I breathe out and think about how he tried to protect me at the beginning of this, and how he's still here now.

"Yes. That's true. So the way forward now would be to let the agency know everything we know about Jimmy Frasier. Anonymously, of course. Tie up all the loose ends with the terror cells."

I point to the screen as a collage of shots of Mark Watson at different ages appears. In one of the pictures he's standing beside a young Juliette at sunset, their arms around each other. Juliette looks sad and I feel sorry for her. I'm temporarily disappointed that Jamie Lewis wasn't Mark. In the back of my mind I'm invested in this, mulling it over and over. But there's no real similarity.

"So do you recognise this man, Juliette?"

"Yes. That's Mark."

"OK. None of this explains why he met up with you. The CIA would be looking for him for the same reasons we are – the missing document. But it looks like he has nothing to do with this. Carey, can you do a face match against known parties?"

He runs a query in the RIPA database and Mark Watson is initially flagged against the missing data investigation. Then his death is flashed on file. Carey and I look at each other as it reveals a huge insurance pay-out to his mother. Then he appears via a face-recognition match as someone called Miles Jansen. Living in Greece, working on a Jet Ski hire, came to our attention when he was involved in a tourism scam. Carey stores this link and flashes up his bank accounts. Mostly empty. A recent police mugshot for petty theft.

I stare at the screen. "So he's not involved at all? He was just on the make when he paid Juliette a visit?"

Carey shuts the screen down. He gets to work, adding information to files and flagging them up. I join Juliette on the sofa in the lounge.

"He was always a liar, Mark. Looking back, he was a cop-out. Good at his job but selfish. Looks like he never hit the big time. Expect he told Jimmy Frazier about our secret in a booze-fuelled episode after I left. Never could keep his mouth shut."

I study her. She looks brighter, like a weight has been lifted from her shoulders. But the sadness still lies heavy in her eyes.

"At least you know he wasn't coming after you. And that he won't again. Time to go home, Juliette. Will you be OK? We'll send someone with you to give you protection."

She looks doubtful. "What will I tell Sandy?"

I touch her arm; she flinches but doesn't move away. "How about the truth? For your own sake. Tell him Sanaa died. Tell him how. He might not be sympathetic but he'll understand how you feel. He sounds like a good man."

For a second I envy her. Someone to lean on. Someone to go home to, to socialise with.

She looks into her coffee cup. "I'm going to make sure that Sanaa's work stands for who she was. I'm going to make sure that everyone knows her value. Now she's dead they can't do anything to her or accuse her of anything. I'll tell them what happened to her and her work will be her epitaph."

For a moment I wonder if Juliette has understood any of this at all. "But what if she was…?"

"A fucking terrorist? Any more than you or me? Jesus, Kate, how many people have died because I kept my mouth shut? And you? Good God. You're a smart woman. Surely you can see it? Surely? Everything she did was to protect her country. Everything. Like I'm sure we all would if we got the chance."

I blink at her. I don't know who is on which side any more. There's a long silence and I desperately feel like explaining everything about my father and what happened. But I can't. Instead, I log into RIPA and type in Sanaa Yazid. The information rolls up the screen. US agents had been tracking her but they'd come up with nothing at all.

Apart from some travel details, some of which coincided with her moving Iraqi art to the UK, and a single meeting with her terrorist ex-husband years ago, they have nothing. That would make her interesting to the security services; his Muj connections sparked the suggestion that they were both involved, but there is no proof she was. None at all. She was either very clever or very innocent but I guess we will never know now.

What I do know is that Riyadh Pachachi is alive and well and is now part of so-called Islamic State. Everything he did was leading to this, all his training and background. I grab his electronic file and push it into Carey's inbox – he'll find a way to weave these connections together and communicate them anonymously.

I scroll back up the page and spin the screen around to show Juliette. She reads it carefully.

Eventually she speaks again, calmer now. "What about you? Family?"

"No family. I was in a relationship but that's ended now. Only recently."

"Anyone else in mind? You could do worse than Carey."

I smile inside. I know this. I've always known. But it isn't my thing. Not now. "He was named after the Joni Mitchell song by his hippie parents. He's a good guy. But I'm not looking for anyone right now."

She sips more coffee and thinks for a moment. "I bet you think I'm weak, don't you? For not telling?"

"You asked me that before. I don't think you're weak. You were young and the decision you made was based on you and how you were feeling. Now you can see the bigger picture and you did the right thing."

She smiles a little. "Is it really that straightforward? I feel like I'm getting away with something. Escaping some kind of punishment."

I think about Belinda and the life she must have led. Like the other eleven, hiding away in the background of life, making herself small so that she would be undetectable to anyone who might come looking for her. Making her husband bigger than her, and him protecting her. Fully bought in. Juliette's life was the same: doing everything to make sure that no one ever found out what really happened to her or connected her with Sanaa. But not compromising their relationship because of it.

"It is that straightforward. You've done enough. It was never your fault in the first place. You reacted to what Mark did. He was the thief. You couldn't have known the full implications. You and Sanaa looked after the document. Whatever else she did or didn't do. And you did that well. So give yourself a break. I've been wondering, Juliette. Wondering if it's all been affecting you?"

She nods and stares into her coffee. "Mmm. Probably. I have been a little bit, um, preoccupied. Yes."

"PTSD. Post traumatic stress disorder. It happens to lots of people. After bad things happen."

She touches my arm and our eyes meet. "I know. It was just that if I had told someone it might have all spilled out. You know. All of it. But I'll try to get help now. I promise. And thanks for saying it. And noticing. I don't think anyone else has even noticed."

She sips her coffee and then unloops one of the clay dolls from around her neck. "Thank you. Thank you so much. It's like you've set me free. I want you to have this."

She holds out the tiny doll, dangling it on its leather thong. I suddenly can't take it. I think about Sammy and Leo and my own choices and I don't feel worthy. "I can't take that. It's... it's..."

"Ibni. I'd like you to look after him. Just to remember him, really, like I remembered Shahid. You're the only other person who knows my story, Kate. No one else really knows what happened. And I'll never be able to tell anyone again. So you're like Sanaa. The truth keeper."

"But I'm not like Sanaa. And I'm not a natural mother."

316

She laughs now. It's the first time I've heard her laugh and it makes me smile. "So what? Neither am I! You know how I felt about it, or the thought of it: that motherhood would be tethering and awkward. You're still capable of caring. I bet there's something you care deeply about, isn't there? Something knotted inside that you can't easily talk about? I bet in your line of work there are lots of things."

I'm blindsided by a sudden memory of my past. The image of my father rushes into my mind. He is leaning against the garden gate, tapping his pipe on the steel turret. My mother comes to stand by him, her apron tied in a neat bow at the back. From the front doorstep where I am sitting I see them, quietly looking out over the horizon. His hand goes over hers and she rests her head on his shoulder. Then the moment is lost as he reaches into his pocket for his lighter, moving her away.

She turns sadly and makes her away up the path. When she sees me she smiles and touches my hair. I watch her as she goes inside and sits at the table, her face momentarily covered by her hands as she takes in a deep breath.

She was the same as all of us. Burdened with a life she didn't choose. Unable to talk about it. She had no real friends and everyone who came to the house was soon deep in conversation with my father in his study.

I take the little figure in Juliette's hand. I'd find a way.

"Yes. Lots of things. But I'm not ready to talk about them yet."

Her eyes tell me that she understands. "Well, whenever you are, you know where I am. Things are different for me now. I can already feel it. No more lying. No more playing for time, having to think about everything I say."

Carey appears in the doorway. "I've booked flights for you, Juliette. You'll need to leave now."

She goes to get her jacket and I stand up and stretch. Carey watches me for a moment. Then he moves very close to me. I think, for a moment, that he's going to kiss me; I don't know what it is about him that makes me think that. But he doesn't. He whispers in my ear: "I've arranged for you to be 'found' in a derelict flat in

Holborn. We'd better get over there and set it up. Then I'll send the message to Karl." I hear him lick his lips and sigh. "I'm still worried, Kate. I'm not sure that you should keep this to yourself."

I turn to face him. I have to look up to look into his eyes and his breath is warm on my face. "But I'm not keeping it to myself, am I? Because you know, too. And if anything happens to me, then you can make the decision about what to do with this information. But for now I think it's safer not to reveal it. It can't be unlocked without Belinda, and only I know where it is. Later on today, when I'm found, everything will reset." He's looking down at me, still doubtful. "It'll be fine, Carey. And if it all fucks up, well, I'll just tell them the truth."

He smiles and puts his hand on my shoulder. "OK. I'll go with that. But if you ever want to talk about it…"

I put a finger on his lips. "I'll let you know. But for now I need to get back into the slipstream. Make it all normal. And so do you."

He backs away and sits on the sofa. Jim and Juliette say their goodbyes and I watch her walk up the pathway. She looks kind of lost, in a shuffling kind of way, a little bit absent-minded. It reminds me how looks can be deceiving. How her decisions, whether she intended to or not, had safeguarded that particular secret and how she had respected Sanaa as a person over the ordeals she had personally been through.

I watch as she waves from the passenger seat of the car, all false smiles as she contemplates the next act of her life. I hold onto the doll she gave me, and she strains to look back at me as the car turns the corner and disappears.

As we stand there on the doorstep Carey's phone rings. He listens and then ends the call.

"Everything's ready. You'll be collected in ten minutes. When you're in place I'll send the information."

Chapter 59

I'm taken to the flat in Holborn in the back of a battered red van. Carried inside in the base of a divan bed and, once in the flat, tied to a chair in the middle of the floor.

"Bit dramatic, isn't it? All this?"

I try to joke with the two men arranging this scenario but they work quickly and silently, and then disappear, after gagging me loosely. I wait and wait, rehearsing what I will say. Thinking about Juliette and hoping she will be OK. Wondering how Carey is getting on with anonymously transmitting all the information. To pass the time I run my mind over some coding and think about the tablet in the museum and how, even at such a young age, I was able to create a cypher that still, to this day, has never been broken.

I suddenly wonder if I've lost my way, if I'd be happier working in some research facility, if that's what I should do next. For a moment I savour the silence and breathe it in, and then my thoughts wander to Elliot and Karl and what happens next. How Elliot and Bees will come in handy, new contacts in the network of my world.

Then I hear rapid footsteps on the stairs and the door panels are kicked through. An operative that I don't recognise points a gun at me. A woman, younger than me, wild with adrenaline. She's followed by a man who scans the room, then goes to the window.

The woman moves towards me. "Are you alone?"

She stops about three feet in front of me, checking for wires. "Any booby traps? Anything else we should know about?"

I shake my head. My eyes meet hers and I see her pity. She unties me and ungags me.

I rub my wrists and rotate my head. "Water. I need water."

She rushes off and fetches a bottle of water. The man murmurs into his radio and less than a minute later Karl appears.

For a moment I think that he's going to hug me but he just stops short and stands directly in front of me. "We thought we'd lost you, Kate."

I look into his eyes. I make my breath short and feign some emotion I don't feel. I need this to be good. "You nearly did. You very nearly did. I've no idea why they let me go. No idea at all."

He's checking me, making sure I'm not lying. Checking for a rapid pulse or tiny beads of sweat. But he's wasting his time because I have it under control. I surprise myself by how calm I am.

"We need to debrief. But not here."

I'm slightly suspicious that Karl wants to take me somewhere but when we get in his car and the driver takes us to a familiar safe house I relax a little.

Karl takes off his camel overcoat and throws it over a leather sofa. He's immaculate, as usual. "Sit down, Kate. Tell me everything."

He clicks on a Dictaphone and places it between us.

I spin a bare bones story about being taken and blindfolded. How they brought me here, probably on a private jet as the airfield was very quiet. Then I was kept in a dark room but treated fairly well. Then brought to the flat.

I wait for his brain to tick over and pick out the meaty bits. The bits that could expose me if I'm not careful.

"'So how long was the drive between the airport and the first place you were held? In the dark room?"

"I don't know. Maybe an hour. But it wasn't the same men. These men had English accents. London and Midlands. The men in New York had American accents."

"Did they say anything?"

"Nothing of interest. Just directions. No names. No locations. No details. I could hear a TV on downstairs but apart from that, nothing."

He's silent for a while. Then he breaks. "I'm sorry Kate. We didn't protect you. We didn't do our jobs. We protect each other."

No. You didn't. But you couldn't, could you, Karl?

"It was a difficult scenario. And, just for the record, I'm not one of you. Like my father, I'm on my own. Freelance. Just for the record."

Of course he knows this. And he knows that I can just walk away any time I want to. It's his job to keep me on side now.

"We hope that you'll continue to work on this case, Kate. Things have moved on since your kidnap. Moved on quite a bit. We're no nearer finding the missing data but the opposing group has killed eleven people now. Just one more to go. We need your help, Kate."

He doesn't mention the anonymous information placed in the service files. He doesn't mention how they've lost Assadi and Belinda. He doesn't mention Carey. He doesn't mention the tip-offs that enabled them to capture Louise and her counterparts across the globe.

"OK. No problem."

He looks at me as if to say 'is that it?' Then he stands and straightens his expensive suit and touches his cuff links. "Good. Glad to hear you're still on board. We won't let this happen again."

I join him by the door. "So I can go back to my flat, then? Everything's been put back in its place?"

He doesn't flinch. Only a slight flutter of his eyelids betrays his irritation. "We only went in there to find out what you needed after Iraq. Nothing more."

"I'll have it swept anyway. I wouldn't want you interfering in my personal life, now would I, Karl?"

He is gone. Without a goodbye, because he knows that he'll see me again very soon in operations. He's confident that he's talked me round. That I've accepted his apology. That there are no real goodbyes in this game unless you're dead.

So I leave and flag a cab. I have a ten pound note tucked inside my shoe and I retrieve it. Once I'm outside the flat I stop and looked up at the pink neon sign still flashing in the golden late afternoon light. The inside of my mind feels battered and bruised with the rolling of the answers to questions that have lingered there too long.

I know that I only have a short time before I'm teamed up with someone else. Someone who Karl, under the pretence of keeping me safe, knows will guard me and make sure that I never disappear again. At least not until they have found the missing data and I have decoded it. I smile a little and savour the knowledge I have. Assadi was right. Like Belinda, I would never be certain that anyone in possession of the 'weapon' would use it for good. But without me no one is ever likely to find it anyway. And even if they did, they couldn't open it without Belinda.

So I climb the stairs and pull the hidden spare key from a crack in the plaster near the skirting board at the end of the corridor. The hair's breadth fishing line I stretched across the door as I last left is gone, of course. As I enter I see that nothing has changed, not on the face of it. But underneath are the signs that people have been in here and meddled. Their DNA would be everywhere. But they will have found nothing at all.

I go over to the hidden panel behind the shower and pull at it. It releases with a fight and even before I pull out the tray of mobile phones and the gun, I know that they didn't find because it wasn't what they were looking for. They were looking for my cypher, the key to my coding. But they could never find that, because it's locked inside my heart.

Chapter 60

I assemble an old Nokia and call Carey. "Mission accomplished. I'm back at the flat. Come over if you want."

He laughs a little too loudly. "That didn't take long."

"No, it didn't."

There's a long pause. I wonder if he has someone there but eventually he speaks. "I'm glad you're back, Kate. It wasn't the same without you."

"You neither, Carey. What now, then?"

"Ah. I'm going to go over some old files and see if I can't dig out some details. Some interesting stuff in those archives. Keep me busy for a while."

"Good. I'm just going to chill. Get a takeaway and maybe watch some TV."

I'm not going to ask him to come over again. He'll turn up if he wants to, all floppy hair and sheepishness and we'll drink diet coke and eat Thai food. And he doesn't mention it either. He's back to the old Carey, somehow satisfied with how this has all concluded, mainly because he feels that both the world and I are safe again. Panic over.

Except my panic isn't over. I pull out my father's gun and run my fingers over it. The smooth steel is cool and I try to understand what he did. Of course, I understand the implications and the noble gesture. But I know this man, my father. I knew him. He was strangely free, and this is what enabled him to become the genius he was. I could never imagine him taking such a decision, to end his own life.

In a way I want to believe it, because it fits with everything that cascaded down the years to a small canister of genetic material buried where the Euphrates meets the Tigris. The fatalistic nature of war, played inside a rule-bound stadium where only those who wear the correct uniform are allowed to compete. All those outside, like Juliette and Sanaa, now must stand silently on the sidelines and ultimately pay the price for their witness.

But my father didn't play by the rules. He hovered above authority, choosing his own path. In the past days I've gone full circle through accidental death to assassination to treachery to suicide. But there's no clear truth in any of it. Nothing to convince me. Assadi didn't see my father die any more than I did. Even so, it's all I have for now.

I clutch the gun close to my chest and doze for a while. I drift in and out of sleep until I wake to find the sky is black and the pink neon sign flashing on and off, lighting my room. I draw the curtain and put on a lamp. Then I shower and change into leggings and a shirt. Just as I am about to open a bottle of wine the buzzer sounds, startling me. Carey. He came after all.

"Hi. Come up. I've got wine."

I hear a deep cough and a voice I recognise. But it's not Carey.

"I bet you say that to all the boys."

Tom Caines. Good God. They didn't waste much time. And Tom. How could they?

"Come up, Tom."

Seconds later, he's tapping on the door. I open it and he stands there, his height making him stoop a little under the low door frame. I raise my eyebrows and step aside.

"I wanted to apologise, Kate, for, well, you know."

Bloody hell. I forgot about how guilty he would feel. And here he is, wanting to make amends. I feel a tingle of amusement and maybe, just a little attraction.

"No problem. No harm done."

"You OK, though? I was kinda worried."

He's cute when he's afraid. I didn't see it before but he has a tiny scar on his chin. His lip quivers ever so slightly, more of a tic, and his eyes are moist.

"Well, obviously, it was an ordeal. But all's well that ends well."

"Except it hasn't ended has it? We need to find the last guy on the list. But the word is that even if they harvest all the fingerprints they won't know where the goods are."

I shrug. "Don't know. I've been out of the game for days. I'll have to read the files tomorrow. Why don't you sit down? I'll get another glass."

He sits on the sofa, leaving me no option but to sit beside him in the tiny room. I pour the wine and bite the bullet. "So, is this a social call or have you been assigned to me?"

He laughs. It makes me smile. "Social. I'm assigned to another agent in London while this case is in operation. So while I was here I called around to see if you wanted to... Look, I thought we had something back there."

Did we? Was it hidden underneath all the mistrust and irritability that operating in close quarters brings? Maybe.

"Mmm. So what do you suggest?"

He leans over a little and sips his wine. "Oh, I don't know. We could catch a late movie. A little dinner, perhaps, or we could stay right here."

He leans further forward and brushes my lips with his. Even though I know why he's here, I'm not expecting it and I feel myself blush red. A second later I know for sure that my relationship with Neil is stone dead. I'd never felt like this about him. A strong attraction, fuelled mainly by physicality. I guess I liked Neil and respected him but I didn't want him that badly.

I pull back a little and Tom leans back and smiles. "I knew it. I knew it. I'm rarely wrong about these things."

I laugh and realise that it's the first time in weeks. Maybe months. "Oh. So you do this with all the female operatives, do you?"

He looks sheepish. Again, very cute. "Not all. But I like to have a little fun. Fool around."

He's drawn the boundary now and he's the Tom I thought he was. Any imagining that he's going to try to have a relationship with me dissolve in the energy between us and I am glad. That's just how I want it. No strings.

He pulls me towards him and kisses me hard, pulling at my T-shirt. It's over my head and I feel a little exposed but free. He's gentle but firm and holds me very tight and whispers that he is sorry he let me get into any danger and that he'll take good care of me. Then he releases me for a moment. "Let's go to the bedroom."

He moves towards my bedroom door and I hurry over to draw the curtains. The pink neon sign lights me up in the window and temporarily blinds me. When I blink out the light I see Carey walking away from my flat towards Euston, his brown mackintosh flowing behind him.

Chapter 61

I wake up in the morning with Tom beside me and a headache. I get up and drink some water and contemplate how I'm going to play this now. I hold the tiny doll around my neck as I brush my teeth and make a mental note to call Juliette as soon as Tom leaves. Then phone Carey.

My heart sinks a little until Tom appears, dressed now, standing in the living room. He looks oversized in the tiny flat and I laugh. "Well. That was certainly a lot of fun."

He smiles widely. "I told you I'd look after you."

He moves in for a rerun but I hold him back. "Later. Plenty of time for that."

"Is that a promise?"

I like this. I like the meaninglessness of it. The flirting. I've missed it.

"Yes. Later. Now go. I'll see you at the briefing."

He's smiling as he backs out of the door and I shut it behind him. I draw back the curtains and watch him walk the same route as Carey did last night. Then I call Juliette. She answers on one ring.

"Hi Juliette. It's Kate. Is it a good time?"

I hear her move around and shut a door. "Yes. Yes, it is."

"Good. I had to find out if you got back OK. And check that you feel protected."

"Well the flight was a little bit bumpy but I'm fine. And someone has moved into Louise's flat and has told me that they've disconnected all the surveillance equipment up there and will look after me. So, to a point, yes. As safe as I will ever feel. Sandy will be home the day after tomorrow. The guy upstairs will explain that I've had some threats and he's my protection; which is true, I suppose."

Yes. It was. It isn't going to be easy for her.

"Great. Look. You'll probably get some more calls about Mark and your time in Iraq. Just continue as you have been doing. Don't tell anyone anything."

"I'm good at that, aren't I? But it's different now, Kate, because I've shared it with you."

"And you can talk to me anytime. Anytime."

I hear the emotion break in her voice. "I can't thank you enough. Look, send me your address. I'd like to send you a gift."

Like Sanaa did. Just like your friend did for you. Paying it forward, no matter what.

"I'll email it to you. Look. I'd better go. I need to phone Carey."

It feels strange, telling another person about Carey. Sharing my secret life with someone else.

"OK. Give him my regards. And Jim. Speak soon. I love you, Kate."

I hesitate. No one has said that they love me since my last conversation with my father. And I haven't said it to anyone else. Love. I'd always thought it was just for family or lovers. But it turns out I was wrong. I suddenly felt love for Juliette, the newly forged friendship bound by a shared secret.

"I love you too. Take care. And call me if you need me."

It's a warm feeling. Love. I use it to force myself to call Carey. I almost hang up as it rings out but then he answers. "Kate.   How's things?"

He seems normal enough. Maybe he didn't see Tom. But who am I kidding? He wouldn't have walked away otherwise.

"Good. You?"

"Yeah. Good. Look, I need to come over. I need to see you before you go back to work. I need to tell you something."

I want to tell him that Tom means nothing, that it was only a bit of fun. But would that make him think I was interested in him? *Was* I interested in him? I had bigger things to consider right now.

"OK. What?"

"I think I'd better come over. Are you alone?"

Silence. I feel bad. Guilty. But then I remember Tom and his gentleness. And why the hell shouldn't I? I'm a single woman. "Yes."

"OK. I'm just over the road. I'll be there in five."

I pull on some jeans and hope this isn't what I think it is. I have to be at Vauxhall Cross by ten and I don't want to misjudge my glorious return by being late.

He arrives exactly five minutes later. I buzz him up and he looks flustered. I almost apologise but he sits down heavily on the sofa.

"I'll cut to the chase, Kate. I came around here last night but…"

"I can explain, Carey. It was just…"

"Oh him. Yeah. I get it. He's a good looking guy. I didn't want to interrupt things. But perhaps I should have." He hands me a thin folder.

"What's this?"

"I was lurking in the coding archives while I had the chance and I came across these."

I sort through the papers, which are mostly printed receipts. The dates go back to 2001 and I flick through them ever more quickly. They are payments to somewhere in Holmfirth, Hattersley Place. My mind doesn't even make the connection until I'm halfway through the thin sheets. And then I see a name. Frank Morden. The Bilton Suite.

Carey watches me carefully and picks up the papers as I drop them onto the floor. My blood runs cold and Carey hurries to me and holds me tight.

"It's OK, Kate. It's OK. He's alive. He's alive."

Chapter 62

We drive at breakneck speed towards the north. Karl rings me every ten minutes and about an hour and a half in I put my phone on silent. Neither of us speaks until we are around ten miles away from our destination. Then Carey pulls over in a lay-by.

"You need to prepare yourself. We don't know what state he's in."

Of course, I've already considered this. I've already run my mind over all the possibilities. But my father is alive and now, in the wake of everything that has happened, it's a miracle. I can't wait to see him.

"Yeah, I know. My expectations aren't high. Let's just see what happens."

Carey regales me with stories about his dead parents and how he misses them. But I'm not listening. I'm watching the golden light play through the trees as the moorland ends and a shady run-up to an old-style house begins. As we near it I expect to see a sign. Nursing Home. Hospital, perhaps. But this appears to be a set of apartments. We pull up to the steep sandstone steps at the front. The entrance is impressive, huge pillars leading to a set of green painted doors.

I sit in the car for a while, and then Carey takes my hand. "Come on. I'll come with you."

So we climb the steps and buzz the Bilton Suite. I see from the door plaques that the suites are merely extravagantly named apartments. From the look of it quite small as the house has been split into twelve of them.

After two buzzes a woman's voice answers: "Hello? Hello?"

I look at Carey. Maybe we've got it wrong. Or maybe the woman is his nurse? "Hi. I'm looking for Frank Morden. May I come in?"

There is a long pause, and my heart beats fast and furious. My father is inside that building.

"I'll come down."

Almost a minute passes and then the green door opens. A young woman stands there. Younger than me by about a decade. Beautiful. Red hair like mine. A face I recognise but can't place.

She stares at me. "Who are you?" She says it in a quizzical fashion, as if she's genuinely curious.

"Kate Morden. I'm Frank's daughter."

She pushes the door shut but Carey puts his foot in it and flashes his security pass. "No point. If you close that door we'll be back with the police. Kate has a right to see her father."

So she lets the door swing open and hurries towards a lift. The open area inside is stylish and clean. The lift is high tech and fast. She stares at me as we ascend and, when the lift stops, she strides out and stops outside the Bilton Suite.

'"He's in here. But first I have to ask you something. Where's my mother? Where is she?"

Her eyes are brimming with tears. Mother? I search my exhausted memory banks for the likeness, for anything that would help me place her, but it wouldn't come. I feel defensive of my own mother.

I say, "I'm sorry. Do I know your mother?"

She shakes her head and opens the door. I hurry in. She points to a door at the end of the lounge. I open it and there he is. Lying in bed. Old and decrepit. Hooked up to a machine with wires extending from under the bed sheets.

She stands behind me. "He had a stroke. He tried to kill himself, years ago, but he failed. The gunshot passed through his skull and he had a brain bleed. He hasn't spoken since."

I shake my head. "No. I saw his death certificate. Why would this happen?"

She comes to stand beside me. "I don't know. There are a lot of things I don't know. But I don't ask questions. I just do what I have to do. I look after my father."

I turn to look at her. My flesh and blood. "But…"

"I'm Elizabeth Morden. Your sister." Her voice breaks with emotion and my head spins with possibilities. "Half-sister, anyway, or so I understand. My mother is Belinda Assadi."

I catch Carey in my side vision, head in hands. Then I reel at the memory of the woman and the girl in my house. When I had finished coding the document, Belinda had come, and brought this girl – this woman – with her. That's when my mother found out. The arguments and the crying. The sadness. That's where my father had been all those times he went away. Not working; he had been with

Belinda and their child. She was born before Belinda tested the modified genetics.

It all makes sense. Belinda's reaction when she saw me. How they both knew my father. How he became involved with coding for her and Assadi. My God. I look at him, an old, old man now. I never knew him. I never really knew what his life was like. Not only had he put my life in danger, he'd deprived me of a sister. But she is here now, so alive. And I am no longer alone.

Then I realise. I have to tell her about Belinda. But I don't have the words now. I don't have the strength. My energy was spent on my mission and all I want to do is see my father. I walk slowly to his bedside and sit down. She stands beside me.

I take his hand and speak close to his ear. "I've found you, Dad, and it's OK. I solved the case. I kept it all safe. Whatever it is you're hanging on for, you can let go now."

But she grabs my arm and spins me around. "Don't say that! I've looked after him for a long time. I've cared for him. He's our father."

The pressure of my feelings begins to erupt. I can feel them rise. I stand up to face her. "You don't know him. You don't know what he's done. What he's put me through. Did you never think of finding me? That I might deserve to know that he was alive? Did you?"

She shakes her head. "My mother didn't want it. She said that it was dangerous. That if you came here things would never be the same. I wanted to but she told me never to contact you. Where is she? Where's Zaki? I've tried their number but they don't pick up."

She's very like Belinda. Her face is solemn and she carries herself with a certain grace.

Carey looks at me and shakes his head. I think hard. That old man in there, my father, is never going to wake up and cause more trouble. If I tell Elizabeth that Belinda is dead, I will be implicated.

Then I think of Juliette and Sanaa. Of their stories within stories, how they could never speak of what had happened yet somehow they managed to communicate their transcendence of the world's troubles deep into their own lives. After all, Elizabeth is my sister. So what is the compromise? I could deny all knowledge and walk out of here without ever telling her. But there has been too much of that. She deserves the truth but it isn't the time.

So I sit her down. I can't tell her my story, or Juliette's, or Sanaa's, or even Belinda's. The time has to be right. After all, like them, I'm a truth keeper. But one day. One day, when the time is right, she will discover the truth, this truth, which I have recorded for her eyes only.

And I say to her: "Elizabeth. A lot has happened over the last few days. Things that I can't explain. But one day I will answer your questions. You'll find out one day. You deserve that, at least."

THE END

Acknowledgements

It is difficult to explain the reasons for writing this book as they were deeply personal and at the same time political. We hear a lot about women in wars in the context of soldiers and filling in for men but hear little of their suffering.

I hope that The Truth Keepers gives a voice to those women who have suffered so much and lost so much.

I would like to thank Michele Brouder and Paula Daly for reading this book. As ever, to Anstey Harris for her patience and for her comments.

To my family, I'm grateful that you understand my need to write and that you make a space for me to do it.

To Eric who listens to these stories as they form and must feel like he knows the characters so well – eternal thanks.

Finally, to you, the reader. You gave this book a chance and that's all I ever wanted for Kate, Juliette and Saana. Thank you for reading *The Truth Keepers*.

Contact and Mailing List

Jacqueline Ward lives in Manchester in the north of England and is the author of several short stories and a speculative fiction novel, *SmartYellow*, under the pen name J. A. Christy. She holds a PhD in narrative psychology and storytelling and is also a screenwriter. *The Truth Keepers* is her fourth novel and the first book in the Kate Morden series. The 2016 bestseller *Random Acts of Unkindness* and its sequel *Playlist for a Paper Angel* were published by Kindle Press as the first two books in the DS Jan Pearce series.

Jacqueline's psychological thrillers *Perfect Ten* and *How to Play Dead* were published by Corvus Atlantic Books.

For more about Jacqueline and the DS Jan Pearce series and Kate Morden series, and to sign up for her mailing list go to http://www.jacquelineward.co.uk. For more information about Jacqueline and her writing

Follow Jacqueline on Twitter @jacquiannc

Printed in Great Britain
by Amazon

10344200R00194